W9-CYD-429

At the edge of ruin...

Ambrose listened intently for any sound from the corridor. He held his breath waiting to see if they would be discovered. After all their near misses to be found here in an indefensibly incriminating position...

She exhaled and it sounded like a cannon blast. He brought his gloved finger to her mouth and pressed against her lips. Now her breath sucked in, albeit much more quietly. He tried not to think of the heat of her mouth seeping through his glove or the gust of her breath against his finger. And he fought the urge to slide that finger into her mouth in the faint hope she might suckle it...

Finally, muted voices came from outside the door. He couldn't hear what they said, but only because his senses were full of Philippa—her lilac-honey scent, the warmth of her body so close to his, the sound of her soft breathing, quickening with each beat of her heart, signaling that her desire—like his—was climbing.

The voices continued, but he was having a hard time concentrating on anything but Philippa's proximity. Because of the tight space, he stood so close to her that if he just inched forward—and as he thought it, he did it—her breasts would be pressed against him.

Instead of retreating as he might have expected, she leaned into him. And then she somehow read his mind—at least partially. She pressed her lips to his finger.

He stifled a groan as he cupped the side of her face and slid his palm down to her collarbone. Her heart beat strong and fast there, and the hot silk of her flesh burned through his glove.

Kissing her was out of the question. But that didn't stop him from lowering his head and inhaling the scent of her hair. He brushed his cheek against hers and bit his tongue lest it dart out and trace a path to her ear, down her neck, then lower to the edge of her bodice.

She nudged her cheek against him and breathed a single word, "Ambrose."

He was a mass of dry, brittle wood and she was the flame that would burn him to the ground.

Also by Darcy Burke

Her Wicked Ways

His Wicked Heart

To Love a Thief (a novella)

Never Love a Scoundrel (Winter 2013)

Scoundrel Ever After (Spring 2013)

Praise for Darcy Burke

"A bad girl heroine steals both the show and a highwayman's heart in Darcy Burke's deliciously wicked debut."
— Courtney Milan, *New York Times* Bestselling Author

"Captivating and romantic. Miranda is my favorite kind of heroine—witty, resourceful, and a little bit wicked—and I loved Fox for loving her as I much as I did."
— Jackie Barbosa, Award-Winning Author

"…a delightful romance mixed with humor, tenderness and love."
— Rogues Under the Covers

"…fast paced, very sexy, with engaging characters."
— Smexybooks

"Sexy and wonderfully romantic. Her Wicked Ways is a debut every fan of historical romance should add to their to-be-read pile!"
— The Season

"FANTASTIC characters…totally recommend this delightful Regency romance…"
— Romancing the Book

"What a wonderful debut! Highly entertaining…the pages sizzle with sexual tension."
— Forever Book Lover

His Wicked Heart

"Intense and intriguing. Cinderella meets *Fight Club* in a historical romance packed with passion, action and secrets."
—Anna Campbell, *Seven Nights in a Rogue's Bed*

"A romance that is going to make you smile and sigh...a wonderful read!"
—Rogues Under the Covers

"The storyline was fresh with a cast of well developed characters. Darcy Burke is an author on the move!!"
—Forever Book Lover

"I loved the book: interesting storyline, wonderful characters, and a touch of humor. 5 stars."
—Booked Up

"You'll love this incredible story of trial and triumph!"
-Kerrific Online

To Seduce a Scoundrel

"Darcy Burke pulls no punches with this sexy, romantic page-turner. Sevrin and Philippa's story grabs you from the first scene and doesn't let go. To Seduce a Scoundrel is simply delicious!"
—Tessa Dare, *New York Times* Bestselling Author

"An enthralling tale of adventure, passion and redemption. At times humorous and at times deeply touching, To Seduce A Scoundrel is a unique tale with a sexy hero you will never forget."

—Leigh LaValle, *The Runaway Countess*

"A great read with a gorgeous tortured hero and a surprisingly plucky heroine, I can't wait to read Ms. Burke's next book."

—Under the Covers Book Blog

"A delicious blend of love and acceptance, humor and angst, action and heat, and a book I would recommend for any historical romance fan!"

—Rogues Under the Covers

"I was captivated on the first page and didn't let go until this glorious book was finished!"

—Romancing the Book

"With refreshing circumstances surrounding both the hero and the heroine, a nice little mystery, and a touch of heat, this novella was a perfect way to pass the day."

—The Romanceaholic

"This novella has it all--action, romance, love and passion...a lovely story!"

—Rogues Under the Covers

DARCY BURKE

To Seduce a Scoundrel

Copyright © 2012 Darcy Burke
All rights reserved.
ISBN: 0615639534
ISBN-13: 978-0615639536

This is a work of fiction. Names, characters, places, and incidents are the product of the author's imagination or are used fictitiously. Any resemblance to actual events, locales, or persons, living or dead, is purely coincidental.

Book design © Darcy Burke.
Cover design © Patricia Schmitt (Pickyme).

All rights reserved. Except as permitted under the U.S. Copyright Act of 1976, no part of this publication may be reproduced, distributed, or transmitted in any form or by any means, or stored in a database or retrieval system, without the prior written permission of the author.

For Jedgie, because you're a fighter.

Acknowledgements

This book would not have been possible without the awesome power of the annual Northwest Pixie Writing Retreat. I don't know what's in the water there (or whatever else we're imbibing), but the words sure flow! Thank you Linda, Kristina, Rachel, Courtney, Becky, Cathy, Kris, Natasha, Joan, and Elisabeth.

I am incredibly blessed with the greatest critique partners in the known universe: Erica Ridley, Emma Locke, and Janice Goodfellow. Each of you offers something unique and I could *not* do any of this without you.

Thank you Jim McCarthy for providing amazing editorial feedback. You knew exactly what needed to happen (or rather, not happen) to make this book sizzle.

I've been very fortunate to be part of a wonderful community of people who have eagerly followed my writing career and who have been nothing short of spectacular in their support. Special thank you to the ladies at ARE, Leslie and Ann. You make me smile on lousy days and for that, you deserve a medal. Hugs to my other ARE "fans," but really I'm YOUR fan: Tina, Jen, Julie, Robyn, Rebecca, Karmin, Erin, and Laura. Thank you for touching my family's lives in the best way possible.

My family's perseverance in the face of my writing-induced-insanity is nothing short of miraculous. Thank you for supporting me, encouraging me, and most of all, loving me. I do all of this for you.

Chapter One

London, April 1818

FROM the comfort of the Herrick coach, Lady Philippa Latham watched her mother alight from Mr. Booth-Barrows' carriage in front of a massive neo-classical house on Saville Street. Booth-Barrows tucked Mother's hand over his arm and they climbed the steps of the townhouse, their heads bent close together. *Like lovers.*

Philippa seethed. Loveless marriage or no, how dare Mother openly cuckold Father? And only days after she'd informed Philippa she must marry this season. How was she to accomplish that while her mother was cavorting about town with a man who wasn't her husband?

Philippa clasped her fingers tightly around the door handle, and before she knew her own mind, she was stepping from the coach. The footman leaped to help her.

With murmured appreciation and a directive to wait until she returned, she dashed across the moonlit street. Nervous energy propelled her along her mother's path. Philippa had never done anything so rash before, but she was intent on convincing Mother to come home immediately.

A black and silver liveried footman opened the front door, and Philippa stepped into a cavernous marble entry. But instead of her mother, other guests, or some sort of receiving line, she found emptiness punctuated by the gentle swell of conversation and muted laughter coming from a chamber on the opposite side of the foyer.

"Would you care for a cloak?"

Philippa turned toward a second footman who held up a voluminous black cloak, complete with a large hood. She frowned. Why on earth would she want to wear a cloak inside? "No, thank you." Puzzled, she turned from the footman and squared her shoulders.

Head high, she strode across the gleaming marble and did her best to appear as if she belonged, though she'd no idea whose house she'd invaded. Not that she cared, so long as she found her mother and took her home. While it was true some women had liaisons outside of their marriage, her mother shouldn't be one of them. Not after twenty-two years of insisting upon propriety and respectability above all else. Philippa's outrage bubbled anew.

She paused at the threshold to the large, dimly lit room beyond the foyer. It was crowded with people. *Masked people.* Faint tendrils of trepidation curled in her chest.

She stepped into the room, seeking her mother's peacock blue gown. In the center, a woman stood on a table in nothing but her chemise and garters. Philippa gaped, completely unprepared for such a shocking display.

She spun about, clenching her teeth. *Curse her impulsivity,* which she rarely indulged. How fitting that on her first foray she'd stumbled into precisely the impropriety her mother had warned against. And how ironic that she'd done so in pursuit of Mother.

A man clasped her elbow. "Lady Philippa." The whisper came next to her ear and sent a shiver down her neck.

Philippa jumped. She turned her head to look at the man, but a dark mask covered the upper half of his face. Panic rooted in her belly. "How do you know who I am?"

He dragged her to the side of the room, deeper into the shadows, and pressed her against the wall. The edge of the wainscoting dug into her lower back. Then he stepped close.

Too close. He put his hands up behind his head. "Quickly, take my mask." He worked another moment then muttered, "Bloody hell, the tie is knotted."

She didn't know what sort of event she'd stumbled into, but clearly it was wicked, and the only thing standing between her and certain ruin was—literally—this bold stranger. Right now, she'd take this man's audacity over discovery.

"Let me." She stood on her toes, for he was quite tall, and found the knot at the back of his head. He smelled of rosemary and sandalwood, very pleasant.

"Where'd she go?" a male voice behind her rescuer asked. "I saw the loveliest creature, dark hair, pale gown—no mask, if you can imagine. She was just here."

Her rescuer leaned his head down so that their mouths were a breath apart. If she nudged up the slightest bit, their lips would touch… Her fingers fumbled as she tried to work the knot free.

"Eh, there she is, against the wall."

Philippa gave up her struggle with the mask and moved her hands to her rescuer's lapels. She pulled him closer so that her bodice grazed the front of his coat. "Don't you dare move."

"I wouldn't dream of it," he murmured, his warm breath caressing her mouth.

More shivers. This time dancing down her arms.

He clasped her waist and she would've jumped back if the wall behind her had allowed any such movement. "I ought to convince the men behind me you are engaged, ah, with me. Pardon my familiarity, but I do believe kissing you is necessary. You might take the opportunity to continue working at the ties of my mask."

Before she had time to make sense of anything he'd just told her, his lips met hers.

The pressure of his mouth was warm and soft. She'd been kissed before—a swift brushing of lips that had left her curious—but pressed against a stranger in a dark corner, this was something quite different. Somehow more than just a kiss. A moment later his advice sunk into her befuddled thoughts. *The mask.*

She lifted her arms, which only served to bring her body up

against him rather snugly. His chest pressed against hers in a
terribly intimate fashion, while he moved his lips slowly,
sensuously over hers. Her sensibilities were scandalized, but her
body didn't care. Her flesh heated, and little whorls of
excitement replaced the panic in her belly.

A dissatisfied grunt came from behind her rescuer, followed
by, "Someone else got to her first." Two sets of footsteps trailed
away.

She plucked at the ties of the mask, and at last it came loose.
He broke the kiss and caught the mask before it fell. Then he
turned it around and covered the upper two-thirds of her face.
He quickly tied the thin strands around the back of her head.
The mask was too large for her, but that only meant it covered
more and she wouldn't complain about *that*. Not when there
were plenty of other things to worry about.

Such as how disappointed she felt that their kiss was over.
Ludicrous! She needed to concentrate on getting out of there
without being identified. "You recognized me immediately. I
suppose it's too much to hope no one else did." She tested the
knot at the back of her head and was satisfied it wouldn't come
loose even as she feared it didn't matter. Though the other men
hadn't referred to her by name, her heretofore pristine
reputation would be ruined if any of them had discerned her
identity.

"You aren't sure if anyone saw you?" The dark timbre of his
voice wrapped around her.

The mask tunneled her vision, and even squinting she
couldn't make out his features in the shadowed corner they
inhabited. "Just the footmen. One of them offered me a cloak.
Oh dear, was that to shield my identity? How was I to know?"

"What were you expecting to find at Lockwood House?" His
tone carried a hint of sarcasm.

"*Lockwood House?*" Dear Lord, she'd marched through the
gates of Hell and straight into Lucifer's bedchamber. "Is this one
of those...parties?" She wasn't even sure what those 'parties'
were—proper girls like her never would—but she'd heard
enough to know that being caught attending one would mean
the death of her reputation.

She reined in her shock to indulge her rising panic. "I have to get out of here. Now."

"I agree." He took her elbow and turned her toward the door.

They took two steps and then stopped short as a group of people stepped inside. He drew her around and guided her along the perimeter of the room. "Sorry, I'd rather not go out that way, particularly since I'm now without a mask."

"I'm sorry to have taken yours. It was very kind of you to offer it, Mr...?"

"Sevrin."

She stumbled as the full reality of her situation permeated her panicked brain. "Lord *Sevrin*." She sounded breathless, but the implications to her reputation were disastrous. And perhaps irreversible.

He clasped her waist to steady her. "As usual, I see my reputation has preceded me."

It most certainly had. Lord Sevrin was nearly as notorious as Lockwood's parties. He'd famously ruined a girl and refused to marry her, but Philippa recalled there might have been even more to the story.

She took a deep breath to calm her raging nerves. "Why are you helping me?"

He kept his hand at the small of her back, but guided her forward. "You seem in need of assistance. Do correct me if I'm mistaken."

"You are not. I appreciate your help even if I am bewildered by it." His touch and his instant recognition gave her an odd sense of familiarity, as if he had been completely aware of her for some time and she'd been oblivious to him. Though she doubted she would ever feel that way again. "How did you even know who I am? We've never been introduced."

"You have a remarkable face, Lady Philippa. I'd wager most men know who you are." The way he delivered the words—as a matter of fact without an excess of pretty compliments—sparked another smattering of shivers along her flesh.

Sevrin led her to a door tucked neatly into the corner. He opened it for her, and they entered a small sitting room. Also scarcely lit, it was currently occupied by not one, but two couples. Philippa's heart beat faster. She began to fully understand the nature of the party she'd unwittingly intruded upon.

Sevrin took her hand and pulled her toward a door on the opposite side of the room. "Pardon us," he murmured.

Though the well-bred miss in her urged her to avert her gaze, she couldn't help but stare at one of the couples as they passed. The woman was sprawled upon a chaise with her head cast back. A man lay over her, his mouth at her exposed breast. Philippa jerked her gaze away and stared at Sevrin's back.

The next room was better lit, but it was full of people playing cards. Without masks. Philippa recognized a handful of faces before Sevrin dragged her out onto the balcony. For once, she was glad to be wearing an indistinct, colorless gown reserved for young unwedded misses like herself. She could be one of any of London's young ladies. Although—and this made her heart hammer even faster—her pale yellow dress could lead anyone to assume she was an unmarried miss. Even that seemingly innocuous bit of information about her identity made her feel anxious.

Once outside, she plastered herself against the cool stone of the house's exterior. She breathed deeply, hoping her pulse would slow. "Good Lord. I'd no idea of the...depravity of Lockwood's parties."

He stood a few feet away. "And you shouldn't."

She gestured toward the house in a thoroughly unladylike fashion. "But my mother is here!"

Sevrin's gaze flicked toward the door they'd just exited. "She is?"

Philippa adjusted the mask, which had drooped over her mouth in her excited exclamation. "I had no idea this was Lockwood House. I followed her."

His brow creased. "Is there an emergency?"

"I wanted to... that is... No, there's no emergency." *Except the danger to her reputation.*

She looked up at him. A sconce on the terrace cast flickering light over the angular planes of his face. Long, dark lashes fringed deep brown eyes. The line of his nose was imperfect, a tad crooked, but it somehow looked right on him. A slightly dimpled chin supported sensuous lips she too-clearly recalled kissing her.

He took her arm, and his touch was oddly comforting, considering he was a scoundrel. "Then let's get you back to your carriage."

Despite his seemingly genuine assistance, she cautioned herself to be wary. She'd spent a lifetime avoiding scandal, and just because she was standing in the dead center of one didn't mean she ought to throw all discretion aside. "You're being very gallant. I'd heard you possessed no such consideration."

He tipped his head toward the light, which brought his good looks into greater focus. "I would tell you not to believe the salacious rumors you've been told about me, but, alas, they're entirely true. Come, let's get you home."

She peered up at him through the mask. "I can't go back through there."

"Of course not. We'll skirt the house." He took her hand again. A pleasant, reassuring warmth stole through her glove and imbued her with a sense of security. He led her along the terrace and down a short flight of steps into the garden.

After a moment he asked, "If there was no emergency, why did you follow your mother?"

"She left Lady Kilmartin's with a gentleman. They appeared," she searched for the right word, "intimate." She looked at the ground where her slippers squashed the damp earth. "I wanted to bring her home before she caused a scandal."

"You think her leaving a ball with someone other than her husband will cause a scandal?"

Philippa paused and looked at him. "I've been raised—by *her*—to think so. You disagree?"

He rolled a shoulder. "It's not as if married women don't have affairs."

Was he defending her mother or merely stating the obvious? "But how can she behave in such a manner while requiring me to comport myself above reproach?"

His lips twisted into a faint smile. "Because life is full of double standards, especially for unmarried women."

"You're right, of course." She continued walking with him through the dark garden. Illumination from the torches on the distant terrace was feeble, but the path was easy enough to follow with a bit of help from a nearly full moon. "Mother's timing, however, is quite poor. I'm supposed to be finding a husband. Her scandalous behavior could drive potential suitors away."

"Perhaps you needn't worry. I'd heard your father had gone abroad to find you a husband. Surely none of them will be aware of your mother's activities."

She cast him a quick glance, but he was eyeing the path. "It appears I am not the only one listening to rumors."

He laughed softly. "Touché."

"The rumors are not, however, completely false. While my father is abroad conducting business, he did threaten to bring a bridegroom home if I didn't select one soon. He was disappointed when I didn't marry the Earl of Saxton last fall."

Sevrin slowed his pace. "And why didn't you? Marry him, I mean. Or anyone else, for that matter?"

She bristled. He might as well have asked her outright if she was settling herself comfortably on the shelf. In this, her fifth season, she'd heard more than one matron musing about her marital prospects. Though she was still young enough, handsome enough, wealthy enough, her failure to accept a marriage proposal—and there had been several—was beginning to erode her standing as one of Society's most sought-after misses. Which was why she'd hoped her courtship with Saxton last fall would have led somewhere. He'd been the first gentleman who'd sought to court her without falling at her feet with flowery platitudes or overwrought declarations of devotion. The first gentleman to whom she might've said yes.

Now, recalling her aborted suit with Saxton, she quashed a niggling sense of disappointment. "He never actually asked me." *The Times* had misprinted news of their engagement, and to protect her reputation—at Saxton's insistence—she and Saxton had put it out that she'd refused his proposal.

"I know."

She stopped abruptly. Only she and Saxton had known the truth. Or so she'd thought. "How?"

His mouth curved up in a reassuring smile as his thumb stroked her knuckles. "Saxton and I are friends. Don't worry he told anyone else—he didn't. And the secret is quite safe with me."

She had to believe he was sincere. If not, he surely would have spread the gossip ages ago. "Thank you."

He tugged lightly on her hand, and they moved along the path. "Were you disappointed?"

"That we didn't suit? Yes, but I had the sense his heart was engaged elsewhere. Why aren't *you* married?" She cringed. In her haste to direct the conversation at him, she'd come dangerously close to the root of his notoriety.

"I'd make a terrible husband."

And then, because as long as he knew one of her secrets she ought to be privy to one of his, she went ahead and asked, "Is that why you didn't marry that girl?"

If he was offended by her question, he didn't show it. "Would you believe me if I told you she didn't want to marry me?"

Philippa thought for a moment. For a sinful rogue, he was charmingly honest and solicitous. "I don't see a reason not to."

He barked out a laugh. "You'd be the first."

She smiled, enjoying their conversation far more than she ought. He was, after all, an utter reprobate. "The first who believed you, or the first you told?"

Sevrin stopped at a five-foot tall stone wall that edged the yard. He let go of her hand and gave her a half-smile. "You're cheekier than I might've imagined."

She couldn't argue with his assessment. Tonight she'd strayed far outside her normal boundaries. If anyone saw her now, she'd be quite thoroughly and incontrovertibly ruined. And while the thought made her a trifle queasy, the sensation was surprisingly overridden by the excitement of Sevrin's company.

She suffered a moment of alarm—why was this exciting? Because it was forbidden? Because it was *Sevrin*? This escapade shouldn't be exciting at all, but with no one here to witness her inappropriate reaction, perhaps she could finally relax her guard. Why not? Her mother certainly had.

The mask drooped again, and she pulled it off, dislodging a lock of hair. The curl grazed her shoulder and sent a tickle along her arm. She brushed at the sensation and then offered him back the mask. "I don't think I need this anymore."

"Keep it," he said. "You never know. An alley runs between Lockwood House and the building next door. We'll take it through to the street. I'm going to lift you up to sit on the wall then I'll climb over and help you down the other side. Are you ready?"

She nodded. Although she expected his touch, she still jumped when his hands came around her waist. "I'm a bit ticklish."

"Lovely," he murmured. The sound, dark and rich, permeated every inch of her. She willed her body to remain unaffected the next time he touched her. Warm hands spanned her waist then lifted her. She held her arms up to grab the top of the wall and bit back a gasp as Sevrin's hands scooped her bottom and raised her higher. She pulled herself atop the stone and watched as Sevrin vaulted the wall with ease.

He reached up and clasped the tops of her hips. She burned where he touched her. When she was on the ground, his hands were gone far too quickly.

"This way." He led her into the dark alley stretching between Lockwood House and the building next door.

They were halfway to the street when two men stepped from the shadows.

The shorter of the two spread his lips in a malevolent grin. "Here's our lad."

Sevrin shoved her behind him and then her scandalous, yet shockingly pleasant evening went completely to the devil.

Chapter Two

AMBROSE Sevrin was no stranger to violence. Indeed, his blood heated at the prospect of a fight.

With Lady Philippa tucked safely behind him, he addressed their attackers. "What do you want?"

The shorter, stockier footpad—for what else could they be?—stepped forward. "Ye're the 'Vicious Viscount', aren't ye?"

Son of a bitch. Anyone asking after him by that name wanted nothing good. Or legal.

He felt Lady Philippa's shallow breaths on the back of his neck. "Not anymore."

The shorter, stockier of the two men shrugged and wiped his hand across his nose. "Don't matter none to me what ye call yerself. Jagger wants ye so ye'll be coming with us."

Who the hell was Jagger? "No, I won't."

The miscreant curled his lip. "I weren't asking." He glanced toward his taller cohort and inclined his head toward Ambrose.

Ambrose tipped his head to the side, but didn't take his eyes from the now-advancing criminals. "Philippa, go back to the house."

He pushed her behind him, his gaze never leaving the two men. The taller one—a massive brute—advanced. Ambrose quickly shed his gloves and threw them to the ground. He lunged forward with fists flying. The first landed squarely against the man's nose, but the second only grazed his jaw.

The bastard was quick for someone so massively built. He retaliated with two fast punches. Ambrose took one to the shoulder, but sidestepped the other.

Ambrose sent three rapid strikes to his opponent's torso and face, but his clothing constricted his movements. He longed to shed his coat, his shirt, everything until he was barefooted and bare-chested, just like at his fighting club where routine bouts fed his primal need for violence.

The man answered with a swift, brutal cut to the back of Ambrose's neck. A rabbit punch, illegal in boxing, but expected in a fight such as this. He ground his teeth and launched himself forward, repeatedly sending his fists into the miscreant's face.

Ambrose split the skin beneath his opponent's eye. The man grunted. The seam of Ambrose's coat tore over his right shoulder.

Dancing backward, Ambrose ripped his coat off in quick, ungainly jerks. The buttons went bouncing over the cobblestones. His opponent took the advantage and advanced with two great strides. He ducked low and grabbed Ambrose around the waist.

Ambrose registered a feminine shriek. He turned his head in Philippa's direction. Christ, he'd all but forgotten his presence in the thrill of the fight. The stocky criminal had cornered her against the side of the house. Ambrose's split-second distraction was more than enough for his adversary to make his move.

With Ambrose clasped in his arms, he leaned close to Ambrose's chest. He brought his head up, striking Ambrose square beneath the chin. Ambrose bit his lip and the metallic flavor of blood filled his mouth. His opponent shoved him back onto the cobblestones, but let go before he fell, too.

Ambrose's back hit the street. The impact knocked the wind from him, but he dug for the energy to roll to the side and miss the man's kick.

Stupid, amateur mistake, but then Ambrose's attention had never been siphoned from a fight. He was always completely in the moment. The fight was everything.

He glanced over at Philippa. The other criminal was upon

her. Ambrose heard the distinct sound of fabric ripping. He'd kill the prick.

Ambrose leapt to his feet and sprinted at the man. With a growl, he grabbed the villain around his middle and threw him to the ground. The thud of his head hitting the cobblestones resonated in the alley.

Ambrose didn't spare him a glance as he turned his attention to Philippa. She stood quaking, her bodice gaping open.

"Are you all right?" He rushed toward her, but was jerked to a stop by the other criminal—the one he'd just left in his furious dash to save Philippa—grabbing his arm and pulling him off balance. Ambrose stumbled over the man lying on the ground as the brute delivered two hard punches to his lower back.

The brute didn't give Ambrose any time to collect himself, not that he expected it. He dodged to the left, escaping the man's meaty fists. Then he sent a merciless series of punches to the man's face. Ambrose's knuckles split. Warm pain blossomed in his hands.

He continued his assault. The man grabbed his waist and wrestled him to the ground. Ambrose rolled on top of the criminal. He landed blow after blow until his lip split and blood ran from his nose.

A piercing scream interrupted Ambrose's beating of the criminal. He stopped in mid-punch. His gaze found Philippa kneeling next to her attacker, but the man wasn't down any longer. He was on his knees and had raised his hand. The blade of a knife flashed in the light of the street lantern.

For the first time in five long years, Ambrose felt fear.

He leapt off his brute of an opponent and dashed toward them. He kicked the man in his ribs. With a loud grunt, the criminal crumpled and let go of Philippa. His knife clattered on the cobblestones. The criminal reached for the weapon. Ambrose kicked the man again, then toed the knife out of reach, and moved in front of Philippa.

The man Ambrose had left—the brute—advanced. While Ambrose would have loved to beat him into the cobblestones, getting Philippa to safety had to be his primary objective, not winning a fight.

He grabbed her hand and hauled her back the way they'd come. They reached the stone wall and he belatedly, stupidly realized she couldn't have scaled it on her own. He hoisted her up with one fluid movement.

With a quick glance down the alley, he saw the larger man bending over his cohort. Satisfied the man wasn't directly on their heels, Ambrose vaulted the wall then grasped her waist. His gaze was drawn to ruddy streaks along her skirt.

"Is that blood?" he asked, panic rising in his throat. "Are you all right?" He gently pulled her down from the wall but didn't let go of her.

She nodded, dazedly.

"Yes, it's blood or yes, you're all right?"

"Both. I want it off. Please." She tugged at her gloves, which were covered in blood. Ambrose finally registered the sticky, wet substance on his own hands.

She dropped the ruined gloves to the ground. Ambrose picked them up, but had no coat pocket to stuff them in since he'd left the garment out on the street. He'd dispose of them inside, in a fire if possible. "Come, let's get you into the house."

She stared up at him. "I can't go back there." Her voice was soft, tremulous.

He tugged her away from the wall, along the dark path toward the house. He cast a furtive glance behind them, but doubted the criminals would follow them into the garden and certainly not into the house.

He paused a moment to catch his breath. "We can't go back that way." In the dim light, he eyed her torn bodice. He grasped one edge. "Here, hold this up. We'll go in through the scullery."

Her eyes were wide, scared. "And then what?"

"There are gowns inside. We'll get you a new dress and get out another way." He eyed the streaks of blood on the lower part of her skirt. "If you're not hurt, is all of that blood his?"

She nodded. "When he fell, he hit his head. He seemed to be unconscious, but then he began to moan and ask for help. I knelt and used my skirt to dab at the cut on his head. It was bleeding terribly." Her voice quavered. "Then he grabbed me. He had a knife." She pressed her bodice more tightly against her chest, and he saw that blood had seeped through her gloves to stain her hands.

He cringed, hating what he'd allowed to happen to her. Hating himself. "Will you come?"

She nodded again and walked beside him while he scanned the back of the house for a servant's entrance. They passed beneath the terrace from whence came muted sounds of conversation and laughter. Finally, when they reached the other corner, there was a staircase leading down to the scullery.

Ambrose led the way, hoping they could sneak in unnoticed. He paused at the door and slowly eased it open. The scullery was empty save a cat curled up on a rug near the fireplace. Its ears pricked as he entered, but other than that the animal didn't stir. He turned back and gestured for Philippa to follow.

She stepped inside and the firelight accentuated her pallor. And the blood caking her skirt. And the deep shivers wracking her frame. Another sharp stab of self-loathing.

He glanced around the scullery in search of a basin of water. Finding nothing, he went into the next room, the main kitchen, where two retainers were working. He spied a basin of water on a table in the corner.

His understanding was that guests at Lockwood House could request the private use of any room at any time. "Good evening," he said, "I need this room for a few minutes."

The retainers merely nodded and left. He turned back toward the scullery. "There's water in here."

Philippa came in, almost silently, her feet scarcely making a sound against the floor.

"It's likely cold," he said, but she had already submerged her blood-dappled hand. Ambrose found a cake of soap and gave it to her. She scrubbed mercilessly for at least a minute, the water turning a murky rust color as she worked.

Finally, she raised her hands. Ambrose searched for something with which she could dry them. His eyes lit on a scrap of toweling hanging from a hook. He crossed the room and grabbed it, then froze upon seeing a girl sleeping in the corner. She'd been hidden by a large worktable.

Lightly, he made his way back to Philippa. He handed her the towel then put his finger to his lips and gestured toward the sleeping girl.

The kitchen fire was low, but he tossed her ruined gloves on top of it anyway and poked them into the coals. They caught and burned.

He went to the basin and cleaned the blood off his hand. His injured knuckles burned as he scrubbed the abraded flesh. He contemplated their next move.

Lockwood House kept a large stock of gowns and other items of clothing. Guests often arrived here after attending other, more acceptable engagements and had need of altering their appearance. They were given cloaks to wear until they donned new costumes in one of Lockwood's dressing chambers.

Ambrose didn't know where any of these chambers were located, but he was aware of a room upstairs filled with a variety of props, including women's gowns. He only prayed the chamber wasn't currently in use.

He took Philippa's hand as she clasped her bodice to her chest once more and led her up the back stairs. He paused on the landing at the top of the stairs. "What happened to your mask?"

"I dropped it. Out in the alley." She glanced away.

Ambrose wanted to reassure her. "It's all right. If we see someone, I'll find a way to shield your identity."

She looked up at him. Her eyes were hooded but held a touch of spark. "Am I to expect another kiss?"

Her tone was light, not derisive or accusatory. This had to be the worst thing that had ever happened to her and she hadn't devolved into a hysterical fit. Quite the contrary. He was impressed. And perhaps even a bit charmed.

While kissing her had been quite pleasurable, he was in no position to indulge such fancy, and definitely not with a proper miss like her. Never with an innocent like her. "I'm certain we can avoid another kiss."

He opened a door and led her into a corridor. He took a moment to get his bearing. He wasn't precisely sure where the prop room was located, but it was rumored to be at the back of the house in the western wing. He turned left and motioned for her to follow. He worried she was still a bit too pale.

Sconces flickered at intervals along the corridor, casting long shadows over the rich cobalt-colored carpet running down the center. A moan floated on the air from behind a closed door. Ambrose glanced back at Philippa who stared at the door. Color flooded her cheeks.

The corridor branched right and left. Ambrose went left and immediately thrust Philippa against the wall as a couple walked toward them. He pressed against her to shield her from view. "Keep your head down," he murmured.

Ambrose turned his head toward the wall, but not before the gentleman, Viscount Heresford, noted him. Heresford gave a half smile and inclined his head before continuing on.

Philippa rested her cheek against his chest, and though it was part of keeping her identity secret, the motion was sweet and trusting. "You could've kissed me again," she said softly. "It was nice, actually."

Ambrose couldn't let her think he—or his kisses—were nice. He stepped back abruptly and turned. At the end of the corridor was a large, curved alcove with a door. He walked toward it without a word, knowing she'd follow.

Two chaises sat against the walls of the alcove—the famed waiting area for those who wanted to use the prop room. Ambrose slowed and quietly said, "There could be someone inside, in which case we'll have to wait."

"Why?"

There were many questions in that one word and he wasn't sure which one she wanted answered, so he gave her just the information he thought she needed. "That room contains dresses."

He tried the door handle but it was locked. A bell pull dangled to the left. Ambrose wasted no time in tugging it, though he was unsure what the result might be.

Behind them, a door—completely hidden in the wall—scratched open. A massively built footman stepped out. "My lord? Do you wish to watch?"

"No. And we don't want to be watched either." He glanced at Philippa, but her head was cast down, her gaze fixed on the carpet. "We're waiting for our turn."

The footman gave a quick nod. "The current occupants are just finishing up."

"Do you have a mask we might use?" Ambrose asked.

"There are masks in the room, my lord."

"Thank you," Ambrose said, inclining his head in dismissal. The footman betrayed no reaction to Philippa's torn and bloodied gown. He likely ignored just about everything he witnessed at Lockwood House. Which was doubly good since Philippa wasn't masked.

She turned and sat on one of the chaises, keeping her head bent. Ambrose sat beside her, careful not to get too close. "You should turn away from the door." She did as he instructed. "Just a bit further, toward the wall almost. Yes, that's it."

"He called you 'my lord.' Does he know who you are?"

Ambrose had also noticed that, but couldn't imagine how the footman might recognize them. "I can't fathom how. He probably addresses everyone that way."

"Yes, though so far it seems as if only retainers have seen me. Presumably they have no idea who I am."

He noted the hint of hope in her tone. "I'm sure you're right. Just keep your face averted when the occupants leave the room."

They were quiet a moment and then Ambrose couldn't contain his regret another moment. "I'm sorry about what happened." The apology was wholly inadequate, but it was all he had.

She kept her face toward the wall, but her eyes darted a glance at him. "Why was that Jagger person looking for you? Are you really the 'Vicious Viscount'?"

A ridiculous moniker given to him when he'd been a prizefighter in another life. "It's an old nickname."

"And you prefer not to discuss it?"

His lips quirked up. Her shrewd assessment immediately vaulted her in his opinion. "Just so."

Besides, he'd no idea who Jagger was. But if he knew Ambrose as the Vicious Viscount, whatever he wanted had to do with prizefighting.

She kept her gaze fixed on the wall. "If you won't tell me

about that, explain what the footman meant by 'occupants.' What are they doing in there?"

Another question he'd rather ignore, but she deserved some semblance of truth after what she'd endured. "Similar to what we saw downstairs."

She turned her head to look at him, her eyes wide. "A woman on a table?"

"More like the other room. With the couples."

"Oh." Her cheeks flared red before she turned back around. She allowed silence to root and grow for a few minutes before asking, "How do people come to be here? At this party, I mean."

"Special invitations."

"So my mother was invited."

"Or her escort. Gentlemen are allowed to bring guests."

"Why were you invited?" She turned her head to look at him and the sconce above them highlighted the unique color of her eyes, a warm golden brown, which he likened to a freshly drawn ale. A single curl feathered against the base of her neck, just above her collarbone, inviting him to stroke its softness. Or, better yet, he could run his fingers along her lustrous skin, which was the color of thick, decadent cream. The kind he loved to lick from the knife after spreading it atop his scone.

Ambrose averted his gaze. For a host of reasons, it wouldn't do to indulge a physical reaction to her, not the least of which was her status as a respectable unmarried young lady and his as a worthless scoundrel.

"Another question you don't want to answer?" she asked.

He gave her a lop-sided, rakish smile. "You know me, I'm the type who's invited to these sorts of parties."

"And I see you attend. But are you the type who participates?"

Ambrose was surprised by the edge of doubt in her tone. He'd planned to participate—at some point—but a five-year-long vow of celibacy was difficult to put aside. Thankfully the door opened, interrupting further discussion on the topic.

She quickly turned back toward the wall as the couple—nay, trio—departed the room. A man and woman arm in arm followed by a heavy-set man whose florid cheeks were just discernable under the edge of his mask.

Once they had exited the alcove, Ambrose jumped up. "Come."

They went into the room and he locked the door behind them. Three black-clad maids cleaned the room in silence. They redressed the bed, fluffed pillows on the various pieces of furniture strewn about, and one busily reorganized the unseen contents of an armoire.

Philippa stood with her back to them. Ambrose let go of her hand. "Almost there," he said.

When he turned back to the room, the maids were gone. Whatever exit they'd used was well hidden. It was as if they'd never been there.

Ambrose went to the armoire, certain he'd find the gowns he sought. Instead, an array of... instruments greeted him. Best if Philippa didn't see them. He slammed the doors shut and turned abruptly. She'd followed him.

"What was all that?"

"Nothing we care about. Ah, there's another armoire over there in the corner."

They skirted the oversized bed draped in rich purple silk. An image of Philippa lying amongst the pile of opulent pillows flashed in his mind. A lovely thought, but one he would never indulge.

He opened the next armoire much more carefully, peeking at its contents before throwing the door wide. Gowns and other garments. He allowed himself to relax for just a moment.

Philippa stopped next to him. He fingered a deep, rust-colored silk and held the skirt out for her perusal.

She cocked her head at him and narrowed her eyes. "Really?"

Foolishly he realized the color resembled the dried blood on her skirt. *Idiot.*

She reached for a dark yellow piped with royal blue. He helped her pull it out and she held the gown to her frame.

"Too long," he said.

She cast it aside while he pulled a vivid rose with cream-colored flounces at the hem. She made a face—clearly she didn't like it—and he thrust the garment back into the armoire.

She ran her fingers along the sleeves of several gowns and then stopped abruptly. "This." She removed a dark emerald velvet and laid it on the bed. She looked up at him dubiously. "You'll have to help me with my dress." She turned her back, but not before he caught bright spots of color on her cheeks.

She was beautiful and smelled of lilac and honey. Fresh, sweet, unspoiled. His lust roared strong once more. The irony of his powerful response—finally—with a young miss like her nearly made him laugh.

She looked over her shoulder, perhaps sensing his hesitation. "Pretend I'm your sister."

"I don't have a sister. Though I do have an aunt in Sussex."

"She'll do." Philippa's shoulders were tense, but her tone was light. She really was trying her best to get through this series of disasters, and he admired her for that.

Reluctantly, Ambrose lifted his hands and unhooked the back of her gown. She turned her face away and tipped her head slightly down. It was a struggle to keep his fingers from brushing her neck as he started, but he managed not to touch her. As he worked to open the gown, his knuckles brushed her stays, but he was fortunate not to come into contact with her skin. The dress gapped open and then fell to her waist. She wriggled a bit and it fell to the floor. Ambrose pivoted away.

While sounds of rustling stirred parts of his body better left ignored, he went in search of a replacement mask for her and hopefully one for himself. For all that he deserved his black reputation, he didn't particularly like walking around Lockwood House with his face exposed.

First he tried the drawers in the armoire. Fripperies and undergarments. He turned to decide where next to look and caught sight of her pulling the green velvet up her body, shielding her partially-clad form from his view.

She stood with her back to him. "Can you fasten the gown?"

It was more time-consuming to dress her than undress her, which gave him more time to contemplate her scent and her softness. Dangerous ground. He hurried at his task, which naturally only served to make the ordeal take longer. Finally, she was clothed, but when she turned to face him, any sense of relief fled.

The dark green velvet draped her form beautifully, as if it had been crafted just for her. The neckline was low, accentuating the creaminess of her skin and the beckoning valley between her breasts. Breasts that were held up and displayed to painful perfection—painful to him, anyway.

"Is it all right?" An honest question, devoid of guile, asked by a young woman who'd seen far more than she ought this night.

It was more than all right. "You'll do. Now, let us find masks."

"What about that?" she pointed a slippered toe at her discarded gown.

"Ah, yes, another bit of fuel for the fire." He grabbed the poker and stirred the coals in the fireplace.

"If we toss the entire thing on the coals, it might douse the fire. Perhaps we should tear it into smaller pieces?"

"What a resourceful girl you're proving to be." He smiled at her, enjoying her company despite the absurdity of the entire evening.

After returning the poker to its stand, he plucked up the garment, grasped the already ripped bodice, and rent it from neckline to hem down the front and again down the back. He dropped one half while he worked to get the other into smaller pieces. It surprised him a little when she picked up the discarded half and viciously ripped the sleeve off and threw it atop the glowing coals.

She caught him watching her and bent her head to her task. "I never liked this dress. My mother chose the pattern and the color." She continued pulling at the fabric, having a more difficult time ripping through it than he did, so when he was finished with his half, he took over hers. She released the tattered silk with a nod. "Thank you for helping me tonight."

He chuckled darkly. "Is that what you call it?"

She lightly touched his arm. "Yes. You gave me a mask and tried to help me escape. It's not your fault we were accosted."

"Save your appreciation for when I actually get you out of here." He tossed the last of the dress atop the coals. The first pieces had caught, and flames now licked at the other remnants.

He handed her the poker. "Stir that while I look for masks."

He started with a small dresser next to the bed. It was filled with an array of cravats, scarves, and long lengths of silk, all of which were suitable for binding. He was immediately grateful she was occupied with the fire.

The next drawer held something mask-like. He held it up.

"Is that a blindfold?" she asked. "Do they play parlor games in here?"

He grinned at her naïveté, glad that she'd no idea. Her innocence—and her curiosity—were refreshing. He quickly tucked it back into the drawer. "Not exactly, no. Someday your husband can explain it to you."

"I see." She returned her attention to the fire, a bit of color again rushing to her cheeks. So sweet.

He pulled another piece of black silk from the drawer, but pivoted his body so she wouldn't be able to see it as he investigated its usefulness. It was a hood designed to completely cover a person's head with cutouts for the eyes, nose, and mouth. He turned toward her. "I've found something that will work." He handed it to her and took over the poker, stabbing the last bits of fabric into the fire.

"Why, it looks like a hangman's hood." She glanced at him with a touch of humor in her gaze. "Not that I've actually *been* to a hanging. Did you find something for you?"

"Not yet." He stirred the embers of her dress and then replaced the poker in the stand.

She stared into the fire. "My mother would hate to see what happened to that gown," she noted, and not without a bit of scorn. "And she'd detest this one." She smoothed her hands over the emerald velvet, drawing his attention to the curve of her hip.

He looked away and was about to continue his search for a mask when the door flew open and disaster fell upon them. Again.

Chapter Three

PHILLIPA froze in mid-stride as the hulking footman who'd earlier bade them wait their turn entered the room. And he was not alone. Quickly, she pulled the hood over her head and hurried close to Sevrin's side.

Sevrin turned to face the intruder, stepping just a bit in front of her. He'd spent the entire evening trying to keep her out of harm's way, yet harm seemed destined to find them.

"My lord, this gentleman insists it's his turn for the room." The footman indicated a tall, slender man. He seemed vaguely familiar, but then her vision was trying to adjust through the tiny eyeholes.

"Our apologies," Sevrin said.

"I should hope so," a dark, feminine voice said.

Philippa sucked in her breath. There was no mistaking the haughty tone of her mother.

The tall man slipped his hand around a woman's waist—Philippa's mother's waist. She'd traded her peacock blue gown for a vivid scarlet. The man had to be Booth-Barrows. Another couple stood behind them. Good Lord, what was her mother going to do in here? Philippa really didn't want to know. She just wanted to leave. Now.

She wound her fingers through Sevrin's and gave his hand a tug.

"We were just leaving. Again, my apologies." Sevrin walked with her toward the door.

A feminine voice—not Mother's, thank goodness—said,

"Why don't you stay, Lord Sevrin. And I suppose your little friend can too."

Philippa nearly gagged.

"How charming of you to invite us, but I'm afraid we have another engagement." His fingers squeezed into hers as he rushed her from the room.

"Lord Sevrin, wait." *Her mother.* Fabric rustled as her mother perhaps approached them in the alcove. Philippa daren't turn around to look. "Your friend seems familiar. Is she your personal guest or one of Lockwood's?"

Philippa froze, her belly churning until she was afraid she'd cast her accounts right into the center of the alcove outside the room.

Sevrin paused and guided her in front of him. Then she felt him pivot. She heard the amusement in his voice and gave him credit for playing his part so well. "Forgive me if I decline to answer your question as the purpose of Lockwood House is to provide anonymity for those who wish it." His voice dropped to a bare whisper. "Isn't that right, Lady Herrick?"

Her mother gasped softly. "How did you know?"

"Your secrets are safe with me," he said quietly. "Enjoy your evening."

His arm came around Philippa's waist and he swept her away down the corridor. The door to the prop room closed behind them.

He led her to the right—back the way they'd come earlier—and then left toward what she thought was the front of the house. Philippa stopped and leaned against the wall, allowing her anxiety to pulse out of her in deep, gasping breaths. She pulled off her mask, needing a greater supply of air.

"Put your hood back on," Sevrin urged. He'd stopped next to her and was glancing up and down the corridor. "Anyone could happen upon us at any moment."

"We'll revert to your kissing stratagem, then. I need a minute to catch my breath."

"I know this has been a trying evening." He kept his voice low.

"'Trying'?" Hysterical laughter bubbled in her chest, but

Philippa fought to keep it inside. "Why did you call my mother by name?"

He looked up as if he were contemplating the question, then his gaze found hers with warm intensity. "I wanted to put her on notice that she is not immune to scandal."

A roguish thing to do, certainly, but he'd done it for *her*, which somehow took the edge off Philippa's panic. She took a deep breath.

Sevrin frowned. "I hear footsteps. Put your hood back on."

She frowned back at him but did as he said. A huge figure circled the corner ahead and walked straight for them. Sevrin pulled her away from the wall and tucked her against the side of his warm body. He was still coatless—why hadn't they thought to get him a new one from that room?

"Sevrin, you've disdained a mask this evening. How bold."

The large man stepped into the light splashing from a sconce and Philippa had to bite back a shocked gasp. He was quite simply the biggest person she'd ever seen. Impossibly tall and massively wide, with hair the color of coal and eyes like a storm cloud. But most unnerving of all was the scar running from the tip of his left eye to the base of his jaw. Was this the mysterious Lord Lockwood? Though he lived—and clearly entertained, if one could call it that—in London, she'd never seen him at a Society event.

"I've nothing to hide, Lockwood." There was a smirk in Sevrin's tone and, not for the first time tonight, Philippa wondered if he really embraced his notoriety or simply had no other choice. What would *she* do if she were a pariah? She'd still be the daughter of an earl, but she'd be relegated to a fringe existence, always clinging to the outside. Never getting in. Never being accepted. She felt a rush of sadness for Sevrin, and more than a surge of panic for her own situation.

Lord Lockwood clasped his hands behind his back, for all purposes seeming as though they chatted at the edge of a ballroom. "Not surprising, but curious since you donned a mask on your other visits. And tonight you brought entertainment, but then my offerings never did catch your eye."

So Sevrin came to these parties but had yet to indulge,

according to Lockwood anyway. However, since he'd taken her directly to that room with the dresses perhaps, as the huge footman had asked, Sevrin merely liked to watch. She peered at him through the slits of her mask, envisioning him watching activities like she'd seen downstairs. Had she ruined his evening's plans?

"A note, however," Lockwood said, his voice dark and deep and mysterious. "A girl like her will draw notice. If you're at all worried about disclosing her identity, you ought to consider covering that mark on her arm. Gloves might have been in order. In fact, if you ask one of the footmen in the foyer, he'll procure a pair for her."

Philippa stiffened in his embrace. She'd earned the crescent-shaped scar just below the crook of her elbow falling from a tree when she was eight. Lord Lockwood was frighteningly observant.

Sevrin stroked her arm, covering the tell-tale scar. She relaxed just a bit.

"We appreciate your discretion, Lockwood," he said. "Thank you for your hospitality."

"Of course." He smiled and it stretched the scar on his face, making him appear more menacing than he already did. Too bad he hadn't encountered the footpads earlier. They'd have taken one look at him and run screaming in the other direction. He clapped a hand on Sevrin's shoulder, and the man's strength carried into Philippa's frame. "Enjoy your evening." Lord Lockwood continued past them down the corridor.

Sevrin took her elbow and pulled her forward. He sounded as if his breathing had become a bit difficult. "We need to get out of here as soon as possible. Your carriage is waiting for you?"

"I hope so." Just when she'd begun to believe she might actually escape this nightmare unscathed, the encounter with Lockwood disrupted her equilibrium. "Do you think running into Lockwood will prove to be a problem? My scar, I mean…"

He didn't slow their pace. "Lockwood designed these parties to be as anonymous and secretive as an attendee deigns. He won't divulge anything."

Philippa wished she could say this alleviated her concern, but how could it? Her entire reputation—indeed her entire livelihood—was at stake.

They rushed down the stairs, but—and she should've expected it really, given how her night had progressed—a group of gentlemen stood in the center of the marble room. In unison, the men turned and watched her and Sevrin descend the staircase. If Lockwood had looked at her appreciatively, these men regarded her with unguarded lust.

"Follow my lead," Sevrin whispered close to her ear. He moved her to his left side, presumably so her scar would be hidden between them. He wrapped her hand around his arm as he guided her down to the marble floor.

"Sevrin," one of them said, "a mask is too good for you, eh?"

He gave them a bland smile, and Philippa was glad her entire face was covered for she couldn't have managed such a feat. In fact, she felt more than a trifle guilty that she was anonymous while Sevrin was not. "I must've forgotten it upstairs," he drawled.

"Your coat too, apparently." It was clear this gentleman thought himself above Sevrin. Unaccountably, Philippa wanted to kick him.

"Who's your friend?" a second man asked. The man was of average height and thick build. He seemed vaguely familiar, but Philippa suspected she knew most of these people and would be shocked by more than a few of them, as she'd been with her mother. He stepped toward Philippa, studying her closely.

"You can't ask that, Blick," the first man said. Philippa recognized "Blick" as the nickname of Mr. Bartholomew Blickleigh, a gentleman with whom she was acquainted and had even danced with once. Would she ever be able to attend another Society event without wondering if she'd met this person or that person at Lockwood House? What a chilling thought.

"Idiot," Blickleigh said, turning his head toward the man who'd identified him. "I'm wearing a mask for a reason."

"As is she," the first man retorted.

Blickleigh appeared to ignore him, returning his attention to Sevrin. "She looks like Quality. He leaned toward her and inhaled. "Smells like it too."

Sevrin pulled her closer against him. "Have you no discretion, Blickleigh?"

"Is she in trade? I'd be willing to pay," said a third man. He stared at her breasts and actually licked his lips. "A great sum."

Philippa shuddered.

"Me too," put in a fourth man. "Come now, Sevrin. She's a beauty. Much too elegant for the likes of you."

The first man moved forward. "She the bit of fluff I saw you with in the drawing room earlier? Too bad you beat me to her. Though, perhaps I may get a second chance." He reached out and grabbed her wrist. Caught unaware, Philippa lurched forward, but immediately pulled back toward Sevrin.

He welcomed her by clasping his arm around her front and tucking her against his chest. His forearm rested against the flesh above her neckline. His embrace was possessive, warm, safe. Still, her heart thundered in her chest. "You lot know I like a good fight," he drawled. He sounded as if he was baiting them. Philippa recalled the way he'd pounded the footpad in the alley. Had he enjoyed it?

"He was kicked out of Jackson's, mate," the third man stage-whispered.

The flesh around the mouth of the man holding her whitened and tiny lines webbed away from his lips. He let go of Philippa and backed away. "Just so."

"Good evening, lads." Sevrin kept a firm arm around Philippa's shoulders as he guided her to the door. She couldn't wait to be free of this place.

The footman let them out, and Philippa practically ran down the stairs to the street where the line of coaches stood queued.

"Wait," Sevrin called. He'd let go of her as soon as she'd started her quick descent.

She pivoted to face him. "What?"

"I presume you came in the Herrick coach?"

Why was he asking ridiculous questions? "Yes, of course. Let's go." She turned toward her family's coach near the back of the queue. She raised her hand toward her hood, eager to rid herself of the visual impediment.

His warm fingers wrapped around hers. "We can't. At least not in your coach. And you can't take your hood off yet. Those men are particularly interested in you and it will be easy for them to learn how we departed."

She dropped her hand. *Hell and the devil, this night is a catastrophe.*

He withdrew his grasp. "We'll have to hire a hack."

"Don't *you* have a coach?" she asked.

The corner of his mouth quirked up. "I'm afraid not."

Right. He was rumored to be light of funds in addition to black of soul.

"But what about my coach? My mother will see it when she leaves and she'll know I was here." Her voice rose in panic. They'd come so close to escape!

"I'll instruct the footman to notify your coachman to return to Herrick House after a reasonable interval of time—say a half hour from now. Will that suffice?"

She glanced at the coach. "Yes."

Sevrin went to a footman standing along the queue. They spoke for a moment and then he came to retrieve her. "All settled. We are now free to go."

"Where's the hack?" Philippa looked up and down the street as if one would materialize precisely because they needed it.

"We'll catch one on the next street."

"Secrecy?"

"Privacy. I prefer it. Especially in this situation." He took her hand and guided her past the queue away from the alley where they'd encountered the men who were waiting for him. She ought to have known Sevrin would consider that.

They left the line of carriages behind and soon turned the corner.

"Now you can remove your hood," he said.

Philippa pulled the fabric from her head and slowed her pace a bit, savoring the relief of being away from Lockwood House. A breeze picked up the curl that brushed her neck and sent a prickle of goose bumps along her exposed flesh. Her gloves were long gone, and she'd left her shawl in the coach before going into Lockwood House. Thankfully, the late March night wasn't freezing, but her body chilled, nonetheless.

"You're cold," Sevrin said. "And I left my blasted coat in the alley."

"It's all right. We'll find a hack soon." She hoped. They'd walked a good block since turning the corner and though there was a bit of traffic, they had yet to see a carriage for hire. Her thoughts turned to the men who'd been looking for Sevrin in the alley. She considered asking him about them again, but doubted he'd be more forthcoming. Her companion was a charming, if a bit wicked, enigma. Instead, she decided to focus on her own problems.

Though she liked holding his hand—it gave her a welcome sense of security—she let go in order to wrap her arms around her middle. She was cold, but the sensation came more from her insides than the temperature.

She'd accepted long ago that her parents existed in a polite marriage devoid of passion. But they'd shared a mutual respect and faithfulness. Or so she'd thought. She couldn't help feeling betrayed by her mother's actions. Mother had strained the fabric of their family, and if it ripped in two... Philippa squeezed herself tighter. "I don't know what to do now that I've learned the extent of my mother's depravity. Should I tell my father when he returns?"

Sevrin put his arm around her shoulders and drew her close. Their proximity slowed their progress, but Philippa was grateful for his warm solicitude. "I don't think I would," he said. "Chances are he'll find out soon enough. Secrets are awfully hard to keep, especially if one isn't particularly careful about hiding them."

Philippa stopped and looked at him sharply. "Don't tell me you were aware of her adultery before tonight? I had hoped to put an end to her behavior before it became known."

He gave a light chuckle. "You sound like the parent."

No wonder, given that Philippa had spent most of her life in the absence of any. She'd begun to assume the role out of necessity. "Someone has to be."

"Well, I wasn't aware of anything regarding your mother. In fact, I'm not sure I could pick your mother out of a crowded ballroom."

"But you recognized her upstairs."

He returned her intense regard, and her heart beat a little faster. "Only from your reaction—and don't worry that you betrayed yourself. I don't think anyone else caught your gasp, and they certainly didn't feel you stiffen."

The things he said seemed so… intimate. Or at least, they weren't the typical things one might notice about another person after just meeting them. She ought to feel concerned or intimidated or *something*. Well, she did feel something, a ridiculously inappropriate attraction.

She started walking again. "You can't identify my mother, but you recognized me within ten seconds of me entering a dark room."

His lip quirked up. "Knowing you and knowing your mother are not the same things."

She gave him a coy smile, knowing she shouldn't flirt, but somehow unable to help herself. She didn't remember the last time she'd met a gentleman who'd so rapidly provoked her interest. Never, she realized. "Any decent gentleman is versed in a young lady's family."

"And that is where you misjudge me." He lowered his voice. "I'm no decent gentleman."

Philippa tried to ignore the shivers dancing along her neck. "You've been incredibly gallant tonight."

"Good God, don't let anyone hear you say that."

She angled her head to look at him. "Why are you so determined for everyone to think the worst of you?"

He stared straight ahead. "This is a highly inappropriate conversation."

"After all we've been through, you find *this* inappropriate?"

"I'm afraid we're going to have to try to forget tonight ever happened. You must treat me as you did before, certainly not as some sort of heroic rescuer."

Was the disdain in his tone directed at her or himself?

"So the next time I see you, I'm to ignore your presence and act as if we hadn't shared the most thrilling night of my life?"

"Is that what you did before, ignore me?"

She couldn't imagine how that could be possible. He'd provoked an intense and startling reaction in her. "I'm afraid I was simply unaware of you. A tragedy, really."

"You flatter me." He withdrew his hand and stepped toward the thoroughfare. "There's a hack." He hailed the carriage and within a few minutes they were inside the marginally warmer interior on their way to Upper Grosvenor Street.

Lanterns hung outside the carriage, but they cast meager light inside. Philippa sat facing forward, while Sevrin sat opposite. She supposed that was the appropriate arrangement, but she missed his warmth.

In the near-darkness his features were indiscernible. They rode in silence for several minutes.

She twisted the silken hood in her hands. "Do you really think no one will determine my identity?"

"I don't see how they could. You were nearly always masked, and when you weren't, only retainers saw you."

"It's a lucky thing you rescued me so quickly." She recalled the way he'd pushed her against the wall, the way his body had fitted against hers, the way his heart had thundered beneath her palm, the way he'd kissed her. "No one has ever…embraced me like that before."

The space in the hack seemed to shrink, but even so, Philippa wished he were closer. Next to her.

"It was a necessary inconvenience."

Philippa felt as if a bucket of water from the Thames in January had been thrown over her. He hadn't experienced the same arousal. But how foolish of her to think he had. He was a man of extreme experience, regardless of what she thought she knew of him after their escapades together. To him, she was a silly Society girl who'd made a very, very stupid mistake. That he'd had to rectify at the expense of his own anonymity. She pulled herself into the corner of the seat, folding her arms into her lap and pressing her knees together.

She looked out the window as they turned onto Piccadilly. She frowned.

Sevrin leaned over and looked outside as well.

Fear laced through her. "We're not going the right way, are

we?"

"It doesn't appear so." The lantern light from outside the door streaked over his face, illuminating his concern. He pounded his fist on the roof of the hack.

She waited for the small door in the roof to open, and when it didn't, her trepidation mounted. "Where do you think we're going?"

"I don't know, but I don't like it."

The coach turned again. Sevrin grabbed the door handle. "Do you think you can jump?"

Philippa blinked at him. "Out of a moving carriage?"

"Yes, we're on the Haymarket. Can you jump?"

She looked down at the cobblestone street. They weren't going terribly fast—she'd gone much faster in a phaeton in Hyde Park, of course—but she'd likely injure herself in the fall. She returned her gaze to his. "I don't know."

As she considered whether she wanted to spend the Season with a fractured leg or arm or both, the door in the roof of the hack finally opened.

A bruised but somehow familiar face looked down upon them. "Evening, milord."

"*You*," Sevrin said, not letting go of the door.

"Me."

Then Philippa figured where she knew him from. The alley. He was the hulking brute Sevrin had fought. "Let go of the door." He pointed a pistol down at them and Sevrin let his fingers fall away.

Sevrin's hand fisted and he moved to sit beside Philippa in a flash. "What do you want?" His warmth infused Philippa, reducing her bone-deep shaking to a light quivering.

"We told ye. Jagger wants to see ye. We're on our way there now. Just sit tight." He glanced at the door and waved the pistol in that direction. "Don't get any ideas about trying to jump. If the fall doesn't break your legs, I will." He cocked the pistol for good measure then laughed before closing the trap door.

Philippa tried to squash herself even farther into the corner, as if the hack would swallow her whole and keep her safe.

Sevrin's arm came around her. "Shhh. I won't let anything

happen to you. I promise."

She knew he would try to keep her safe. He had kept her from harm all night, hadn't he? "It would appear that danger is intent upon us this night."

He pulled her head against his shoulder. "There's no need to be melodramatic."

Melodramatic or not, it seemed to be the truth. She'd been careful to keep herself above reproach in every aspect of her life. Suddenly, with one impetuous decision she'd put everything at risk. Deep shudders wracked her frame. She nestled closer to Sevrin, seeking his warmth to calm her quaking body.

Sevrin stroked her arm. "Take a deep breath. If you can."

The coach turned once more. She thought they might be traveling along the Strand. Silence filled the interior, and she imagined Sevrin's mind was churning. "Are you formulating a plan?" she asked.

His body was tense beside her. "Trying to."

She looked up at him, but he stared at the opposite seat. "Would you care to enlighten me?"

"I would, when I have something to share. It all depends on where we end up."

"Have you a weapon of any kind?"

He turned his head to glance at her. The barest hint of a smile haunted his lips. "Save my fists? No."

After watching him fight in the alley, she had to agree his fists qualified as weapons. The hack made two more swift turns—away from the Thames—and then came to an abrupt halt.

"Stay close to me," Sevrin said against her temple. His warm breath was comforting.

She turned into him and slid her arms around his waist. "They'll have to pry me off you."

Something brushed against her forehead. His lips?

The door swung open. The man from the alley stood with a lantern held high. His face looked even worse than before. Sevrin had done quite a bit of damage.

"Get out."

When they didn't immediately move, he reached up and grabbed Philippa's arm and pulled. She half-fell from the hack, but Sevrin came right after and snatched her up against him.

"Don't touch her." He bared his teeth at their captor.

The tall man sneered. "I'll do as I please." He sent a fist into Sevrin's gut, causing him to double over and loosen his hold on Philippa. The villain wrapped his hand around her upper arm and tugged her away from Sevrin.

She looked up and around. They were within a very small court surrounded by ramshackle tenements. A woman leaned against the railing of a balcony one story above them. She held a lantern, by which Philippa noted her ragged gown and pockmarked face. Philippa averted her gaze just as two men standing at the door pulled her into the dimly lit interior.

The low-ceilinged room wasn't large, but it was filled with men. There was a massive rectangular table suitable for a formal dining room—which meant it was completely unsuitable for its current location—at the back. Behind it sat a man in a gilt chair. He was more finely dressed than the others and appeared engrossed in whatever papers were laid out before him.

The two men led Philippa toward the table. She tried to look behind her to see what happened to Sevrin, but the men jerked her forward. Once they had her positioned in front of their apparent leader, she didn't try looking back again.

After the longest minute of her life, the man finally looked up. A lantern atop the table illuminated his features. He was only a few years older than she, with dark, grayish-brown eyes and nearly jet black hair that waved back from his face with far more style than a man in his position ought to possess. He raked her with unabashed interest, his gaze lingering on her too-low bodice. She cursed her vanity in choosing this dress from Lockwood House.

"This is the girl?"

The man Sevrin had fought stepped forward. "Aye, Jagger."

Jagger. The man who wanted to see Sevrin.

Jagger turned his attention to his employee. "Where's Sevrin?"

A commotion behind her drew her to turn, or at least try to. Once again the men tugged her back around, but not before she saw Sevrin tussling with a couple of the men.

"She's mine. No one touches her." His voice reverberated off the low ceiling, sending a thread of hope into Philippa's shriveling insides.

Jagger leaned back in his chair and settled a hard-edged stare toward the opposite end of the room. "Bring him."

Philippa heard more struggling noises and then Sevrin entered her line of sight. Blood trickled from his lip. Her legs threatened to collapse from under her, but she held herself upright and even pulled her arms from the too-tight grasps of the men beside her.

Sevrin looked over at her and gave a little nod—a tiny bit of encouragement, which she greedily accepted.

Jagger frowned at him. "You've caused me quite a bit of trouble this evening. You should've just come with my men earlier."

Sevrin curled his lip. "I was otherwise engaged."

"So I see." Jagger rolled his gaze to Philippa and regarded her with heavy-lidded appreciation. "I might've ignored me, too. But," he slapped his palm on the table and sat upright once more, "you're notoriously unencumbered when it comes to females. In fact, I'd heard a rumor you might prefer men... Any truth to that?"

"Let her go," was all Sevrin said.

Sevrin purportedly liked men? Preposterously, she wanted to voice her opinion—based on empirical evidence of course—that Sevrin most certainly did *not* prefer men, but what did she really know about the bounds of his depravity?

Jagger turned to a man standing just behind him and Philippa realized it was the man who'd attacked her in the alley, only now he sported a bandage wrapped around his head. He stepped forward, leering at her. A tremor shuddered through her frame.

Jagger spoke to her attacker. "Swan, take her upstairs while the viscount and I discuss our business." He looked back at her. "Let's hope your lover is amenable to my business arrangement. If he's not... Well, there are other *business arrangements* I could make with you." He gave her a thoroughly wicked grin.

Before Philippa had a chance to voice her dissent or her bone-piercing panic, her assailant grabbed her forearm and dragged her toward a rickety staircase, passing in front of Sevrin. She tried to dig her feet into the floorboards and struck out at Swan.

"Tell your lady to go along nicely. Swan won't touch her." Jagger lowered his brows. "Yet."

His dark gaze met hers. "I'll come for you." His voice was low, with a menacing quality that made her shiver. Not for her safety, but for their captors. She'd seen him fight, and if the rage in his eyes was any indication, he was eager to do it again. She went along, taking hope from Ambrose's promise.

The men who'd flanked her followed behind, one of them pushing her up the narrow stairs, while Swan pulled her. The wood creaked and bent as they climbed up one story, then two, then a third. She was breathing heavily by the time they reached the third landing. They went to a door at the end of a short corridor and threw it open.

Swan cocked his head to the side. "Better hope yer gentleman does what Jagger asks. Otherwise, I'll get me way." His gaze dipped lewdly over her form and his grip tightened on her arm. "I like yer new dress."

Her stomach heaved as the criminal laughed. Roughly, he shoved her into the room. The door closed and the heavy, sinister sound of a bolt being thrown filled the small space.

The room was dark, save slivers of light sneaking in through the battered shutters over the lone window. Philippa peeked through the slats, seeking the light source. She made out a lantern hanging just outside the window. A shadow passed by and she jumped back, her heart thundering.

She turned and made out a chair near the window, a small, wooden affair that looked as if it might hold something as insignificant as a mouse. Against the far wall was a cot. Narrow, low to the floor, strewn with a few scraps that were perhaps meant to serve as blankets. Her blood ran cold. The bed represented what could very well happen to her if sevrin didn't rescue her. Again.

Chapter Four

AMBROSE struggled against the three men holding him as he watched Philippa's forced ascent up the staircase. His body teemed with frustration and pent-up violence. He threw his arms out, hands fisted, uncaring who he hit, so long as he damaged someone.

"Sit." Jagger waved a hand and a chair appeared.

The men pulled and shoved Ambrose until he sat. One delivered a blow to the side of his head that ought to have clouded his vision, but Ambrose only saw red.

Jagger inclined his head toward the staircase. "Who is she?"

Ambrose glared at him.

Jagger threaded his fingers together and set his clasped hands on the table. "Ah, no matter. She clearly means something to you, which is helpful to my cause."

She meant nothing to him, at least not personally. Never mind his body's reaction to kissing her. But he'd dragged her into this dangerous scenario, and he wouldn't turn his back on her. "How could she possibly help you?"

"She'll ensure *you* help me."

Ambrose itched to fight. Any of them would do. "Leave her out of it. What do you want?"

Jagger rested his elbows on the arms of his gilt chair. "Yes, let me get to it. Perhaps you'll readily agree. You look as though you want to throttle me, so my request may be more than palatable. Shame you didn't just come with my men earlier."

Throttling the criminal held infinite appeal. "Out with it."

Jagger inclined his dark head. "I need a prizefighter. I watched you fight four or so years ago in Dirty Lane. You were unbeatable. You could've taken the title. Why'd you quit?"

Because while he'd thrived upon the physical punishment—both giving and receiving—he'd hated the accolades and the admiration. He didn't deserve to be cheered or lauded for any reason. "I was bored."

Jagger gave him a skeptical look, but didn't press him. "My prizefighter was to fight the Irishman Patrick Nolan a week from tonight, but he broke his hand. I need you to take his place."

A dark thrill shot up Ambrose's spine. Fighting at that level had been brutal. He missed it. He dug his fingernails into his palms. "I don't fight anymore."

"The hell you don't." Jagger's stare was piercing. "I know all about your little club off the Haymarket."

Ambrose gritted his teeth. "I don't fight for profit."

Jagger curled his lips in a snarl and narrowed his eyes. "What the hell do you fight for then?"

Ambrose pressed his heels against the chair legs. He couldn't explain how fighting kept the demons at bay, how the physical pain kept him from falling into the abyss of his tragic, reprehensible mistakes, how without it, he withdrew to the point of bare existence where misery and regret ruled his soul.

The muscles of his shoulders bunched into tight knots against the back of the wooden chair. "My answer is no."

The villain arched an ink-black brow. "I have your woman. Surely a single fight—something at which you excel—is nominal in exchange for her well-being."

Put like that, it seemed a simple choice. But of course it wasn't. "What do you mean 'her well-being'? Speak plainly about your intentions."

Jagger shrugged. "I'm using her as leverage. Agree to my terms or she'll suffer the consequences."

What consequences? "You can't mean to kill her. You'll hang."

"Who said I was going to kill her? I needn't do anything so messy. I have only to inform a few key newspapers of her whereabouts this night." His stare was charged with innuendo. "Lockwood House. With *you*."

Ambrose wasn't certain Jagger possessed the misjudgment to murder Philippa, but knew he'd ruin her in a trice. Over a prizefight. "You can't."

Jagger exchanged looks with the men surrounding Ambrose. They broke into laughter. After a moment, Jagger wiped a finger over his left eye. "Of course I can. I *could* even kill her if I chose, but I don't have to. I'm sure you'll agree social murder for someone like her is devastating enough. Go on, run to the magistrate and say you were kidnapped from one of Lockwood's orgies with Lady Philippa Latham. The papers will love that even more."

It took every scrap of self-control not to throttle the son of a bitch. If Ambrose went to the authorities, the entire evening would have been for naught. She'd be ruined. "How did you discover her identity?"

"You were kind enough to provide her address. Only one young woman like her resides at Herrick House. The Earl of Herrick's daughter." Jagger's eyes narrowed. "I'm quite serious. Think carefully before you answer."

The chair seemed to melt from under Ambrose. He'd spent the entire evening trying to keep her safe and he couldn't stop now. He'd abandoned a woman once—God, how could he even compare the two situations? Still, he had a chance to save someone now, and he'd be damned if he failed her. "I'll fight the Irishman, but no one else."

"That's not what I'm negotiating. I require your prizefighting services indefinitely. I want you to fight Belcher this summer when he returns from Derbyshire."

He glared at Jagger. "One fight." He prayed he could manage one fight without falling back into the abyss that had claimed him three years ago, but more than that he didn't dare.

"Perhaps I should just take the woman." Jagger nodded at a man in the corner who nodded in return then started toward the stairs.

Goddamn Jagger to hell. "I'll find you a prizefighter," Ambrose blurted loudly. He hated that he sounded strained, almost desperate.

The villain steepled his hands on the table before him and

contemplated Ambrose over the points of his index fingers. "Who?"

"I don't know, but there are dozens of fighters who would grasp at the chance."

Jagger laid his palms flat. "I've watched them all. None are as good as you."

"I'll train him to be."

He stared at Ambrose a moment then held up a hand at the man who was poised at the base of the stairs. "I accept your proposal, but this prizefighter must be acceptable to me. And you'll fight for me until you satisfactorily train him. If you don't, I'll ensure Greater London knows she accompanied you to Lockwood House."

He should've felt at least a moment's relief at settling things, but until Philippa was safely in his keep, he was ready to spring into violence. "Is this to be a fair fight or will I win easily?"

Jagger's mouth ticked up. "A reasonable question. Yes, this is a fair fight, one I expect you to win. Keep an eye on your woman. Until you fight Nolan and deliver me an acceptable prizefighter, I will be watching your every move." His lips spread in a cold smile. "And hers."

God, Ambrose wanted to hit someone. He thought of simply starting in on one of the men beside him, but knew a half dozen or more would descend, and he'd hurt worse than he already did. The wounds he'd suffered from resisting his captors were more numerous than he'd thought. His lip had stopped bleeding, but was now swollen, as was one of his eyes. He was fairly certain his ribs were bruised. If he was going to fight in ten days' time he'd need to allow himself to heal, which meant no fighting in the interim.

"Your days are numbered, Jagger. You can't threaten a gentlewoman and not expect repercussions."

Jagger smiled his infuriatingly smug smile, but his eyes were pure malice. "There will be no repercussions for me. But the damage to her will be incontrovertible. Her reputation rides on *you*. Fighting *for me*."

"God damn it, just bring me the woman!" Ambrose thundered, his tolerance past its limit.

Jagger chuckled. "Impatient bastard, aren't you? I would be too if I had her at my fingertips. And what a cheeky fellow you are—shagging a respectable girl right under the *ton*'s noses. But then that's what you do, isn't it?"

Ambrose leapt across the table and slammed into him. They hit the gilt chair, knocking it backward. The top just cleared the wall, but he and Jagger went crashing into the paneling. Before he could land a punch, Ambrose was viciously pulled away. A fist drove into his lower back and he grunted in pain.

"Stop," Jagger gathered his balance. "Don't hurt my new prizefighter. I see I salted a wound, Sevrin. I'd no idea you were a man of such strong emotions."

He hadn't been in a long time. Though Jagger's account of Ambrose's history was true, it wasn't the entire truth. Regardless, he was as surprised by his reaction as Jagger had been. Apparently there was at least a scrap of honor buried somewhere inside him. There had to be, or he never would've helped Philippa tonight.

Jagger brushed off his clothing. "Take him upstairs to get the woman and then put them in a hack to Upper Grosvenor Street."

The men holding Ambrose pulled him toward the stairs. He wrenched his arms free as they passed the bastard who'd attacked Philippa in the alley. He gave Ambrose a sharp, sinister stare. "Keep hold of yer girl. Never know when something bad might happen."

Ambrose lunged toward him, but the other men grabbed him and pushed him toward the stairs. One led the way while the other kept shoving him in the back as they climbed the creaking stairs. The smell of rotting wood and cloying dust accompanied them. On the third landing, he was led to a door at the end of a short corridor.

The first man threw the bolt and opened the door. The room was pitch black save weak light filtering in through the closed shutter over the single window. Ambrose strained to see, but couldn't make out a figure in the small chamber.

He pushed past the criminal into the room. "Philippa?" He couldn't keep the concern from his tone. Didn't even try.

"Sevrin?" She stepped from behind the door and he heard something clatter to the floor.

Ambrose slammed the door in the faces of the criminals and then gathered Philippa in his arms. "Are you all right?" He pressed his lips to her temple, unable to stop himself. Somehow they'd gone from complete strangers to something else in the span of a few hours.

Her arms came up around his neck and she pressed into him as if she meant to join her body with his. Need and want speared through him. He clasped the sides of her head and kissed her.

It wasn't a gentle kiss, but a savage claiming borne of fear and danger and soul-shattering relief at finding her whole. His lips slanted over hers and demanded entrance into her mouth. She opened for him and he devoured her. She tasted of desire and courage. He licked and ate at her mouth as if he'd die without possessing her in this moment.

That she kissed him back with open-mouthed hunger should have shocked him, but he reveled in her response. She clutched at his neck, her fingers twining into the hair at his nape. Her tongue met his with probing, delicious strokes. Her lips moved with increasing urgency. Her body cleaved to his perfectly. He wrapped his arms around her, pulling her breasts against him until his body was shamelessly aflame with lust.

"Ye want us to leave ye alone?" came a voice from outside.

Ambrose slowed the kiss with great reluctance then ended it with a soft brush of his lips against hers. He knew he had to let her go, but couldn't. Not yet.

He rested his forehead against hers as they breathed into each other. "I'm so sorry," he said. "Are you sure you're all right? I'll kill them all if they've hurt you."

She looked up at him, her eyes wide in the dim light. She looked a bit dazed, and he hoped it was from the kiss and not anything else. "I'm fine." She shuddered, but it was much different from the spasms she'd suffered in the hack earlier. Her body thrummed with energy, and it was all Ambrose could do not to prolong their embrace. "I'm just glad it was you, though I was prepared to defend myself." She glanced at the floor where a piece of wood lay.

He followed her gaze. "What's that?"

"Part of a slat from the bed in the corner. The furniture's in horrible condition, but it provides a ready weapon."

He laughed, as much to release everything pent up inside him as to see her smile in return. And she didn't disappoint him. "You're the bravest girl I know. No other woman could've endured tonight."

"Is it over then?" The hope in her voice drove him to squeeze her tightly against him.

"Yes, we're going to Herrick House now."

"What did he want from you?"

"I'm to help him find a prizefighter." He wouldn't tell her about the threat to her reputation. There was no need for her to worry over something that would never come to pass. He wouldn't allow it.

She blinked at him, her ale-colored eyes wide. "That's it?"

He pulled her against his chest to avoid looking in her eyes. "Yes."

"And you can do that?" At his nod, she clutched at his shirtfront and rested her cheek against his pounding heart. "Thank you."

A quarter hour later they were ensconced in the hack that had brought them and were traveling back the way they'd come.

"What time do you think it is?" she asked.

They sat together on the forward-facing seat. She leaned against him, and he curled his arm around her shoulders.

"I'm not sure, but morning can't be too far off. Will your mother be home already?"

"I don't know. Last night—rather, this morning, no I suppose that was *yesterday* morning now—she didn't return until after I'd risen."

"I imagine the servants will inform her of your late arrival. I'm sorry this will cause you trouble."

"It won't." She yawned behind her hand. "The night footman is half-blind and typically too sleep-addled to remember what time I came in, and my maid will say whatever I tell her to."

"Convenient."

"Very. Though I'd trade the convenience if it meant my

mother would cease her scandalous behavior." They lapsed into silence for a few minutes. The wheels of the hack rattled over the cobblestone streets; street lanterns glowed at intervals. She yawned again. "You never answered me about why you let others think the worst of you."

Her head rested against his chest and he gave into the urge to stroke her hair, which had all but come out of its elaborate style. "Because everything they think is true."

"I don't believe it. Especially the part about you liking men."

"God, no. At least that isn't true."

She gave a single, lethargic nod. "Everything you did tonight was heroic."

He couldn't allow her to credit him. They couldn't be friends. They couldn't be anything. He stopped stroking her hair and ought to have set her against the squab, but couldn't bring himself to dislodge her—an utterly unheroic gesture. "Philippa, I'm not some knight meant to rescue you. I've done many things that are far beyond the pale."

She lifted her head and looked up at him. "Such as ruin a girl and not marry her."

"Yes." And so much worse.

She laid her head back down and snuggled against him. "Next time I see you, you can tell me what really happened because I don't believe the story is that simple."

He was unnerved at both her faith in him and her ability to vault the carefully constructed wall around his past. He ought to say there wouldn't be a next time, that when he saw her again, he would turn and walk away as if he didn't know the luscious feel of her body, or the heartwarming sound of her laugh, or the delectable taste of her mouth. Instead, he listened to the deepening sound of her breathing and caressed the gentle rise of her shoulder.

All the anger he'd felt, all the self-loathing drifted away. His body relaxed in time with hers, and he surrendered to the comfort of just being next to her. He would cherish this moment of absolute peace, knowing it was the only one he might ever have.

Chapter Five

THE following day, Philippa nervously paced her mother's sitting room. She'd tried to complete her morning's correspondence, but penning letters to her married friends couldn't hold her attention. Letters to her aunts and cousins even less so. She was far too consumed with her mother's outrageous behavior. Leaving Lady Kilmartin's with Booth-Barrows. Going to Lockwood House. Engaging in some sort of illicit activity with Booth-Barrows and *two other people*.

She shuddered to think of the scandal if anyone discovered her mother's perversion. Her pace quickened along with her pulse.

Mother wouldn't appreciate Philippa taking up residence in her personal chambers. However, Philippa was determined to see her as soon as possible. *Assuming she came home.*

The clock on the mantelpiece ticked loudly, announcing the time to be nearly half past noon. Noon! Mother had never stayed out so long.

Philippa wished the window overlooked the street instead of the rear garden. She supposed she could go down and wait on the doorstep.

Was that the faint sound of a coach? She stilled and listened intently for the sound of the front door opening. There it was. *At last.* She perched on the edge of the burgundy damask settee and composed herself, mentally rehearsing what she meant to say.

A moment later the door opened, but it was her mother's

maid, Ellis. She inclined her head. "My lady." Her soft, crinkly face—Ellis was well past middle age—was pinched, showing a bit of displeasure.

Philippa doubted Ellis's expression was due to her presence in Mother's sitting room. Rather, the maid was disturbed by Mother's staying out all night. Ellis was nothing if not staid and proper. "Good afternoon, Ellis. I need to speak with my mother privately."

"Certainly. I'll just wait in her dressing chamber."

Philippa nodded. The maid disappeared into her mother's bedchamber and presumably the dressing room beyond. A few minutes later, the door opened again. Philippa's heart rate increased.

Her mother closed the door and turned. Her face was lined, exhausted, but a smile lifted the edges of her mouth. She stopped short upon seeing Philippa, and the smile faded.

"Mother, I need to speak with you."

"It will have to wait, I'm afraid. I'm simply dead on my feet."

"It can't wait." Philippa refused to be pushed aside until a more convenient hour. She pressed her damp palms against her lap. "Mother, you can't continue to behave like this."

Rather than react to what Philippa had said, her mother had the audacity to stifle a yawn. Perhaps that *was* her reaction. "Like what? Really, I must insist we discuss this later."

"No, we'll discuss it now."

Her mother's eyes narrowed and her mouth drew tightly into an expression of disapproval. Her tone dripped ice. "I do not appreciate your disrespect."

Philippa stood, her legs quivering in anger. "*My* disrespect? I'm not the one cavorting about Town with a man who isn't my husband!" *Not to mention attending orgies*, but she couldn't bring herself to verbalize that.

Her mother stepped toward her bedchamber, giving no indication she registered—or cared—about Philippa's outrage. "Your insinuations are insulting. I'm a grown woman. If I choose to stay out all night with my friends, it's none of your affair."

Philippa shouldn't have been surprised by her mother's

indifference. She'd long ignored any concerns her daughter might've had. Her primary goal had been to see Philippa married, and the longer Philippa took to find a husband, the less interested Mother became.

Weary of her mother's selfishness, Philippa blurted, "I followed you to Lockwood House." Immediately, she wished she could draw the words back into her mouth.

Her mother's gasp filled the chamber. She turned abruptly. "Never say you were there."

No point in refuting it now. She forced her quaking frame to still. "I was."

Mother stepped toward her, the exhaustion stripped from her features. "Why would—"

Philippa notched her chin up. "I'm afraid I deluded myself into thinking I could talk you into coming home with me and honoring your marriage to Father. Only think, if I'm aware of your activities, who else is?"

Mother's lips disappeared into a tight line. "I don't love your father, and he doesn't love me. He doesn't care what I do."

While her parents' marriage had never been one of passion or love, hearing Mother plainly say so made Philippa's heart ache. She'd spent years—a lifetime—convincing herself that behind closed doors her parents shared some sort of *feeling* for one another. What a fool she'd been. Even now, she searched her memories for happy times, love-filled moments, care and consideration, but there was nothing. Just a cold void where a family ought to have been.

She forced her pain into her anger. "I'm certain Father would care you were at *Lockwood House.*"

Mother smoothed her skirt with quivering hands. "No one knows. Lockwood House is private, and I can't imagine you'll tell anyone."

Philippa struggled to accept that her mother wasn't just her mother, but also a woman who was apparently trying to find happiness. Even so, her mother's actions affected her. How could they not? "Of course I won't, but doesn't it matter to you that *I* know?"

Her mother came to stand before her. "You mustn't be

disappointed. Your father wouldn't be. Our marriage has never been based on love or affection."

"What was it based on then?" Philippa's voice sounded as small as she felt.

"A marriage must be based first and foremost on a shared regard. A husband should be kind and likeable, if at all possible."

Philippa had heard all of that before, but had never thought to ask her mother, "Is that how you found Father?"

Silence descended, and her mother stared at some point beyond Philippa's shoulder. "No," she whispered. "I loved your father, but I was a fool." She blinked damp eyelashes then looked at Philippa. "I don't want that for you." Her features tightened. "But neither do I want you at the center of an outrageous scandal. Tell me exactly what happened last night. Did anyone see you?"

Only one of England's most notorious scoundrels. Just thinking of Sevrin sent a pleasant shock through Philippa's frame. She forced her thoughts away from her handsome rescuer and contemplated how to answer her mother. Obviously, she needed to lie. "Once I realized I was at Lockwood House, I returned home." She had to trust the eyesight-challenged footman and her loyal maid wouldn't reveal the actual time of her arrival at Herrick House—which was of course several hours later.

Her mother exhaled audibly. "Thank heaven for that. Philippa, if you'd been seen… you'd be finished. No decent man would wed you." She pursed her lips. "Since you decided to call this tête-à-tête, I must remind you that you *will* marry this Season."

Philippa ought to have realized her mother would turn the conversation around. Her defenses prickled. "You've made it perfectly clear."

"I hope so. However, after rejecting—what, six?—offers in the past five years, you need to make it known that you're serious now. That you *will* accept an offer."

"I've always been serious." Serious enough to risk rejecting suitor after suitor because she hadn't loved any of them. She knew how her repeated refusals appeared, but she couldn't enter into a marriage that might be as cold and stilted as her parents'.

Mother sniffed. "I can't imagine what you're waiting for."

To fall in love. However, Mother's revelations now gave her pause. Mother had fallen in love, and it had brought her nothing but misery. Suddenly Philippa's dream seemed childish and all but impossible. "Why didn't Father love you back?"

Her mother blanched just as they heard a commotion from downstairs. It sounded like an arrival, but they didn't have any appointments today. Philippa would know since she'd managed the household the past few years after her mother had simply stopped doing so.

Her features drawn, Mother went to the door of the sitting room and opened it a hand's width. Multiple voices from downstairs carried into the chamber. Then a louder voice, just outside the door. "My lady, his lordship has returned from abroad." Pigeon, their butler paused a moment, then added, "He's brought guests."

The door closed and Mother turned. Her face had been pale, but now bright flags of red stained her cheeks. "You want to know why your father didn't love me back? Go downstairs and see for yourself."

A thunderous pounding on the door pulled Ambrose from sleep. He opened his eyes, squinting at the daylight working its way around the edges of his curtains, and guessed the time to be well past noon.

The noise stopped a moment then started more vigorously. Ambrose forced his aching body from his bed, cursing whoever had roused him. His head throbbed in time to the smacks on the door as he made his way across the sitting room. At last, he pulled open the door and then had to jerk backward as a massive fist came toward his face in mid-knock.

"Where the hell were you last night?" demanded Hopkins, a wide, heavily-muscled man a decade older than Ambrose's twenty-eight years. He was Ambrose's right hand man at his fighting club, which met nightly downstairs in the back room of the Black Horse Tavern, and was one of three people Ambrose tolerated speaking to him like that.

"I was detained." For the first time since he'd started the club more than two years ago, Ambrose had missed an evening of bouts.

Hopkins eyed Ambrose's battered face. "I can see that. Tom take care of you?"

Ambrose nodded and then stepped aside to allow Hopkins to come in. Tom was the owner and operator of the Black Horse Tavern, though Ambrose owned the actual building. In addition to making the best ale in London, Tom was a skilled healer, but he confined his "practice" to the members of Ambrose's fighting club.

Ambrose closed the door. Hopkins went to the table situated at one side of Ambrose's sitting room. His apartment consisted of two chambers. The first was the sitting room where he greeted very few guests, and the second was his bedchamber, where he greeted no one save Tom's daughter who cleaned it. That a viscount lived in such lodgings was scandalous. Or it would be, if anyone knew.

Hopkins deposited himself in one of the four chairs that surrounded the table. Covered with letters from his steward, correspondence from his secretary, and various other business materials, it was rarely used for dining. Ambrose piled the papers in a corner. "You want a drink?"

Hopkins nodded. "Ale, if you have it."

Ambrose always kept a jug of Tom's ale in his cupboard. He poured two cups and handed one to his friend before joining him at the table.

After they'd both taken large draughts, Hopkins shook his head. "Don't suppose you're going to tell me where you were last night."

Ambrose preferred to keep his private matters private, even with Hopkins, who was his closest friend in London. Despite that, he recognized he'd have to tell him what happened. He needed Hopkins's help. "Actually, I would like to discuss it, and in fact I require your assistance."

Hopkins had been raising his cup to his mouth, but now his arm froze in mid-drink and he peered at Ambrose disbelievingly. "You want my help?"

Ambrose grinned at him even as he knew Hopkins's reaction was genuine. "Surprising, I know. I'm to fight in a prizefight in less than a fortnight."

Hopkins clanked his cup onto the table. "Thought you gave that up."

He had. Though he could have sought the championship, he couldn't bear the praise. Even so, he missed that kind of fighting. His club was a decent replacement, a necessity for his sanity, but a truly visceral bout where winning or losing was everything? Nothing could compare.

Ambrose only said, "I'm doing a favor for someone. Bloke called Jagger."

Hopkins's eyes widened. "That gutter rat? How'd you get mixed up with the likes of him?"

"You know him?" Ambrose's first order of business today had been to learn all he could about the jackanapes. To have information fall readily into his lap was most convenient. He wrapped his hands around his ale cup and settled back in his chair. "Tell me everything."

"I don't know him personally, mind you. He runs a group of thieves, pickpockets, and the like. Plus a band who'll obtain an object for a price."

"I could hire them to steal something?"

Hopkins nodded. "I heard he owns a brothel or two as well, maybe an interest in an opium den."

"Sounds like a charming fellow." Plenty of criminal interests and now he wanted to back a legitimate prizefighter? Something didn't make sense.

As if he'd heard Ambrose's thoughts, Hopkins said, "Never heard of him backing a prizefighter before. Why do you owe him a favor? What's he got on you?"

Ambrose should've expected Hopkins to figure that much out. He was far more astute than most people gave a huge brute like him credit for. Still, he wouldn't mention Philippa. The fewer people who knew about his connection to her the better. "Nothing. Believe it or not, I'm actually looking forward to fighting."

And he was, save the part where everyone cheered and

heaped glory upon him when he won. He'd grown up with an overabundance of such distinction, as his father's favorite, the district's pride, and his brother's hero—all roles he'd felt entitled to. And all roles he'd proven he didn't deserve.

Hopkins regarded him with an expression of disbelief. "Well, you must have a reason beyond that. Can't see you getting into bed with the likes of Jagger unless someone needs your help."

Again, Hopkins was smarter than Ambrose wanted him to be—at least about this. "You're giving me far too much credit."

Hopkins shook his head. "No, you've helped plenty of men. Like me. This club has saved a lot of blokes."

Ambrose shifted in his chair, uncomfortable with Hopkins' words. He'd never said anything like that before. "Don't fool yourself. This club is my little hobby. I just let all of you in so I have someone to fight."

Hopkins rolled his eyes. "Right then. You don't help anyone. Except Tom. You'll at least admit you helped him?"

He supposed he'd "helped" Tom when he'd purchased the building that housed the Black Horse from a brutal, money-grubbing jackass. But Ambrose had also bought it for his own selfish reasons. He'd just started using the Black Horse's back room for his fighting club when the landlord had threatened to evict Tom. Since Ambrose preferred to deal with Tom, he'd just bought the damned building.

"Fine, I surrender. But keep that to yourself. Back to Jagger." Ambrose wanted to learn all he could about Jagger—assess the true depth of his threats. He didn't doubt the man would socially ruin Philippa, but would he take things further? He'd certainly implied that he could, without fear of meeting the hangman. "Sounds like he's not a brutal criminal? I like to know what sort of man I'm getting involved with."

Hopkins cleared his throat. "Mayhap you should've thought of that before you agreed?" At Ambrose's quelling stare, he shrugged. "Haven't heard of him to be a murderer, if that's what you're getting at. Though he's pretty tight with Gin Jimmy, and he's a nasty sort. Wouldn't want to cross him." Hopkins took another gulp of ale.

Now Gin Jimmy Ambrose had heard of. He was one of the

largest gin producers in London and owned several opium dens and brothels. He preyed on people's vices and addictions to their absolute destruction, and never looked twice at the bodies he left in his wake. If Jagger was a bosom friend of Gin Jimmy, Ambrose had cause to worry.

Hopkins set his empty cup on the table. "What does this mean for the club? You disbanding it?"

"Lord, no. Last night's absence was a one-time occurrence. Though, I suppose I'll miss the night of the prizefight."

"Won't matter. All the men will go to watch it anyway. When and where?"

Ambrose had received the specifics of the bout from Jagger before leaving last night. "Dirty Lane. Friday the sixteenth."

"You need me to help you train?"

"Probably." One couldn't be too prepared. "You ever see this Irishman—Nolan's his name—fight?"

"That your opponent?" At Ambrose's nod, he continued, "No, but I've heard of him."

Ambrose had heard of him too, but was hoping someone had actually seen him. Nolan had lost only three fights in his entire career, and none for the past two years. He had his eye on battling Belcher for the title, which was why Jagger needed Ambrose to win. Why he'd recruited Ambrose in the first place.

Recruited. More like forced. Jagger had dragged Philippa—an innocent—into this, and it was up to Ambrose to ensure her safety. He felt compelled to see her—something he hadn't planned to do.

Hopkins stood. "I'd best be on my way. Just wanted to make sure you weren't dead."

Ambrose smiled. "I appreciate that. I'll need a few days to recover, but then you can start drilling me in the evenings, if you don't mind?"

"It's not as if I need to get home to my family." Hopkins was a confirmed bachelor, though unlike Ambrose he partook of female company from time to time. One of the reasons Ambrose counted him among his few friends was his complete silence regarding Ambrose's lack of skirt-chasing.

Speaking of friends… the Earl of Saxton, Ambrose's sole

friend outside the working class, had returned to London the week before. He could certainly arrange for Ambrose to be invited to select events that would allow him to observe Philippa and ascertain her safety and well-being. He could even speak to her without drawing notice. *Hell.* No, he couldn't. They hadn't been properly introduced. Well, Saxton could arrange that, too.

After Hopkins departed, Ambrose cradled his mug and outlined his priorities. Protect Philippa. Fight the Irishman. Find a prizefighter.

What would he have said to Jagger's men if he hadn't been with Philippa when they'd come looking for him? He would've declined just the same, and without Philippa, Jagger never could have forced him into agreeing.

Philippa. The crux of all of this. Ambrose frowned into his mug. His reaction to her was quite troubling. Kissing her to shield her identity? Sweeping her into a thoroughly debauched embrace? Five years he'd kept himself from women. Five years of well-deserved penance threatened by a genteel miss on the hunt for a husband.

He drained his cup, wishing he'd poured something stronger.

Chapter Six

SITUATED on a pale green settee across the drawing room, Abigail, Lady von Egmont, the source of misery in Philippa's mother's marriage, laughed at something Philippa's father whispered in her ear. She was precisely one year widowed, which is why Father had chosen this moment to bring her back to England, her homeland.

For the past three days, Philippa had suffered the woman's intrusion on their household and her father's obvious affection for her. The way they fawned over each other—in plain sight of everyone at Herrick House—made Philippa want to toss up her accounts. It also made her eager to escape. As in permanently leave Herrick House behind. Suddenly her parents' edict that she marry this season had acquired a quite tolerable taste.

Hence, her husband hunt had been revised to *The Necessary and Most Immediate Husband Hunt* and would be launched tonight at Lady Dunwoody's ball.

Armed with a list of potential suitors, Philippa meant to narrow her field to five or less. Then she would do her best to glean the marriageability of each one. She couldn't hope to fall in love quickly, so she'd have to dispense with that life-long goal and settle for someone who would be faithful, with the hope they might build something more. But how could she possibly be certain of a man's fidelity? During courtship, they would behave in whatever manner necessary to gain the prize they sought—Philippa and her ten thousand pound dowry.

Sickened by the spectacle on the settee, she turned her gaze to Lady von Egmont's son, Pieter, standing at the windows. Tall with gently waving blond hair and an athletic physique, he presented a handsome figure. He was also charming, intelligent, and witty.

Father had invited them to London—ostensibly—to see if Lord von Egmont and Philippa would suit. However, both she and von Egmont knew the real purpose behind the von Egmonts' visit: their parents' intent to carry on their decades-old affair now that Lady von Egmont was a widow.

Father had also indicated he was providing "assistance" to an "old friend" given the strife in their French-occupied homeland. Philippa just wasn't sure blowing in Lady von Egmont's ear was the type of assistance an old friend ought to provide. Particularly when one's wife was upstairs.

Philippa clenched her fists, outraged on her mother's behalf. Mother scarcely spent any time at Herrick House, and when she did, she kept to her room. She professed a headache, but everyone, including the servants, knew the truth.

That was why, when the countess entered the drawing room a moment later, four heads turned to her in complete shock. To her mother's credit, she simply smiled serenely at everyone and murmured, "Good evening."

They'd gathered in the drawing room before going to Lady Dunwoody's ball. Tonight was to be Lady von Egmont's first foray into Society since returning to London. She'd grown up here and it was, in fact, where she'd met Philippa's father. Unfortunately for them, she'd already been betrothed; otherwise their history—as well as Philippa's—would have been written quite differently.

Philippa gave her mother a warm smile meant to convey support. "Good evening, Mother. You look lovely." A dark purple feather arced from her upswept hair, and her form appeared long and slender beneath the graceful drape of her amethyst gown. Despite the trials of the past few days, she was the epitome of vibrancy and beauty.

"I'm taking the carriage to Lady Dunwoody's, Philippa, if you'd care to join me." She narrowed her eyes at her husband. "Herrick, I presume you will escort the von Egmonts and help them acclimate. You'll forgive me if I focus on Philippa this evening." This made sense even if it wasn't for the monstrous chasm that now divided her parents. Lady Dunwoody's ball was one of the premier events of the Season and would be Philippa's best opportunity for culling her list of suitors. That her mother wanted to personally supervise her this evening spoke volumes about Mother's priorities. She wanted Philippa married posthaste.

Philippa stood and smoothed the skirt of her aquamarine dress. "I'm ready, Mother." She turned and gave a nod to her father who was now scowling a bit darkly.

"I'd hoped for Philippa to arrive with me and the von Egmonts."

Philippa noted her mother's heightened color and intervened. "Now, Father, it wouldn't be at all fair to the other gentleman if I arrived on the arm of Lord von Egmont. But I shall save him a dance." She flashed a smile at their houseguest who gave her an infinitesimal bow in return.

Her father pursed his lips, and while he didn't look pleased, he made no further complaint. With that, Philippa left the drawing room with her mother, and they were soon situated in the carriage on their way to Lady Dunwoody's.

"Did you mean what you said about arriving with von Egmont?" her mother asked. "May I correctly interpret you are finally getting to the business of securing a husband?"

Philippa wished she didn't sound so cold and calculated about it, but then she herself was going about this in a far more calculated manner than she would ever have thought. "Yes."

"I'm pleased to hear it. The sooner the better, in fact." She paused and inhaled deeply. "There's no easy way to say this, so I'll just come out with it. I've let my own townhouse. I'll be leaving Herrick House in thirty days' time."

Mother's selfishness was deeper than Philippa had thought. Philippa flexed her hands against her skirt and refused to allow her chest to burn. "You couldn't wait until after I was betrothed?"

"I would've preferred to, yes, but the situation at home is intolerable. And I couldn't be sure you would wed." She shifted her gaze away. "I still can't."

Philippa straightened, stung by her mother's lack of trust and patience. She wholly understood her mother's position regarding the atmosphere at Herrick House, but how could she put a timeframe on Philippa's future happiness? She could hope her mother's defection from Herrick House wouldn't cause a major scandal, but it would be enough to deter most suitors—those worth having, anyway—from pursuing her.

It seemed her *Necessary and Most Immediate Husband Hunt* required another revision: the *Direly Important Crusade to Marry Before Scandal Ruined Her.*

"Mother, the likelihood of my marrying in the next thirty days is nearly impossible. I'd have to become betrothed in the next few days in order to allow time for the banns to be read. And I can't imagine my betrothed seeking a special license to accommodate your whim."

"You don't have to wed, you only have to become engaged. Your groom won't cry off because your mother moved into her own residence."

One could hope. But it appeared her mother had no sympathy for her situation—a situation *she'd* created.

Her mother turned her head and regarded her with open curiosity. "Who do you have your eye on this evening?"

Though Philippa had given this plenty of thought, she didn't want to discuss it with her mother. Their motives were far different even though they sought the same end. She wondered if Mother wouldn't just marry her off to the first man they came across at Dunwoody House.

Still, she offered a couple of names to avoid further pestering. "Lord Vick and Lord Allred."

Mother nodded. "Allred's an excellent choice. Vick isn't bad, though I'm surprised you'd consider someone of his age." Vick was a widower north of thirty, but he was charming and intelligent, and possessed a love of horses, which Philippa shared.

Another name rose unbidden to her mind. Sevrin. Ha! As if he'd even be at Lady Dunwoody's.

He couldn't be on Philippa's list of suitors. Aside from his ghastly reputation, he'd made it clear he wasn't the marrying kind. Even if he were, he wouldn't be the kind she'd want. His kisses were toe-curlingly delicious, but the darkness and violence simmering beneath his attractive exterior didn't bode well for a happy union. If nothing else, Philippa meant not to repeat her mother's mistake. If she had any inkling at all that a man would make her miserable, he was off the list.

At last the carriage arrived at Dunwoody House. Her mother prepared to alight. "I shall do my part to advocate you to Allred and Vick. Allred's grandmother is delightful and will take kindly to your attention—make sure you visit with her. At the end of the evening you'll need to return to Herrick House with your father."

Philippa wasn't surprised by this pronouncement, but again saw exactly where her mother stood with regard to their crumbling family. "I'm sure I'll find my way home. Please don't concern yourself."

Her mother pursed her lips at the edge in Philippa's tone, but Philippa kept her chin elevated. After her mother departed the carriage, Philippa exhaled and prayed the evening would go on much better than it had started.

Once inside, they greeted their hosts and then parted ways without saying a word. Upon entering the ballroom, Philippa was immediately hailed by her friends Lady Lydia Prewitt and Miss Audrey Cheswick.

Lady Lydia, the epitome of a young London miss with her warm brown eyes and pale blonde hair, drew Philippa away from the doorway. Philippa barely had time to register the fragrant lilies blooming in profusion about the ballroom or the ivory and gold decorations swathing the walls.

"Goodness, Philippa, we feared for your health after so many days away," Lydia said. "We've been so bereft without you—our shining leader." Lydia, ever dramatic, placed her hand over her heart.

"'Shining leader'?" Philippa laughed and shook her head. "Pray, you aren't going to start calling me that."

"You know very well Audrey and I are lost without you," Lydia said. "We simply fade into the background without your sparkling wit and charm to remind people we exist."

Philippa felt heat rise up her neck. "Stop, you're making me out to be far too important."

Audrey, a quiet young woman whom most would term a wallflower, nodded in agreement. "It's true. You always make sure we're included in conversations, and you endeavor to secure us dance partners. You're a true friend. We missed you."

Philippa gave Audrey's hand a squeeze. "I missed you, too."

Lydia leaned forward. "Yes, well, so many things have happened. Saxton has returned with his bride. There's a rumor she's increasing." In addition to her penchant for drama, Lydia thrived on gossip. She narrowed her eyes and regarded Philippa shrewdly. "Is that why you stayed away? Of course I would completely understand. Losing Saxton to her of all people..." She shook her head and rolled her eyes.

Philippa ignored Lydia's spite. Lydia possessed a wealth of time, a dearth of hobbies, and a harridan of an aunt who encouraged her to obtain and spread gossip at a breakneck pace. It was because of her poor example that Philippa sought to affect Lydia in more positive ways. She smiled and gave a light shrug. "You know I declined his suit, Lydia."

Audrey pursed her lips at Lydia. "Philippa isn't bothered in the least by Saxton or his bride."

Lydia looked unconvinced, but said nothing more on the subject. "The other morsel you missed has to do with Viscount Sevrin."

Her heartbeat gained speed. Sevrin? She couldn't help but inwardly cringe as she thought of the scandalous way in which they'd met and spent their evening at Lockwood House. For a moment, her blood ran cold as she wondered if she was somehow part of this gossip. But, no, surely her friends would have told her immediately, or visited her before now.

Forcing her voice to remain calm and even, she asked, "What morsel is that?"

Lydia glanced around to ascertain if anyone was listening. When her gaze settled briefly on a pair of matrons within earshot, she raised her voice. "He was seen at Lockwood House."

Philippa's stomach flipped over, and heat suffused her body. Again, she tried to maintain her equilibrium. "Why is that news?"

"Surely you know what Lockwood House is." Lydia rolled her eyes again. "Goodness, Philippa, I'm beginning to think you were actually ill."

Audrey shook her head at Lydia. "Can't you just tell her?" She turned to Philippa, but did not adopt Lydia's too-loud tone. "He was there with a *woman*."

Philippa recalled what the criminal Jagger had said about Sevrin the other night. Did people really believe he preferred men? She couldn't imagine that was true. He'd kissed her. Twice.

"Why is this notable? I should think someone like him would be expected to visit Lockwood House."

"Yes, but he's never been seen there with a woman. Though she was masked, rumor has it her form was quite beautiful. There are at least a dozen wagers at White's as to her identity."

Philippa's interest sharpened as her insides twisted. "Who do they think she is?"

"Most of the names are courtesans. But there's a wager she's Quality." Lydia gave her a sly smile. "And unmarried, to boot."

Philippa's discomfort vaulted to full nausea.

Audrey shook her head again. "Absent a specific name, this is all ridiculous conjecture. Honestly, men will wager on the color of the sky."

Lydia patted her immaculate hair. "I, for one, am determined to learn the identity of this mystery woman."

Philippa nearly choked.

Audrey's expression turned sympathetic. "I feel sorry for her, whoever she is."

"Oh, don't," Lydia said. "She had the wherewithal to attend a party at Lockwood House. Like as not, she's looking for a bit of notoriety."

Philippa finally found her tongue. "If that were true, don't you think she would have foregone a mask?"

"You would think, but apparently that just isn't *done* at Lockwood House. Unless you're Sevrin, but then he's made it clear he doesn't follow the rules."

"And what will you do when you identify this poor woman?" Audrey asked.

Lydia blinked. "Accept the accolades for discovering her, of course."

"Oh, well, I only wondered if you meant to somehow collect on the wager at White's." Audrey winked at Philippa. They often provoked Lydia—good-naturedly—about seeking notoriety.

"Of course not." Lydia grinned. "That would be incredibly gauche."

Audrey shook her head. "I still don't understand why you would focus on Sevrin of all people. He's so far outside our circle—I'm certain you can count the number of times you've seen him on one hand. He's a *scoundrel.*" She shuddered. "The things they say he did."

Philippa snapped her attention to Audrey. *Things* plural? "Refusing to marry the girl he ruined, you mean?"

Lydia's eyes lit. "Oh, there's a bit more to the story than that—"

Further discussion was cut off by a dull roar spreading through the ballroom. It seemed to originate at the door, which could only mean the arrival of a Terribly Important or Interesting Person. Philippa swung her gaze with the rest of the crowd. *Or a Terribly Scandalous Person.* For standing in the doorway garbed in devilishly dark attire, his sable hair combed back from his handsome face, was none other than the scoundrel himself.

Chapter Seven

AMBROSE had braced himself for his arrival at Lady Dunwoody's ball, but he'd clearly underestimated the effect of his presence. After his hostess stuttered her way through their greeting and his host glanced nervously away while Ambrose executed a formal bow, he thought he'd seen the worst of it. Now, however, with three hundred of the *ton's* most elite citizens staring wide-eyed at him, he was quite…perturbed. Why had he decided to suffer this again? Oh, yes, Philippa, and her peculiar absence from Society the past three days. Since their night at Lockwood House and beyond. He'd grown concerned.

He scanned the ballroom for her form and found her standing off to the side with two other young women. She might be the only person in the room who wasn't slack-jawed. His lips curved into a smile. But he didn't move toward her. Yet. He had to do this correctly.

He searched the cavernous room with its fussy decorations and cloying scent of lilies for the tall, blond Saxton. There, in the opposite corner, naturally. Which meant he had to cross an entire ballroom of gaping, prurient ninnyhammers in order for Saxton to formally introduce him to Philippa.

To hell with Society and their rules. He was the Vicious Viscount, and he did whatever he damned well pleased.

He was halfway to Philippa before he stopped. He couldn't just walk up to her. He could ignore Society's demands, but she could not. He was helping her for that very reason, wasn't he? To approach her without proper introduction would damage her reputation in just the way he was trying to avoid.

He turned on his heel and went toward Saxton instead. Thankfully the grinning jackass had the grace to meet him part way.

The sonorous rise in conversation that had heralded his arrival had drifted to near silence, save the music, but damn if the dancers hadn't fumbled as they'd strained to see the commotion. Now there was a sharp and boisterous return to regular discourse—about him, he'd wager—given the frequent glances directed his way.

"You do know how to make an entrance," Saxton said.

"I merely walked in. Perhaps I should have leapt through the balcony doors. Or sprung from behind the refreshment table."

"Yes, that would have been much better." His grin faded. "You only drew such notice because of the wagers at White's."

Dread stole up Ambrose's spine. "What wagers?"

Saxton's brows rose. "You haven't been to White's today?"

"Not at the top of my agenda." Saxton knew better than to mistake him for a dandy.

"Right." Saxton led him to the side of the room, not terribly far from where Philippa stood.

"There are a handful of wagers about the woman you were seen with at Lockwood House. It's notable you were there with… a woman." He averted his gaze for the briefest moment, but Ambrose caught it. They'd never discussed his lack of female companionship, but Saxton had to wonder. "The wagers center around her identity. Some say she's a courtesan, others Quality, and others…" he glanced away again, "assert she's not a woman at all."

Clearly none of the latter wagers had been placed by anyone who'd been there. There could be no question his companion had been a woman. And an exceedingly beautiful one at that. His gaze found Philippa, but he could only see her back. However, instead of aquamarine silk, he saw the gently curved expanse of pale flesh he'd glimpsed at Lockwood House as she'd changed her gown.

He turned his attention back to Saxton. "I don't allow innuendo to trouble me, so you needn't either. Given everyone's reaction, I assume the masses are aware of these wagers."

Saxton inclined his head. "A fair assumption. Given that, I wouldn't blame you if you left."

"But I won't."

"I can't imagine why you wanted to come here in the first place. When I dragged you to a few events last fall, you complained bitterly."

"Not true. I only complained the first time. Then I rather enjoyed watching you make a cake of yourself over Lady Saxton."

His pale blue eyes frosted, but they lacked the icy heat of his pre-marital days. Saxton was a happily married man, and it showed. "I'm glad I could provide you entertainment. If you won't leave, what do you plan to do? The card room is through those doors." He pointed to Ambrose's left.

"I want you to introduce me to Lady Philippa Latham." Ambrose hadn't bothered stating his goal when he'd asked Saxton to secure his invitation. He'd doubted Saxton would have done it if he'd known what Ambrose had planned.

Saxton's eyes narrowed. "No."

"Yes."

"No."

"Why not?" He knew why not, but also knew he had to convince Saxton why he *should.*

Saxton exhaled, darting a glance at Philippa's back. "Because I like her, and introducing you to her would be presumptuous. She's the daughter of an earl, you're a—"

"Viscount, in case you've forgotten. It is precisely because she is such an estimable young woman that I want to make her acquaintance. However can I redeem myself in Society—as you've so often encouraged me to do—if I don't aim high?"

Saxton shuttered his eyes briefly and when they opened, there was a hint of mirth. "You're a cunning bastard." His expression grew serious. "But I'm warning you not to play with her. She's a nice girl, and I owe her better than to leave her to you."

"I don't mean to damage her reputation at all." *I'm trying to keep it safe.*

"Fine, but Olivia's coming with us."

"Excellent, I'm delighted to pay my respects to your better half."

Ambrose spent the next hour watching Philippa dance with a parade of men. Short men, tall men, fat men, too-handsome men, old men, young men—in fact, her current partner looked as if he was barely out of university. Ambrose leaned toward Saxton. "Who's she dancing with now?" He didn't have to identify the "she" in question since they'd been awaiting the proper opportunity to orchestrate their introduction. Primarily, they'd been waiting for the fervor surrounding Ambrose's presence to die down.

They were still waiting.

"I'm not entirely certain, but rumor is he's her houseguest. Her father returned from the continent a few days ago with company in tow."

Ambrose followed Saxton's line of sight to Philippa's father, the Earl of Herrick. He was standing quite close to a petite blonde whose high, tinkling laugh carried much too far in a crowded ballroom. Watching their intimate behavior—the way she gazed up at him, Herrick's casual stroking of her arm— Ambrose immediately understood why Philippa's mother had sought companionship elsewhere. Ambrose felt a wave of sympathy for Philippa and cursed his weakness for her anew.

Perhaps he should go. He could see that she was fine and well, untouched by Jagger. Why the devil did he need to actually speak with her? Just as he was about to cry off, the music ended and she and her partner were close enough for Saxton's lady to intercept them as they left the dance floor.

"Lady Philippa, you look lovely this evening," Olivia said with a bright smile. Though she'd been raised by one of London's most notorious courtesans, Saxton's bride was the epitome of charm and grace. Saxton didn't deserve her, but then scoundrels like them rarely did.

Philippa paused, her hand curled annoyingly around the arm of that moon-faced boy. "Lady Saxton, what a pleasure to see you. May I present Lord von Egmont from Amsterdam?"

The boy bowed and lightly took Olivia's hand. Ambrose dared to look at Philippa and was surprised—pleasantly so—to find her studying him with her delicious ale-colored gaze. "I'm delighted to make your acquaintance."

Olivia turned her head and gestured for her husband and Ambrose to step forward. "Saxton, meet Lord von Egmont." The two men nodded in greeting. "And this is our dear friend, Lord Sevrin." Olivia turned to Philippa with just the right amount of innocent curiosity. "Lady Philippa, have you met Lord Sevrin?"

Philippa's gaze widened just slightly, but probably only Ambrose caught it. "I have not." She dipped into a curtsey and lowered her gaze. The submissive gesture stoked a primal, lustful, thoroughly inappropriate reaction. Ambrose shifted his weight and prayed for a cool breeze from the open doors, which were much too far away.

He forced himself to take her hand though he knew touching her was bound to increase his discomfort. He was not mistaken. Though their hands were gloved, the spark that leapt between them was both palpable and disconcerting. Her gaze came up too quickly, and her lips parted in response.

Hell, hell, hell. He said the next stupid thing that came to mind. "May I claim this dance?"

Of all the foolish, disastrous, wrong-headed things to do. But he couldn't take it back now. He could only pray they wouldn't become the most talked about thing in the ballroom. Though he suspected he had a better chance of obtaining eternal salvation, which was to say nil.

If Philippa registered any of the shock he felt at his outrageous question, she didn't show it. "Yes, you may."

She withdrew her arm from the boy with a smile. "Thank you for the dance." A warm, genuine smile that made Ambrose perversely jealous. Which was absurd since he didn't want such affection from a woman.

The boy nodded at her. "My pleasure."

Ambrose resisted the urge to roll his eyes. Surely Philippa could do better than that green lad. More absurdity. He shouldn't care who Philippa danced with and resolved at that moment not to.

After the boy left, Ambrose presented his arm as the music

started. He shot a glance at Saxton whose gaze held a smidgeon of glower. Just the right amount to remind Ambrose of his place—far beneath that of his dance partner.

He swept her onto the dance floor, ignoring the enticing heat that radiated from her palm clutching his sleeve. "A minuet? I hope I can recall the steps." It was the sort of self-deprecating comment he made without thinking, but he actually nursed a touch of anxiety. He hadn't danced in years. Five, to be precise.

Philippa's brow creased. "Lady Dunwoody always includes a minuet—it's her favorite dance. Would you prefer to leave the dance floor?"

"Not at all. I shan't embarrass you." He winked at her to let her know he was jesting, but by the twinkle in her eye, she already knew. How could she know him after just one—albeit long—night?

She looked at him closely. "Are you wearing cosmetics?" Her eyes narrowed in scrutiny. "Yes, you're wearing face powder. To cover the remains of your bruises. Were you terribly hurt?" She raised her hand as if she meant to touch his face then dropped it quickly as she realized she couldn't. Not here. And the fact that he wanted her to made her the most dangerous woman of his acquaintance.

His mouth curved up. "Your ability to see right through my façade is more than a bit unnerving." In so many ways.

As they moved into position, she dropped her voice to a whisper. "I heard about the wagers. Should I be concerned?"

Glancing around to gauge the distance of the other couples, he adjusted the volume of his voice accordingly. "No. It's nonsense men participate in to amuse themselves. No one is ever going to learn the real identity of the woman I was with at Lockwood House."

She'd told him only retainers had seen her face, and he was nearly certain he'd been the first to see her in the drawing room. Because he was only *nearly* certain, he was concerned. But he wouldn't worry her.

They touched and stepped away and touched again. Each brush of her fingertips sent a wave of desire racing through his long-deprived body.

When they came together again, she said, "My friend, Lady Lydia Prewitt, is determined to discover your mystery woman's identity. I wish I possessed your confidence, but you don't know Lydia." She peered up at him inquisitively, as if she were assessing his worth. He hated to disappoint her, but he surely would. "If only you weren't so interesting to people. You've created quite a stir just by coming tonight."

Yes, and he was stoking the fire into a full-blown blaze by dancing with her. "I'm quite boring, actually."

She arched a slender brow. "Somehow I doubt that. What with your fighting skill, visits to Lockwood House, and scandalous background. Pity you don't have any normal hobbies, such as riding." She blinked. "Do you ride? I've never seen you in the park, but surely you must."

Ambrose inwardly flinched. She'd asked a benign question, completely unaware of the unwanted memories it provoked. But then people often asked probing, intrusive questions—did he ride (he didn't), where did he live (over a tavern), and why didn't he marry the girl he'd ruined (because he hadn't wanted to)— which he chose to ignore. Indeed, he rarely answered anything at all. Though he liked Philippa better than most, he didn't plan to answer her either.

"Who told you about the wagers?" he asked.

If she was bothered by him ignoring her question, she didn't show it. Likely because returning to the topic of the wagers had caused her forehead to crease with concern. "Lady Lydia told me," she said. "She knows everything."

He heard the anxiety in her voice. "She doesn't, and she'll never know about that night."

He danced away from her. He'd keep an eye on Lady Lydia and somehow ensure she discovered nothing. He knew precisely how rabid a gossip on the hunt could be. It was just such a scandalmonger who'd eagerly shared news of his past transgressions when he'd come to London. How much about that did Philippa know? Surely she wouldn't be dancing with him if she knew the truth.

Dancing with her reminded him of the life he'd forfeited. The life he could never return to. The life he didn't deserve. Christ, he despised such maudlin thoughts. He fought to push them away, annoyed they'd even intruded.

They came together again and he asked, "How are things at Herrick House? I couldn't help but notice your father and Lady von Egmont seem close."

Philippa's eyebrows drew together but she forced her features into a serene smile. "Soon all of Society will be well aware of my parents' affairs." Her smile faded and a bit of the scowl crept back. "And they expect me to find a husband in such an environment."

"Is that what you've been doing with your dance partners tonight? Husband hunting?" The notion filled him with a disturbing sense of nausea.

"Yes."

They danced apart again, and Ambrose took the opportunity to mentally review the men he'd watched her with. When they came together, he said, "That foreign boy, you danced with him out of obligation, not because you're considering his suit?"

She smiled up at him, her ale-colored eyes sparkling beneath the glow of hundreds of candles. "Oh, stop. I'm not considering his suit, but he's perfectly charming."

"Charm is your chief requirement in a husband?"

Her body moved with precision and grace. "Along with honor and kindness."

"You might do better with a dog."

She laughed as they danced apart again. Such a warm, lovely sound. He would miss it.

When they came together, she gave him a contemplative look. "Is there a breed you recommend?"

"Something loyal who's ready to defend you."

"Like you?" She gazed at him alluringly and he had to work to focus on the dance steps.

"That is not how I'd describe myself." *Unfaithful, selfish, arrogant...* those were far more accurate adjectives.

"But your ability to defend me and my honor is well-established. And here you are with me again tonight." She shook her head, her lips set firmly together. "I'm dubbing you loyal."

He leaned forward slightly and lowered his voice to just

above a whisper. "Please, stop. You're going to reverse my black reputation. I can't have that."

She winked at him and then whispered saucily in return, "Then you have only to tell everyone I am your mystery woman and abandon me without a second thought."

Though meant as a flirtation, her words chilled him to the bone. What would he do if her identity became known? He couldn't think of a way to salvage her reputation in that instance. He needed to distance himself from her. Now.

Thankfully the music was drawing to a close.

"Pity the dance is ending," she said. "I don't suppose you'd walk with me on the terrace?"

Christ, no. They'd drawn more than enough notice. "No. I'm leaving." He offered his arm to lead her from the dance floor. Softly, he said, "Don't expect me to dance with you again. You know we can't be friends."

She glanced around them at the interested looks directed their way. "Regardless, I shall think of you that way." She flashed him a brilliant smile before whispering, "Privately, of course."

Privately, he would try not to think of her at all.

Philippa watched Sevrin stroll through the ballroom, his tall, athletic form cutting through the throng of people with careless grace. People stared, some covertly, others with unabashed interest. And those who weren't watching him were looking at her. Wondering why he'd asked her to dance. Would anyone who'd been at Lockwood House somehow realize she was his masked mystery woman? Her head felt light, and her breathing shortened. She shouldn't have danced with him.

And he shouldn't have danced with just her. She held her breath, willing him to dance with someone else. Anyone.

As if he could hear her thoughts, he lingered on the other side of the room with Saxton and his wife. Saxton introduced him to a group of people and a few minutes later, he led Miss Lucinda Clark onto the dance floor.

A stab of jealousy overshadowed Philippa's relief. No, it was good he was dancing with someone else. Necessary, even.

Hadn't she just wished for this very thing?

She mentally shook herself. She couldn't feel jealous. Not even for a moment.

Instead of meeting von Egmont as promised, she decided she needed air. And privacy.

She threaded her way toward the terrace doors, but was cut off by her mother of all people. Her expression was dire. "Let us take a quiet stroll on the terrace, Philippa."

So much for privacy.

Philippa exited the ballroom with her mother who led her to a dim corner of the terrace. She'd barely come to a halt before Mother had turned on her with eyes spitting fire. "What do you think you're doing dancing with Sevrin?"

"The minuet?"

Mother pursed her lips in disappointment. "You're supposed to be looking for a husband, not squandering your precious time with wastrels. And you were doing so well before that. Lord Allred's grandmother had already given you her stamp of approval, now she may rescind it."

As if it were an actual stamp emblazoned on Philippa's forehead. She fought to keep her temper in check. "Remind me again why I need to find a husband yesterday? Oh, yes, *your* impending departure from Herrick House. I hope you plan to give Father this same dressing down. His behavior with his mistress is appalling. If it weren't for the both of you, I could manage quite well."

Mother's lips tightened even further until the flesh around her mouth was so pale as to be translucent. Words didn't come, however, and why should they? Philippa spoke nothing but the truth.

"If we're finished here, I'd like to get back inside." She gave her mother a cool stare. "I've a husband to find."

Mother's features softened, and she lightly touched Philippa's arm. "I'm sorry. Sevrin's just so inappropriate. He would only make you miserable."

If the rumors about him were accurate, she was right. But so far Philippa had only seen a man who'd gone to great lengths to spare her reputation and keep her safe. This simply didn't conform to what everyone said about him.

Was she prepared to defend an association with him? He'd just finished telling her they couldn't even be friends. "Mother, there's nothing between me and Sevrin. I met him after dancing with von Egmont, and I had a vacancy on my card. He was only being polite."

Mother's eyes narrowed. "Men like him are never polite. I'm sure there was some hidden agenda. Do yourself a favor and stay away from him."

What was the point in arguing? After all, Philippa *was* going to stay away from him.

Philippa returned to the bright, sultry ballroom, and immediately felt weary. However, she still had a few more men to evaluate this evening before she could go home. Her gaze found her father and *that woman* and she realized she had to wait until *they* were ready to go home. Or perhaps they'd send her home alone. She could only hope.

In the meantime she turned toward the refreshment table only to be cut off once again, this time by Lydia and Audrey.

Lydia linked her arm through Philippa's. "Come, you must tell us *everything*. What did you discuss? Why did he dance with you? Does he smell divine?"

While Philippa had expected this from Lydia, she'd really hoped to postpone the interrogation until tomorrow. She was on a firm deadline and there were still three men she needed to speak with.

"Well?" Lydia blinked at her as they stopped at the periphery of the ballroom.

"We discussed the weather. He danced with me because I had a vacancy, and he just happened to be there. He smells..." The words caught in her throat as she recalled his scent. Sandalwood and sage—unique and incredibly stirring. Horrified, she realized she'd ceased speaking. "He smells normal." At Lydia's frown, she added, "What is he supposed to smell like?"

Lydia rolled her eyes. "Never mind. I can't believe you only discussed the weather. If I had him alone like that I would've asked about his scandalous past. Why he refused to marry that girl after ruining her so thoroughly. And—"

Philippa recalled that Lydia had been about to impart some information earlier and leaned slightly forward in case she meant to disclose it now, but a gentleman was bearing down on them. It was Sir Reginald Johnson, one of the men Philippa had hoped to see. She affixed a welcoming smile, but he approached Lydia and asked her for the next dance.

After she'd gone, Audrey sidled closer. "I'm surprised he asked Lydia to dance, but glad. I was sure he'd come to dance with you."

"I was too." But she was pleased he'd asked Lydia to dance.

Audrey shook her head. "Oh, you shouldn't. He's awful."

Had she misunderstood Audrey? "But you just said you were glad he's dancing with Lydia. Yet you don't want *me* to dance with him?"

"I'm glad he asked Lydia because she never receives enough invitations. But I would rather you both stay clear of him. He has a terrible gambling problem, and he's horridly mean when he's in his cups."

Philippa turned all of her attention to Audrey. "Does Lydia know that?"

"Yes."

"Then why would Lydia dance with him?" As soon as the question left her mouth, she knew the answer. "She just wanted to dance."

Audrey nodded. "She and I don't have many choices. Or *any* choices. At present anyway." She smiled, taking the gloom from her words. "We're not like you. You can choose any of them. If you want."

Unfortunately, want had become need. "How do you know about Sir Reginald?" She expected the answer to be Lydia and was already thinking how she might enlist Lydia's help with potential husband evaluation.

"My cousin told me. He was at university with Sir Reginald. Before my cousin bought his commission, he warned me about certain blackguards I was to avoid at all costs."

How lovely to have a caring family who looked out for each other's best interests. All Philippa had were two self-involved parents. Suddenly she felt overwhelmed by her plight. Find a decent husband in the next thirty days who wouldn't make her miserable for the rest of her life. She'd always found Sir Reginald to be charming and witty. She could very well have accepted his suit or even a proposal of marriage. And then where would she be?

She couldn't do this.

Would it be so awful if her mother left her father? It might ruin the rest of the Season, but what was another year? Philippa had waited this long to marry already. But then she'd be stuck at Herrick House with Father and *that woman*. She supposed she could move in with Mother, but if she was carrying on with Booth-Barrows, such an environment would reflect poorly on Philippa. She'd be damned no matter where she lived.

Hang them all, she simply needed her independence and the only way to attain it (or at least more than she currently enjoyed) was through marriage.

She turned toward Audrey. "Are there other gentleman you can warn me about?"

Audrey nodded enthusiastically. "Certainly." She proceeded to list several gentlemen, including three others on Philippa's rapidly dwindling list. When she finished, she said, "I'm sorry I never told you before. I wasn't sure you wanted that sort of information."

"Of course I do. I would hate to find myself leg-shackled to a profligate or a fortune hunter."

Audrey's gaze grew guarded. "Why haven't you married? You've had a few very good offers."

They may have seemed good, but they hadn't been good enough. Each man Philippa had rejected had fallen short in some way. "I wasn't sure I could love any of them. And I'm worried I'll never find someone I can. Or worse, that I'll love him and he won't love me back."

Audrey smiled softly. "I understand. Why marry at all then?"

Philippa pondered her astute question a moment before asking, "Why do you want to marry, Audrey?"

"Because every girl does. Or should." She shrugged, her smile broadening. "Oh, I don't know. Because there's nothing else to do?"

Philippa laughed. "That is what we're meant to believe. I'm still hopeful, but I'd be ever so much more so if I had someone like your cousin to help me. Someone who could ferret out the Sir Reginalds so I don't make a ghastly mistake."

"You've been selective so far." She regarded Philippa with something akin to admiration. "I'm confident you won't make a mistake."

Philippa watched Lydia dance with Sir Reginald and was relieved to have avoided him. But her mind ran over the remaining men on her list and she wondered if any of them were mistakes. One face rose in her mind—Sevrin. Oh, he'd be a mistake of catastrophic proportions. Too bad because he'd been so kind and considerate, a right hero if the truth were told.

A hero… he could help with her search! As a gentleman—or at least as a man—he could gain information about her potential suitors that she could never hope to attain. Information that could mean the difference between a happy marriage and a mistake.

The idea gained traction in her brain until she was convinced it was her best approach, given her ridiculously short timeframe. But how to request his assistance? She'd no idea when or if she'd see him again.

She'd just have to find a way. Secretly of course. The thought caused a tremor of anticipation in the pit of her belly. And warning bells in her brain.

In the interest of adhering to the deadline her mother had imposed, she chose to ignore them both.

Chapter Eight

THE following evening Ambrose went to one of his favorite places to watch a good pugilistic bout. He cut through the main room of the Lamb and Flag Tavern toward the boisterous shouts coming from the back room where fights were held—the notorious Bucket of Blood.

Sometimes he felt a pull to fight, but not tonight. He'd already spent a grueling two hours sparring with Hopkins at the Black Horse, his first bout of training for the prizefight that would take place in a little over a week.

The Bucket of Blood was filled to its walls with spectators. Ambrose recognized only one of the combatants. Presumably the other was new to the sport—and since Ambrose had been a part of London's pugilistic community the past five years, he would know.

He worked his way through the throng of working class men—and a few women—seeking a better vantage point. A large-bosomed woman stumbled against him. "Pardon me, milord." She raked him from head to foot and licked her lips. "You here to watch the fight or something else?"

She was attractive, but Ambrose had spent too many years fighting his baser urges. Now that he could recall Philippa's scent and touch and taste, he didn't have to work very hard to ignore this woman's advances.

"I'm here for the fight. Excuse me." He brushed past her.

"Sevrin." His name came from a few yards distant, a deep, dark voice he knew well.

Ambrose moved to stand beside the massive speaker. "Lockwood."

They'd met here a few years ago, but had kept to themselves, each preferring his own company to that of anyone else. It was that shared preference for solitude that had perhaps finally drawn them together several months ago, when Lockwood had invited Ambrose to one of his vice parties. Ambrose had been surprised because while his reputation was rotten, he wasn't known for bed-hopping or skirt chasing. When Lockwood had quietly informed him that his parties offered opportunities of every flavor, the implication had been clear—Ambrose could indulge his proclivity for male companionship, if that was his choice.

It wasn't. He'd chuckled, not the least bit offended. His lack of philandering since coming to London had been noted— everyone expected a known ruiner of women to leave a trail of discarded females—and explained by a sudden preference for men instead. At least by some. They reasoned his mistakes in Cornwall had changed him so that he now sought the company of men instead of women, not that anyone had ever *seen* him with a man. The irony was that his mistakes *had* changed him, but not in the way they imagined.

While he wasn't interested in men, he'd kept himself from being interested in women. Which hadn't been difficult following the catastrophe that was Lettice. The thought of bedding another woman had sickened him—not physically, but mentally. Fighting was a much less complicated and disastrous way of exercising one's physical needs.

However, when Lockwood had invited him to his party, Ambrose had wondered if he'd abstained long enough. He'd certainly felt lust for women over the years, but had always tamped it down by beating the pulp out of someone instead.

After mulling over the invitation a few months, he'd decided to go—just to see if he was ready. If not, he'd at least enjoy the high stakes gambling with no harm done. Except within ten minutes of entering the sexually charged drawing room, he'd been propositioned by a woman. A curvaceous blonde who'd borne a striking resemblance to Lettice, even though he couldn't see her face. Or maybe he'd simply recalled Lettice since she was the last woman he'd lain with. For whatever reason, he'd left immediately and hadn't returned until four nights ago.

That visit had gone much better, for he'd gone straight to the card room, simply bypassing the drawing room. After an hour of emptying his opponents' pockets, he'd departed—without thinking—via the drawing room.

Where he'd seen Philippa.

He couldn't say what had caused him to rush to her side. Her beauty? The lost look in her eyes? Her palpable sense of uncertainty? All of it. But he hadn't *really* needed to kiss her, had he? A moot question because he'd been powerless to resist. The lust he'd subjugated for five long years had roared back, and he'd indulged for just a moment. With the most unattainable of women. He could no more capitulate to his desire for her than he could ever return to Cornwall.

He turned his mind to the fight, which was just starting. "You see this new bloke—Ackley—before?"

Lockwood shook his head. "My money's on Locke, though."

The din rose loud enough to obscure further conversation, so they fell silent to watch the fight. Though clearly less experienced, Ackley was fast. Locke was a heavier man and his punches were powerful and precise. Ackley dodged the first several, but one finally caught him on the side of the head. Ambrose winced.

Dazed by the blow, Ackley stumbled into the rope strung around the ring. Locke pushed forward and drove two more punches into Ackley's middle.

Ambrose's gut tightened as he watched the young man struggle to stay in the fight. Ambrose had always been drawn to the weaker, less experienced fighters, which hadn't always won him much money when he wagered. However, the money was nothing compared to that jubilant feeling when the fighter he backed was victorious—almost as heady as his own win. And it was no secret, at least to him, why he supported such men. Growing up with a brother like Nigel meant he looked out for the weak, the ridiculed, the disdained. Not that such concern had stopped him from dealing Nigel the ultimate injury. He pushed his mind away from the painful memories and focused on Ackley.

He was holding his own now, not fighting offensively at all, but no longer stumbling. Locke was a massive brute who used his weight to try and corner Ackley. But the younger man's spry frame worked to his advantage as he danced around his bulkier opponent. Suddenly he sent a quick jab to Locke's chin. His head snapped back and Ackley drove two more punches into Locke's middle. Locke then leaned forward a bit, which opened him up to receive several more blows to his face. He tried to react defensively, but Ackley was too fast—and Locke too slow.

Ambrose realized his fists were clenched, and he was subtly moving his arms in silent encouragement of Ackley. With a half smile, he crossed his arms over his chest.

When Locke finally got his head up his eyes were unfocused. He shook his head, but Ackley was merciless. He drove his fist up into the bottom of Locke's chin and then pummeled his ribs. Locke grunted and tried to push Ackley away. Ackley danced to the side and landed another punishing blow to Locke's face, this time catching him square in the eye. Locke went down on one knee. Ackley threw his fist into Locke's nose and Ambrose heard the crack. Blood gushed, and Locke went down all the way.

Ackley, breathing heavily, watched his opponent, but gave him space. The referee started the count to thirty. Locke wasn't unconscious, but blood ran so freely from his nose that Ambrose doubted he could continue the fight if he wanted to.

The count finished, and Ackley was declared the winner. He nodded to the spectators, but Ambrose didn't see satisfaction in his gaze. He saw hunger. God, how he remembered feeling that way.

When he'd first come to London after Nigel's death, he'd done his best to immerse himself in the worst the city could offer. He'd drunk and gambled excessively, but the hollow ache in his chest never dissipated. He'd considered tumbling a woman, but the thought of touching one after what he'd done... he couldn't do it. Didn't want to do it.

Then he'd gone to see a fight, and a new lust had been born. He'd seen fights before—in Cornwall—but he'd never wanted to be in one. He'd been so enraptured by what he'd witnessed, he'd promptly started a fight outside the pub. That was the first time his nose had been broken. Still, he'd felt alive in a way he hadn't in months. He'd glimpsed a future that contained more than despair and unworthiness. Oh, he'd still despised himself for what he'd done—still did now—but he could focus on something besides regret.

Ackley possessed that same desperate, searching look. Add that to his natural talent and clear commitment to winning, he might make a hell of a professional fighter. And Ambrose needed a professional fighter.

He was considering how and when to approach the young man when Lockwood nudged his arm. "Good fight."

"You lost."

Lockwood shrugged. "A few pounds, but I was entertained. Ackley's good. I won't make the mistake of betting against him again." He directed his attention to Ambrose, his gaze assessing. "Speaking of wagers, you created quite a stir with your masked ingénue at my party the other night."

"So it would seem." He struggled to appear uninterested when he really wanted to demand why Lockwood was mentioning it.

"I heard about your dancing with Lady Philippa—"

Ambrose turned toward him, perhaps too abruptly. "How do you know about that?"

"The paper this morning. You're quite the interesting topic this week. You had to know dancing with her—with any young deb—would draw notice and speculation. She bears a resemblance to the woman—"

"Don't." Heat spiked up Ambrose's spine, making him anxious and unsettled.

Lockwood held up a hand. "I only mean to warn you that if I might be wondering, others may be too."

He knew he shouldn't have danced with her. And if he were smart he'd go to the nearest ball—except his invitations were sparse—and dance with a handful of other debs just to distract the masses.

Ambrose narrowed his eyes and gave a slight nod. "Point

taken." He pivoted away just as Jagger entered the Bucket of Blood, flanked by two impossibly large men.

Lockwood exhaled what sounded like a curse. Ambrose turned his head. Sure enough Lockwood's already fearsome visage had darkened.

Ambrose leaned toward him. "Do you know him?"

"Barely," he said through gritted teeth.

Intriguing. "How do you know a criminal like him?"

Lockwood's tension was palpable. "I like boxing. Apparently he does too. I see him around. More and more it seems." The animosity in his tone was unmistakable.

"You know anything about him?"

Lockwood tore his gaze away from Jagger and planted it on Ambrose. "Why?"

Ambrose weighed whether or not to tell him the truth, but reasoned there was no point hiding it. Very soon everyone would know. "I'm fighting for him next week."

His dark grey eyes reflected surprise. "A prizefight? I thought you quit years ago."

Ambrose had shared all he meant to. He only shrugged and gave an enigmatic smile. "What can I say? I love a good fight."

Lockwood's gaze was intense, serious. "Be careful with him. He's not to be trusted." And then he cut into the throng and disappeared.

Ambrose turned his attention to Jagger who was now moving directly toward him.

"Sevrin, good to see you here." Jagger turned to address a younger man trailing him. "Put those up on the walls."

Ambrose watched the lackey post an advertisement for the prizefight: the Vicious Viscount vs. the Irishman. He considered saying something to Jagger about Ackley's potential, but decided to wait until after he'd spoken to the young man.

"You here scouting?" Jagger asked.

"A bit."

"Shouldn't you be practicing? I expect you to win. I should hate to think of what might happen to your lady if you don't."

Ambrose wanted to practice right that moment. By driving his fist into Jagger's face. A thousand times. "You've made yourself clear. I'll win."

"Excellent. I'd hate for her escapades with you to become public after the lengths you've gone to protect her."

Was he behind the wager? Ambrose had his hands curled around Jagger's throat before he could censor himself. The two burly henchmen pulled him away leaving both his hands and his need for satisfaction quite empty.

Jagger pulled at his cravat, his eyes flashing. "Don't hit him. I need my champion in perfect condition." He narrowed his gaze. "Besides, I know how to hurt him in other ways."

The implication was clear. Ambrose fought to keep his hands at his sides as the men let him go. "I'll win your goddamned fight and you'll leave *my lady* alone."

"After you get me a fighter. Until then, *your* lady's a nice piece of insurance."

Ambrose glared at him a moment before quitting the Bucket of Blood. Jagger's laughter echoed in his head as he made his way outside into the damp night. He'd taken a hack earlier, but now he walked, letting the darkness close in around him. He'd walked a lot those first long months in London, when his pain and regret had been too much to bear. Now the familiar sensation of moving but going nowhere was back, and he cursed Jagger anew for foisting this fight upon him.

But no, it wasn't Jagger and it wasn't the fight. It was Philippa and his desire for her. He couldn't have a woman, and especially not her.

Much later, he approached the small Black Horse Court off the Haymarket. He stopped short as a liveried footman greeted him in the street. He recognized that livery…

"My lord, Lady Philippa desires a conversation with you." He gestured to the vehicle parked on the corner. "In that hack. Will you come with me, please?"

The door to Philippa's hired hack opened, and Sevrin climbed inside.

The lantern highlighted his drawn brows, his dark eyes, and the furious set of his lips. "What the bloody hell are you doing here?"

She'd expected him to be surprised, but not angry. "I need your help."

His eyes widened, and he leaned forward from the opposite seat. "Are you all right?"

His concern warmed her. She'd made the right decision in seeking his help. Without it, she could very well find herself in a loathsome marriage. She may still, but reasoned her chances were far better with an ally like Sevrin weeding the field of suitors. And it had to be him. He was the only man from whom she could expect total honesty. The only man she trusted. Which was why she'd risked coming here. "I'm fine. I've come to ask for your assistance with finding a husband."

He blinked at her. Slowly, he settled back against the squab. "You took a chance coming here. I thought we were trying to preserve your reputation."

"Which is why I'm in a hired hack. And it's not as if anyone in polite society knows where you live. Except Saxton."

"I presume he gave you my direction?" At her nod, he continued. "I'll give him hell for that."

"If you must. Now, if you'd let me present my request, we could go our separate ways. May I speak?"

Wordlessly, he gestured for her to go on. Then he folded his arms across his chest, pulling the wool of his coat tight across his broad, muscular shoulders. Lamplight slashed across his imperfectly handsome nose and his sensuous lips.

Heat stole up the back of her neck. "I need to find a husband right away."

His eyes narrowed and he frowned. "Philippa, I can't marry you."

His quick refusal stung, which was ludicrous since she wasn't even proposing *that*. "I'm not asking you to marry me. I need your help to find a husband."

His jaw didn't drop per se, but it visibly drooped as if he only just kept himself from gaping. "I'm not a matchmaker, I'm a scoundrel."

Her body shivered at the word *scoundrel*. Despite his all-around unsuitability—she was still hopelessly attracted to him.

Sitting with him here in the dim hack reminded her of their first night together, snuggling close to his warm body on the ride home. She shouldn't think of such things. He was an inappropriate match even if he were interested in marriage. Which he wasn't.

She straightened her spine and did her best to ignore how much she liked being with him. "You don't have to find potential candidates. I have a list. I want you to discover their true natures—the things they don't show the woman they're courting."

He settled back against the squab. "I doubt I would know anyone on this list of yours."

"Perhaps, but I'm confident you can still glean the information I need." She arched a brow at him. "As you so kindly reminded me, you're a scoundrel. I'm sure you'll be able to identify any kindred spirits on the list."

"What a cunning female you are." He grinned, and she felt like they were back at Lockwood House enjoying each other's company despite the disasters they'd encountered at every turn. They'd performed like a team. She'd never realized how good it felt to have someone with her. Someone watching out for her and keeping her safe. Not just that—someone sharing experiences.

He stretched his arms out along the top of the back of the cushion, putting his stamp on the meager space in the coach. "Now, tell me why you're in such a hurry all of a sudden."

"My mother is moving to a new townhouse. She's leaving Herrick House in less than thirty days."

"Pardon my shortsightedness, but why does that matter?"

How could he miss the obvious? "Because she'll be living separately from her husband and conducting a liaison with another man. Just as my father has a very public mistress. Perhaps you saw them at Lady Dunwoody's ball?"

He nodded, his lips pressed into a thin line. "I did. I'm sorry."

And now she felt shrewish for thinking he didn't understand. She took a deep breath and explained the situation with her parents. She couldn't expect him to react the way she would or the way her friends would. He was a man—a scandalous man—who said he didn't want to be friends. Regardless, he was listening to her and now displaying—yet again—consideration. Which was precisely why she knew she could trust him to help her, regardless of whatever he said or whatever he'd done in the past.

"So you want to rush into a marriage? That doesn't sound particularly sensible, and you seem like a sensible girl—" he arched a brow, "—your presence here notwithstanding."

"I *am* a sensible girl, which is why I've weighed my options and determined this to be the best course of action. I've also approached the process of finding a husband with logic and care. Will you help me or not?" She held her breath, waiting for his answer. She'd decided to put her faith, her *trust* in him. Would he trample it as her parents had, or would he support her?

He fell silent a moment, turning his head to gaze out the window. She watched his hands, which were splayed atop the upper edge of the back of the squab. His position was so very relaxed, yet commanding in the way he took up the entire seat. Again, she recalled nestling against his chest, within the crook of his arm and wished she could move to sit beside him. To draw from his strength and his protection.

He looked at her again and her face heated. Could he read her thoughts? But he only asked, "Who are these men, and what am I supposed to learn about them? Wait, I think I know. You want a lapdog, if memory serves." His tone was light.

He was going to agree. She released the tension from her shoulders and rolled them back against the squab. "That was *your* assessment. I'd like a husband I can respect and admire, and who will be faithful."

"Unlike your father."

Very astute. "Yes."

He unfolded his arms and rested them on his knees. His gaze was direct, piercing even. "And what of love? Don't you want to love your husband?"

The air in the coach seemed to heat, the space between them to decrease. Hearing him talk of love only heightened her arousal. Had he loved someone? What role had love played—if any—in his past, with the girl he'd refused to marry? And why did he care if *she* loved? "I had hoped to, but that is not a requirement. In fact, it might be best if that emotion weren't involved at all."

"I have trouble imagining that for you," he said softly, his voice a dark caress.

Heat coiled in her belly. He was so perceptive. "I would also prefer a husband I'm attracted to. Someone with whom I might share…" She glanced away lest he see the obvious truth in her eyes—that she was recalling his kisses. "Passion."

Sevrin shifted in his seat, drawing his coat tighter around his middle. "I see. And how do you plan to discover the depth of a man's passion?" He sounded strained and he'd leaned forward just the smallest bit.

"I will kiss them, and if they kiss like you—"

"Philippa, don't." His tone was dark, dangerous, his eyes hooded. "You can't talk to me like that."

Her blood warmed and her skin tingled. The air in the coach crackled with something almost tangible. "I know it's not terribly appropriate, but you must agree our relationship is anything but appropriate."

"We don't have a relationship. I've told you—we can't be friends."

He could resist all he liked, but they already were. And why was he resisting? Did he prefer emotionless acquaintances? She was beginning to think he needed her and the connection they'd forged at Lockwood House. "Does this mean you won't help me?"

He scowled at her. "You can't go around kissing all of the men on this list."

"I won't. I'll narrow it down to two or three and start by kissing one of them."

He scrubbed a hand over his face. "I can see I'm already a bad influence on you."

"Not at all. You weren't the first man I kissed."

He dropped his hand and stared at her.

She hastened to assure him. "You shan't corrupt me. Unless I'm unable to find someone who is up to your standards. In that case, I may have to curse you." She smiled at him, but he only continued to stare, his eyes dark and impenetrable, his frame still as the surface of a frozen pond.

While she waited for him to say something, she realized his gaze was focused on her mouth. The warmth in her veins stoked into something brighter, hotter.

"Give me your list," he said.

She fumbled through her reticule and withdrew the list of names and handed it to him. He was careful to keep his fingers from touching her as he took the paper. She exhaled in disappointment.

He studied the parchment beneath the glow of the lantern. "I don't know any of these men personally."

She had wondered if he would. The only man of stature she'd ever seen him with was Saxton. She supposed she should also count Lockwood, but his title was as useful to his reputation as Sevrin's was to his. "I think you might be able to find information about the men on my list at White's. You do go to White's, don't you?"

"Occasionally." He still hadn't looked up from the list. "D'Echely's French, surely you can do better than that." He shook his head and lifted his gaze to hers. "Finchley, isn't he a young dandy?" She nodded. "Vick and Allred. Isn't Vick a bit old for you?"

"You can see my options are few. I ruled several gentlemen out during my previous Seasons. However, if you find anyone you think may suit, do tell me."

His lids drooped, making him look unbearably seductive. "I told you I'm not a matchmaker."

Her pulse quickened. "You don't want me to marry someone awful, do you?" She sounded breathless. Which made sense since she felt as if she couldn't quite fill her lungs.

Their gazes locked. "I'm not sure I want you to marry at all," he said softly.

Her breath caught and held in her constricted chest.

He coughed, breaking the spell between them, and pressed back against the squab. "But I see why you must. I'll conduct this investigation and deliver my findings as quickly as possible."

"Thank you." She willed her body to relax fully—but it wouldn't. She felt taut and warm and quivery.

He grasped the door handle. "You will *not* contact me, is that clear? I'll deliver my information to you. If you can't agree to that, I won't help you."

Tonight's excursion had been a necessary risk. One she didn't plan to repeat. "I agree. I'll send a note if I require assistance or information." She put her hand over his. The shock of the touch stole her breath again. He turned his head to look at her. "You've done nothing but help me since we've met and I'm very grateful."

He was staring at her mouth again. She leaned forward and licked her bottom lip, which had gone completely dry.

He took her hand from his and placed it in her lap, bringing his upper body toward her. His scent of sandalwood and sage stirred her senses. "Don't kiss anyone until you hear from me."

"I won't." And now she was staring at his mouth, wishing he'd kiss her again.

Then he opened the door and stepped down from the coach. He closed the door and the vehicle moved before she settled back against the squab. Little tremors of anticipation rioted through her.

If one of the men on her list could elicit half the reaction sevrin did, she might just make a go of it. Things were moving along exactly as they should. Why then did she feel unsatisfied?

Chapter Nine

THE following evening, Ambrose scowled as the third bout of the night at the Bucket of Blood concluded. All of the fighters had been bitterly disappointing, and to further blacken his mood, Ackley wasn't about and no one seemed to know how Ambrose might find him. He'd been counting on successfully recruiting Ackley in order to endure the rest of his evening's agenda: he was going to White's on behalf of Philippa and her dash to find a husband.

With a muttered curse, he left the Lamb and Flag and hailed a hack to St. James. Fleetingly, he considered directing the driver to the Black Horse, but he couldn't fight at his club. Not with the prizefight less than a week away. He growled "White's" at the driver instead.

His body felt brittle, anxious, incendiary. He couldn't fight, and yet he *needed* to fight in order to keep his lust for Philippa at bay. Her surprise visit last night and the ensuing coach ride had only stoked his desire for her. When she'd spoken of kissing him and then of kissing other men, envy had nearly sent him sprawling on top of her. Then she'd touched him and God, he'd almost been lost.

He'd simply been too long without a woman. What had once been a repentant endeavor had become torture in the last week. A torture he could perhaps end by simply purchasing professional services at the end of his interminable errands this night.

God, he really was a scoundrel. Take away his pugilism and

he was desperate for sex.

The hack stopped in front of White's. Ambrose alighted and marched up the steps. A footman opened the door wide and Ambrose strode inside. He took in the dark wood, the pungent smell of smoke and liquor, the warm sounds of conversation and game play—a true gentleman's haven, so different from his club at the Black Horse. So far removed in fact, that he was always a trifle astonished he was allowed within these hallowed walls. Except, he was a member so they *had* to let him in.

Ambrose surveyed the room. Men, young and old, wealthy and indebted, quiet and verbose—all united in this club that had been founded on chocolate and politics over a century ago. Could his fighting club last that long? Hell, it didn't even have a name. Sevrin's? The Black Horse, after the tavern in which it met? The London Pugilism Society? He smiled to himself as he thought of the men in his club belonging to anything with the word 'society' in the title.

He'd considered asking one of them if they were interested in becoming Jagger's prizefighter, but he didn't want them mixed up with the criminal. Just as he hated Philippa's involvement in this muddle.

Bloody hell. What was he doing tangled up with her? If only he'd walked right past her at Lockwood House, none of this mess would be happening. At least to him. Philippa's reputation would have been ruined while he was happily ensconced with his men at the Black Horse, pummeling Hopkins or someone else into merry exhaustion. He cringed at the thought. His soul might be black, but he couldn't wish that on her. If he had it to do over, he'd make the same choice. And suffer the same consequences.

He scanned the main chamber for the men on her list. He was only vaguely aware of what the Frenchman and Finchley looked like, but would easily recognize Allred and Vick. Since he didn't see the latter two, he set about trying to determine if any of the others were the former.

Finchley was within a year or two of Ambrose's twenty-seven years and pale-haired, if memory served. D'Echely was French, so he was likely sallow and outspoken.

"Sevrin!" called a dark-haired man from a table near the betting book. Ambrose had no idea who he was, but strolled in that direction anyway. He had to start somewhere.

"Evening, gentlemen," he said, perusing the three faces at the table. His gaze settled on a man with a somewhat handsome countenance, he supposed, though his chin was a bit small and too rounded. He was almost certain that was Finchley.

"How goes it?" the man who might be Finchley asked. "Please sit. Why not give Brock and me the name of your lady?" He nodded his head toward the dark-haired man who'd hailed Ambrose.

Brock chuckled. "Finchley, you assume she *is* a lady."

Finchely's identify confirmed, Ambrose took one of the empty chairs and poured himself a glass of whisky from the bottle on the table.

"She's definitely a lady. Goodwin saw her with him," Finchley gestured toward Ambrose, "at Lockwood House. And since Goodwin wagered she's Quality, I'm betting he's right."

Ambrose had to assume Goodwin had been one of the men in the foyer that night.

Finchley looked up at Ambrose with a sly wink. "What say you, Sevrin? I've got my eye on a new phaeton, and that wager gets me a lot closer to my goal."

This dolt would never do for Philippa. How had he even made it onto her list in the first place? Whatever the reason, he was officially stricken from it now. "Finchley, you do realize this is a bet no one can actually win? It's not as if I'll just give one of you the woman's name so you can collect. Play your little game until you grow bored."

Like a child, the younger man stuck his lower lip out. "You're pissing in our ale. We're just having a spot of fun."

Ambrose was saved from having to extricate himself from their table by the arrival of Saxton. He entered White's with the air of someone who'd been born and bred to command respect and admiration. In other words, someone very like Ambrose had once been.

That similarity wasn't what had drawn them together, however. Saxton had joined Ambrose's fighting club last fall after trying out in a street fight in the Black Horse Court. Ambrose held the tryouts regularly, for there was never a dearth of men wishing to join, and had been surprised when Saxton had not only showed up, but then proceeded to demonstrate an enormous amount of skill and fire. Unpredictably, to Ambrose anyway, they'd become friends.

Saxton made his way directly to their table. "Sevrin, I didn't expect to see you here." There was a question in his tone. He knew Ambrose was usually at his club at this time of night.

"Just enjoying a drink. Excuse me, gentlemen." He nodded at his tablemates and stood, glad to be presented with an easy and polite departure from the table.

He walked with Saxton to a smaller table in the corner, where they would have a modicum of privacy. Once they were settled, Saxton signaled for a bottle of whisky and a glass from a footman. It arrived almost immediately, which led Ambrose to believe the staff had readied it as soon as Saxton had arrived.

"You get excellent service," he remarked as Saxton poured three fingers into his glass.

Saxton took a drink. "I just came from the Black Horse. I hear you're to take on an Irishman in a prizefight next Saturday. What's that about?"

Never one to answer a question he didn't want to, Ambrose instead asked, "How long will you be in Town?"

Saxton stretched his legs out to the side of the table. "A few weeks. Olivia prefers Yorkshire, and we have preparations to oversee for the baby."

Ambrose had already congratulated him on their impending parenthood, but decided it bore repeating. "Congratulations, again." He lifted his glass, and they both drank.

Saxton set his glass down. "Let me try another tack. What was that stunt with Lady Philippa about the other night?"

"I told you. Dancing with a paragon like Philippa will elevate me in the eyes of Society."

One of Saxton's brows arched high on his forehead. "'Philippa?'"

Ambrose gripped his glass tightly and emptied the contents down his throat.

Saxton drummed his fingers atop the table. "If you're not careful, you'll soon be married like me."

Ambrose poured more whisky. "Never. And certainly not to her." She deserved someone who could love her, and Ambrose had utterly failed at that emotion.

"Why not? If it can happen for me, it can happen for you."

"I've told you before that we are not that alike," Ambrose said. Saxton believed that because they'd both ruined girls and not married them, they shared some sort of black-hearted connection. Ambrose didn't argue they were both scoundrels, however Saxton had loved his girl and his failure to marry her was through no fault of his own, but due to his father's ruthless machinations. Ambrose's crimes were far worse than stealing an innocent's maidenhead.

Saxton's brow furrowed. "Nonsense, we've plenty in common. Aside from the whole scoundrel business, we're both spares who inherited. Tragic, that."

Yes, tragic. Ambrose didn't want to think about Nigel. That way lay stark pain and soul-crushing regret. "I never mention him for a reason, Sax. Leave it."

Saxton's fingers stopped their rhythmic tapping. He lowered his voice. "I understand what it's like to be second. Never good enough, never expected to succeed."

Ambrose curled his fingers around his glass with a tightening grip. "And that is why we are not alike. I was plenty good enough." Better, in fact. Everyone at Beckwith and on the Roseland Peninsula remarked at how Nigel should've been second born. His lesser intelligence, his physical weakness, and his awkward manner resulted in a viscount who engendered nothing but pity, while his younger brother reaped all of the attention and all of the praise.

Saxton's gaze turned to frost. "I'd no idea. And here I thought we were cut from the same cloth. Clearly I was mistaken."

Bloody hell. "I didn't mean it like that, Sax. Just...don't ask me about my brother."

Saxton drummed his fingers again. "All right, I surrender. But I'm afraid that leaves me just my original topic. Why are you fighting the Irishman? If you don't tell me, I'll beat it out of you. And I don't give a damn that you've got a prizefight in six days."

Ambrose knew he'd try it, too. "Since you're proving to be so persuasive, I'll tell you. Though it's not very interesting. I was asked to fight and said yes."

Saxton arched his brow. "Hopkins said he's to be your second. I'm affronted you didn't ask me."

"I would've, but you'll be in the throes of your father's annual house party at Benfield."

Saxton frowned. "Which you were supposed to attend."

He'd never committed to any such thing. Horses, which he avoided like the pox, a woman (Philippa would be there) he couldn't touch, and the anxiety of competing in a prizefight that night. He couldn't think of a worse way to spend a day. "I'll try to come by for a brief while. Will that stop you from conducting this inquisition?"

"I suppose. Though I should point out that participating in a prizefight may impress some gentlemen, but it won't improve your social standing." He frowned again, as if he were trying to deduce Ambrose's motives and failing miserably.

Making a trip to Benfield, which was just an hour outside London, would give Ambrose the opportunity to ensure Philippa's safety the day of the fight. He wouldn't put it past Jagger to try something nefarious.

Saxton was staring at Ambrose's hand, which, due to his firm grip around his glass, had gone quite pale. Ambrose tossed back the last of the whisky and deposited the empty glass on the table.

A gentleman swaggered toward their table. He stopped beside them and grinned at Ambrose. "Lady Lydia, eh? Don't know how you managed that, but I suppose you'll have to marry the chit."

Ambrose looked up at the man, who, like most of London, seemed to know him while he doubted they'd ever been introduced. "I don't marry anyone, or don't you know that about me?"

The man's smile faded. "Someone's just entered Lady Lydia Prewitt's name in the book. Are you refuting she was your mystery woman at Lockwood House?"

Ambrose's body tensed, but he forced himself to appear impassive. "Most certainly."

Saxton shot the intruder a quelling stare. "This has gone too far. It's one thing to make ridiculous wagers, but quite another to slander a young, unmarried woman. Who wrote her name down?"

The man who'd so gleefully delivered the news now looked quite pained. His face flushed, and his forehead glistened in the lamplight. "Some bloke called Tweedy."

Saxton's eyes narrowed as he scanned the room. "Who the hell's Tweedy?" he asked in a loud, commanding voice. Conversation wilted and died. Heads turned—first to Saxton and then to a young, slight man standing off to the side of the betting book. His face reddened beneath a smattering of freckles. Ambrose almost felt sorry for him.

"Come here," Saxton bellowed, and of course the lad wobbled his way to their table. "Everyone else go about your business," Saxton directed to the room at large. The men immediately turned their heads, but conversation was stilted and slow.

"Now," Saxton began, his frigid gaze impaling the poor young Tweedy, "why did you write Lady Lydia's name in the book?"

"I-I w-w-was at the Pinnocks' rout earlier. It w-was just a rumor I'd heard. I thought I'd be the f-first to get to the b-book." And bask in the praise for such a wager. He blinked and Ambrose caught the moisture in the lad's eyes. "So it's n-not her then?"

Ambrose interceded before Saxton delivered a set-down that would likely cower the boy until he was middle-aged. "No, and you must be careful about bandying young women's names about. Lady Lydia doesn't deserve to have her name sullied by some baseless wager."

Tweedy nodded, his eyes still damp and his cheeks bright red. "Yes, my lord."

"Sevrin, you could be lying about the gel's identity to protect her." Finchley, simpleton that he was, had approached the table and apparently overheard their discussion, despite Saxton telling everyone to mind their own business. "How're we to know the truth?"

Saxton opened his mouth, but Ambrose held up a hand. "Please, allow me." He turned his attention to Finchley. "How do you know it's not the truth? If I start a wager about who you shagged last Tuesday, would I be wrong if I entered the name of a Covent Garden whore?"

Finchley sucked in a breath. "You most certainly would."

Ambrose curled his lips into a taunting sneer. "Prove it."

There were a few snickers—clearly more than just Finchley had ignored Saxton's directive—and one loud bark of laughter. Finchley reddened then turned and went back to his table.

Again, Ambrose wondered how such a featherbrain had found his way onto Philippa's precious list. If she hadn't enlisted his help, would she have found Finchley adequate? After all, she was only looking for the bare minimum. And passion, she wanted passion.

Suddenly his blood returned to the boiling point. It took everything he had not to stalk to Finchley's table and smash his fist into his face.

Saxton was watching him again with that same narrow-eyed concern. He quickly turned to the young Tweedy. "Remove your wager and take yourself off. I don't want to see you betting on anything again, do you hear me?"

Tweedy nodded, his carrot-colored hair flopping across his forehead. He turned and went directly to the book where he scratched out his wager. Then he left the club as quickly as his matchstick legs would carry him.

Normally Ambrose would've teased Saxton about the manner in which he'd frightened the boy, but he was too angry. Too pent-up. Too in need of physical release. He stood abruptly.

Saxton also stood. "Where are you going? You look... well, I've never seen you like this before." As loud as he'd spoken earlier, his voice was now nearly a whisper.

"Where's your favorite brothel?" At Saxton's shocked gaze, he added, "From before you were married?"

"I've never known you to visit a brothel."

"You've also never known me to dance with debs. I'm feeling

adventurous this week. Give me the name of a brothel."

"The Red Door."

"Excellent. Evening, Sax." He turned and strode away from the table, his body teeming with frustrated energy.

He knew everyone turned to watch him leave, but he didn't care. He'd grown used to condemnation and scorn. Indeed, he'd feel strange without it. Maybe that was what was wrong with him. For the first time in five years someone was treating him like he was some sort of hero—and he absolutely was not. He really ought to disabuse Philippa of her belief, but he couldn't walk away from her now. Not until after the prizefight.

But he could—and should—let her judge her own husband's merits. He'd become far too entwined with her and no good could come of it. He'd track her down tomorrow and tell her she was on her own.

In the meantime, it was time to relinquish his self-torture and take a woman to bed. He walked down the steps to St. James and immediately hailed a hack.

Only the words that came out of his mouth weren't "Red Door," but "Black Horse." It seemed old habits died hard.

⁂

Two nights later, Philippa arrived at Lady Anstruther's ball in the company of her father, *that woman*, and Lord von Egmont. She immediately scanned the ballroom for Sevrin, but couldn't find him. He was either not here or hidden amongst the crowd. It was likely the former, since she'd looked for him every night and he had never been in attendance after Lady Dunwoody's ball. This shouldn't have surprised her since she was fairly certain his polite invitations were few and far between.

Resigned, she instead looked for Lydia who was returning to Society tonight after her name had been wagered at White's as Sevrin's mystery woman. Horrified, she'd taken to her bed and was only here tonight because her great-aunt had demanded she show everyone she couldn't be cowed by a ridiculous—and untrue—wager.

A group of people were clustered around Someone Very Interesting in the far corner. Philippa's breath caught as she wondered if it might be Sevrin. But it couldn't be. People didn't fawn over him, they stared at him from across the room. He was interesting, but dangerous.

"What do you suppose is going on over there?" she asked von Egmont.

"Let's find out."

He escorted her through the crowd until they were near enough that she could finally make out the person of interest. Lydia! Their gazes met and Lydia smiled widely. "Excuse me," she said to those around her. "I must speak with my dear friend, Lady Philippa." She cut through the people and Philippa met her.

"Come and walk with me," she said, taking Philippa's free arm and casting a glance at von Egmont.

Von Egmont disengaged himself from Philippa and stood aside.

Lydia pulled her away from the throng. "Can you believe it? I'm the most popular girl in London. All because some nincompoop wrote my name in the betting book at White's. I was certain my reputation was doomed, but no one believed it. Indeed, it's given me an air of excitement. My dance card is nearly full, Philippa, full!"

Philippa smiled at her friend's exuberance. She deserved to bask in this moment. "How lovely that tragedy has turned into victory."

"Aunt Margaret is beside herself and of course taking all the credit." Lydia adopted a high, scratchy voice, "'If I hadn't dragged you out of your room, you'd still be crying into your pillow, silly gel.'" She rolled her eyes.

Margaret was a spinster universally feared for her sharp tongue and ability to ruin anyone. That her great-niece hadn't blossomed into one of the ton's most sought-after young ladies had been a particular source of bitterness—at least according to Lydia. How satisfied she must be feeling now that her protégé was suddenly the toast.

Philippa was less concerned with Lydia's aunt's reaction than with the wager itself. She naturally held a personal interest in what happened with it. Specifically, that *her* name wasn't written down. "I wonder why your name was entered, though. Peculiar, isn't it?"

Lydia cocked her head to the side. "Perhaps not. Sevrin's mystery woman is rumored to be a debutante, after all."

A fact that made Philippa a bit nauseous. "What nonsense. The woman was supposedly masked."

"Also rather young and possessed of a certain air."

Philippa cringed. If someone had—correctly—deduced Sevrin's mystery woman was a deb, what else had they discerned? The scar on her elbow perhaps?

The flesh just below the hem of her glove suddenly itched.

Lydia shrugged. "Ah well, I daresay that may be the last we hear of the wager after Saxton castigated the young man who wrote my name."

Philippa would cling to that hope. "I heard about that. I almost feel sorry for the man if Saxton turned his icy Sinclair Stare on him." If people feared Lydia's aunt, they were positively petrified of running afoul of Saxton's father, the Duke of Holborn. The males in their family were so renowned for their ability to cut, that their trademark look had been coined the Sinclair Stare.

"I do not. Feel sorry for him, that is. Serves him right for sullying my name." She lowered her voice to a whisper. "Though, I may thank him in my prayers tonight." She giggled softly.

They'd circuited half the ballroom, drawing interested looks and smiles as they progressed. Lydia inclined her head at people and smiled in return, clearly enjoying her notoriety. All the while, Philippa was dreadfully aware of how close she'd come to utter ruination. If someone had written her name down, would everyone assume the charge was false and clamor for her attention? Or would they somehow divine the truth? A cold shiver slithered down her spine.

Lord Allred intercepted them. "Good evening, ladies." His gaze settled on Philippa. "I expect you to save me a dance, Lady Philippa."

She dipped a slight curtsey, forcing her mind away from a disaster that would likely never be. "I'd be delighted, my lord."

"The set after the next?"

"Perfect."

"Until then." He bowed to them and they continued on.

Lydia squeezed her arm. "He's so handsome—all that muscle from his sporting activities. He's quite the cricket player, but then you'd know all about that. He seems interested in you."

"Yes, we've danced together the last two nights."

Lydia smiled knowingly. "He's courting you."

"Not formally." But perhaps he would, provided Sevrin found him acceptable. Where was Sevrin anyway?

"Do you want him to? I mean, are you really looking for a husband? Aunt Margaret says you enjoy stringing men along." Lydia turned wide eyes toward her as the color drained from her face. "I'm so sorry, Philippa. I never meant to insult you."

It was nothing she hadn't heard before—not directly, but via whispered gossip that invariably made its way back to her. "Apology accepted. Just promise me you don't say that to anyone else."

"Of course not. But you could marry anyone and yet you don't."

"I plan to marry soon. Why don't you tell your aunt that?"

Lydia gave Philippa an earnest look, clearly trying to make up for her faux pas. "If you want me to, I will."

Philippa patted her hand. "It doesn't matter." If she didn't marry, she needn't worry about what the Aunt Margarets of the *ton* would say—they'd be too scandalized by her mother's public separation from her father.

They returned to where they'd started and were immediately set upon by people wanting to talk with Lydia. The commotion was so great that Philippa didn't see Sevrin approach until he was upon her.

He was garbed in rich navy blue with a wine-colored waistcoat. Allred might be handsome, but Sevrin was devastating. His dark eyes glittered beneath the thousands of candles illuminating the ballroom—and they focused solely on her.

Silently, inconspicuously, he handed her a small scrap of paper and then turned without a word. In fact, the encounter was so brief as to perhaps not even have occurred. However, his departure through the ballroom, his form standing out like a prize stallion among a field full of nags, evidenced that it had.

Belatedly, she realized he'd given her a note. With shaking fingers she unfolded the parchment.

Remove Finchley from your list. I can no longer help you. Best wishes with your endeavor.

She turned the paper over looking for more. That was it?

The warm fuzziness that had pervaded her a moment before evaporated like a bead of water over an open flame. He couldn't mean to simply give her a note and walk away? He'd committed to helping her! Maybe he'd carelessly abandoned that girl in Cornwall, but she wasn't going to let him do the same to her.

Livid, she stared after him, wishing she could run him down and demand an explanation. Covertly, she glanced around and then surreptitiously made her way to the perimeter of the ballroom. She marked his progress as she surveyed her own path to ensure no one was paying undue attention to her. He reached the exit and she quickened her pace as much as she dared. Just a few more steps and she'd be free of the ballroom.

At last she stepped into the—fortunately empty—corridor and strode to intercept him. She caught his sleeve between her fingertips. "What is the meaning of this?" she hissed, holding up his ridiculous note.

He turned. *And tried to shake her off.* "Go back to the ballroom. You know we can't be seen together."

"Then find some place private because I'm not leaving until you explain yourself. You said you'd help me."

"I did help you, but now I can no longer do so."

Suddenly she felt as if the world were pressing down on her, like she couldn't breathe.

"You can't abandon me. How am I to know d'Echely's or Vick's or Allred's true natures?"

"I can't help you." He sounded strained, annoyed. And he still didn't look at her.

She grabbed his lapels. "Look at me!"

He did and there was something in his eyes—regret maybe. Whatever it was, it gave her pause. "I can't help you," he said again, with an edge that didn't match his gaze.

Voices sounded from behind her.

"Bloody hell," he breathed. Then he grabbed her elbow and pulled her to the nearest door, which he opened. He pushed her over the threshold and followed her inside drawing the door closed behind them.

Darkness enveloped them, but she'd seen they were in a small closet. A very small closet. That from the smell of it contained candles.

The voices grew louder and louder and then they just stopped.

Her body quivering with barely-checked panic, Philippa closed her eyes and waited for ruin.

Chapter Ten

AMBROSE listened intently for any sound from the corridor. He held his breath waiting to see if they would be discovered. After all their near misses at Lockwood House to be found here in an indefensibly incriminating position...

She exhaled and it sounded like a cannon blast. He brought his gloved finger to her mouth and pressed it against her lips. Now her breath sucked in, albeit much more quietly. He tried not to think of the heat of her mouth seeping through his glove or the gust of her breath against his finger. And he fought the urge to slide that finger into her mouth in the faint hope she might suckle it.

His cock roared to attention and the small closet surged in temperature.

Finally, muted voices came from outside the door. He couldn't hear what they said, but only because his senses were full of Philippa—her lilac-honey scent, the warmth of her body so close to his, the sound of her soft breathing, quickening with each beat of her heart, signaling that her desire—like his—was climbing.

The voices continued, but he was having a hard time concentrating on anything but Philippa's proximity. Because of the tight space, he stood so close to her that if he just inched forward—and as he thought it, he did it—her breasts would be pressed against him.

He closed his eyes in ecstasy. This was the closest he'd been to a woman in five years. His previous kisses with Philippa notwithstanding.

Instead of retreating as he might have expected, she leaned into him. And then she somehow read his mind—at least partially. She pressed her lips to his finger.

He stifled a groan as he cupped the side of her face and slid his palm down to her collarbone. Her heart beat strong and fast there, and the hot silk of her flesh burned through his glove.

Kissing her was out of the question. It would only lead to God-knew-what, and he couldn't go there with her. But that didn't stop him from lowering his head and inhaling the scent of her hair. He brushed his cheek against hers and bit his tongue lest it dart out and trace a path to her ear, down her neck, then lower to the edge of her bodice.

She nudged her cheek against him and breathed a single word, "Ambrose."

He was a mass of dry, brittle wood and she was the flame that would burn him to the ground.

Which was what made him step back. Not far, because the closet simply wouldn't allow it.

He picked up the sound of fading footsteps in the corridor and took that to mean those outside had left. He allowed himself to exhale and so did she, their breath warming the already steamy interior of their confined space.

With each breath he took, reason returned. And anger—at himself, but he'd never been very good at directing it.

"Philippa, you shouldn't have followed me." Though he whispered, he injected a firm dose of urgency.

"I'm to just let you abandon me?" Her whisper was far less fierce. In fact, he wondered if she wasn't upset, but in the darkness, he couldn't tell.

He couldn't let her get to him. He'd had his fill of lowering his defenses around beautiful, alluring females. Or rather, one beautiful, alluring female. "I'm not abandoning you. You don't need me to find a husband."

"Apparently I do if you think I should remove Finchley from consideration. He seems perfectly acceptable to me. Just yesterday I saw him in the park and we had the most diverting conversation about his latest purchase at Tattersall's—"

Christ, maybe she did need him. Or someone anyway. "I take your point, however, I can't be the one to help you."

"What's wrong with Finchley? I'd like to know."

He was careful to keep his voice low. "He's an idiot. For one, he's far too interested in my mystery woman."

"But surely that will die down after what Saxton did to that boy who wrote Lydia's name in the book."

"Perhaps. If anyone can keep scandal to a minimum it's Saxton or his father. But just as they can tamp it down, others can stoke it. Every moment we spend together is a moment we risk your reputation."

She was quiet, which allowed him to be painfully aware of her proximity again, of the heat emanating from her delicious body. And also of the distance that really stretched between them, regardless of how close they now stood. He could dream of her the rest of his days, but he could never, ever have her.

"You should go," he said, while the dark recesses of his mind thought of how he could raise her skirts, lift her against the wall, and slide into her.

Her hand found his cheek in the darkness and stroked his jawline. "'Tis a pity things aren't different. If you weren't who you are…"

He grabbed her hand and pressed a hard kiss to her gloved palm. "Go. And if I had to pick one of your suitors right now, I'd choose Allred. From what I can discern, his reputation is sterling."

"Are you giving me permission to kiss him now?"

Jealousy cut through him. "Yes." He forced the word through the tight muscles of his throat.

The space around him moved, and he felt her lips against the side of his mouth. He held her close a moment and spoke softly against her ear. "But don't be cruel. Don't kiss him if you don't plan to marry him. He'll spend the rest of his life cursing his loss." He felt her shiver, but ruthlessly pressed himself back as far as the closet would allow.

"Oh no, Allred," she said at full voice, which nearly sent him into a panic. "I'm supposed to be dancing with him."

She cracked open the door and peered outside. "It's clear."

She threw a glance over her shoulder, but he couldn't read her eyes. Then she was gone.

He pulled the door closed and immersed himself in darkness once more. He rested his forehead against the door and took deep, even breaths until his cock relaxed and the sexual tension in his body dissipated. Somewhat. It never went away completely these days, and he could only hope a return to fighting would improve his condition. Just three more days.

After another moment, he opened the door and stepped into the corridor, coming face to face with Booth-Barrows who was on his way from the ballroom. One of his dark brows made a slow climb up his forehead as he contemplated Ambrose. Ambrose gave him an equally studious stare. They communicated more silently than they could ever have hoped to with words.

Booth-Barrows, *I saw you at Lockwood House.*

Ambrose, *And I saw you.*

They both inclined their heads and went their separate ways. Ambrose had decided he'd best walk the direction Booth-Barrows had not, which meant he was headed back to the ballroom. Just as well, since he figured he should dance with another debutante who wasn't Philippa.

Who to choose? He scanned the wall next to where he entered and immediately saw one of the girls who'd been with Philippa at Lady Dunwoody's. They hadn't been introduced, but what did he care? He made his way to her.

"Good evening, I believe we met the other night, Lady...?"

She blinked up at him with pale sea-green eyes. They reminded him of the water surrounding the Roseland Peninsula back home.

"Miss Cheswick," she supplied. "I'm not sure—"

"Would you care to dance?" While he didn't frequent London balls, he was certain of her wallflower status by the way her eyes lit.

"I would, my lord." She dipped a brief curtsey and then he led her onto the dance floor.

The line for the dance was forming, and it was the devil's luck—or his own—to find himself standing next to Lord

Goddamned Allred who was partnered with Philippa.

She looked flushed and lovely. Her delectable lips formed the slightest O of surprise at seeing him, but she quickly masked it by shooting Miss Cheswick a questioning look. Miss Cheswick simply shrugged and gave a mildly bewildered smile. He was glad he'd asked her to dance above anyone else. He only hoped his attention wouldn't solidify her wallflower status.

The music started as Allred nodded at him. "I say Sevrin, is it true you're to fight in Dirty Lane on Friday night?"

He hadn't spoken very loudly, but his voice carried to Philippa, whose head snapped in his direction. Her eyes widened, and he could fairly see the questions trying to tumble from her mouth.

Ambrose nodded. He was a bit surprised Allred would broach this topic in front of ladies in the middle of a dance. "It is."

"Shame I'll be at Benfield. I would've liked to see you. I've heard tell you were quite the contender a few years back."

"So some say."

A couple danced between their lines.

"Don't be modest, man." Allred gave him an admiring smile, which made Ambrose more uncomfortable than he already was watching Philippa with him. "I recognize a superior sportsman when I see one. You're obviously quite fit."

The whole while they conversed, Philippa clearly strained to hear. When they reached the top of the line she stepped out with Allred, but nearly stumbled as her gaze was still pasted on Ambrose.

This wouldn't do. He sent her a stern glare as he took Miss Cheswick's hand.

Philippa pursed her lips, but shifted her attention to Allred with a smile. A captivating smile that sent an envious stake straight through Ambrose's gut.

"I'm pleased to hear you'll be at Benfield, my lord," she said. And now Ambrose was the one hanging on her every word. "I so look forward to His Grace's annual party."

Allred smiled dashingly, damn the man. "His horse flesh is a wonder to behold."

"Most definitely. My father has a stallion from His Grace's stud. He's going to breed him this year."

Horses. Which normally wouldn't interest Ambrose at all—he despised thinking of the creatures, wrapped up as they were in his own transgressions—but from her lips, they became as fascinating as the strategy of boxing.

"We shall take a ride on Friday," Allred said. "I can't resist sampling Holborn's finest mounts."

She nodded demurely, flirtatiously. "I should be delighted."

And suddenly it became imperative that Ambrose attend that infernal house party.

This obsession with a woman he could never have was becoming troublesome. But going to Benfield would allow him to verify her safety, he reasoned. Surely no one could fault him for doing *that.*

Afterward, he'd beat the Irishman to a pulp and recruit Ackley to be Jagger's champion. Then Philippa would truly be out of his hair, and they'd have absolutely no reason to cross paths.

How disappointing that sounded.

Philippa worked very hard to concentrate on her conversation with Allred and on the dance—a typically easy endeavor that had become nigh impossible with Sevrin dancing behind her. With every turn and tip of her head, she saw him and remembered the way he'd fitted so deliciously against her just a quarter hour ago. How he smelled of sage and sandalwood and man, and how she regretted not kissing him in that closet.

How could she possibly kiss someone else now?

She looked at Allred. With dark russet-colored hair and bright hazel eyes, he was pleasing in his regard, but he simply didn't spark the sensations that a mere glance from Sevrin ignited into a full conflagration.

She shook her head and tried to focus on what Sevrin had told her. He'd reminded her countless times in word—and in deed because no gentleman would have kissed her like that— that he was an unrepentant scoundrel unworthy and unwanting of her company.

Fine.

And he was right. She shouldn't want his help. She should've run as far away from him as possible, and she certainly shouldn't have risked being caught alone with him. If only he hadn't written that provoking note.

It didn't matter. She had to marry, and Sevrin was nowhere in that equation. He was correct that Allred was her best choice, and she resolved right then to pursue the match with everything she had. It was that or embrace spinsterhood.

The dance came to a merry conclusion. Philippa was a bit out of breath from the last series of turns. Allred—the consummate athlete—was an excellent dancer. Sevrin, she noted, was every bit as skilled. More importantly, Audrey was smiling giddily. Philippa couldn't remember the last time her friend had danced. She covertly watched Sevrin as he led Audrey from the dance floor. He could've danced with anyone in the ballroom—or no one. Yet, he'd chosen Audrey. For a man who swore he wasn't a hero, he certainly performed his share of chivalrous acts.

Allred drew Philippa away and she had to turn from Sevrin. "I confess I'm quite looking forward to Benfield now that I know you will be there. Are you staying for the entire party?"

The party was due to last four days. "Yes."

"How fortuitous." He gave her hand a squeeze as he wrapped it around his arm.

The rest of the ball passed without note. After her dance with Allred, she'd tried to find Sevrin in the ballroom, but he'd disappeared. Later, she'd spoken with Audrey who'd waxed besottedly about dancing with him. He was so handsome and urbane and witty, and she couldn't understand how he could still have such a bad reputation. Surely people could forgive him his past behavior if he was reformed?

But was he reformed?

Philippa had become consumed with this thought for the remainder of the evening. The real question was what he was reforming from. She sensed there was more to the story than simply ruining a girl and recalled that Lydia had been about to tell her. She looked over the ballroom for Lydia.

Her mother came up beside her. "Are you ready to leave, Philippa? I am."

Philippa turned toward her mother, annoyed at being interrupted. "I'm not quite ready. But please feel free to go on without me. I can ride back with Father."

"Your father has already left. Besides, I've a matter to discuss with you."

Since "a matter to discuss" meant suffering a mountain of criticism, Philippa would've rather walked home. But alas, that wasn't an option. "I suppose."

Once they were ensconced in the carriage, Mother wasted no time launching her offensive. "You disappeared for a while this evening."

Philippa's breathing quickened. What did she know? "Yes."

"I couldn't help but notice your departure from the ballroom came directly after Sevrin's. You assured me there was nothing between you."

Philippa placed her shaking hands on the cushion beside her legs and hid them beneath the folds of her skirt. "There isn't. I went to the retiring room. I'd no idea he left at the same time."

Mother's eyes flashed. "Don't lie to me! Walter—that is, Mr. Booth-Barrows—saw you fleeing down the hallway just before Sevrin stepped from a closet. He is an exceptionally smart man, and he put one and one together. You're Sevrin's mystery woman. That is how you knew I was at Lockwood House."

Finally. Though she hated that her mother knew the truth, she was—in a peculiar way—relieved. She was also ready to defend herself. "I didn't go there with him."

"But you don't deny being there with him." She frowned deeply and folded her arms over her chest. "Tell me everything."

Her mother's outrage was more than a bit sanctimonious. "Including the part where I saw you go into that room with three other people? Good heavens, Mother, what's happened to you? Why are you treating me like I've done something hideous when you've gone beyond the pale?"

"This is not about me! And you can't compare our situations." Her face was flushed and her light brown eyes spat fire. Philippa had seen her disappointed, irritated, frustrated, but never this livid. "What were you doing with him at Lockwood House?"

"I told you why I went there. I followed you. But I had no idea where I was. How was I to know you'd gone to a *vice party*? I went inside, and Lord Sevrin was kind enough to help me escape without my identity being discovered."

"*Yet*! We've no idea how this will play out." She sucked in a breath and pressed her hands to her cheeks. After a moment, she spoke more evenly. "Your tale might be believable if not for the fact that you were with him in the prop room."

"Only so I could change into a new dress." Oh, this didn't even sound believable to her, but then the entire evening had been fraught with events one might expect to find in a novel instead of real life. And though it was the truth, inviting a known scoundrel to play the role of lady's maid was scandalous regardless of the location. But she'd done the best she could, and she wouldn't apologize for it.

Mother's stern gaze brimmed with censure. "You're ruined."

She suffered a moment's panic. Her chest felt tight, and she worked to draw a deep breath. "I'm not. No one knows."

"Then it seems you've more than one reason to seek a hasty marriage. Mark my words Philippa, this will not remain secret forever. Someone else will figure it out, especially if you keep drawing attention to yourself with Sevrin. Dancing with him at Lady Dunwoody's? Leaving the ballroom tonight in close proximity to him? These mistakes may yet prove fatal."

"Forgive me if I find your counsel hypocritical, given your own behavior." Even so, Philippa couldn't deny she was treading dangerously close to indiscretion. She liked Sevrin, was attracted to him, would encourage his suit if he offered it.

Her mother sucked in a breath and then shook her head. "Your lack of respect is horrendous."

"I'm happy to give respect where it's due." She narrowed her eyes, having had enough of her mother's needling over the years. "For you to behave as you have after alternately ramming propriety and grace down my throat and ignoring me... It's unconscionable. Would you at least do me the courtesy of leaving off being critical? I think we're quite past that. Either way, I'll no longer be your problem in less than thirty days."

"You will if you don't marry."

"I doubt you'll give me a second thought. I'll continue to live at Herrick House and put up with Father and," she shuddered thinking of a lifetime that stretched before her, "*that woman.*"

She turned her head and stared out the window, seeing nothing. Her desire to fight fled with the realization that she didn't even know what she was fighting for. Her mother's integrity? Her own reputation? Permission to spend time with Sevrin, who'd made it clear he wouldn't spend time with her?

After many long minutes during which time Philippa had almost convinced herself she was alone, the coach slowed. Before the door opened, Mother took her hand in a surprisingly fierce grip. Her eyes were bright, her mouth drawn. "Promise me you'll stay away from Sevrin."

A moot request since Sevrin had pledged to keep his distance, not that her mother knew that. "I will, if you stay at Herrick House."

Her mother dropped her hand. "I can't promise you that."

"Then I believe we've nothing more to say, Mother."

Chapter Eleven

AMBROSE sat at a table in the back room of the Black Horse Tavern where his fighting club met nightly. The low ceiling and battered wood floors gave the space a small, well-worn atmosphere, like a favorite pair of boots past their prime, but still too comfortable to relinquish. He downed a second glass of gin as he waited for Ackley to arrive.

Hopkins had finally tracked him down that day and invited him to attend the Black Horse this evening. Ackley had been intrigued if only because he'd heard of Ambrose's private fighting club and knew that invitations were never offered—they were sought.

The boisterous cheering of the club soothed his nerves as much as the gin, but neither was enough to keep him from thinking of Philippa. From lusting after her with every breath he drew.

The club's second bout of the night finished up. Typically, Ambrose would participate in the selection of fighters for each match, but tonight he just couldn't muster the will. He couldn't even watch, for it was torture to see but not feel.

The door from the main room of the tavern opened and in walked Ackley. At last.

He paused just over the threshold and took in his surroundings. Hopkins greeted him and led him to Ambrose's table.

Ambrose looked up at him. "Evening, Ackley. Glad you could join us. Sit." He indicated another chair at the table.

Thomas Ackley was young—but not too young. He was of average height and build, but his appearance was deceiving. For buried beneath that unassuming frame was power and stealth and pugilistic grace. He eyed Ambrose as he slowly sat.

Ambrose nodded at Hopkins who fetched two more glasses from a sideboard. He brought them back to the table and took one of the remaining two chairs.

"Gin?" Ambrose offered. At Ackley's answering nod, Ambrose poured some in both glasses. Then he raised his glass in a silent toast.

After everyone had taken a draught—Ackley's was more accurately a sip—he got right to the point. "What are your aspirations with regard to fighting?"

Ackley wrapped both of his hands around his glass. His fingers were long, his knuckles bruised and scabbed. His angular face was also bruised, but his nose was straight and perfect. Unbroken as of yet. Ambrose's had been cracked no less than three times.

"I like fighting," Ackley answered with a shrug. "You want me to fight here?" He turned his head to look at the two men who were preparing to duel.

"Perhaps. But I'm looking for a different kind of fighter. I'm looking for a champion."

Ackley's brown eyes flashed with surprise. "My lord? Aren't you in contention for the championship?"

"No, I'm fighting on Friday as a favor to someone whose fighter was injured. He's looking for a permanent replacement. When I saw you at the Bucket of Blood the other night, I thought I might have found that replacement. If you're interested."

Ackley's nostrils flared and his eyes brightened. He sat up a bit straighter. "I might be." His casual words belied his obvious enthusiasm.

"I need to be sure you're good enough. I want you to fight Hopkins." He inclined his head toward their other tablemate. "Tonight."

Ackley visibly swallowed as he contemplated Hopkins. Ambrose didn't blame him. Hopkins was huge. His hands alone would make any fighter quake in fear.

Ambrose sought to reassure the young man, but not in the way he probably preferred. Hopkins was going to pummel him, and that was all right. "Don't worry that I expect you to beat him. You won't." Ambrose smiled. "It took me a long time to do so. I only want to judge your technique."

Ackley looked between them. Then he drained the rest of his gin, slammed his glass on the table, and stood. "Let's go."

Ambrose admired the lad's spirit. He inclined his head at Hopkins and they rose from the table in unison.

"Hold," Ambrose called out to the men in the ring. He made his way to the center. "My apologies mates, you can fight in a bit. I've invited a new bloke to try out tonight." There were murmurs as this was not how men typically came to audition. "This is Ackley. I saw him fight at the Bucket of Blood. Hopkins is going to give him a go."

Wagers began changing hands immediately. Hopkins had already stripped to his waist and was now removing his boots and stockings.

Ackley paused in the process of drawing his shirt over his head. "Why is he baring his feet?"

"We fight barefooted here," Ambrose explained. "You'll soon see the difference."

A few minutes later both fighters were bare-chested and barefooted.

They entered the makeshift ring—which was only a chalk outline in the middle of the room—and met at the scratch, a chalk-drawn square yard in the center.

"Now, we don't have seconds or referees here," Ambrose said. "We fight. No kicking or hitting below the waist—we prefer our manhood intact." A few men chuckled. "And when you go down, we only count to twenty." Ackley nodded.

Ambrose took a step back. Hopkins was a good head taller than Ackley and half again as wide. But what Ackley lacked in bulk, he could more than make up for with skill and speed. Precisely what Ambrose had learned to do.

He left the ring and assumed a position just outside the chalk. Then he nodded to Timmons, who held the bell. A loud peal filled the room, and Hopkins delivered a quick blow to Ackley's cheek, knocking his head back. He hadn't been expecting such a rapid attack. Hopkins grinned.

Ackley danced away, employing the neat footwork he'd used at the Bucket of Blood. Fighters used this method instead of standing in place as they once did, but Ambrose hadn't seen anyone—save himself and he really couldn't testify to what he looked like—who'd learned to move the way Ackley did.

Hopkins was also good on his feet. Though not as fast, he moved with precision and surprising grace. He landed two more punches to Ackley's middle before Ackley was able to defend a third.

The members of the club cheered and continued to wager—all of it good-natured. Ambrose immersed himself in the comfort and familiarity of being amongst his passion, his very livelihood. He couldn't imagine where he'd be today without this club. Without the fight.

Ackley sent a jab toward Hopkins's face that was easily deflected. But then he moved left and connected his fist with Hopkins's gut. It was a bold, nimble move, and exactly the reason Ambrose had chosen him in the first place. He leaned forward, anxious for Ackley's next attack.

Hopkins advanced on his opponent and delivered two hits to Ackley's shoulders. Ackley moved away, but Hopkins kept after him and continued punching. Ackley deflected most, but Hopkins's speed overcame him. He landed one good blow to Ackley's eye, then his ear, finally a bruising jab to his middle.

Ackley retreated, but his rhythm had been broken. Hopkins mercilessly followed him and punched him again. And again. And again.

A cut formed near Ackley's eye, and blood trickled down his cheek. He swiped at it—he'd have to work on focus—and it was all Hopkins needed to deliver several vicious blows to Ackley's torso. Ackley stumbled backward, but, to his credit, didn't fall. However, neither did he advance. Normally, Hopkins would've continued, but he glanced at Ambrose who shook his head. *Keep going.*

Hopkins went after Ackley anew, swinging wide at Ackley's

sides and connecting once, twice—then Ackley skittered out of the way. A bit graceless, but he'd regained at least a little speed. He kept moving around the edge of the ring. Hopkins cut across the middle and headed him off. Ackley tried to get his hands up in a defensive position, but Hopkins cut them down with two swift blows.

Ambrose respected Ackley's effort, but he hadn't yet built up the ability to sustain his speed against someone as powerful as Hopkins. They'd fix that. Time to let the boy rest. He inclined his head toward Timmons, who rang the bell.

Ackley dropped his hands, clearly fatigued, but he frowned at Ambrose. "The fight's not over."

"You really want to keep going?"

"I do." The fire was there in his eyes—a smoldering need to win that Ambrose knew well.

He nodded in return and shot a glance at Timmons. The bell pealed once more, and the fight resumed. The short break had revitalized Ackley a bit, but he was sluggish and drooping where Hopkins was surefooted and sound.

They circled a few more times, but Hopkins seized the upper hand. He landed a blow to Ackley's mouth, splitting the lad's lip. Ackley sent an excellent shot to Hopkins's chin, but it was too little, too late. Hopkins delivered one final blow to Ackley's ear, and the younger man went down to the floor.

Ambrose started the count and reached ten before Ackley lifted his gaze and shook his head. Ambrose signaled to Timmons to ring the bell.

Hopkins helped Ackley to his feet as Ambrose announced, "Brothers, our newest member!"

Voices swelled in cheer and camaraderie. The men welcomed Ackley who, though clearly bemused judging by the dazed look in his eye—or probably he was still recovering from that last series of blows—smiled with blood-streaked front teeth.

Ambrose guided a heavily-breathing Ackley to a chair outside the ring. He signaled for another member to hand him a towel and provided it to his new protégé. "Your membership comes with a price."

Ackley swiped the towel across his face and neck then looked up at him in question.

"You'll train with me and then you'll fight for the championship. There will be other fights first, but later this summer you'll go up against Belcher. Does that appeal to you?"

As soon as he'd said Belcher, Ackley's eyes narrowed—one of which was rapidly blackening—and brightened with hunger. He was already nodding. "Definitely." He wiped the towel over his chest and then wrapped it around the back of his neck so that it hung over his shoulders.

"Your footwork is damned fast," Ambrose said. "If I didn't know better, I'd say you were a student of Mendoza."

"My father was. God rest his soul."

Perhaps that was behind the boy's passion. Ambrose thought of his own father who would've been ridiculously proud of Ambrose's pugilistic achievements—as he'd been with everything else Ambrose had done. Ambrose's chest compressed. "Is he the reason you fight?"

Ackley nodded. "He would've been champion, but he was run down by a coach and four." His eyes grew bright for a moment then darkened with promise.

Ambrose knew from personal experience the mental aspect was often more important than the physical. Would he have fought so well if he hadn't been driving every painful regret from his brain? "Then we'll have to make sure you're the champion."

Ambrose clapped Ackley on the shoulder then turned and went to Hopkins, who'd deposited himself in a chair. He mopped his face and chest with a towel before looking up at Ambrose.

"He's better than you. Or at least he will be when you train him up."

Ambrose's blood stirred. For the first time in days he'd forgotten about Philippa and her tempting curves. He had something else upon which he could focus. Or obsess, as it were.

"We start tomorrow."

Friday morning, Philippa suffered the nauseating company of her father and *that woman* on the ride to Benfield. Thankfully

Lord von Egmont's presence provided a slight buffer, and Philippa turned her attention toward him as much as possible.

Still, Lady von Egmont babbled incessantly about her memories of London while Father smiled—more than Philippa had ever seen him smile—adoringly from the opposite seat. Her emotions jumped from disgusted to jealous to sad (for her mother) and back again.

When they finally arrived at their destination, Lord von Egmont helped Philippa from the carriage and made to escort her away. However, *that woman* stopped them with her overly high voice. "Just look at it, Pieter!"

Von Egmont turned toward his mother with a questioning, if slightly harassed look.

Lady von Egmont blinked beneath the brim of her large hat, which featured a plethora of silk flowers, a handful of feathers, and a tiny fake bird. "Oh, my goodness, I've only been to Benfield that one time." She'd told them all about her first visit to Benfield at the age of seventeen. "Truly, I'd forgotten its magnificence."

"It's very nice, Mother," von Egmont said as he guided Philippa along the shell-packed drive.

'Very nice' didn't begin to adequately describe Benfield. Built first during the late medieval period, the house had been enlarged and improved on two subsequent occasions, the last being during the middle of the previous century. The property had been in the possession of the Dukes of Holborn since the early seventeenth century, except for when Cromwell stripped it from the family for its loyalty to King Charles. The house and surrounding parkland—including a large pond, but minus the stables, which had burned—had, of course, been restored to Holborn.

That all of these were facts she'd memorized in preparation for marriage to the future Duke of Holborn didn't change her appreciation for the diamond-paned windows glistening in the sunlight, or for the pink-tinged sandstone mined from the family's quarry in Wiltshire and painstakingly assembled into a majestic façade.

Lady von Egmont took Philippa's father's arm. "Herrick, I

declare this to be the most perfect day." The two exchanged a look of mutual admiration, and for the first time Philippa felt a pang of sorrow for their plight. Von Egmont had explained to her that his mother had fallen in love with Philippa's father, but she'd already been promised to von Egmont instead.

Philippa turned away. Their affair was becoming more palatable, which only served to frustrate her. She didn't want to accept her father's infidelity. But really, why not? Did she want to go back to the silent dinners with her parents, the (now) obvious discomfort they felt with each other? Why not let them live the lives that made them happy?

Such contemplation only increased Philippa's anxiety about finding her own happiness in marriage—something she simply had to do in…three weeks. It was as if a clock had been implanted in her brain, and it constantly ticked away the minutes of her freedom.

They rounded the side of the house. To the south, a gentle slope rose and about fifty yards distant stood the impressive stables Holborn had enlarged and refurbished a decade ago.

The Earl of Saxton greeted them when they arrived outside the stables. As Holborn's son and truly one of the best horsemen in England, he was always present at this event. "Good afternoon, Lady Philippa."

Philippa felt no regret or remorse upon speaking with Saxton. Indeed, she was quite pleased for his happiness. She'd sensed he'd needed it most desperately. Last fall he'd been tense, but now he appeared relaxed and content. A man in love. She felt a rush of envy.

She dipped a curtsey to Saxton. "Good afternoon, my lord. You remember our guest, Lord von Egmont?"

Saxton nodded. "I do. Welcome to Benfield."

"I'm delighted to be here." He gestured toward one of the penned areas. "That's a splendid bay. Full-bred Arabian, or was he bred with a Cleveland Bay?"

Saxton grinned. "You've an eye for horses. Conqueror's from Holborn's Arabian stud. His dam is indeed a Cleveland Bay."

"His sire is Prince?"

Saxton nodded, but then Philippa's attention was drawn to

her left as Sevrin came to a halt beside them. Her heart beat faster, and her stomach fluttered. She hadn't seen him since the other night when they'd been closeted together.

"Afternoon, Sevrin," Saxton greeted him. "Lord von Egmont, this is my good friend, Lord Sevrin. Sevrin, this is Lord von Egmont. I was just about to take him to see Holborn's latest breeding triumph, Conqueror. Would you care to join us?"

Sevrin's gaze flicked to Philippa, but only for the briefest moment. "I would." He returned his gaze to Saxton. "Allow me to escort Lady Philippa so you two can continue your discussion."

Von Egmont gave Philippa a questioning look, which Saxton must've also noticed because he said, "Let him. Sevrin couldn't give a fig about our breeding program. Come."

Sevrin offered his arm, and she took it. She purposely walked very slowly so that they were several steps behind Saxton and von Egmont when she said, "Why are you participating in a prizefight?" She realized it was Friday. "Goodness, is that tonight?"

He kept his voice low, matching her subdued tone. "Yes. I used to fight a lot. I missed it."

She wasn't surprised at his background given the skill he'd exhibited the night she'd met him. "That's it? You simply decided to take up fighting again?"

"I never really gave it up. I operate a private fighting club."

"You do?" Her voice had climbed, so she hushed herself before adding, "Where?"

"At the Black Horse." The tavern where he lived.

They entered the cool, dim stables. Saxton and von Egmont were completely lost in their discussion, oblivious to her and Sevrin.

"Are you staying for the entire house party?" Sevrin asked.

"I am. Will you be returning after your fight?" She tried to sound nonchalant, but she would be worried all night. And tomorrow—until she knew he was safe.

"No. I only promised Saxton I would come by. A house party focused on horses isn't my favorite pastime."

She frowned. "What's wrong with horses? Wait, I just

realized I've never seen you ride in the park. Or anywhere else. In fact, I think I asked you about riding the night we met and unless I'm mistaken, you never answered me."

"I don't ride."

For the first time, she mentally gave a point to Allred over Sevrin. She loved to ride and couldn't imagine a mate who didn't.

Blast! When had she begun to consider Sevrin as a potential mate? Since she'd started looking for a husband. Since Sevrin had rescued her and kissed her. Depressingly, she wondered if she'd compare them forever. She couldn't. Not if she hoped to build a better marriage than her parents had. Marrying Allred while wanting Sevrin made her no better than her father.

It was past time for her to put Sevrin from her mind. He'd already stated his intent to do the same when he'd rescinded his help. No more comparisons. No more recollections of the way he kissed her, or the way he made her feel—like a valued partner.

She gently withdrew her hand from Sevrin's arm with the knowledge that she'd never touch him again. "I wish you good luck tonight." *Be safe*, her mind screamed, but she didn't voice the words.

"Thank you." He looked deep into her eyes, as if he might communicate more, but he said nothing.

They'd reached the center of the aisle between the stalls. Corridors branched between the stalls to exterior doors placed at the midpoint of the stable. Sevrin bowed to her and left through the right-side door.

A cool breeze from the door closing wafted across her neck, icing her flesh. Her chest felt hollow. Though their acquaintance had been brief, their meeting had been profound. At least for her.

A half hour later, Philippa left von Egmont to meet Audrey and Lydia who were strolling in the rose garden. She joined them with a smile, resolved the day would end better than it had started.

"Good afternoon, isn't it a beautiful day?" The sky sparkled a brilliant blue, and trees bloomed pink and white all around them.

The scent of hyacinths and roses filled the air.

Lydia linked her right arm through Philippa's and her left through Audrey's. "Yes, it's a spectacular day. I daresay this has been the best week of my life." She was clearly enjoying her newfound popularity, and Philippa only hoped it continued. Perhaps she and her friend would get married this Season, and then they need only find a husband for Audrey. She peered around Lydia at Audrey.

Taller than most girls—she had at least three inches over both Philippa and Lydia—Audrey wasn't what one would call dainty. She possessed beautiful hazel eyes and a thick head of light brown corkscrew-curly hair that was almost impossible to capture in a hairstyle, but Audrey did try. Though often termed "unremarkable," Philippa found Audrey quite lovely. And she was certain she wasn't the only one who thought so.

Audrey caught her gaze and smiled. "I saw you with Sevrin a bit ago. I'm glad to see he's here."

"Unfortunately, he's already gone," Philippa said.

Audrey's smile faded, and her eyes clouded with disappointment. "Oh. That's a pity."

"It isn't," Lydia said with a firm shake of her head. "Philippa, whatever were you doing with him again? First you danced with him, then there's talk you might have left the ballroom with him at Lady Anstruther's, and you were with him today?"

Philippa bristled. She didn't need Lydia telling tales. "You know there's nothing between Sevrin and me. Allred is courting me, and I'm quite pleased with that."

"I'm glad to hear it, but you must be careful. Rumors can ruin someone, whether they're true or not. I was lucky to have escaped scandal. Do you think anyone actually verified the story that paints Sevrin as such a scoundrel? It's not as if anyone can ask his brother what occurred, and who knows what happened to the girl."

Blast, Philippa had forgotten to ask Lydia about Sevrin's past, but she at least knew his brother had died. "Why would anyone want to talk to his brother?"

"Because the girl he ruined was his brother's fiancée." Lydia blinked at her. "Didn't you know?"

Speechless, Philippa blinked in return.

"*I* didn't know," Audrey said, her eyes wide.

He'd ruined his own brother's fiancée and refused to marry her? That didn't sound like the Sevrin she knew, but how well did she really know him? Her flesh chilled.

"I've also heard he and his brother fought a duel," Lydia added.

Oh, God. Philippa's stomach dropped to her toes. "Is that how he died?"

Lydia shrugged. "No one seems to know for sure, but Aunt Margaret insists Sevrin killed him. And you know how seldom she is wrong."

It was true. Aunt Margaret was the premier gossip of the realm for a reason—unparalleled accuracy.

Philippa thought of all the self-deprecating comments Sevrin had made during their acquaintance. His insistence that he wasn't a hero, despite his actions and behavior to the contrary. Did a man who ruined his brother's fiancée and killed him rescue hapless females? Did he ask wallflowers to dance?

Apparently he did.

She struggled to refute it, but reason told her he was guilty of those crimes. If only because of the remorse he'd evidenced in the subtle things he said and did. A man without regret didn't live in a tavern or hide on the fringe of Society.

It was good she'd severed their acquaintance, particularly if speculation about them was mounting. Furthermore, her mother's dire prediction that she'd be discovered as Sevrin's mystery woman could hopefully be put to rest. While all of this was quite sensible and cautious, she still couldn't help regret what might've been.

Just then Allred entered the rose garden. He strode toward them with a charming smile lighting up his handsome face and offered a deep bow. "Good afternoon, ladies."

Lydia giggled demurely. "Good afternoon, Lord Allred. I presume you're here to collect Philippa."

He regarded Philippa and presented his arm. "Indeed. It is time for our ride. I hope you don't mind, but I've invited some others to join us."

Philippa saw a small group of people standing just down the path. She'd thought they would be going for a private ride. However, given the weight currently burdening her head and heart, she didn't particularly care.

Chapter Twelve

THOUGH invigorating, the ride did nothing to ease Philippa's anxiety about Sevrin. She still couldn't make sense of him killing his own brother. Over a woman. For any reason!

That Allred had paid more attention to his two male friends than to her on their ride had been a blessing since Philippa's conversational skills had fled upon hearing Lydia's pronouncement. She had to get herself together before dinner. Perhaps a nap would help restore her composure.

After a brief, troubling sleep, Philippa woke to the sounds of someone treading upon the carpet. She stretched beneath the coverlet and opened her eyes. She froze.

A filthy hand tasting of she-didn't-want-to-know-what slapped over her lips. The despicable visage of Swan—the man who'd accosted her in the alley outside Lockwood House—filled her view. With his free hand, he brought a long knife to his mouth, urging her to silence.

"Best be quiet now, else this blade'll slip right between your ribs."

Her heart throbbed painfully, but at least it reminded her she was alive. For now. She nodded, and he slowly withdrew his hand.

"That's a good girl." The villain was wearing Holborn livery.

A hundred scenarios about what this intruder could want invaded her mind, but only one rang true. Given their last encounter—when he'd ripped her dress and grabbed at her flesh—she had to assume he meant to rape her. She forced herself to take a breath, but it was shallow and inadequate. "What do you want?"

"That's no proper greeting."

Her mind scrambled for a means of escape.

He shook his head. "Now, now. I see ye looking around, but don't think to run. I've insurance to keep ye in line." He grinned, revealing a disgusting array of brown teeth, as his gaze dipped to her chest.

With shaking fingers, she clutched the coverlet tighter. "What does that mean? What sort of insurance?"

"Yer lordship. Sevrin. If ye don't cooperate with me, the boss'll have his head by morning."

Sevrin could more than take care of himself. "That's absurd."

Swan shrugged. "He's fighting for Jagger tonight. If he loses, he's dead for sure. But if he wins, he'll save his hide—and yers. Unless ye try to get away from me, and then all deals are off."

Philippa's mind swam. What deals? Why was Sevrin fighting for Jagger?

"I'm hoping his lordship loses," Swan said as his gaze dipped down to her chest. "I'm dead certain Jagger'll let me have ye, and I've been dreaming of that every night since we met." He leered at her again and dragged a callused finger down her arm. "If ye don't get up, I might take yer dawdling as an invitation."

She scrambled off the other side of the bed, her gaze never leaving the wicked blade in his hand. "What do you want me to do?"

"Get dressed. Yer coming back to London to watch the prizefight. Jagger's orders."

She was finally able to take a deeper breath. Her virtue, at least, was safe for now. But none of this made sense. Sevrin was fighting for Jagger as some sort of deal? Was it about her? "Why do I need to go?"

"Just as Sevrin's our insurance you'll come along nicely, you're our insurance he'll win the fight."

Her knees went weak. *What did Sevrin do?*

Swan waved his knife. "Go on then, get dressed. We're on a schedule, much as I'd like to loiter here with ye." He raked her again with his vulgar gaze, and she scurried to the armoire where her new ball gown hung.

Think, Philippa, think. She shuddered before turning to face her captor. "I'm expected downstairs this evening. The entire house party will know I've disappeared."

"Ye won't 'disappear.' Ye're ill and have decided to go home."

An unfortunately plausible explanation, and one she'd warrant his boss, the nefarious Jagger, had come up with. She simply couldn't credit this villain with that much forethought. "Still, I can't get dressed without assistance."

"I was hoping ye'd say that." His tongue darted out and slathered his lower lip.

She had to work to keep herself from gagging. She turned away from him and drew her corset on over her shift, then quickly laced it up the front. Next came her petticoat, which she also fitted herself. Unfortunately she couldn't fasten the back of her dress and so she'd have to allow him to do it. With quaking hands, she pulled the dress over her head and settled it on top of her undergarments.

He came toward her, but she held up a hand. "I'll need to see to my hair first."

Working quickly, she pinned her hair up into a basic knot. She wished she had a hat with a veil—she'd no idea who would be at the fight, but surely there would be men who could identify her. Better yet, she wished she had that hood from Lockwood House.

After donning her stockings and boots—with her back to her captor—she took a wrap from the armoire. She'd use it to conceal her head at the fight.

Gathering her courage, she looked over her shoulder. By the lascivious look on Swan's face, he'd watched every movement she'd made.

She clenched her teeth together and forced herself to say, "Now you may fasten the back of my gown."

Though she steeled herself, the first stroke of his fingers against her back came like a snake slithering over her skin. She squeezed her eyes shut as if that would somehow block out the hideous sensation.

"Pity the boss told me not to touch."

"Then stop touching!" she snapped, unable to keep her emotions in check another moment. "I'd be delighted to inform Jagger how you ignored his directive."

"Ye'd do that too, ye bitch." He roughly pulled the sides of her dress together.

"Careful you don't tear it!" *You great oaf.*

He grumbled, but gentled his grip. It took him several minutes, but she was finally garbed.

She skittered away from him and turned.

"Very nice," he said, his gaze as invasive as ever. "But I liked ye better in yer underthings. I'll remember that a long time." He leered once more.

"May we go now?" She'd no idea how she'd endure the hour-long ride back to town in his presence and was eager to get it over with.

"Not a word when we get downstairs, ye understand?" He'd set his knife on her dressing table, but now plucked it up as a reminder of how he planned to keep her captive. "Remember, yer lordship's fate rests with him."

Ambrose. She understood perfectly. She wrapped the thick, woolen shawl around her shoulders and preceded him from the room.

Her legs quivered as she walked down the corridor and then the massive staircase. It was early for the evening's activities, so she doubted they'd encounter anyone. Even if they did, what would she say? She could likely save herself, but what would Jagger do to Ambrose if she failed to arrive at the prizefight? Indeed, what was in store for Ambrose anyway? And why had he entered into an agreement with this criminal for her?

Fear for his safety was joined by a ridiculous thrill at the risks he continued to take on her behalf. For a scoundrel, he was deceptively wonderful. At least to her—she couldn't forget what Lydia had told her that afternoon. Still, her mind couldn't equate the man who'd stolen his brother's fiancée and likely killed his brother in a duel with the man who'd gone above and beyond what any gentleman might do to protect not only her honor, but her life.

At last, they reached the foyer where a footman greeted them with a bow. She forced herself to smile at the young man and noted that behind her Swan kept his head bent. She paused in front of the footman. "Will you please convey my apologies to Lord and Lady Holborn and inform Lord Herrick that I've returned to London? I'm afraid I'm not feeling well."

"Indeed, my lady. Godspeed to you." He bowed again.

"Thank you." She darted a glance at Swan, adorned in his certainly-stolen Holborn livery. She returned her gaze to the footman, who had absolutely no idea she was being abducted under his very nose.

She could scream right now and consign Ambrose to who-knew-what, perhaps death. Surely he could defend himself. But doubt prevented her from opening her mouth, and soon she was through the doorway and in the drive where a coach awaited them.

"Took ye long enough." Another presumed criminal in another set of stolen livery opened the door of the coach.

He helped Philippa inside, crushing her elbow in a bruising grip. She sat in the forward-facing seat and pushed herself into the corner. When the door closed leaving her alone, she audibly exhaled in relief. Following that came deep, bone-shaking chills.

What would happen to her? To Ambrose? The ruin of her reputation was—at last—guaranteed, but that paled beside other concerns. What if Ambrose failed to win this fight? What if her captor failed to follow his employer's orders?

Though it provided no warmth—nothing could—she pulled her wrap closer about her shoulders. And prayed.

At half eleven that night, Ambrose and Hopkins exited a hack in the Strand and made their way to Dirty Lane near the Thames. Ambrose had attended many pugilism bouts at this address before, including a few he'd fought in, when he'd first come to London.

"This it, Sev?" Hopkins asked, gesturing toward a large warehouse with peeling whitewash. Men loitered about the entrance, and a few women hawked their bodies.

One slattern winked at Ambrose and sashayed to greet him. "Evenin', milord." She smiled, but didn't show her teeth—likely to keep him from seeing how many were missing. "Two pence."

"No, thank you." He strode past her into the warehouse. Hopkins followed. Two burly men stood sentinel at the entrance to the main fighting room. A slender fellow pushed away from the wall and approached them.

"Follow me, my lord." He led Ambrose and Hopkins down a dark corridor to the right. It turned and ran parallel to the fighting room. Ambrose could hear the gathering crowd.

The man opened a door to the left, and light spilled into the corridor. They walked inside.

"You left it a bit late, didn't you?" Jagger stood from a chair in the corner. He was dressed in a fine wool coat and gleaming Hessians. If he removed just one of the four gold rings he wore on his fingers, he might pass for a polite London gentleman.

Ambrose shrugged. "No reason to arrive too early."

"I take it that means you haven't brought my future prizefighter." He frowned. "A week with nothing to show for your efforts?"

Ambrose didn't look at Hopkins, but could see from the corner of his vision that his second was regarding him with curiosity. "You presume much. As it happens, I've found your prizefighter."

"You should have told me sooner. For incentive, I invited a special guest this evening."

Ambrose's stomach plummeted to his feet. Hadn't he feared this very thing? "You didn't bring her here."

Jagger nodded, and Ambrose advanced on him with a snarl. "You son of a bitch." Hopkins grabbed his arm and held him back—not that Ambrose couldn't have broken free in a trice if he really wanted to hurt Jagger. God, how he wanted to hurt him. But not now.

Jagger grinned. "Absolutely. Now, win me this fight. I put five hundred pounds on you."

Hopkins sucked in air between his teeth, creating a soft whistle.

Jagger looked to Hopkins. "Get your man ready. The fight's

in less than half an hour."

Ambrose clenched his fists. "Where is she?"

"My private box."

Where everyone would see her. His took another step toward Jagger. "I made this bargain with you to keep her safe, and yet you're parading her in front of countless gentlemen who will gleefully spread news of her presence."

Jagger held up his hand. "I'm a man of my word. She's masked." He leaned forward and curled his lip, meeting Ambrose's attempt at intimidation. "You'd best fulfill your part of our bargain."

Jagger quit the room, closing the door behind him.

Ambrose growled and turned toward a bewildered Hopkins who asked, "How the hell did you get mixed up with a lowlife like Jagger?"

"Unfortunate circumstances."

Hopkins shed his coat. "Who's the skirt you were talking about?"

"An innocent." Ambrose's mind worked. The need to brutalize Jagger overwhelmed him.

"Come on, we'd best get out there." Hopkins reached to help Ambrose out of his coat.

Ambrose suddenly had to see Philippa as soon as possible. He handed Hopkins his coat, waistcoat, and cravat. He'd wear his shirt and take it off out there. He ought to remove his boots, but he was too anxious to get to Philippa.

Hopkins laid Ambrose's clothing over the back of another chair. "You're wearing boots?"

"Not sure they'll allow bare feet, and anyway, I want to get out there." Ambrose shifted his weight, anxious to see Philippa.

"Fair enough. You can always change your mind." Hopkins said. "What happens if you don't win?"

"An innocent will be ruined." Ambrose pushed the thought from his mind, vowing it would never come to pass. "Ready?"

With a nod, Hopkins picked up the bag he'd brought with him. Inside were towels, a large flask of water, a bottle of gin, and perhaps the most important item: a vial of Tom's healing tonic. Applied to bruises and cuts, it repaired injuries twice as fast as without. Tom's recipe for the tonic was as secret and effective as his recipe for ale—and Ambrose's club survived on a steady diet of both.

Hopkins led him from the small, dingy room into the narrow corridor. They turned left and after a quick right, entered the arena. The place had changed since Ambrose had last been to a fight.

The fighting stage was still in the center, but wooden railings had been erected around the square. In addition, a balcony had been constructed around the perimeter of the arena with boxes built into the center of each. They were not luxurious by any means, but they contained chairs, whereas the rest of the balcony did not. Ambrose immediately caught sight of Philippa, clad in a pale coral gown and a dark mask that covered her face from her hairline to her upper lip, in one of the boxes on the opposite wall. Beside her, Jagger looked down at him smugly. Ambrose dug his fingernails into his palms.

His gaze surveyed the other boxes and arrested. *Bloody hell.*

The Duke of Holborn held court in the box on the opposite side of the ring from Philippa. Around him were several gentlemen Ambrose had seen at Benfield that afternoon: Allred, Finchley, even Philippa's bloody houseguest from the continent. He searched for Saxton but couldn't see him. He was more than a bit surprised his friend hadn't come since the rest of the damned house party had.

Hopkins had continued on, breaking his way through the crowd. Ambrose hastened to catch up. Men turned to look at him as he passed and he heard several murmurs of "the Vicious Viscount" and some of the names of his past opponents.

He'd fought in a half-dozen prizefights and had won four of them. The first two had been brutal losses, but he'd learned how to better defend himself, and more importantly who not to fight. One of his opponents had been an incredibly dirty fighter, throwing rabbit punch after rabbit punch to the back of Ambrose's head. The bout had ended with Ambrose tossing up his accounts over the side of the ring.

Shortly after that had been his discovery of barefooted fighting. He'd practiced his movements and had steadily improved. The first victory had been cathartic, effectively banishing his regret and despair. With his subsequent wins, he'd all but forgotten what he'd done in Cornwall.

Which was bad.

He didn't want to forget. He didn't deserve to forget. And he sure as hell didn't deserve to be a celebrated pugilistic champion.

He'd set up his own fighting club at the Black Horse. A haven for miscreants, failures, and sinners alike. A place where fighting meant physical and mental release, not glory. A refuge for Ambrose to bury the painful mistakes of his past.

He reached the side of the fenced square, where Hopkins was already arranging their things on a small table.

Ambrose looked up at Philippa whose head was turned toward him. He could imagine her ale-colored eyes wide with concern, her flesh pale with apprehension. His gaze flicked toward the box of Benfield men. Had Philippa seen them? Of course she had. How could she not? Ambrose wanted to choke the life from Jagger for bringing her here.

A chant of "Sevrin, Sevrin," drew his attention to the opposite side of the square. A group of men—*his* men from the Black Horse, led by Saxton—were moving en masse to join him.

Two men stepped to the other side of the ring. It was obvious which was Nolan—a massive-shouldered, ham-fisted bloke with a long nose and ginger hair. He pulled his shirt over his head. A nasty scar ran down his left arm. Nolan flexed his bicep and cast a glance at Ambrose as if to say, "I'm not afraid to get hurt."

Ambrose didn't bother stifling his answering smirk. He removed his own shirt and rotated his left shoulder where a round, puckered scar made its permanent home. Nolan registered the blemish and gave a slight nod.

Hopkins walked through a gap in the fencing around the square. Nolan's second did the same, and they met in the middle. They exchanged a few words and then nodded. Each returned to their fighter.

"Now we choose an umpire," Hopkins said.

Right. Saxton came up beside him. "Good thing I showed up."

"What the devil are you—and all of them," Ambrose jerked his head toward the Benfield box, "doing here?"

Saxton shrugged. "Couldn't keep them from coming. Several of them are great supporters of the sport."

Like Allred. God, if he somehow recognized Philippa. If any of them did... Ambrose could only hope they assumed she was merely Jagger's masked paramour.

"You ready?" Saxton asked.

"More than." All of his rage at Jagger would be directed at Nolan.

Hopkins went back into the square. Nolan had chosen his umpire, a squat, older fellow who now stood on their platform. Nolan's second entered the square, and Ambrose and Nolan followed. The room hushed.

A boy came into the square and drew the scratch—a square yard etched in chalk. Hopkins led Ambrose to one side and Nolan went to the other. The seconds nodded at each other, and with a final clap on Ambrose's shoulder, Hopkins exited the square.

A bell sounded. Memories of previous fights assailed Ambrose. The cheers of the crowd, the tension between him and his opponent, the hunger to win.

Nolan's shoulders twitched then he raised his hands in a defensive posture. He held his fists high. Ambrose wondered if that meant he'd be able to get to the man's gut. Only one way to know.

He moved forward. The floor felt strange because he was wearing boots , but he couldn't remove them now. Disregarding the sensation, he delivered a quick jab to Nolan's middle. His opponent dropped his arms, but it was too late. Ambrose's fist connected with Nolan's flesh, eliciting a grunt from the Irishman.

Ambrose picked up a faint feminine shriek. He glanced up at Philippa, but was instantly sorry as Nolan came at him with both fists in a quick one-two punch. One caught Ambrose in the ear with a deafening pop, and the other grazed off his left shoulder as he danced out of the way.

Ambrose shook his head. *Concentrate.*

They circled each other a few times, gauging one another's position and movements. Ambrose studied Nolan's features, looking for anything that would reveal his next strike. Nolan came forward and jabbed with both fists again. Ambrose brought his hands up and defended the attack, then launched his own assault, catching Nolan's side beneath his left arm.

They continued like this for several minutes. Sweat trickled down Ambrose's face, his neck, his torso. His feet were unbearably hot in stockings and boots, and Ambrose regretted keeping them on.

It was time to get this bout going and bring it to a hopefully rapid end. He rushed at his opponent and volleyed him with punches to the face and gut. However, it wasn't that simple. Nolan was better than anyone Ambrose had fought. He deflected most of Ambrose's blows and landed a few of his own. Pain sliced Ambrose's cheekbone from Nolan's well-directed and powerful right hook. Nolan drew his hand back for another strike, but Ambrose spun about and Nolan's fist landed at the base of his neck.

The bell on Ambrose's side rang. "No rabbit punches!" Saxton yelled.

Nolan held up his hands and backed to the side of the square. "I didn't mean to. He moves fast is all." He grinned, revealing a gap in the upper right of his mouth.

The bell rang once more, and the fight resumed. Evenly matched, they traded blows for several minutes—or maybe it was an hour. Ambrose lost track of time, of place, of everything but the pulse of his blood and the analysis of his opponent and where to strike next.

It was wearying. Sweat ran into his eyes. Blood trickled from his lip, and his battered knuckles ached. He recognized the same in Nolan and dug deep for an attack. He danced forward and landed his fist against Nolan's chin. Nolan staggered backward and Ambrose followed, sending another punch to the side of his opponent's head. Then another to his cheek. Then another and another, to his side and middle.

Nolan slumped and then dropped to his knees. The bell sounded. He was down. His second rushed into the square.

Ambrose backed up to the scratch and waited. *Thirty seconds. Stay down thirty seconds and it will be over.* His mind counted as the umpires did the same.

Three, four.

Ambrose looked up at Philippa. She sat at the edge of her chair, one hand raised part way to her mouth.

Seven, eight.

Nolan's second bent down and spoke to him softly, words Ambrose couldn't hear. Nolan shook his head, sending droplets of sweat and blood splattering to the floor. He already sported a bruise on his cheek, a bloodied nose and lip, and his knuckles looked every bit as destroyed as Ambrose's felt. But he refused to look at his wounds or indulge his pain. Not yet.

Twelve, thirteen.

More whispering from his second. Another head shake from Nolan. The second rubbed Nolan's shoulders, dabbed at his sweat-covered neck and face.

Eighteen, nineteen.

Hopkins came into the square and gave Ambrose a towel. He swiped it over his face and chest, the back of his neck. He thrust the sweat-sopped cloth back at Hopkins.

Twenty-three, twenty-four.

Nolan leaned forward and laid his palms on the floor. Ambrose's blood surged with imminent victory.

Twenty-seven, twenty-eight.

Nolan sprang to his feet. His second shoved him toward the scratch, getting him to the line just before Ambrose would've been declared the winner.

He wrenched his mind back from the brink of victory and refocused. Nolan shook his arms out and then pounced. He did what Ambrose had just done—fists flying with a precision that should have been dulled at this point in the fight, especially after going down as he did. But had he really gone down, or had he just taken a respite?

Ambrose deflected, but he was tired. A blow caught him beneath the chin, snapping his head back. Then a series of punches landed against his middle, where he still wasn't completely healed from his trip to Jagger's. He managed a glancing blow off Nolan's head, but the answer from his opponent was punishing. Damn, but his right hook was merciless.

Bright light flashed as Nolan's knuckles pummeled Ambrose's eye. Another hit to the side of his head and another to his mouth. He bit his tongue and blood gushed. He coughed against the bitter taste and then he slipped. Down he went, his knees hitting the wood.

He pitched forward and couldn't quite catch himself. The rough-hewn planks of the wood floor scraped his cheek. The hardness welcomed him as pain enveloped his mind. The cacophony faded around him. He closed his eyes and found peace.

Chapter Thirteen

PHILIPPA screamed and jumped to her feet. She rushed to the edge of the balcony and gripped the rough wooden railing. Jagger came to her side while people stared up at her from below.

"Sit down," Jagger whispered close to her ear. "You don't want to draw unnecessary attention to yourself." No, she didn't, particularly when Swan had stolen her shawl as some sort of trophy.

She looked down at Ambrose's body lying halfway over the scratch into the center of the square. Nolan stood over him, a grin splitting his battered face.

Ambrose's second kneeled beside him, and Saxton stood nearby. Philippa curled her fingers around the railing and wished she could go down and pull Ambrose to his feet. When Nolan had collapsed she'd learned that a fighter had half a minute to get himself back up to the scratch or his opponent would be declared the victor. They were already at fifteen seconds, and Ambrose hadn't stirred.

And while waiting for the fight to begin, Jagger had made it very clear that Ambrose had to win. He'd made a bargain with Jagger for her reputation and losing would nullify the deal. If Ambrose lost, Jagger would remove her mask. Her gaze moved to where several of Benfield's partygoers—including Allred—were seated. Several of them—again, including Allred—had already looked in her direction. What did they see?

"Get up!" her mind screamed.

She leaned further over the side, and Jagger clasped her arm and drew her back. "Can't have you falling over." He kept his hand around her bicep. His grip was firm and as the seconds ticked by, his fingers bit deeper into her arm.

Twenty-three already!

"Drag him up!" someone yelled. Philippa's gaze roved the crowd, and she spotted a man near the square cupping his hands around his mouth to be heard above the throng. "Drag him, Hopkins!"

Hopkins must be his second. The large man pulled Ambrose to his feet, but he was limp. They were already at the scratch, but Ambrose's head lolled back. Hopkins grabbed the hair at Ambrose's nape and tugged.

Ambrose's eyes fluttered.

Twenty-nine.

His shoulders squared.

Thirty!

Ambrose's eyes opened, and he lifted his head.

Nolan's umpire tried to call the fight for Nolan, but Saxton surged forward, his glare positively glacial. "He was up to the scratch."

"No, thirty seconds had passed."

"It was precisely *at* thirty seconds."

The crowd yelled their own opinions, drowning out the debate between the umpires. Jagger squeezed her arm, and she turned her head sharply.

"You're hurting me."

He released her with a murmured, "Sorry," his gaze never leaving the spectacle below.

While the umpires argued, Hopkins mopped Ambrose's face and neck. Philippa willed him to look up so she could affirm he was all right, but he didn't.

Saxton towered over the other umpire, but the shorter man stood on his toes and waved his hands. Finally, the other umpire nodded and stepped back. Both umpires spoke to the principals and their seconds. Then everyone left the square but Ambrose and Nolan.

The bell rang.

Philippa sagged with relief for the briefest second, but then her body coiled with tension once more as she watched Nolan strike out.

Ambrose tried to answer, but his movements were sluggish compared to his opponent. Over the next few minutes, he managed to maintain a defensive posture and mostly protect himself, but he wasn't causing any damage. The fight had already lasted forty minutes, how much longer could they go before fatigue and injuries completely claimed them?

Ambrose danced backward and sat down in the corner. The bell chimed, and again the umpires came out and started counting. Philippa stared in disbelief as he pulled his boots and stockings from his feet and tossed them at Hopkins. He jumped back up and was leaping toward the scratch before the count reached twelve.

The umpires retreated from the square, and the bell sounded once more—Philippa prayed for the last time until it signaled the fight was over.

Ambrose launched forward as if the loss of his footwear had somehow restored the strength and energy sapped from him over the course of the bout. Nolan jerked back, but Ambrose followed. He dropped his defenses and simply attacked. He drove Nolan back with blow after blow. A sickening crunch came after a particularly brutal strike to Nolan's nose, and blood flowed over his mouth and chin. One of his eyes was nearly swollen shut. Ambrose continued on, and Philippa bit her lip to keep from calling for him to stop.

She watched, transfixed, as he viciously attacked the other man, causing horrific damage to his face, not to mention the series of jabs to the man's ribs. She wrapped her arms around herself protectively, as if the fight were somehow hurting her too.

Nolan tried to protect himself, but his hands fumbled ineffectually between him and Ambrose. Then he simply sagged and fell back against the railing. Philippa held her breath, waiting to see if he might pitch over into the spectators, but he slid down and then slumped forward.

Ambrose took a step back, his chest heaving. He wiped his

hand beneath his nose and then flexed his fingers. The umpires rushed forward and began the count. Philippa prayed the man wouldn't get up. And she prayed he was all right. How could men watch this for enjoyment? How could men *do* this for sport? She felt sick.

She watched, motionless, as the seconds counted by. It seemed several minutes before they reached thirty, but when they got to that number, Nolan was still on the floor. Saxton raised Ambrose's arm, and cheers filled the hall. Philippa held her hands to her ears.

Ambrose turned and looked up at her, then shifted his gaze to Jagger. He narrowed his eyes.

Jagger nodded and then spread his lips in a wide grin. He pulled Philippa's hands from her ears. "Come, dearie, time to see your lover."

"He's not my lover," she spat, never taking her eyes from Ambrose.

Saxton and Hopkins practically dragged him from the square. Outside the railing, they helped him don his shirt before leading him through the crowd. They could barely move forward, however, as men rushed to congratulate him.

She turned to look at Jagger who was still grinning. "I knew he'd win," he said.

"Yet you abducted me to intimidate him anyway."

Jagger shrugged. "What do you care? No one saw you."

Though the fight below had sickened her, she wanted very much to punch her captor. Perhaps everyone had a breaking point at which violence became acceptable. Had something happened to Ambrose that made brutality easy? Perhaps he *had* killed his brother. The idea repelled her, but also made her want to know why. She had to see him, ensure he would be well. "Take me to Sevrin."

Jagger turned to one of his men and said something. Philippa couldn't hear what they discussed—the sounds around her were far too loud and distracting. Jagger nodded to the two men who'd brought her there, though they were no longer garbed in Holborn livery. They took her arms and guided her out of the box onto the balcony. Up ahead was a staircase that would take them down to the main floor.

The balcony was narrow and choked with men. Swan walked behind her while the other led. Neither let her go. The air was hot and reeked of sweat and alcohol. A surge from behind jostled her forward into the back of the man in front of her. She couldn't put her hands up to keep from crashing into him. The man behind her pulled her back so she was upright once more, and they continued on in this fashion until they reached the staircase. The rickety wooden steps creaked as she descended, and she worried the stairs weren't meant to carry so much weight at once.

Finally they were on the floor making their way through the crowd. If the jostling had been extreme on the balcony, it was far worse down here. Large, smelly men fell against her, and she had to struggle to keep her footing. She tripped and stumbled, but a man gripped her elbows and kept her from falling. She looked up expecting to see one of her captors and froze.

Allred stared down at her.

A loud buzz blocked all sound from her ears, and motion seemed to slow around her. Allred cocked his head to the side, contemplating her as if… Did he recognize her? She swallowed with difficulty.

"Ho, ho, it *is* her! By heaven, it's Sevrin's mystery woman!" A gentleman—one she recognized from the foyer of Lockwood House—stepped next to Allred.

Allred's brows drew together.

Finally one of her captors—and she couldn't believe she felt even a second's gratefulness, but she did—snatched her against his side. "Hands off!"

They pulled, not that she wasn't eager to go, her away through the crowd and a few moments later pushed into a corridor. The air was a bit cooler, and no one followed them. This was clearly some sort of back area where the masses were not admitted.

Swan shoved her up against the wall, startling the breath from her in a loud gasp. The blow jarred her spine. He put his face a scant inch from hers so that all she could smell was his stale, fetid breath. She tried to turn her head to the side, but he gripped her chin and forced her to look at him.

"Yer lordship may've won, but I'll still find a way to collect from ye. Maybe not tonight, but soon. Soon."

"Swan!" The other man pulled Swan's arm. "Jagger told us not to touch 'er."

Swan cursed as his cohort grabbed Philippa and dragged her to a door. He opened it and shoved her inside.

She was shaking from her encounter in the corridor, but her fear of Swan quickly morphed into concern for Ambrose. He sat slouched in a chair with Hopkins dabbing at his left eye, which was puffy and nearly purple. Saxton stood nearby, his gaze now firmly planted on Philippa. Did he recognize her?

She wanted to rush to Ambrose, but given her audience, she moved slowly, demurely toward him. The blood had been cleaned from his face, and now his wounds glared stark against his pale flesh. In addition to the black eye, he sported a split lip, an abrasion on his right cheek, a bruise on his left cheek, and a reddened ear. Somehow they'd gotten his stockings and boots back on his feet.

He looked up at her from his one open eye. He frowned. "Are you all right? Let me see your face."

She glanced at Saxton, unsure if she ought to remove her mask or even speak. Saxton would surely recognize her voice. They'd been too familiar when he'd briefly courted her last fall. But really, did it even matter now? There was no way she'd escape this night without at least him discovering her identity. "What about him?"

"He won't say anything," Ambrose growled. His voice sounded as bruised as he looked.

She untied the mask and slipped it from her face. "I'm fine."

"Blood of Christ," Saxton swore. "What in the bloody hell is she doing here?"

Sevrin waved a hand as if he couldn't be bothered to respond.

Philippa supposed breathing took effort at this juncture, so she answered Saxton. "Jagger abducted me from Benfield."

"Who's Jagger?"

"The man Sevrin fought for," Hopkins supplied.

Saxton looked from Ambrose back to Philippa. "Why would he take you from Benfield? And how? Someone's about to be sacked, I can promise you. You shouldn't be here at all."

"She wasn't supposed to be," Ambrose managed. "Jagger brought her here to entice me to win." Saxton still looked furiously perplexed, but Ambrose sent him a single-eyed glare that silenced further questions. "Now that she's here we can go," Ambrose rasped. "Let's be quick about it." He turned his gaze toward her. "Put your mask back on."

"Go where?" Saxton asked. "You need to get home, and Lady Philippa, good God, what are we going to do with you?" He stared at her as she fumbled with retying the mask around her head.

Her fingers wouldn't work and strands of her hair kept getting tangled in the ties of the mask. "I told one of the footmen I was ill and returning to Herrick House. You could take me there."

He shook his head then took over tying the mask. "Not if you want to avoid a scandal. I heard the men talking before I left the box." She'd seen him with his father and the others when she'd first arrived. "They think you're Sevrin's mystery woman. If any of them connect you with her—your hair is completely uncovered for Christ's sake. No, you have to be seen at Benfield. We'll pretend you never left. That the footman was mistaken. You were merely ill tonight. Tomorrow you'll arrive for breakfast as if you were at Benfield the entire time. I'll have Olivia and my sister say they visited you."

That could work. She prayed it would work. She nodded. "Thank you."

Saxton wrapped his hand around Ambrose's upper arm. "My coach is outside." He inclined his head toward Hopkins who helped him pull Ambrose out of the chair. Ambrose winced and his hands went toward his middle.

Philippa spotted Ambrose's other clothing draped over the back of another chair and plucked the garments up. She folded the coat, waistcoat, and cravat over her arm.

She opened the door for them but two burly men stood in the corridor. One held up his hand. "Can't leave till Jagger gets here."

They started forward once more, but the two men stepped together, blocking their departure. Saxton snarled. "You don't want to fight us. I'm nearly as good as Sevrin and this one," he pointed at Hopkins, "is better."

He was nearly as good as Ambrose? And Hopkins was better? Were they all fighters?

The men looked at each other then stepped apart and allowed them to leave. The corridor was—thankfully—almost entirely devoid of people.

Saxton left Ambrose in Hopkins's care and took Philippa's arm. He stared down at her, his eyes like shards of ice. "What is between you and Sevrin?"

Despite what they'd shared and the friendship they'd forged, the answer was still, "Nothing."

"That can't be true or Jagger wouldn't have been able to *entice* Sevrin to do anything."

Philippa looked straight ahead as they neared the end of the corridor. They left the building and stepped into the cool night air. The dank smell of the nearby Thames filled Dirty Lane, which was little more than an alley that ran off the Strand. They made their way toward the thoroughfare, but Ambrose stumbled.

Philippa cringed. "Help him," she said to Saxton.

Saxton moved up to take Ambrose's other side. "My coach is just there." He gestured toward the Strand, and a few moments later they'd reached the crest-emblazoned carriage. His footman held the door as Hopkins and Saxton half-lifted Ambrose inside. They helped Philippa in after him, and she took the forward-facing seat beside the slumped Ambrose.

The other men joined them inside, and they were on their way. She pulled off her mask once more then turned toward Ambrose. He barely resembled the handsome man she'd met at Lockwood House. His eyes were shut, and even in the dim light of the carriage lamp, his pallor disturbed her.

She wrapped her hand around his, but he flinched and drew it away. He really didn't want anything to do with her. But that didn't make sense, given he'd just fought to safeguard her reputation. Even so, he'd continually rejected physical contact with her, which also didn't signify since she was all but certain their attraction was mutual. Vexed, she turned from him.

Everyone remained quiet until they turned onto the Haymarket. Saxton looked to Hopkins. "I'll help you get him upstairs. Philippa, wait here and then we'll return to Benfield."

Though she ought to return to Benfield immediately, she had to talk to Ambrose. She wanted so badly to understand how a man with his background could be her champion. Following Saxton's example, she adopted her haughtiest tone. "Not until after I ensure Ambrose's well-being."

Ambrose opened his good eye. "The hell you will. Do as Saxton says."

Still stung that he'd withdrawn from her touch, she snapped, "You're in no position to order me about." She immediately regretted her tone—the man was wounded, for heaven's sake.

He closed his eye again. "A quarter hour. Not a minute more."

The coach stopped at the mouth of the Black Horse Court. The door opened. Hopkins and Saxton stepped out. She followed them, still clutching his garments, and then watched as they helped Ambrose to the street. He groaned as he climbed out. His movements were slow as they made their way to a tavern bearing a sign with a black horse rearing on its hind legs.

"Can you get the door?" Saxton asked.

Philippa did as he bade. The common room was low-ceilinged, and at this hour there were only a handful of patrons seated at the various tables.

An aproned woman rushed forward. "Is he all right?"

"Aye," Hopkins said, readjusting his grip on Ambrose. "Fetch some of Tom's tonic and some hot water."

She nodded and disappeared through a doorway at the base of the stairs. The barkeep stepped from behind the bar. He was a grizzled man of about fifty. "Tell me ye won. I had ten pounds on ye."

Ambrose offered a weak smile. "Yes, Tom, I won."

Tom gave a single nod. "Get upstairs then. Ye want anything to eat, drink?"

"Just some whisky, if you please."

"I'll bring it," Philippa said.

Tom turned and looked her over with an inquisitive eye. He shrugged then led her to the bar where he gave her a bottle and a glass. "Room's upstairs on the right."

She wove her way through the tables and went up the stairs the men had climbed a few moments before. She turned to the right and went to an open door. She stopped short and surveyed Sevrin's lodgings.

The room was small, but comfortably appointed with three stuffed chairs situated around a fireplace, a well-made table cluttered with papers, and a pair of cupboards against one wall.

She heard commotion from an open doorway in the right wall and followed the sound. Into his bedchamber. Her skin suddenly heated as she caught sight of Ambrose's bare legs just before Hopkins drew the bedclothes over them.

"Does he have a valet?" she asked.

Saxton shook his head. "No."

What manner of viscount didn't have a valet? And lived in two rooms over a tavern? The manner that ruined women and dueled with their brothers. She had to stop forgetting he was anything other than that. Perhaps she could if he weren't saving her reputation and fighting on her behalf.

She laid his clothing on a chair in the corner and then deposited the whisky and glass on the table.

Hopkins poured a generous dose and handed it to Ambrose, who downed the contents, albeit with difficulty. His movements were slow, his face drawn in pain.

Hopkins went to the door. "I'll go down to the club and talk to the men. I'm sure they'll all be headed back here."

The fighting club.

"Sax, go check on the tonic, will you?" Ambrose asked.

Saxton frowned, clearly reluctant to leave her alone with him.

Ambrose arched the brow over his uninjured eye. "Just what exactly do you think might happen in my current state?"

With a gusty exhalation and a parting glare, Saxton quit the bedchamber, though he didn't close the door. A moment later, she heard the outer door close.

Philippa moved his clothing to the other side of the room where he had a small dressing area. She then came back and drew the chair to the side of the bed. A branch of candles on the bedside table cast enough light to illuminate his beaten face. Her chest constricted.

"It's not that bad," he croaked.

She looked up to see him regarding her with his good eye. "Oh, Ambrose." How long had she been thinking his Christian name? "Why did you do this?" Tears threatened the backs of her eyes. Scoundrel or not, she owed him so much. "I know why—Jagger told me—but, I'm just…humbled by your efforts to protect me from scandal."

He glanced away from her. "I've fought before."

Why? How did a viscount become a prizefighter? *After he killed his brother*, her mind answered. But she wanted to hear it from him.

"Do you want any more whisky?" she asked as she took the empty glass from his fingers.

"No."

Her gaze fell to his hand, the knuckles were red and scraped, the flesh stained with blood. Suddenly she knew why he'd pulled his hand away in the coach. She'd hurt him. But no more than he'd hurt himself. "You like to fight. Tell me why."

He rested his head back against the pillow and closed his eyes. "It's complicated."

"You stopped engaging in prizefights for a reason and then did so again tonight. Was it just to save me, or do you plan to fight again?"

He kept his eyes closed. "I was to find Jagger a permanent fighter."

"And did you?"

His eyes opened—the uninjured one anyway—and he regarded her with a pupil as dark as midnight. "Yes."

"So you're done fighting?"

"In prizefights. I will always fight in my club."

She still couldn't fathom why men would do this to each other willingly. "Is it like this?" Her gaze flicked to his injured hands before resettling on his battered face.

"No. We're friends. We spar, but we don't beat each other mercilessly."

Friends who fought for fun? "Why?"

"It's different for everyone."

He was doing his level best to discourage her, but she wasn't having it. "I want to know what it is for you."

He was silent several moments. The candlelight cast shadows across his face, drawing her to the intricacies of his wounds, the marred beauty of his features. "It's a release. A comfort. It's home."

There was no mistaking the wistfulness in his tone. She'd never heard him speak like that. The door to the outside chamber creaked, followed by footsteps and the appearance of the woman from downstairs.

"Come in," Ambrose called.

She entered with a tray and set it on the bed. She removed a stack of towels and placed them next to the tray, then put the bowl of steaming water and a jar of tonic on the bedside table.

Philippa picked up the jar and glanced at the woman. "What is this?"

"Apply that to his wounds. It will help him heal."

Ambrose wrinkled his nose then grimaced. "Hopkins coated me with that noxious brew earlier."

The woman sniffed. "Good, then you're about due for another dose." She looked at Philippa. "Don't take any rubbish from him." After a nod from Philippa, she took her leave.

Philippa dipped a cloth into the water and resumed her seat. "May I?" she asked and gently lifted his hand.

His good eye regarded her steadily. "Yes."

She began to wipe away the stains of blood on his fingers and on the back of his hand. He winced a bit as she moved the cloth over his abraded knuckles.

She glanced up at his face before returning her attention to his hand. "Is Saxton a member of your club?"

"Yes."

"That explains a few things."

"It does?" Ambrose arched a brow, and she smiled.

"I noticed he sported a few bruises last fall. It was odd." She bent her attention back to her work, finishing up his first hand and moving on to the next one.

She felt alarmingly at ease, alone with him in his bedchamber, when she ought to have been scandalized. As she cleaned a nasty scrape, he drew in a sharp breath. Pausing, she looked up at his face. "Are you all right?"

"Fine," he ground out through clenched teeth.

"Ambrose," she said softly, wanting to take all of his pain away.

He exhaled slowly and seemed to relax a bit. He stared at her intently, intimately. Her body tingled with awareness. She returned to her ministrations, careful to dab gently at his wounds.

Time for another question. "Why is my reputation so important to you? That you'd fight to protect it?"

He shrugged, but grimaced for the effort. "Jagger would've found a way to get me to fight."

She peered askance at him. "So my reputation means nothing to you? I don't believe that. You protected it before you even met Jagger."

He wrapped the fingers of the hand she was tending around hers. "You don't deserve to be ruined."

His touch was warm, wonderful. She shivered beneath the dark intensity of his stare. "But the girl in Cornwall did?"

He looked away and removed his fingers from atop her hand.

With slightly shaking fingers, she resumed her work. She finished with his other hand then studied his face. "Is anything broken?"

"I don't think so. A surgeon looked me over after the fight. Before you arrived."

"Was this a reputable surgeon?"

"I'm fine. Aside from the way I look." His mouth quirked up, and despite his injuries, her heart still flipped over.

She fetched a clean towel from the foot of the bed and dipped it into the water before retaking her seat. Slowly, carefully, she cleaned his facial wounds again. Quiet settled over them as she worked, binding them in a silent, intimate cocoon. Every part of her was hyper aware of every part of him. Did he feel the same?

When she was finished, she got a fresh towel and the tonic. First, she soaked a corner of the cloth and held it over his swollen eye. "Does it hurt?"

His one good eye met hers. "Yes."

"I'll be gentle."

"I know." The dark timbre of his voice heated her blood.

He was right—the tonic smelled awful. Like day-old cabbage the head groom liked to feed the horses at Wokeham Abbey. She dabbed at the swollen flesh and summoned the courage to ask, "That scar on your shoulder, what's it from?" She held her breath, wondering if it was from the duel he'd purportedly fought with his brother. The one in which Ambrose had killed him.

He scowled. "It's an old wound. Leave it. Please."

She didn't want to let it go, not now. This was as close as they'd ever been, might ever be. And she wanted to know. "There must be more to it than that. No, there must be more to *you* than everything I've been told. I simply can't reconcile your reputation with the man I know. I can't believe you killed your brother."

His gaze sharpened. "Can't believe it or won't? I've told you innumerable times I am not your hero."

Her emotions tumbled over into anger. "Why won't you defend yourself?"

His eye flashed. "Because the things I've done are indefensible. Including ruining you."

She held her hand poised next to his face. "I'm not ruined."

"Not yet."

Oh, he was maddening. "Saxton's plan is sound. I'll return to Benfield shortly, and no one will know I was gone."

He turned his head from her. "You have far more faith than I do."

She dabbed at his eye. "I suspect you lost yours somewhere around the time your brother died." He stared stoically ahead, and she knew he would say nothing more. What did it matter? They had no future together. This—right now—was all they may ever share. She didn't need to know his secrets, but how she wanted to.

She finished with his eye and then doused another corner of the cloth. With great care, she tended to his other wounds, finishing with his knuckles.

"You should go now. You're right—Saxton's plan is good. You'll be fine."

She folded the towel and set it on the table. "Do you really think so?"

He turned his head and the intensity of his gaze startled her. "I do. You've a wonderful life before you. Our acquaintance is finally at an end. I've satisfied my bargain with Jagger. You're safe. Free."

She gently laid her hand atop his. "Thank you."

And then because it was the right thing to do, the thing she'd been raised to do, Philippa stood to go. She plucked the soiled towels from the table to take them downstairs. "Good night, Sevrin. Take care of yourself."

She turned to leave, knowing she'd never be alone with him again, never share this closeness. Her throat constricted, and her legs felt wooden. As she made her way to the door she heard him murmur, "I liked it better when you called me Ambrose."

Chapter Fourteen

THE following day, Ambrose managed to get himself bathed and dressed, despite the lingering pain of his wounds. He hurt in places he hadn't injured, given the effort he'd exerted. Though he fought regularly, he rarely fought that long and never that hard.

He'd just donned his second boot when there was a knock on his door. Slowly, agonizingly, he made his way to the outer chamber and answered the summons, splaying his hand against the jamb to support his weight. Upon seeing his caller, he cursed his decision to leave his bed.

Jagger swept his hat from his head. "You're looking better than when I saw you last."

Ambrose gripped the jamb as if he'd pull it from the wall. "What the hell do you want?"

"Better, but you still look like shit." Jagger raised his brows. "May I come in?"

Ambrose threw the door wide and stepped to the side.

Jagger strolled inside, lightly swinging an ivory-handled walking stick. "You live here?" he asked, perusing the meager furnishings. "I live better than this."

Ambrose strode to the middle of the room where Jagger stood judging. He turned to say something else, but Ambrose silenced him with a fist to his mouth.

"Christ, Sevrin." Jagger lifted his fingers to his mouth and wiped his lips.

Ambrose shook out his hand. *God, that hurt.* But it was worth the pain. "That's for Philippa."

Jagger stroked his jaw. "I'm surprised Nolan lasted as long as he did if you hit him that hard."

"Oh, I could hit you much harder." And one day he just might.

"Then it's just as well you've found a prizefighter and our association is nearly at an end. Who is he, and when can I meet him?"

"Ackley. Perhaps you've seen him fight."

Jagger thought a moment and shook his head. "Doesn't sound familiar. But he's good?"

"Quite, but more importantly his potential is excellent."

"Brilliant. Who's to train him?"

"Me."

Jagger's obsidian eyes flashed with surprise. "You're willingly going to continue our affiliation?"

"Not because I'm particularly fond of you—I still haven't decided if I'm going to beat you senseless yet. That depends on what happens with Philippa."

"Ah, such tender feelings you bear this girl. One might wonder why you don't marry her."

God, how this bastard's needling rankled, especially because his taunts hit far too close to the mark. He cared far too much for Philippa. "That's precisely the kind of blathering that will see you thrashed. Do it again, and I'll show no mercy."

Jagger held up his hands in supplication—one of them still clutching his hat and walking stick.

Ambrose continued, "I'm training Ackley to be a champion, but not due to any desire to help you. My involvement is solely about Ackley's potential and my personal interest in his success." Ambrose had drafted the lad into this, and he wouldn't abandon him to the likes of Jagger.

Jagger's eyes narrowed. "What do you want?"

"Calm yourself. I don't want a share—I'm not foolish enough to think you'd part with that. I merely want control of his training, and you'll leave me and my associates—including Philippa—*entirely* alone."

Jagger's forehead relaxed, and he sprouted a conceited smile.

"Done. Since you're in charge of his training, I'd like for him to fight in an upcoming bout."

Ambrose had been thinking of whom to pit his protégé against. He needed to acquire more experience before he faced Belcher. "Who, when, where?"

"Isling, May 12, Truro."

Bloody, bloody hell. Truro. Isling would be an excellent opponent to prepare for Belcher. They had a similar fighting style. Ackley would learn much from the event. But go to Truro? Ambrose had avoided Cornwall and his responsibilities there for five years. He'd be as welcome at his estate, Beckwith, about as much as he wanted to return there, which was to say not at all.

He felt ready to break into a thousand pieces. He supposed he'd known he'd have to return some time, and why not now? There would never be a "right" time to face his mistakes, to seek forgiveness from those he'd left behind. Perhaps he never could. But didn't he owe it to Nigel to try? Anguish filled what was left of his soul. "We'll go."

"Good. I'll join you there a few days before the fight. Now, when am I to meet this Ackley?"

They'd skipped their training last night. Ackley had come to watch the prizefight, and they were scheduled to discuss it—reviewing technique and strategy—that evening. "He's coming here tonight if you'd care to join us."

"I would. Thank you." He regarded Ambrose warily. "Am I always going to feel as if you're just a breath away from pummeling me into oblivion?"

"Probably."

"And will you?"

Ambrose smiled slowly, menacingly. "Probably."

"Ah, excellent. Just so I know. Perhaps you should train me as well."

Ambrose's smile faded, and he glared at the criminal.

Jagger arched a dark brow. "Too much? Right. See you tonight, then." He turned and left.

Ambrose sank into one of the stuffed chairs situated by the cold fireplace. His ribs ached. His face and head pounded. His knuckles were on fire. But all of it paled next to the pain he'd felt when Philippa had interrogated him last night.

She'd somehow learned the truth—that he'd killed his brother. She may not know the details, that he hadn't done it in a duel, but his actions had absolutely caused Nigel's demise. The look in her eyes—disbelief, followed by horror, and then regret—had dredged up the old emotions so that he'd barely slept. She hadn't had to say it: if only he hadn't behaved so abominably, his life could be so different.

But he had done those things. He'd seduced his brother's fiancée and driven Nigel to his death. He was everything people said and more.

Another knock on his door drew him from his pathetic reverie.

He couldn't be bothered to get up. "Enter."

The door pushed open, and Saxton stepped inside. "You're dressed."

"I'm not a complete invalid."

"You looked as if you would be. I'm glad to see you're well." Saxton's perusal was followed by a look of pure sympathy. "Or rather, well enough."

He didn't want Saxton's pity. He accepted everything that happened to him—especially a good beating—as just and right. "What are you doing here? Aren't you supposed to be at a house party preserving Philippa's social standing?"

Saxton's glanced away, stirring Ambrose's concern. "That's partly why I'm here. There's still a bit of speculation."

Ambrose gripped the arms of his chair, but let go as his knuckles burned in protest. "Did someone see her at the fight?"

"Not that I can tell, but Finchley has made it widely known that your mystery woman was there. He's also noted that Philippa was not in attendance at Benfield's soiree last night."

He wanted to kill Finchley and may just dredge up the necessary capacity to do it. "Neither was half of your father's bloody house party given the lot that showed up in Dirty Lane."

Saxton's gaze turned dark. "This isn't anything to make light of."

"I'm sure as hell not. What are you doing to fix this?"

"Since when did I become your housekeeper? Clean up your

own goddamned messes." Saxton's pale blue eyes flashed, but then he exhaled and seemed to rein in his temper. He went to stand behind one of the other stuffed chairs and drummed his fingers on the top. "As it happens, I have an idea."

Of course he did. Saxton was rather good at managing things. He'd been quite successful at keeping the true nature of his wife's birth—she was the daughter of a notorious courtesan—completely unknown. "Tell me."

"You'll need to come to Benfield—the sooner the better."

"I'm in no condition to travel. At least not today."

"Come tomorrow then. And you'll need to bring a guest. Someone who looks enough like Philippa to fool people into believing she's your mystery woman."

Ambrose understood Saxton's plan and had just one quibble. "And where am I to find such a woman? Stop by Covent Garden at a courtesan stall?"

Saxton gave him a suffering glare before speaking. "There's a demimondaine I know. I'll send her a note explaining the circumstances—that she's to pretend to be your mistress—and ask her to be ready to travel to Benfield tomorrow morning."

Ambrose couldn't keep from grinning. "You *are* my housekeeper."

Saxton arched a brow, his fingers stilling. "Someone has to be."

"Won't everyone be scandalized I've brought a courtesan to their precious house party?"

"Not as scandalized as if they found out you were at Lockwood House with Philippa."

True enough. Why couldn't this threat just *die*? "You think this will work?" Ambrose asked.

"It could. It will certainly put an end to the speculation and the wagers."

"So would beating the shit out of Finchley and a few others, but I suppose that's a bad idea."

Saxton's mouth curved up. "Tempting as it is, I doubt your pummeling would end anything except Finchley's enjoyment of the party. However, the situation is also helped by Philippa's courtship with Allred. Things are progressing quickly. In fact, the rumor is that he may propose to her today."

Ambrose was glad he was sitting because this information came like a blow to his gut. Which was asinine since he'd all but pushed her into Allred's arms. God, had she kissed him yet? Ambrose already cursed his loss.

Saxton sat in the chair next to his. "You care for her."

This was a dangerous conversation, and one he didn't want to have. "Of course, but not in the way you think."

"I'm not blind. Furthermore, I saw the way she was with you. She clearly cares for you too—I can only imagine the depth of your acquaintance." Saxton's unspoken question hung in the air. "Perhaps you should marry her."

Ambrose wouldn't bother denying their mutual attraction. He couldn't look at her, couldn't think of her without wanting to end his five-year sexual drought by burying himself between her thighs. "I can't."

"Of course you can. I didn't think I could marry Olivia either, but some friends of mine," Saxton gave him a pointed stare, "convinced me otherwise." Like quicksilver, his eyes turned frigid. "Don't be a fool."

He'd be a fool—or more accurately a prick—*if* he married her. She deserved a husband who would love and cherish her, not a selfish brute who took what he wanted and thought nothing of the consequences. And who didn't know the first thing about love.

"I can't marry her. Don't speak of it again." Ambrose stood up from his chair with surprising ease. Guilt, it seemed, was a useful healing tonic.

Philippa caught up to Allred who'd beat her handily in their impromptu race.

He grinned at her. "You're an excellent seat, Lady Philippa. I'd heard such, but given your gender, I had to reserve judgment until I saw your skill for myself."

Allred occasionally made similar comments regarding womanhood, insinuating frailty or lesser ability. Though they pricked Philippa's nerves, he said them with an air of such charming ignorance that she permitted herself to overlook them.

She inhaled the fresh spring air and smiled, exhilarated by their ride on such a fine day. It was almost enough to make her forget about last night's events. Almost.

Saxton had planned things perfectly for her return. He'd secreted her up the back stairs and this morning she'd been flanked by Lady Saxton and Saxton's sister, Lady Miranda Foxcroft, who'd testified to her presence at Benfield the previous night. The ruse had worked as several people had asked if she was feeling better. No one even suggested she'd left Benfield, at least not that she had heard, but then the bulk of the conversation had been focused on Ambrose's prizefight.

The men were in awe of his pugilistic skill and were already clamoring for how they might convince him to impart his fighting strategy. Winning a prizefight just might vault him from shameless blackguard to exciting rogue. Not that such promotion helped her cause.

What cause? She had no cause where he was concerned. Their acquaintance—no matter how delightful—was over. She had to stop thinking of him, particularly when she ought to be enjoying an outing with a man who was courting her.

"Shall we walk for a bit?" Allred asked.

She nodded and he climbed down from his horse then helped her from hers. They were riding two of Holborn's stock. Beautiful, superior creatures.

He took his horse's reins and led his mount. Philippa did the same with hers. "I'm glad you're feeling better today," he said. "I would've hated to postpone our scheduled ride."

She wanted to ask him about the prizefight, but it felt odd. Since she'd been there.

They were silent a moment as they tracked across the spongy, spring ground. Birds chirped in the trees around them, and the scent of lilac wafted in the air. It really was a lovely day, but Philippa couldn't shake a sense of foreboding. Of change.

"I think we both know why I arranged this ride today."

She nodded, her muscles tensing. She felt anxious, her nerves pulled as tight as an overdrawn corset. Here was the moment she'd been working toward, the moment that would ensure her security. The moment that suddenly felt wrong.

He paused and turned toward her. "Shall we make things formal, then? I'd be pleased to make you my wife."

While it wasn't the proposal she'd dreamed of, it was the one she needed.

Even so, panic rose in her throat. He didn't love her. She'd made a career of rejecting proposals just like this one. But she was out of time. She had to marry now or she might not get another chance.

Allred took her hand. "We're well-suited, Philippa. This is an excellent match."

She took a deep breath, willing herself to think rationally. It *was* an excellent match. He would take care of her and give her precisely what she expected: mutual admiration and respect.

He leaned forward and pressed a kiss to her lips, surprising her. "I'll speak with Holborn and your father about announcing our betrothal tomorrow night."

So soon? *Of course, you ninny. You're the one who needs a quick trip to the altar!* She wondered if Allred would even care that her mother was about to create a scandal, not that she would tell him.

They took up their horses' reins again and walked a bit before remounting and heading back to the stables. By the time they entered the house, her rioting pulse had calmed and she felt almost normal. Her betrothal would be announced, and all would turn out as it should.

Belatedly, she realized she'd never given an Allred a proper answer. But then, he hadn't waited for one either. A chill ran down her spine. What manner of marriage was this going to be?

Chapter Fifteen

AMBROSE arrived at Benfield the following afternoon at nearly three o'clock. The drawing room was overrun with people drinking tea and sharing gossip. In other words, they were starved for his arrival.

The moment he entered with Miss Cordelia Mathison on his arm, the room buzzed.

Saxton stepped away from his position near the windows overlooking the garden and came to meet them. "Afternoon, Sevrin, you're looking well." A bald-faced lie given the purple bruise around his left eye and the puffy redness of his cheek.

"May I introduce my guest, Mrs. Mathison?" She wasn't really a Mrs., but it wouldn't do to introduce her as Miss *and* his guest. It was only a matter of time before everyone determined—if they hadn't already—that she was a demimondaine, someone who wouldn't normally be accepted in such a drawing room as Benfield's, and he needn't help them along.

Miss Mathison sank into a respectable curtsey, but her eyes twinkled as she looked up at Saxton. But then, she already knew him. Whether carnally or otherwise, Ambrose didn't care to speculate.

To Saxton's wife's credit, she promptly came over and also received an introduction. Then Saxton's sister, Lady Miranda Foxcroft did the same. Others followed—mostly men—while the women regarded Miss Mathison with a mixture of hostility (yes, they'd already figured her out) and curiosity because of the resemblance she bore Philippa. Ambrose was suddenly aware of the potential risk involved with all but declaring that his mystery woman *looked* like Philippa.

To compare them side-by-side, one would note Miss Mathison was a bit taller than Philippa and that her hair was nearly the same color. Their shapes were alike enough, provided no one stared too closely at Miss Mathison's larger bosom. He'd had to caution his borrowed courtesan not to show her teeth when she smiled, because they weren't nearly as straight as Philippa's. He'd no idea if anyone would catch that small detail, but he didn't want to bungle things with something so avoidable as revealing her crooked teeth.

Finchley came directly to them with a sly grin. He pulled Ambrose away from Miss Mathison and whispered, "This is your masked woman then?" His use of the word woman instead of lady was not lost on Ambrose. The cad.

"Yes," Ambrose answered calmly, though he longed to further torture his wounded hands by pounding Finchley into the carpet.

Finchley's perusal of Miss Mathison was thorough and lingering. "And I was so certain she was…never mind. Guess that settles the question, then."

He had the audacity to look disappointed. What had he been about to say? That he'd been sure Philippa was his mystery woman? That was what Saxton had warned him would happen, was indeed why he'd brought Miss Mathison to Benfield. That Finchley was upset because he would've preferred the perversion of ruining a young lady only made Ambrose want to hit him more.

He flexed his hands, trying to work the tension from his muscles.

Apparently Finchley's declaration had settled the issue because what followed was a swarm of men peppering him with compliments and questions. "Excellent footwork." "Wicked upper cut." "Any chance you'd give some lessons later?"

Hell, no. As soon as he was done with this nauseating errand, he'd dash from Society and go back to the warmth and familiarity of his life at the Black Horse. One night. He could endure one night of this nonsense.

For Philippa.

He hadn't seen her in the drawing room, but now he scanned the space again for her dark hair and elegant features. Definitely not here.

It was just as well. He'd hoped to keep their interaction to a minimum. Was it too much to hope he might escape without having to see her at all?

While the men swarmed him, he became separated from Miss Mathison. A quick survey of the room found her still standing near the doorway wearing a bemused expression. Where he was overcome with unwanted attention, she was perfectly alone. Ignored. Apparently she wasn't used to being ignored by men.

But then Lady Saxton approached her and guided her from the room. She'd served her purpose. Hope surged in his chest. Did that mean they could leave? Ambrose searched for Saxton. He was back at the windows.

Ambrose murmured a few words of excuse and left his circle of admirers. He pinned Saxton with a harassed glare, which incited Saxton to meet him in the corner.

"Yes?" Saxton drawled.

"Get me out of here. Your wife saved Miss Mathison, now it's your turn to save me."

"Go out the door here." He flicked a glance to the left at the door to the terrace. "If you want, you can go for a ride."

Ambrose glowered at him. The bastard knew he didn't ride. Anymore.

He turned and left, crossing the terrace and striding down the stone stairs to the garden as if Satan were behind him. Hell, he supposed Satan was always behind him given the things he'd done.

He walked with no intention of going to the stables. However, he could practically feel spectators watching his every move. A quick look over his shoulder confirmed his suspicion.

The stables then. At least there he'd be away from over-curious eyes.

He strode into the cool darkness of the stable and nodded at a groom as he passed. If only he could hide out here until tomorrow. Until after everyone returned to London. Until after

Philippa returned to London. He really preferred not to see her. How many more times would he be able to keep his hands to himself?

Despite his injuries from the fight, the presence of her next to his bed the other night had been nearly enough to send him over the edge. That dangerous precipice where denial met indulgence. Where lust overrode regret and self-recrimination. A place he didn't dare go.

His selfish impulses had ruined one woman and killed his brother—he wouldn't let them destroy Philippa as well.

He neared the end of the long aisle between the stalls. This part of the building was blessedly devoid of cattle. To the left was an open door to a tack room. Perhaps he could spend the night on a saddle blanket in there. So blissfully removed. Quiet. Perfect.

He walked to the door and stopped cold. Standing against the far wall was Philippa. Not standing precisely, more like teetering on a rickety stool.

Ambrose crossed the small room in four quick strides. "What the devil are you doing up there?" He grabbed her by the waist and swung her to the floor.

"Oh!" She gasped. Her eyes widened as their gazes met. "I was, ah, trying to reach that bridle on the hook up there. The grooms are all busy, and I thought…" Her voice trailed away to nothing.

He'd get her bloody bridle. Or at least he meant to. Really, he did. He wanted to let go of her waist, to stop looking into those riveting ale-colored eyes, to cease thinking of the way her lilac-honey scent tantalized him beyond reason.

But he did none of those things.

He was at the edge, staring out over the void where there was no reason. No discipline. No regard for anything but his most primal needs. The place where fighting took him. And since fighting was currently out of the question, he seized the next thing he could: Philippa. He tightened his grip on her waist.

She stood on her toes and touched her fingers to his bruised cheek. "Does it still hurt?"

The stroke of her hand and the concern in her eyes undid

him completely.

"Philippa," he murmured, turning his face so that her palm rested against his flesh. "You should go."

She laid her other palm against his other cheek and looked into his eyes. "I really should." But she didn't, and it was all the invitation his starving body needed.

He kissed her.

Her lips were soft, a balm moving gently over his bruised mouth. One brush. Two. A third time and her mouth lingered against his, her breath teasing its way into his mouth.

He tightened his grip on her waist, his body raging with barely checked desire.

Then she lowered herself and dropped her hands to her sides. He didn't let her go, and she didn't break free. Her brow furrowed. "I'd almost forgotten how nice it is to kiss you. Allred kissed me yesterday, and I'm afraid—"

No, no, no. He didn't want to know that. Couldn't think of another man touching the woman he so badly craved. With a groan, he pulled her against him and took her mouth with open lips.

Her hands came up again, wrapping possessively, savagely around his neck. She pulled him tight against her as she rose up and pressed her chest to his. She was perfection and agony rolled into one irresistible woman. His body scorched with a need he'd denied for five long years. No, that wasn't right. He wasn't sure he'd ever experienced a need like this. There was no comparing her to Lettice, a woman he'd desired and taken. Philippa was life's most fundamental requirement—like air or water. His soul ached to possess her.

Her kiss was innocent and ravenous, sweet and hot. Her tongue danced with his, and she tilted her head to probe deeper, taste more. He held her closer and answered her questing mouth, losing himself in rapture.

She pressed her hips up against his until he could fairly feel the heat of her through all their layers of clothing. Too damned much clothing. He cupped her bottom through all those frustrating layers and brought his other hand around to her breast, sliding his palm over the lush curve.

He tasted her response as she seemed to melt against his mouth. She pushed into his hand and it was all he needed. Lightly, he swept his thumb over her nipple. It instantly peaked beneath her bodice.

Still too many damned clothes.

He unbuttoned her riding jacket with feverish, fumbling hands. She pushed his coat from his shoulders and tangled her fingers in his cravat, tugging at the linen clumsily, desperately.

Her shirt had buttons at the collar and he pulled at them madly. One popped free and bounced against the wooden floor. He broke their kiss to look down at the creamy flesh he'd exposed. Her chest rose and fell deeply with her breathing. He cradled both breasts, one step closer to her lustrous skin without that damned coat covering her. But the shirt was still an impediment. He pulled the neckline down, but it wasn't enough to expose her. Heedless of any consequence, he tugged the linen until it split past her breasts.

She gasped, and he swallowed the sound with a kiss. She pulled the ends of his cravat free and used them to urge him closer. His hands remained between them, kneading her soft breasts. She moaned into his mouth.

He needed more.

He worked to unlace the top of her stays enough so that her breasts came free and rose above the lace edge. He pulled away from her mouth reluctantly, but he desperately needed to see and taste her.

She tipped her head back, baring the pale column of her throat, leading him down a path to her glorious breasts, the tips dark pink and pebbled with her arousal.

Though hunger drove him to devour her, he cautioned himself to be gentle. She deserved to be worshipped. Adored. He ran his thumbs over both nipples. A soft moan whispered past her kiss-dampened lips. His mouth went dry as he lowered his head and stroked his tongue across her hot, supple flesh.

He lightly tugged on one nipple as he closed his lips over the other and suckled. Her legs quivered and she sagged. He moved a hand to support her back as he licked and sucked her. His cock raged, reminding him how long he'd been without a woman.

How long he'd been without *this* woman—forever.

"Philippa?" The word came from the corridor.

Fuck.

"Philippa?"

Christ, the door was still open. Ambrose tore himself away from her and clasped her shoulders. "Someone's coming," he whispered.

"Philippa?" came the questing voice again.

Her eyes grew wide. "Allred. He must've learned I was in the stables."

Fuck, fuck, fuck.

He rushed to pull the door closed, not that it would help. Allred was looking for her, and she was right here.

She fumbled with her stays as she pushed her breasts back beneath them. With shaking fingers, she pulled the strings and tried to tie them. He brushed her hands aside and accomplished the task, but the footsteps sounded outside the door.

He took one look at her flushed cheeks, her pinkened, swollen lips, her heavy-lidded eyes and knew there would be no avoiding scandal this time. The pathetic irony of being caught *in flagrante dilecto* a second time was not lost on him. Indeed, it crushed what remained of his soul.

There was a knock on the door followed by the creak of old hinges.

Ambrose closed his eyes and didn't even bother to repair his clothing.

"Philippa?" The sound came from the doorway. "Good God, Sevrin, what are you doing with my fiancée?"

Fiancée? *Son of a bitch.* He'd done it again. He'd seduced another man's fiancée and hadn't even possessed the grace to avoid getting caught.

Philippa shoved her arms into her coat sleeves and drew the garment tight about her in an effort to cover her ruined blouse. Slowly, warily, she raised her gaze to Allred's outraged countenance. She blinked and willed strength into her suddenly water-filled legs.

Of all the brainless, reckless, scandalous things to do! But the moment she'd turned and seen Ambrose she'd been lost. Her betrothal to Allred, which had already felt wrong, had become impossible. She couldn't marry one man while she wanted another. And Allred didn't deserve to be treated the way her father had treated her mother.

Summoning a courage she didn't feel, she squared her shoulders and faced Allred. "I'm so sorry. I'd planned to tell you we won't suit after all. Before the betrothal was announced. You deserve better than this." How trite and inadequate that sounded.

"Damned right I do." Allred's hazel eyes turned frigid. "I thought you were an impeccable young woman. How appalling to discover you're nothing but a harlot."

Ambrose's gaze darkened. "There's no call to insult her."

Allred sneered. "*I've* insulted her? You're the one alone in this tack room with her, looking like... *that*."

Philippa cringed.

The flesh around Ambrose's mouth had gone pale. "Allred, I understand your anger. You've every right to it. But think of Philippa. She hasn't publicly embarrassed you. No one needs to know."

"You're quite right. There's no need for me to make her transgression my problem." Allred glared at her, his lip curling. He looked so different from the charming gentleman who'd courted her the past fortnight. "Why did you accept my proposal if you wanted this blackguard instead?"

She supposed she owed him an explanation, but finding the right words was difficult. "It seemed appropriate for you and me to wed, but I don't love you. And I don't think you love me."

Allred's gaze turned condescending. "Love is not intrinsic to marriage." He threw a harassed look at Ambrose. "I do believe you've saved me a regrettable trip to the altar."

Philippa gaped at him. She'd never imagined he could be so cold, but then she'd never imagined she would do what she'd just done with Ambrose. She had no right to judge Allred or his reaction.

Ambrose moved closer to Allred, his eyes narrowing. "She's

apologized, and since your betrothal was not formally announced, you can simply walk away."

Allred's hands balled into fists and for a tense moment, Philippa wondered what he might do. But then Allred relaxed, perhaps recalling Ambrose's status as a premier fighter. Allred turned to Philippa. "I'll be courteous despite your *debauchery*." The word came out like a knife—sharp and meant to inflict pain. "If anyone asks, I'll deny I ever proposed."

Though she was horrified by his hurtful words, his accordance to keep the incident secret was more than she deserved. "Thank you."

Footsteps sounded against the wood floor outside the door. "Allred, where'd you go? Ah, there you are." Finchley appeared behind him. "What, ho? Who've you found here?" His eyes grew wide as he surveyed the interior of the tack room. He slapped his hand against his thigh. "I was right!" he crowed loud enough for all of Benfield to hear.

Philippa wanted nothing more than to dissolve into a puddle and seep through the cracks in the floor. She turned her back to the doorway. From the corner of her eye, she saw Ambrose's fists clench and the muscles of his arms flex.

"Finchley, get the hell out of here." Ambrose's tone was low, menacing.

Philippa looked over her shoulder so she could watch what happened next. She was afraid Ambrose might go after Finchley.

Finchley jabbed Allred in the shoulder. "I knew she was Sevrin's mystery woman. After I saw the masked woman last night at the prizefight and learned Lady Philippa had been 'ill,' I concluded it was she. Right size, right shape." His gaze lingered on her backside. Philippa felt nauseous.

Allred's jaw dropped. "Philippa, was that you at the prizefight?"

She turned slightly. "I—"

"And at Lockwood House?"

There were reasonable explanations for both of those things, but what of today? Shame clogged her throat.

"Leave it," Ambrose growled.

Finchley stepped around Allred. "I think she owes him the

truth. Why the little slut was trying to entrap him—"

Ambrose punched Finchley square in the jaw and again in the eye. Finchley fell back against the doorjamb with a howl.

Philippa slapped her hand over her gaping mouth.

"Ow, my eye!" He pressed his palm to his eye and then grimaced. He turned to Allred. "Am I bleeding?"

"Not yet," Ambrose said. He hadn't moved back, and his fists were still raised. His waistcoat pulled tight across his upper back. His face was flushed, and his eyes glittered darkly.

Philippa shivered.

Finchley stared up at Ambrose another moment, spun on his heel, and practically ran from the tack room.

Ambrose dropped his fists, but his frame remained tense, his expression grim.

"You're not planning on hitting me, too?" Allred asked cautiously.

"You're not planning on insulting her again?" Ambrose's tone was sharp, dangerous.

Allred's features hardened. "When you asked me to spare her reputation, were you threatening me?"

"No, I was asking a favor. Finchley's been begging for my fist since he started carrying on about this wager like a stallion after a mare."

Allred looked from Ambrose to Philippa. "Just as you've been rutting after each other." His eyes lit, and he stared at Philippa in shock. "*Were* you trying to trap me into marriage? Because he won't marry you?" His face paled. "God, are you carrying his bastard?"

Philippa wildly shook her head. "No, no, *no*. There is nothing between us. At least nothing beyond what happened here. Which was a mistake. A terrible, thoughtless mistake." She glanced at Ambrose. His face was hard, stoic. His gaze was fixed on Allred.

Allred straightened his spine. "I've no cause to believe you, but I'm enough of a gentleman to let the matter lie. Do not expect Finchley to do the same." Then he turned and quit the tack room.

Philippa watched his retreat and pressed her hand to her

mouth lest a sob escape. He'd been less than gallant, but what did she expect? She'd done him a terrible wrong. And for what? A few minutes of bliss?

No, it had been more than that. What she felt for Ambrose was a bone-deep need that had blocked everything else from her mind—propriety, commitment, consideration of anyone but herself. It was terrifying in its magnitude and in its similarity to her mother.

Ambrose picked up his coat and drew it on. "I shouldn't have kissed you."

Philippa paused in buttoning her jacket over her ruined shirt. "I shouldn't have kissed you back." Her fingers shook as she worked to push each button into its hole.

"I didn't know you were betrothed."

She looked up at him. "Would it have mattered?"

His gaze was full of anguish. "It would've to me."

She stared at him a moment, her heart thudding in response to the dark emotion in his eyes. He turned away.

With shaking hands, she secured the last button and pulled the top edges of her shirt together, making sure she was as decently covered as possible. "He only asked me yesterday, and I didn't feel right about it. Then I saw you here and realized I couldn't marry him. But that doesn't excuse what I did."

"What *we* did. You are not alone in this." His words gave her a bit of comfort. "I'll marry you."

She jerked her gaze to his. Did she really want that? Did *he* really want that? "I know you don't want to marry, but why not?" She turned toward him, hoping for once he might give her a direct answer. "You're a viscount. You should beget an heir."

Her words stirred no reaction. "What I should do is not often what I choose to do. Which is only one of the several reasons you probably shouldn't marry me. I'd make a terrible husband. I'm thoughtless, selfish, and I haven't the slightest notion how to love. Nor do I want to learn. You deserve better than that."

"You're not selfish or thoughtless. You never would've tried to save my reputation—or my life—at Lockwood House if you were those things."

He arched a brow. "Are you forgetting I seduced my

brother's fiancée? Or that I just publicly ruined you?"

"We were carried away." A paltry excuse. They'd both behaved selfishly.

His lips flattened into a grim line. "What I did is indefensible." He leaned against the wall and crossed his arms. "But if you want me to marry you, I will."

That wasn't the proposal she'd dreamed of either.

She wanted him—at least physically, but what about emotionally? Whether she loved him or not, he'd just said he couldn't love her and didn't even want to try. Despite the scandal she was facing, she was unwilling to chance an unhappy marriage.

Saxton burst into the tack room with a furious glower directed at Ambrose. "What the devil have you done?"

"Ah, Saxton," Ambrose said in a deceptively serene voice. "Will you arrange a carriage to take Philippa back to London? She won't be returning to the party."

He was still working to protect her. And she was grateful. She couldn't face anyone now.

"Tell me what happened first," Saxton demanded.

Ambrose gave Saxton an equally intimidating stare. "Philippa needs to leave. Have her things sent later. Just get her out of here now."

Saxton finally looked at her. He pursed his lips and shook his head. How his pity stung. She'd become *that poor girl*. He returned his frigid gaze to Ambrose. "I assume you'll make this right."

Ambrose sent her a questioning look. "I offered to."

If only Ambrose's proposal had been driven by love or affection instead of obligation. She wouldn't marry based on that. She gave Saxton a level stare. "I don't believe we'll suit."

Ambrose's eyes widened briefly. Then he looked down at the floor as the side of his mouth curved up. It wasn't an amused half-smile, but one of self-deprecation.

Saxton turned startled eyes to her. "Don't be foolish, Philippa."

Elevating her chin, she attempted to make her gaze as frost-laden as Saxton's. "Was I foolish when I agreed to make it known the announcement of our marriage last fall was a mistake?" Saxton flinched, and she almost smiled. "No. I did it because I didn't want to marry you. I didn't love you, and you didn't love me. The same is true with Sevrin." Her chest felt heavy, and her eyes stung. Unfortunately, this situation wasn't the same. She'd been falling in love with Ambrose. She thrust her emotions away. "What happened here was regrettable—and forgettable. Saxton, do fetch me a coach as I'd like to escape Sevrin's presence as quickly as possible."

Head high, and without looking at Ambrose, she turned and strode from the room—and didn't stop until she reached the other end of the stable.

She was vaguely aware of grooms rushing to ready a coach. In the meantime, she stayed in the shadows and didn't look toward the house. She imagined people crowding out on the terrace, clamoring for a glimpse of the fallen debutante. *That poor girl.*

Alone now, she allowed her emotions to return. Her body shook, and her throat itched with unshed tears. Her head began to pound, and heat flooded her cheeks. She wouldn't cry. Not now. Not yet.

There'd be time for tears later. A lifetime.

Chapter Sixteen

ONE week and nearly three hundred miles hadn't dimmed Ambrose's regret. Regret for both Philippa's downfall and because they'd been interrupted. When he wasn't brooding over the ways he would've made love to her in that tack room, he tried to focus on fighting. Unfortunately, for the first time in five years, violence failed to distract him from his lust.

A perplexing problem since he now found himself at Beckwith, precisely where that lust had caused *his* downfall.

He looked at his sleeping coach mate, Thomas Ackley. He ought to wake him, but Ambrose needed a few minutes of solitude as they passed Beckwith's gatehouse.

The coach rambled up the drive of his centuries-old converted castle. Once, long ago, it had been an impressive fortress overlooking the bay and protecting Cornwall from invaders crossing the sea. Now it was a collection of ruined and crumbling structures, including the manor house that had been renovated from the living quarters in the north wall during the sixteenth century.

Their father had wanted to build a new manor house, but the estate hadn't been profitable enough to undertake such a project. Ambrose hadn't accepted that. Why couldn't they make it profitable? He'd returned from Oxford with plans for increasing their sheep herd and thus their wool production. He'd done a decent job too, but regrettably their father hadn't lived to see it. He'd died while Ambrose was at school. Nigel—the new viscount—however, had stood by and watched while Ambrose single-handedly turned the estate around.

Single-handedly.

Why hadn't he ever solicited Nigel's input? Why had he been so eager to manage everything himself? Because their father—a man Ambrose had admired—had always encouraged him. "Ambrose, you're the future of Beckwith." He'd even gone so far as to say, "You should've been the heir. If only the fever that took your mother had taken…" He hadn't uttered the rest, but the meaning had been clear. If the fever had claimed Nigel, he would've been spared his sickly, wretched existence.

But not even that was wholly accurate. Nigel had been sickly, but not wretched. He'd been fairly ineffectual at Beckwith, but when their father died, he'd been eager to take up his position in the House of Lords. Not that Ambrose had minded—he'd been happy to have Nigel remove himself to London, thus leaving Ambrose in total control of Beckwith. Just as Ambrose had always expected.

Until Nigel had returned with a new attitude—that he would run Beckwith. To everyone's surprise, he'd also brought a fiancée, the overtly flirtatious daughter of a merchant, Lettice Chandler. Upset with his brother's sudden desire to remove Ambrose from his managerial position, Ambrose had returned Lettice's attentions. Nigel had taken Ambrose's birthright—or what he'd been led to believe was his birthright—and Ambrose had selfishly sought revenge.

Because Lettice was staying at Beckwith, their affair was easy to conduct. And she hadn't been an unschooled virgin. In fact, she'd drawn him to most of the places in which they'd had sex— sometimes within earshot of the servants. When her advances became bolder—touching Ambrose overlong at the dinner table, casting openly admiring glances, accompanying him on his afternoon rides—Nigel grew suspicious. Ambrose knew the affair needed to end, and indeed he'd grown rather tired of the game. But he'd indulged himself one last time, and Nigel had paid for it.

One afternoon, Ambrose and Lettice planned to ride out to one of their favorite spots, a vacant cottage on the periphery of Beckwith's property. As they'd left the house, Nigel had watched them progress across the keep to the stables. Uneasy, Ambrose had suggested Lettice remain at Beckwith, but she'd cajoled and promised a sinfully decadent afternoon. She'd convinced him Nigel didn't know, and even if he did, why would he care? Unlike Ambrose, he hadn't shown the slightest interest in bedding her, a fact that made Lettice pout. Furthermore, it was unlikely Nigel would follow them. He rarely rode because he'd never mastered the sport.

In the end, Ambrose hadn't been able to disappoint her—or his prick—and they'd set out for the cottage. Immersed in her skillful ministrations, Ambrose hadn't heard his brother arrive on horseback. When the cottage door opened and revealed Nigel's devastated countenance, Ambrose had shriveled both inside and out. He practically shoved Lettice from where she knelt before him and drew on his breeches before following his brother outside.

Thinking back, he was more horrified than ever at his cavalier behavior. He'd always done as he pleased—such as managing Beckwith—and Nigel had let him. Until Nigel had returned from London intent on fulfilling his role as viscount, which meant taking control of Beckwith away from Ambrose. Ambrose had been more than angry; he'd been out for revenge. And Lettice had given him the perfect avenue.

Though he might not have done it if Lettice hadn't made it so easy. Not to diminish his fault in the matter, but refusing her would have required self-discipline, as well as a will to ignore his impulses that Ambrose simply hadn't possessed. He'd wanted her. She'd wanted him. Nothing and no one else had mattered.

Nigel's hurt and outrage had satisfied the part of Ambrose that was jealous of his brother's position. However, remorse quickly worked its way into Ambrose's mind. He'd tried to assuage Nigel by assuring him Lettice meant nothing to him. That had only made things worse, prompting Nigel to respond, "She means something to me and that's why you did it."

And then the most shocking thing of all had happened. Nigel had pulled a gun from his saddle bag. He'd pointed it at Ambrose. "You think I'm stupid. As weak-minded as I am weak-bodied. But I guessed the truth. I came here to demand satisfaction."

Ambrose had shaken his head. "I don't have a pistol."

"Then I'll just shoot you."

"You wouldn't. Please, stop for a moment, Nigel."

He'd fired. Searing pain had exploded in Ambrose's shoulder, driving him to his knees. Nigel had rushed forward, his face paling as he realized what he'd done. Then a scream had sounded from behind Ambrose. Nigel had looked beyond Ambrose, and his features had hardened into a mask of despair. Lettice had donned clothing and ran to Ambrose's side.

Ambrose could see the scene as if it played before him now. Nigel had wiped his hand across his nose—an achingly familiar action Ambrose recalled from their childhood—and turned. Only he hadn't gone to his horse—a placid mare. He'd gone to Ambrose's horse, Orpheus, awkwardly mounted, and set off at a reckless pace.

Struggling to his feet, Ambrose had called after him to stop. Nigel couldn't handle Orpheus. Lettice had begged Ambrose to come into the cottage so she could see to his wound. Hot blood flowed over his shoulder, down his chest and arm, but he hadn't cared. He'd raced to Lettice's mount, because it was faster than the mare Nigel had ridden.

Garbed in only his breeches and dripping blood, Ambrose had chased after his brother. Nigel had tried to ride fast, but Ambrose was quickly upon him. Nigel turned back and yelled something. He never saw the branch that swept him from Orpheus's back. Or the rock that broke his skull.

Shaking, Ambrose shook the memory from his head and stared at the massive façade of Beckwith's manor house. Then he jabbed Ackley in the knee. "We're here."

Ambrose climbed from the carriage. No one was waiting for them in the drive, but then he hadn't notified anyone he was coming. Not his steward, not his housekeeper, no one.

Regardless of that, the door of the house opened. His housekeeper, Mrs. Oldham, a slender woman just entering middle age stepped forth, her mobcap impeccable, her apron starched and white. She watched him warily but didn't advance.

He'd been certain of the welcome he would receive.

Everyone despised him for what he'd done. Not only because Nigel had died, but because Ambrose had evicted Lettice from Beckwith without thought to her reputation or welfare.

Mrs. Oldham had been the most disappointed. She'd spoiled and fussed over Ambrose and Nigel their entire lives. That Ambrose had destroyed their family with his selfish behavior was unconscionable, and his treatment of Lettice had only sealed his fate. Mrs. Oldham had—justifiably so—consigned him to hell.

He was a blackguard, but he wasn't a coward. At least not about this. Throwing his shoulders back, he went to stand before the housekeeper. "Good afternoon, Mrs. Oldham. It's good to see you."

She blinked up at him. The day was bright and warm. He'd forgotten how fair Cornwall was compared to London. "Master Ambrose? I mean to say, my lord." She dipped a curtsey.

He'd scarcely been Lord Sevrin before he'd gone. A fortnight after Nigel had been laid in the churchyard, Ambrose had gone to London.

Not knowing what to say, Ambrose pivoted and gestured for Ackley to come forward. "This is Mr. Ackley. He'll be staying with us."

She glanced at Ackley and dipped another curtsey. "Mr. Ackley." Tentatively, she returned her gaze to Ambrose. "For how long, my lord? That is, how long do you plan to be in residence?"

The prizefight was in a little more than a fortnight. "Three weeks at most."

"I don't have rooms prepared, but it won't take long. Would you care to come into the solar for refreshment?"

"Yes, thank you. Will you let Fisher know I'm here?"

His steward would be shocked to see him. They corresponded regularly. Fisher often requested Ambrose return—at least for a short visit—but Ambrose always ignored that portion of Fisher's letters.

Mrs. Oldham nodded. She started to turn, but paused. "It's good to see you too, my lord." Then she disappeared into the house.

Ambrose walked inside. Nostalgia assailed him and slowed his pace. The entry hall contained a portrait of his mother. Beautiful and serene, she gazed down at him. He scarcely remembered her, but he remembered this portrait. Nigel, four years his elder, had told him stories of her grace and sense of humor. She'd played soldiers with him and read him books in a variety of accented voices. Nigel had imitated her accents, often sending Ambrose into fits of giggles. He couldn't look at that portrait without thinking of Nigel.

His throat burning, he turned from the portrait and strode into the great hall, which served as an interior drawing room. The stairs to the second floor were situated at one end. Beyond the great hall was the solar. Three hundred years ago it had been the master's bedchamber, but now it was a comfortable sitting room used by the family for intimate occasions. Wide windows faced the former keep and the bay beyond. The view was breathtaking. He was pleased to see how well the gardens inside the keep had been maintained. Indeed, everything looked precisely as he remembered it.

Including the portrait of his father over the fireplace. Looking at that provoked an even stronger reaction than the portrait in the hall. Whereas Ambrose only remembered his mother via Nigel, he'd shared a close and loving relationship with his father. A relationship that now made him feel sick. Father had said Ambrose would be the heir, and as a boy Ambrose hadn't realized for that to happen Nigel would have to die.

"Sevrin, did I hear your housekeeper mention refreshment?"

Ambrose startled. He'd forgotten Ackley. "Yes. Ale or something stronger?"

"Whatever's convenient." Ackley went to stand before the windows. "You grew up here? Can't imagine why you left."

Nor would Ambrose enlighten him. He went to the sideboard on the right wall and found a bottle of whisky. It looked familiar. Had anyone touched these bottles except to remove the dust?

He uncorked it and poured a glass then handed it to Ackley.

Ackley accepted the drink. "Are we starting today?"

Their trip had taken just four days due to favorable road conditions and cooperative weather. During the journey, they'd participated in a raucous fight in the yard of an inn, resulting in a fresh black eye for Ackley.

"We'll start tomorrow. Give your eye a day to heal."

Ackley nodded. "That tonic of Tom's is dead useful though."

That it was. Ambrose thought of the Black Horse. He'd left Hopkins in charge of the club. Though he'd been disappointed not to make the journey with them, he was pleased to manage things while Ambrose was gone.

"Where will we practice?" Ackley asked before sipping his whisky.

Ambrose had given this some thought. There was a tower at the end of the manor house built into the corner of the keep. Though it hadn't been updated with the house, its rooms were in serviceable condition, and there was a large chamber on the first floor that would suit their needs. "The southwest tower."

"Gor, this is a real castle."

"It was." Ambrose gave him a brief history of the building, and then Mrs. Oldham arrived with a footman.

"I'm afraid we don't have a butler to show you to your rooms," she said.

Their butler had died three years prior, and Ambrose hadn't seen the point in replacing him. No one was in residence, nor did anyone visit. In fact, the entire house was run with minimum staff. Belatedly he wondered if his unannounced arrival was a hardship. He silently chastised himself. Ever the selfish ass.

"Whatever you've arranged will be more than satisfactory," Ambrose said. "I must commend you on the state of Beckwith. You've kept things beautifully, Mrs. Oldham."

"Let's see if you still say that after you take a tour." She paused, her gaze sharpening in question. "If you want to take a tour, that is."

"I shall. Tomorrow." He gestured toward the young man beside her. "Can this footman, ah…?"

"Ned," Mrs. Oldham supplied.

Her son? How he'd grown in five years. Ambrose remembered him as a lanky boy. "Ned, please show Mr. Ackley to his room."

"Certainly, my lord. This way, sir." He led Ackley, who still clutched his whisky, back into the great hall.

"Your son is quite a strapping lad," Ambrose said, utterly unsure of how to behave with her.

Small flags of color heightened her cheeks, not from embarrassment—judging by the angle of her chin—but from pride. "He is, thank you. I've put Mr. Ackley in the largest chamber in the northern wing. If you'll come with me, I'll take you upstairs. Unless you'd prefer to go alone. I presume you recall the location of the viscount's chamber."

Hell. He hadn't given a thought to where he'd lodge, but of course he'd inhabit the viscount's chamber. His brother's room. Ambrose wished he'd drunk his whisky.

He stood thinking for a minute—of ways to avoid using the viscount's bedchamber, but it all came down to him being a coward. His muscles tensed, and he again chastised himself. He'd caused his pain, and he'd bloody well endure it.

"Thank you, Mrs. Oldham, I can find it."

She nodded, but something flickered in her eyes.

"Is there something else?" Ambrose asked. He tried not to think of Mrs. Oldham baking biscuits for him and Nigel when they were boys, of how she'd played king of the castle with them, of how she'd loved them. That was all in the past. "I realize my presence here might be difficult. I want you to speak freely." He deserved to hear anything she had to say, though nothing could be worse than the diatribe she'd heaped on him before he'd run to London.

"Why have you come back? After all this time?"

He wished he could say his conscience had finally driven him, but that wasn't the truth. "Our houseguest, Mr. Ackley, is a prizefighter and I'm training him. He's fighting in Truro week after next."

She nodded slightly and then tipped her head to the side, as if judging him in a new light. "I see, and how is it you came to train prizefighters?"

"I was a prizefighter myself."

Her eyes widened and her jaw dropped. "Goodness me, you

weren't!" She studied his face, perhaps noting that his nose was no longer as straight as it once was. "Why would you do that?"

Her care and concern made him uncomfortable. He didn't deserve them. He preferred her loathing and disappointment. "Because it suited me. If that's all…" He didn't wait for her to respond, but walked by her into the great hall.

He finally let out his breath as he climbed the stairs, but didn't dare look down to see if she was watching him.

He was a nasty brute. Hadn't he come—at least partly—to seek forgiveness? How could he do that if he behaved badly?

At the top of the stairs he turned right toward the western wing. The viscount's chamber was at the end of the hall with glorious views of the bay. With halting steps, he made his way to the chamber and opened the door. A small sitting room greeted him. Decorated in blues and greens, it was the same as when their father had inhabited the space.

The bedchamber would be different, however. He moved through the sitting room and paused in the doorway. He'd expected to see Nigel's shorter bed, but of course Ambrose's own furniture had been moved here at some point during the last five years. It wasn't as if Nigel would be sleeping here again.

Ambrose turned toward the opposite wall, in the center of which was a massive fireplace. He froze. Hanging over the mantel was a portrait of two boys. Nigel sat in a chair in front of a tree while Ambrose perched on a low branch above him. He remembered his aunt painting that portrait. He'd been what— eight years old? And full of energy. He hadn't wanted to sit still for a painting. He'd wanted to run, ride, play. Nigel, however, had been a bit sick that day—as he was so often—thus sitting complacently in a chair had been no trouble at all.

Though Nigel was scarcely twelve in the portrait, he didn't look much different than the day he'd died at twenty-seven. But then Ambrose had always seen him as smaller, weaker, less of a man. Ambrose closed his eyes and welcomed the hatred he felt for himself.

Eventually, he turned and left the sitting room. However, instead of exiting into the corridor, he took the wrong door and entered the viscountess's chamber, which connected to the sitting room.

He never came into this room. Scarcely remembered it existed, in fact. No one had inhabited it in, what, nearly twenty-five years? The furniture was covered, but the room was clean. Mrs. Oldham hadn't let it deteriorate into forgotten filth.

Suddenly he pictured Philippa sitting at the dressing table in the corner, standing at the windows, reclining on the bed. He couldn't think of her without picturing her naked breasts, her kiss-swollen mouth, her dazzlingly lustrous eyes. Eyes that looked at him with unchecked desire.

His cock rose. What was she doing now? After leaving Benfield, he'd immersed himself in training Ackley and preparing for their trip to Cornwall. Saxton had visited him once to verbally eviscerate him. Philippa hadn't been seen since she'd left the house party. She'd closed herself up at Herrick House and saw no one—not that anyone was clamoring to see her. Lady Saxton had tried, but the rest of London had abandoned her as if she'd contracted syphilis.

Ruination was like that. Ambrose ought to know.

He closed his eyes, hating her suffering. He'd worked so hard to keep her safe from ridicule. But in the end his lust had won out—again—and created another catastrophe. If he'd ever needed further reason to continue ignoring his prick, he had it now.

Perhaps in time, people would forget and she'd find her place again. She was beautiful and vivacious. He couldn't imagine her living a life of solitude. He didn't want that for her at all—not that what he wanted mattered in the slightest.

He swiped a hand over his face and exited into the corridor.

He went downstairs in search of Mrs. Oldham to instruct her to have the portrait of him and Nigel removed. Then he'd visit the southwest tower to investigate the room they'd use for sparring. He stopped short in the great hall at the sight of a massively wide man striding toward him.

Mr. Oldham. His housekeeper's husband and the groundskeeper.

He barreled straight at Ambrose and lifted his fist to hit him in the face. Ever the fighter, Ambrose moved at the last second, but the blow grazed him on the cheek. Ambrose brought his hands up but didn't strike.

Oldham glowered at him beneath bushy black brows. "How dare ye show up here without a word and make Mrs. Oldham cry?"

Christ, he *was* a nasty brute. "I didn't mean to. I'm just…never mind, there's no excuse. I'll convey my apologies straightaway."

Oldham narrowed one eye. "What're ye really doing here? Mrs. Oldham says ye're training some fighter, that ye were a fighter." He looked at Ambrose's still elevated fists. "Though I guess I can see that for meself."

Ambrose glanced at his hands and then dropped them to his sides.

"Ye fight anymore?"

"I have a fighting club in London, but I don't prizefight any longer." His fight with Nolan notwithstanding.

Oldham nodded slowly. "Found some solace in that, I'll reckon."

How very astute. And discomforting. Ambrose didn't want to discuss this. "Where is Mrs. Oldham now?"

"In the kitchens." Ambrose moved to pass him, but Oldham grabbed his elbow. "Ye're going to have to make an effort if ye want to stay here. I know this is yer house and I can't throw ye out, but ye've left everyone stranded here. Mrs. Oldham was devastated enough when yer brother died, but to lose ye at the same time?" He shook his head. "It wasn't right of ye to leave. And to add five years of silence to that injury? Make it right. If ye can."

Make it right.

How could he ever make anything right? It wasn't as if this was a solitary mistake. He'd gone and done it all over again—minus anyone dying, thank God. Still, he nodded. As he'd resolved, he owed it to Nigel to try.

On the first day after the Disaster at Benfield, Philippa buried her head beneath the covers of her bed and hid.

On the second day, she read the newspaper.

On the third and fourth days, she went back to hiding under her coverlet.

On the fifth day, Father summoned her to his office. Directed into a stiff leather chair before his desk, Philippa sat straight and expectant whilst he gazed out the windows.

Tall and mostly fit (he'd developed a bit of a paunch in the last few years), the Earl of Herrick resembled Philippa only in that she'd inherited his golden-brown eyes. He possessed light brown hair that had thinned on top, but which had apparently tried to compensate by sprouting an overabundance of eyebrows instead.

It was the drawing together of these impressive swags of hair over those familiar golden eyes that preceded his Awful Pronouncement.

"You're coming to Wokeham Abbey with us."

Oh, she *couldn't*. She shook her head. "I can't come with you."

"You've no choice." He moved to the front of his desk and paced, his hands clasped firmly behind his back. "Your life in London is over."

It was, unfortunately, not a melodramatic observation. Indeed, every single one of her invitations had been rescinded.

She watched him make a few passes before lifting her chin. "Perhaps. However, I've no desire to accompany you and *that woman* to Wokeham Abbey."

He stopped and sent her a furious glare. "I should've forced you to accept one of those other proposals. Like Saxton." *Which would have required you to actually pay attention to me...* He took a deep breath and tugged at the bottom of his waistcoat. "It's lucky for you I have saved your future."

Dread snaked up her spine. She hated to contemplate what her father might consider "lucky." "What have you done?"

"Sir Mortimer Stinson has professed his continued desire to marry you."

Oh no, anyone but him. Sir Mortimer was a widower—at least forty—who lived near Wokeham Abbey. He was eager to sire children—many, many children, he'd said—and he was less than kind to his horses. He'd offered for Philippa three years ago, to which she'd politely declined. Other young women had also refused him, so Philippa understood why he might be willing to overlook her scandal.

Could her father be so cruel? "You can't mean to marry me to him?"

Father's bushy brows drew together, which truly didn't take much effort given their breadth. "You've no other choices, and I won't allow you to become a spinster."

That was preferable to marrying Sir Mortimer. Still, she recognized her father's efforts to see her married, even if she didn't want them. "I really don't wish to marry him, Father. I'm sorry I've disappointed you, but in time things will—"

Father leaned over her and bared his teeth. "You've run out of time, gel! You'll marry Sir Mortimer, or I'll banish you to some remote cottage with barely enough income to subsist. You've embarrassed this family, and you'll bloody well do what's necessary to make it right!"

She'd never seen her father so angry, but she was angry too. She pushed up from the chair and stood before him, though her forehead only met his chin. "I've embarrassed this family? What of you and *that woman* promenading about town? Isn't that the real reason I've run out of time? I could perhaps wait out my mistake, but you and Mother can no longer keep your own scandalous behavior in check."

"It's not at all the same!" he thundered.

They both stood glaring at each other. Philippa was shaking with a multitude of emotions—outrage, disappointment, hurt.

He lowered his voice and shook his head disdainfully. "You stupid chit. When are you going to realize life isn't fair?"

"Right about the time you force me to marry Sir Mortimer," she muttered. Or removed her to the edge of nothing.

He gave her a gimlet eye and tugged on his waistcoat again. "I'm not completely unreasonable. I'll allow you to say goodbye to your friends—if they'll see you." Reasonable, but unfeeling. "As soon as your mother leaves, you'll depart for Wokeham Abbey. I'll expect you to arrive in a fortnight. Then the banns will be read, and you and Sir Mortimer will be married three weeks later."

That had been the truly Awful Pronouncement.

The next day Philippa read in the newspaper that Ambrose had left London and returned to Cornwall. While she was nursing this disappointment in the upstairs sitting room, Mother entered.

"I came to speak with you about your future," Mother said through lips so tight they might split. She sat in a chair near the windows overlooking the street.

Seated on an adjacent settee, Philippa stiffened as she waited for her mother's lecture.

Mother smoothed her hand over her lap. "I will be relocating to my new townhouse next week. And as such, it's good you'll be going to Wokeham Abbey."

Good? How typically unfeeling of her. Didn't she realize Philippa would hate having to marry Sir Mortimer? Unless she didn't know the extent of Father's plans. "Do you know what Father has organized?"

"I do."

"Then surely you know that I'd rather do anything *but* go. I might even consider coming to live with you."

Mother pursed her lips. "You could, but I don't think you want to, nor would it be wise."

Philippa couldn't argue with her there. Living with a mother who'd left her husband's townhouse might be the lesser of two dreadful circumstances, but dreadful was still, well, dreadful.

Mother sat straighter, stretching her spine as she'd so often instructed Philippa to do. "I'm very sorry for what this has cost you. I know you were only trying to protect our family—such as it was—when you went to Lockwood House. That your naïve efforts caused such a catastrophic downfall—"

She didn't need her mother's overview of the entire scandal. She was quite well-acquainted with every step of her social demise. "Thank you, Mother. I think that's enough."

"Marriage to Sir Mortimer won't be so terrible. You'll have a lovely household to manage."

"He's mean to his horses," Philippa muttered, feeling her world closing in.

Mother leaned forward in her chair. Her expression was earnest, caring. Which was more than a bit suspicious. "What happened with Sevrin? If what I heard is true, you were caught in a rather compromising position and yet you declined his proposal? That makes you look like a lightskirt, and I can't believe that of you. Not after the way you've attacked me for my behavior." She paused to take a breath. "Is there a chance you possess a tendre for each other?"

It was quite possible *she* did (she couldn't help but recall the ways in which he'd championed her, nor could she deny the physical pull between them), but Ambrose? He at least found her desirable, even if he'd managed to convince her marriage between them would be a regrettable mistake.

She finally answered her mother's question. "Perhaps."

Mother gave a firm, decisive nod. "Then you should follow him to Cornwall."

Her mother's concern was shocking. "You're saying I should ignore Father?"

"What's the worst that could happen? He'll drag you back to Wokeham Abbey and force you to marry Sir Mortimer?"

Since that was already in store for her, Philippa could hardly argue with Mother's logic. "I don't know, Mother. Following him to Cornwall is so…forward." So *her*.

"Your reputation won't suffer," Mother said wryly, and Philippa almost laughed. Mother reached out and took her hand. It was a remarkable gesture. Philippa's throat constricted. "Love is worth any risk."

Philippa swallowed the sharpness away. "Is that how you convinced yourself it was acceptable to pursue your liaison with Mr. Booth-Barrows?" The question wasn't meant to be hostile. She truly wanted to know what had motivated her Mother.

"I tried not to at first. Truly, I did." Her smile was soft and tinged with regret. "But I'd been alone for so long, and he was so lovely. I should've been stronger—for you." Her gaze grew sharp, intense. "If you think for even a moment you might find happiness with Sevrin, go after him."

"I don't love him," Philippa said quickly. And he certainly didn't love her.

"Then just think about your future. Would you rather marry Sir Mortimer and never know what might've been, or take a risk and see what happens?"

Two days later, Philippa hadn't yet decided what to do, but she'd had enough of being cooped up in Herrick House. She sent a note to Audrey—one of only two people (the other being Lady Saxton) who'd called on her in the past week. Audrey had arrived shortly thereafter, and they went for a walk to the park.

Philippa breathed deeply of the warm spring air, glad to be outdoors. Perhaps she'd go for a ride tomorrow.

Audrey looked askance at her and smiled. "I'm so happy you decided to get out today, Philippa."

"As am I. Thank you for coming to rescue me. Your parents don't mind?"

"Mother's not terribly pleased, but it's not as if my social worth will be impacted. I'm not exactly popular." Audrey's tone was matter of fact. She never complained about being a wallflower, and she'd never made Philippa feel bad because she wasn't one.

"Still, if you think associating with me will negatively affect you, I insist you stop."

Audrey shook her head. "Nonsense. I'm not in the same position as you. I'm in no rush to marry, and my family is supportive of me." Whereas Philippa's family could scarcely wait to throw her out the door.

As they neared the park, they passed three ladies. Instead of pausing to exchange pleasantries, the trio averted their gazes and hurried past.

Philippa kept her head up. She knew all three women quite well.

"I'm sorry, Philippa," Audrey murmured.

"It's fine." But Philippa's chest squeezed nonetheless.

They crossed the street to the gate. "Do you want to go in?" Audrey asked.

She had, but now she wasn't so sure. It was before the fashionable hour, but there would still be people who would cut her or perhaps worse. It was one thing to be ignored, but to be publicly ridiculed?

Her courage had reached its limit. "Let's go back."

They turned and retraced their steps. A brougham passed on the street. Inside were Lydia and her Aunt Margaret.

Lydia turned to look down at Philippa and Audrey as they passed, but Aunt Margaret quickly drew her around.

"I haven't heard from Lydia at all," Philippa said, her lungs tightening so that her breathing felt short and harsh.

"Her aunt won't allow her to write you. She did say to tell you she missed you."

Philippa missed her too. She missed parties, she missed dancing, she missed the reliable if cold routine of her family before her parents had gone mad with their personal desires. And, tellingly, she missed Ambrose. His charming laugh, his imperfect nose, his kisses, and the way he made her feel. Cared for. Desired. There was a reason he held himself back from her—both physically and emotionally—and she wanted to find out what it was.

It seemed her decision was clearer than she'd thought.

She hurried her pace as they crossed the street.

"Slow down," Audrey called.

"Sorry, I've just decided I must get home."

"Whatever for?" Audrey smiled bemusedly. "It's not as if you have an appointment."

Philippa laughed, because really, there was nothing else to be done in her situation. Besides, she was weary of hiding and cowering beneath a blanket of fear. She was ready to take a risk that might have a positive outcome instead of the foolish choices that had led to her current circumstances. For the first time in over a week she felt a sliver of hope. "No, but I need to pack. I've decided to go to Cornwall."

Chapter Seventeen

A WEEK after his arrival at Beckwith, Ambrose felt almost normal, whatever that was. He vaguely recalled how things had been before he'd maligned his brother. Before he'd fallen from grace.

Over the last several days he'd developed a routine of sorts. In the morning he met with Fisher and reviewed the estate's business. Fisher, as expected, had done an excellent job of managing the sheep herds and wool production. He'd also kept the estate in as good of repair as one could keep a centuries-old castle without its master present.

After their meetings, Ambrose went on a strenuous walk with Ackley as part of his training exercises, followed by luncheon and an hour or so of working on technique and strategy. In the afternoon, they'd assist Oldham or another retainer with some task around the estate—just as Ambrose had done before he'd left. After dinner they sparred in the tower fighting room.

Though Ambrose fell into bed exhausted at the end of each day, it had taken seven long nights before he'd finally succumbed to a sleep without dreaming of Philippa. At last, he'd driven her from his mind.

This afternoon they were repairing the east wall. Fisher had ordered stone from a quarry near Tregony, and Oldham was overseeing the repair. The wall of the keep had deteriorated over the last few centuries and they were not only rebuilding it, but installing a gateway since the stables were in the northeast corner of the keep.

The day was quite warm. Oldham mopped his brow. "Wondered if I might watch yer sparring practice this evening."

Ambrose set another rock onto the wall and turned to his groundskeeper. "You're more than welcome."

Oldham squinted at him. "Ye haven't been down to Gerrans since ye returned, have ye?"

Gerrans was the nearest village, less than two miles away. It was also where Lettice Chandler resided in a small cottage her father had demanded Ambrose purchase for her. Ambrose preferred to avoid running into her. "No."

Oldham nodded. "I was at the pub last night. Folks are anxious to go to the prizefight in Truro now they know ye're training one of the fighters."

Why? Were they hoping to see him fail? He couldn't imagine any of them wishing him well. Perhaps they were merely curious since he'd been gone so long.

"Ye might be surprised at how people treat ye," Oldham said. "Five years is a long time."

Was Oldham saying people had forgiven him? How could that be possible when he'd yet to forgive himself?

Mrs. Oldham strode toward them from the solar, her dark skirt blowing in the soft breeze. She was the one part of Beckwith that hadn't become part of his routine. She still regarded him a bit warily, and they had yet to regain the closeness they'd once shared. She came to stand before Ambrose and shaded her eyes as she looked up at him. "You've a visitor, my lord."

Ambrose's gaze shot toward the house. He caught a glimpse of a green gown in the window of the solar. It could be only one person. Ambrose contemplated escape, but reasoned he'd have to face Lettice Chandler some time. Resigned, he trod forward.

Mrs. Oldham followed him.

The closer he got to the house, the more his apprehension grew. The sweat on his forehead turned cold, and the remains of luncheon in his belly turned to lead.

He opened the door. Prickly heat drove away his icy

foreboding. It was not Lettice, but Philippa. Had it really been a fortnight since he'd seen her? It seemed it had been only moments or perhaps an eternity. Time didn't matter, just her. He feasted on her presence like a beggar at his lord's table.

Reality saturated his senses. God, why had she come? She'd refused him—wisely so—and he couldn't imagine what would bring her all the way to Cornwall.

"Good afternoon, Ambrose." Philippa stood on the opposite side of the room. Curls of dark wavy hair peeked from beneath her bonnet. Her ale-colored eyes were warm and assessing. She was draped in a pale green muslin gown that accentuated her breasts—or perhaps he was merely recalling their last meeting when he'd touched and tasted them.

He was such a beast. After all that had happened, and after she'd journeyed this far, all he could do was pant after her like a dog in heat? He tamped down his lust. He wanted to know why she'd come. "You've ventured a long way for an afternoon call."

She smiled at him, and his too-rapidly-aroused body stretched even tighter. "Indeed, but London has become a bit stuffy of late."

Ambrose was vaguely aware of Mrs. Oldham lingering behind him. He pivoted. "Philippa, this is my housekeeper Mrs. Oldham. Though I daresay she's already introduced herself, Mrs. Oldham, allow me to present Lady Philippa Latham."

Mrs. Oldham curtseyed. "A pleasure to formally make your acquaintance, my lady. My lord, she's come all the way from London." She turned her gaze to Ambrose and narrowed her eyes.

Philippa looked between the two of them. "Would it be too much trouble for tea?"

"Not at all." Mrs. Oldham bestowed a pleasant smile upon Philippa. "I'll see about getting your things settled in a room. I presume you'll be spending the night—at least—given how far you've come."

"Yes, thank you." Mrs. Oldham exited, and Philippa gave Ambrose her full attention, her gaze hovering in the area of his loins—or did he imagine that? "Your housekeeper is lovely," she said.

If lovely meant perturbed, then yes, she was. He deserved Mrs. Oldham's ire—Philippa's too, if she wanted to give it—and so much more.

Regardless of what he deserved, Ambrose gravitated toward Philippa. Not too close, but close enough that he could smell her familiar scent. He inhaled deeply, both relishing and disbelieving her presence at the same time. "Why have you come all this way?"

She lifted her chin and regarded him with a defiant edge. "I've reconsidered your proposal. I'd like to determine whether we might actually suit."

She'd come to court him? His pulse quickened as he realized one of the reasons he'd come to Cornwall was to escape her allure. "My opinion hasn't changed. You'd be miserable with me."

She inclined her head. "You're entitled to think that, of course. However, I must see for myself." She strolled to the windows and looked out at the gardens. "We clearly get on quite well, as evidenced by our quick friendship. And surely you won't argue the attraction between us. I think we can both agree our mutual... desire," her cheeks blushed a delightful shade of pink, "would be enough to visit the vicar. Indeed, marriages have been based on far less."

If his body had been aroused before, she'd stoked him to raging lust by murmuring a few well-chosen words. What she didn't understand was that his uncontrollable *desire* had been his ruin—and hers. He could well imagine how things might turn out this time. They'd marry, she'd fall in love with him, and he'd do something to crush her. Growing up, Nigel had been the person he'd loved most in the world, and look what he'd done to him. Ambrose clearly didn't know how to love someone, or how to keep his passion from destroying people.

He joined her near the windows, again not getting too close. "Your logic seems sound except for one pesky fact—you want love, and I can't give that to you."

"So you say, but I am also not convinced of that. Although, I invite you to persuade me otherwise." She blinked up at him with impossibly long, seductive lashes. Had she always been a siren?

Persuade her that he couldn't love her. She was far too clever for her own good, but he could play her game. "I'll only be in residence another ten days."

"Until your prizefight is concluded?" At his questioning look, she tipped her head. "I know about the prizefight next week. I believe I'll have my answer regarding our suitability by then."

"You do?"

She nodded, turning her head toward him. "If we aren't betrothed by then, I will take my leave, and you may bid me farewell forever."

Forever? He didn't like the sound of that at all, which was asinine. He'd left her ruined in London. Had he really ever expected to see her again?

Perhaps not, but that didn't mean he hadn't wanted to.

And therein lie his real fear. If she was here to court him— and she most certainly was—how on earth could he defend himself?

With the truth.

"Let me be clear about the things I've done." He leaned forward, wondering if he might be able to intimidate her. "I seduced my brother's fiancée, then I caused his death, and then I abandoned her. Why the devil would you want to marry me?"

"Because I've seen another side of you. Perhaps you've changed. Would you do those things today?"

He blinked at her. "I ruined you."

A gentle shrug. "And were prepared to marry me in London, so you *have* changed. I'm here to ascertain how much."

Christ, she wasn't courting him, she was investigating him. The apprehension he'd felt earlier returned tenfold. "And now I've changed my mind. I won't marry you."

She turned from the windows, her skirt billowing gently around her ankles. "I don't believe you. You're a better man than you think. You made mistakes, and from what I can tell you've been reeling from them for five years. But now you're here, and maybe I can help." She gave him a placid, daring look.

He'd had quite enough of this charade. In two quick strides

he was standing before her. "Don't push me, Philippa. I will humor your visit, but you will leave in ten days exactly as you arrived. Alone and unwed."

Her gaze remained steady. "We'll see."

She moved infinitesimally closer so that her breasts barely grazed his chest. It was enough—more than enough—to remind him how badly he wanted her, and how torturous the next ten days would be.

He stepped back from her, letting go of her arms and willing the charge between them to dispel. It didn't. How easy it would be to kiss her, to strip her bare, to tumble her over the back of that chair. He swallowed as Mrs. Oldham entered with the tea tray.

"Enjoy your tea." He spun on his heel and quit the house.

PHILIPPA'S chest rose and fell steadily as she fought to refill her air-deprived lungs. He'd been so close and the look in his eye so full of promise. A kiss had seemed certain, but then he'd pulled away, and she'd been left as wanting as that day in Benfield's stable.

She'd come hoping to determine if the spark between them would be enough to sustain something more, and she had just ten days to find her answer. She glanced at the door Ambrose had departed through and sank into a chair. Breaking down his defenses was going to prove difficult, but since he hadn't immediately thrown her out, she had hope.

The housekeeper set the tray on a table between a collection of two settees and two chairs. "His lordship returned to work?"

Unfortunately. She looked up at Mrs. Oldham and summoned a smile to warm the air Ambrose had turned frigid with his abrupt departure. "Yes, I didn't mean to interrupt him. We'll talk at dinner."

Mrs. Oldham nodded and set about organizing the tea implements. She'd greeted Philippa a half hour earlier and had apologized for the lack of a butler. "Where is your butler?" Philippa asked, curious for any morsel of information about

Ambrose and his surroundings.

"He passed on, my lady."

"I'm so sorry."

Mrs. Oldham looked up at her. "It was three years ago. Cream and sugar?"

"Yes, please. One spoon of sugar." Three years and they hadn't hired a replacement?

As if Mrs. Oldham had heard Philippa's question, she said, "His lordship runs Beckwith with minimal staff. He spends little time here."

No time, from what Philippa could tell. Her next question was probably too forward, but she'd come here for answers. "Is that because of what happened with his brother?"

Mrs. Oldham had been preparing to pour, but she stopped and looked at Philippa with wide eyes.

Philippa immediately regretted her impudence. She shouldn't have invited the housekeeper into her problems. "Please accept my apologies. I know your loyalties lie with his lordship."

Mrs. Oldham poured Philippa's tea, added the cream and sugar, and stirred. "My loyalties have been tested over the years." She pursed her lips as she handed Philippa her cup. "Now it is I who must apologize. I did not mean to speak above my station."

Philippa had the sense Mrs. Oldham was of the servant-as-family variety, much like Philippa's first governess, who'd died when Philippa was just eight. "I would prefer you speak freely. You have to be wondering what I'm doing here. A young, unmarried miss traveling all the way from London to see one of England's most notorious scoundrels."

Mrs. Oldham sat on the settee adjacent to Philippa's chair. "Is that how Master Ambrose is viewed?"

Philippa pinched the handle of her cup. "Of course." Her heart sped up at the prospect of learning more about him. "Shouldn't he be?"

The housekeeper frowned, and her eyelids drooped with sadness. "Yes, he should. He was a scoundrel, and I'm deeply afraid he's continued to be since you're here. Pray tell me he didn't ruin you too?"

Philippa rattled her teacup on its saucer and silently chided herself for starting this inquisition. No, she had to accommodate herself to the way things were. She *was* ruined. "It's a bit complicated. Suffice it to say we both made mistakes, but I must claim the bulk of the blame. I allowed myself to be in the wrong place at the wrong time." Except that if Ambrose was half the man she hoped he might be, she'd been in exactly the right place at the right time.

Mrs. Oldham eyed her intently. "You seem a reasonable and intelligent young lady. I'm sorry for your situation."

"Don't be, I'm trying to make the best of it. I shall see if Ambrose and I might suit. And if we don't, well, I have other options. Though, I'd prefer you didn't tell him that."

Mrs. Oldham inclined her mobcapped head. "As you wish, my lady. I'll just go and see about preparations to your chamber, then I shall come back and show you up."

"Thank you for being so welcoming."

Mrs. Oldham departed, and Philippa sipped her tea. Ten days in which to make Ambrose fall in love with her. For that was surely her goal. Though she'd told her mother otherwise, she *did* love him, despite his faults, or maybe because of them. Like his imperfect nose, he'd been broken and haphazardly repaired, but forever changed. And not necessarily for the worse.

They'd shared plenty of wonderful moments, and she would endeavor to create several more. She'd show him he could trust her, that she could help him overcome the past and embrace the future. Together.

Failure meant not only going to Wokeham Abbey and marrying Sir Mortimer, it also meant leaving Ambrose to battle his darkness alone. All the more reason to make the most of these ten days.

She mentally recalculated her timeframe. Her father would be expecting her at Wokeham Abbey in a few days, and she would, of course, disappoint him. When she didn't arrive, Father would send word back to London, demanding she come posthaste. A few days prior to the prizefight in Truro, he'd receive a response from Herrick House stating she'd gone to Cornwall. He'd be furious and would likely come to fetch her personally, probably arriving the day after the fight. At which time, Philippa would be betrothed or ready to face the fate her father had dictated.

AFTER a dinner during which Ambrose spent more time mentally making love to Philippa than he did eating, he was more than ready to engage Ackley in the tower sparring room.

Oldham had joined them this evening and was now situated on a wide bench. "Mrs. Oldham told me about yer lady friend."

Ambrose paused in removing his waistcoat. He could well imagine what Mrs. Oldham and the other servants were saying about Philippa, a lone woman from London who wasn't his wife come to visit him. "She 'told' you about her or demanded you ask me about her?"

"Both."

"She's merely touring Cornwall."

Oldham snorted. "What rot."

Ambrose fixed him with a Saxton-worthy glare. "She's here for the prizefight and then she'll be on her way."

"Indeed?" Ackley had tossed aside his boots and now pulled off his stockings. He looked over at Ambrose, his eyes wide with interest. "She came for the prizefight?" They'd discussed a variety of things at dinner—the weather in Cornwall, the journey from London to Cornwall, and the history of Beckwith—but they hadn't touched on the prizefight at all. "She came to see me?"

Oldham chuckled. "Though I've yet to meet the lady, I'd wager she's here to see him." He jabbed his thumb toward Ambrose.

Ackley nodded, albeit glumly, then finished removing his stockings.

Oldham looked at Ambrose expectantly. He sat on the opposite side of the bench and removed his boots and stockings, purposefully ignoring his groundskeeper. He didn't want to talk about Philippa. Indeed, he wanted to try to forget her for at least an hour.

Ackley went to the table in the corner upon which lay two

pairs of boxing gloves. They'd used the mitts for practice, so as not to injure each other overly much. However, tonight Ambrose needed the feel of his bare knuckles, wanted the true challenge of fighting a worthy opponent. But he'd have to be careful. In his frame of mind, he could easily damage Ackley enough to cripple him for a few days and that wouldn't help him win next week.

Ambrose stood. "Let's skip using those tonight." He prowled to the table and clapped Ackley's shoulder. "I want to see your progress without the gloves. Just be careful."

Ackley arched a brow. "You're telling me that? You're the professional."

"Professional, eh?" Oldham asked.

"As good a prizefighter as I've ever seen," Ackley vowed. "You should've seen him against Nolan a few weeks back."

Ambrose inwardly squirmed beneath the weight of Ackley's admiration. "Was that before or after he nearly knocked me out?"

"Don't minimize your abilities." Ackley shot Oldham a speaking glance. "He always does that."

Oldham's brows elevated. "Does he now?"

This conversation was growing far too personal. Ambrose walked to the center of the scratch he'd drawn on the floor at the start of their first session. "Let us focus on you, Ackley. You're going to be a far better fighter than me."

Ackley joined him at the scratch. "Are we still sparring, or will this follow the guidelines of an actual match?"

Ambrose hadn't considered having a formal bout. In the past, they'd fought, but interrupted the exercise to discuss strategy. However, since they were going bare knuckle, they may as well follow the rest of the rules. "We'll make this a fight, but the goal isn't to knock each other down. We'll go ten minutes, break, then another ten, break, then another ten." Ambrose pivoted toward Oldham. "Can you give us a signal?"

Oldham put his fingers in his mouth and whistled. "That do?"

"Perfect." Ambrose turned back toward Ackley and then nodded. Oldham's piercing whistle filled the high-ceilinged room and reverberated off the stone walls.

Ackley moved quickly—Ambrose had instructed him to deliver the first punch if possible. It set a tone for your opponent. It said, "I'm ready."

However, Ambrose also expected his right jab. Ackley had forgotten to alter what he started with. If anyone studied his fights over time, they'd learn to expect it.

Ambrose easily deflected the strike and drove his fist into Ackley's gut. Not full-power, but enough to make him jump back. Ackley nodded, realizing his mistake. They circled each other a moment, but Ambrose took the offensive and drove Ackley back with several swift strikes. He deflected all but the last. His speed and reflexes were improving with each fight. Ambrose was pleased with his progress.

As the first stretch wound down, Ambrose wanted to press Ackley. His fingers were also itching to feel more than the light hits they were trading. But he had to remember this wasn't a fight to drive his demons from his body or to purge Philippa from his mind. Frustration mounting, he dashed to the side and landed a powerful jab to Ackley's ribs. Then he spun about and sent one to the other side. As Ackley reacted, Ambrose caught him on the chin. He hadn't meant to hit him hard, but Ackley moved at the same second and Ambrose's knuckles caught Ackley's jaw with a resounding thud. His head snapped back. He retreated and shook his head. His eyes narrowed, and he attacked.

Ambrose got his hands up, but Ackley was relentless—just as Ambrose had taught him to be. He drove Ambrose back with his fists and his fast footwork. Ambrose worked to keep up, but staggered backward. God, if he could unleash himself, he'd have Ackley on the floor in a trice. In the span of that thought, Ackley punched him in the gut and again in the cheek. Already off balance from the quick assault, Ambrose fell back and sprawled on the floor.

A loud gasp from the doorway drew everyone's attention.

Philippa stood staring with her hand over her mouth. Then she immediately rushed forward and knelt beside Ambrose. "Are you all right?"

"Fine." In truth, his cheek throbbed. He wondered if Ackley's chin pained him the same. Perhaps sparring without gloves had been a poor idea.

"Ackley?" Ambrose asked as he sat up.

Ackley shrugged, though he rubbed his chin. "Fine."

Oldham whistled.

Ambrose and Ackley both turned to look at him. Oldham shrugged and needlessly said, "Time's up."

The touch of Philippa's hand on his cheek drew Ambrose's attention. "You're hurt," she murmured.

"You've seen me much worse." He got to his feet and extended his hand to help her up.

She put her fingers in his and the contact almost sent him back to the floor—on top of her.

Ackley went to the table and plucked up a towel. Ambrose turned to Philippa, blocking her from the other men. "You can't be in here. How did you even find us?"

"I asked Mrs. Oldham. Why can't I be here? I've watched you fight before." Her gaze fell to his chest. He watched her lips part to reveal the dainty pink tip of her tongue. For the second time that day, he cursed his lack of garments in order to shield his erection.

Keeping his back to Oldham and Ackley, he led her to the door. "You have to go."

She put her back to the doorjamb and stared defiantly up at him. "Persuade me."

His blood stirred at the idea of persuading her to do any number of things, and not one of them involved leaving his presence. "Will you settle for a tour of Beckwith tomorrow?"

Her dark lashes swept over her glittering eyes and her mouth curved up in a slow smile. "I would."

He braced his hand on the doorjamb over her head, tormenting himself by leaning over her and inhaling deeply of her soft, feminine scent. "In exchange, you'll stay out of this tower. Understood?" By God, he'd need a haven from her if he was going to maintain his vow.

She dropped her gaze and when she again looked into his eyes, her smile broadened. "Perfectly."

Chapter Eighteen

THE following morning Philippa stepped from the solar and squinted into the bright sunshine. The rear yard had once been the castle's keep, and was now a very large walled garden and pasture area. With the sound of seabirds and the gentle breeze from the ocean, it was a beautifully serene setting.

Mrs. Oldham had instructed her that Ambrose was waiting for her in the stables, which were built into the northeast corner of the keep. Philippa followed a path in that direction, eager to see him.

Last night hadn't gone as planned—him tossing her out of sparring practice was a setback since she'd intended to spend time with him—but she'd been encouraged by his reaction to her. While vexing him wasn't her goal, she'd take it above indifference. His emotional response at least showed he felt *something* for her.

The path branched to Beckwith's stables. She stepped inside where the smell of hay and the nickering of horses greeted her senses. This pleasant moment was instantly overridden by the sound of two male voices raised in argument.

"Milord, ye can't take a cart!"

"Just hitch the damned thing!"

Philippa strode to where Ambrose was towering over a much shorter, stockier man with a shiny, bald pate. The head groom, perhaps.

Upon seeing Philippa, the man smiled broadly, revealing a gap between his front teeth that, well, a cart could drive through.

"Good morning, my lady."

"Good morning," she said warmly, though she shot an inquisitive glance at Ambrose who was currently glowering at his retainer. "Is there a problem?"

"Not if you don't mind bumping around Beckwith in a cart." The retainer eyed her riding habit. "I'd wager you're a horsewoman, my lady."

She inclined her head. "I am, thank you. What's this about a cart?" She looked between the two men.

"His lordship is planning to take ye on a tour of his fine estate in a cart. That would be acceptable if ye stuck to the dirt track, but to truly appreciate the beauty of Beckwith and the Roseland Peninsula, ye'll want to go on *horseback*." He threw the last word at Ambrose like a dagger.

Philippa thought it more than fair to torture Ambrose just a bit, given his treatment of her. "Oh, but I understand his lordship doesn't ride."

The groom gaped, first at her and then at Ambrose. "What? I understood why ye might be avoiding Orpheus, but ye don't ride at all anymore?"

Anymore. Which meant he'd ridden once. Why had he stopped?

Ambrose glared at his retainer. "Saddle Demetrius."

The smaller man looked a bit surprised, but nodded before turning to Philippa. "And I'll saddle Matilda for you, my lady. I'm Welch, by the way."

"Thank you, Welch," she said, her gaze straying to Ambrose.

Welch took himself off to the other end of the stable.

A vein pulsed in Ambrose's neck. He looked furious, but also something else. His face had gone a bit pale.

"We don't need to ride if you don't wish to," she said softly. He was clearly upset about having to ride, and she didn't want him to be.

"No, I'll ride." His lips barely moved, and he didn't look at her.

"Really, we can take the cart," she insisted. "Or walk."

"Come, let's help Welch." He didn't wait for her, but started down the row of stalls. As he passed one in particular, the horse within neighed and danced. Philippa came abreast of the animal and paused. He was a gorgeous black Arabian, and even now he whinnied and strained over the door to watch Ambrose though he'd already passed.

Gingerly, she reached out to stroke his nose. "There, you beautiful lad. You're all right, aren't you?"

The Arabian nuzzled her briefly, but stomped his feet.

Philippa startled as Ambrose—he'd apparently doubled back—gripped her wrist and pulled her hand from the horse. The Arabian neighed loudly and pushed forward, toward Ambrose, but Ambrose dragged Philippa away. "Don't touch that animal."

His tone was so sharp, so fierce, his hold on her wrist so tight, Philippa merely nodded.

Ambrose let her go and turned abruptly, passing Welch who was leading a dark brown mare.

Welch shook his head behind Ambrose's back and handed the reins to Philippa. "Here's Matilda. There's a block in the yard if ye'd like to mount up."

She nodded, thinking it best to give Ambrose a few minutes to recover. She'd never seen him so rattled, not even when he'd faced Jagger and his men the night they'd met.

She led Matilda outside and found the block. Five minutes later, Ambrose came out of the stable leading a spirited gray gelding.

He paused for a moment in the yard and Philippa held her breath. How long had it been since he'd ridden? Perhaps not since he'd left Beckwith.

He swung himself onto the horse's back and walked the animal toward her. Whether it was five years or five minutes since Ambrose's last ride, Philippa couldn't tell. He appeared as natural on horseback as she felt. He also looked unbearably handsome in a dark blue coat and buff breeches, a stylish beaver pulled low over his brow, shading his eyes.

"Are you ready?" he asked.

She nodded. They guided their mounts out of the keep. Last night he'd talked of the wall they were repairing and the gate they were building. It looked as if there was quite a bit of work to be done, certainly more than could be accomplished in the next week. Would he leave before it was finished? Or would he stay beyond the fight? She had so many questions to ask him, and not because she wanted to judge. She only wanted to *know*.

They walked their horses a few minutes, and she came abreast of him. He looked over at her, but she couldn't see his expression beneath the brim of his hat. However, when his horse picked up speed, she understood it was time to move faster.

Philippa spoke softly to Matilda and took her to a trot. The air was so pure and lovely, the breeze from the ocean so fresh and crisp. There was truly nothing better than riding on a glorious day. She laughed with pure joy as she passed Ambrose and took Matilda to a full run.

She raced along the cliffside. Below, the pale beach stretched along the ocean's edge, an endless stretch of dark green-blue water intermittently dotted with white. A sound came from behind her, and she turned in the saddle.

Ambrose was bearing down on her. Now she could see his face perfectly. He was livid.

He brought his horse beside hers and snatched the reins from her grasp. Philippa gasped, as shock mingled with a bead of admiration. Though, now was not the time to reflect upon his superior horsemanship.

"What the hell do you think you're doing?" he demanded, as he brought his horse to a halt. Watching his muscles tighten and his eyes flash furiously, she was all too aware of the strength of his body and the fragility of his temper. Still, she was weary of him constantly getting angry with her.

She summoned her own ire and glared at him. "Riding a horse. What the hell do you think you're doing?"

"That's how you ride a horse? At breakneck speed along a path you've never ridden before? And then you *turn around*?" The flesh around his mouth turned pale. He was afraid.

Philippa instantly gentled. She reached out and touched his hand. "I'm an excellent rider. You've no need to worry."

He jerked back, unsettling Demetrius, who danced beneath them. Ambrose tossed her the reins. "Since you're such an excellent rider, I'm sure you can find your way back to the stables." He pulled his reins.

She tried to touch him again. "Wait, don't go."

He gave her a pained look, then turned and rode off, throwing dirt and grass in his wake. He cut across the field, away from the cliff.

That hadn't gone at all as planned. She'd scared the wits out of him somehow. She wanted to follow him, but thought it might be better if she approached him later. After he had a chance to work through whatever her actions had stirred.

Resigned, Philippa clutched her reins and leaned over Matilda. "Let us continue. I'm not yet finished with our ride, and you seem to be enjoying yourself too."

After walking a few minutes along the cliff path, Philippa led her mount away from the breathtaking view of the ocean and cut through a lush green field. With the wind rushing over her face and the scent of the sea behind her, she could almost forget the daunting task she'd undertaken in coming here. But then the tall spire of a church rose before her and she was instantly reminded of where her life was headed—to the altar with a man she'd no desire to wed.

Slowing Matilda, Philippa entered the town of Gerrans. At least she thought it was Gerrans. Mrs. Oldham had described Gerrans as being on the hill and Portscatho down on the bay—really not much farther away to warrant being a separate town, but it was.

She passed the medieval church on the right, which was surrounded by a large yard. Headstones marched neatly across the back. Was Ambrose's family buried there? His brother?

Further on were cottages and shop fronts, a small inn with a tavern. Then an open area with a few market stalls.

Curious, she dismounted and tethered Matilda to a post. The first stall offered baked pastries and sweetmeats. The delicious scents wafted in the air. So far the wonderful smells of the Roseland Peninsula were unparalleled.

The next stall was operated by a fishmonger, a red-cheeked woman perhaps ten years older than Philippa. She and her customer, a petite and voluptuous woman with blond hair, grew quiet and turned as Philippa approached.

"Good morning," Philippa greeted.

"Good morning," the fishmonger said. She gave Philippa a quick, inquisitive perusal. "Ye're new to town?"

Philippa nodded, unable to keep from glancing at the blond woman. She was quite striking with sparkling, cat-like eyes and full pink lips. Philippa returned her gaze to the fishmonger. "I'm visiting Beckwith."

The fishmonger's eyes widened briefly—so briefly, Philippa might've missed it. However, there was no mistaking the silent communication between her and the blonde.

The blonde offered a brilliant smile. "Allow me to introduce myself. I'm Miss Lettice Chandler."

Miss? She had to be at least a few years older than Philippa. Why was a beauty like her unmarried? *Maybe for the same reasons as Philippa.*

Pleased to meet a—perhaps—like-minded woman, Philippa returned her smile. "I'm Lady Philippa Latham."

Miss Chandler gestured to the woman in the stall. "Lady Philippa, this is Delores, our beloved fishmonger. You'll not want for fresh seafood on the Roseland Peninsula."

Philippa perused the array of fish and other creatures laid out behind Delores on a shaded table. "I can see not."

"Are you visiting from London, Lady Philippa?" Miss Chandler asked. "I'm from London."

"Indeed?" Two unmarried misses from London meeting all the way in Cornwall—what were the odds of such an occurrence? "Your family relocated here? That's quite a distance."

Delores made a small sound and bent her head. Miss Chandler shot her a glance, but Philippa couldn't determine if they were exchanging any sort of meaningful communication.

"I came here to marry," Miss Chandler said, "but unfortunately my betrothed passed on." How sad, yet why wouldn't she have returned to London? Philippa was curious, but possessed too much tact to ask. Lydia would ask, if she were here. Miss Chandler added, "It was long ago, and I'm betrothed again. Just recently in fact."

Long ago? Perhaps Miss Chandler had merely fallen in love with the Roseland Peninsula. Philippa could well understand that happening. She was already halfway there. "Congratulations."

Miss Chandler gestured toward the High Street. "Would you care to stroll?"

Why not? It wasn't as if Ambrose was waiting for her at Beckwith. "Yes, thank you."

They both nodded toward Delores before starting along the High Street.

"You're Lord Sevrin's guest?" Miss Chandler tipped her head and looked at her askance. "How is he?"

This wasn't a simple conversational question, based on the subtle glint in Miss Chandler's eye. A glint Philippa likely would've reflected in her own gaze if she'd asked that question. Suspicion inched up Philippa's neck.

How to answer? *He was an angry reprobate who'd ruined and abandoned her?* Philippa wanted to answer with her own question—*how should he be?*—but wasn't sure she wanted to know. Nervously, warily, she said, "He's well. He's training a fighter for a bout in Truro next week."

"I'd heard that. I'd no idea he was a pugilist." Clearly then, Miss Chandler had some knowledge of him.

Could she possibly be the woman Ambrose had ruined? Nigel's fiancée? Though Philippa had come to Cornwall for answers, now faced with Ambrose's past in the form of this beautiful woman, she couldn't quash the anxiety rising within her breast. "Miss Chandler, how do you know Sevrin?"

Miss Chandler stopped and turned toward her. "You haven't heard of me?"

There could be no question as to Miss Chandler's identity now. Philippa tensed. The sun seemed to grow hotter, the air more still. "Not by name, but I gather you're the woman he ruined." Well, the *other* woman he'd ruined, but she needn't share that information.

Miss Chandler reflected no surprise, no outrage. But then she'd lived with this blemish for years. Unlike Philippa, who still cringed whenever she thought of the day Lydia and her aunt had cut her on the street. "He's told you all about me then?"

"No, he has not." For that would involve a depth of trust they didn't share. If they did, she would've told him about her impending marriage and what she was really hoping to gain from this visit. "I know you were... lovers." The word nearly stuck in her throat. Heat raced up her neck and burned her cheeks. She glanced away. "And I know you were betrothed to his brother who apparently died by Ambrose's hand."

Miss Chandler's eyes widened. She raised her hand to her open mouth. "That's not what happened."

Philippa's heart raced. "Any of it?"

"We were lovers, yes, and I was betrothed to Nigel, but Ambrose didn't kill him."

"They say Ambrose and Nigel dueled. That Ambrose killed him."

Miss Chandler shook her head. A sheen of tears glistened in her eyes. "Forgive me." She withdrew a handkerchief from her pocket and dabbed at her eyes.

Philippa wanted to dislike the woman who Ambrose had chosen above his own brother, a woman who'd cuckolded her fiancé. However, Philippa recalled her own treatment of Allred and felt a peculiar connection to Miss Chandler.

Philippa gestured forward. "Come, let's walk."

Miss Chandler walked beside her. "Are you and Ambrose, that is... I should think you would hate me, but perhaps you don't possess a tendre for him."

Other women might've hated her, but Philippa wanted to get to the heart of Ambrose's pain and this woman could help her do that. "I'm here to see if Ambrose and I might suit."

"You're not betrothed?" Miss Chandler smiled ruefully and shook her head. "Of course not, Ambrose didn't even propose, did he?"

She felt a stab of pity for Miss Chandler. He'd given Philippa far more consideration than his former lover. "Actually, he did. I refused him."

Miss Chandler's mouth dropped open. "Why?"

"I didn't think he'd make a very good husband. And I'm still not sure. Why didn't he propose to you?"

"He didn't want to. But even if he did, I don't think he

would've married me. I'd only remind him of Nigel, of how he—how we—wronged him."

Philippa noted Miss Chandler said nothing of love. "But he took care of you. I mean, you're here, and you seem to be all right." It was really none of Philippa's business how Miss Chandler survived, but she was curious nonetheless.

"Yes, Ambrose purchased a cottage for me." She glanced away. "My father didn't want me to come back to London."

"I'm so sorry." Philippa wondered if her father would treat her the same if she refused to marry Sir Mortimer.

"He was so proud I was to marry a viscount. I hadn't given him much hope, you see. Plenty of men were interested, but none of them offered for me. When Nigel patronized Father's shop—he's a tailor—and fell in love with me, Father was thrilled. He could hardly wait for us to go to Cornwall and marry, which was Nigel's preference."

"And when you didn't marry, he didn't want you to return home."

Miss Chandler shook her head. "I haven't corresponded with him in five years."

"I'm sorry to hear that."

"Don't be. I created my own mess. I don't blame my father. He had high expectations for me, and I failed him."

Just as Philippa's father had expectations of her. She appreciated his concern for her to marry, not just for her family's reputation, but also for her future. At least, she hoped such thoughts motivated his actions. Still, Philippa was reluctant to marry Sir Mortimer when she didn't love him and doubted she ever would. She looked at Miss Chandler. "Did you love Nigel?"

"Regrettably, no. He deserved so much better than I gave him. I needed to marry, or at least I thought I did." Her cheeks flushed scarlet. "Pardon me, I'd rather not speak of it. Some things are better left buried, especially my past behavior."

"I didn't mean to pry." Philippa recognized their conversation had become overly personal, but Miss Chandler had been quite forthcoming. However, Philippa didn't wish to cause her pain.

"It's all right. I know you're only trying to learn about what happened. It must matter to you since you're trying to determine his suitability."

It did matter, but not at the cost of Miss Chandler's comfort. "Don't feel as if you need to share anything further with me."

"No, I think it's good you understand Ambrose's behavior at that time. Though, of course, I've no idea how he is now."

Philippa couldn't keep herself from asking, "How was he then?"

Miss Chandler glanced up at the sky with a wistful expression. "Wickedly charming, overwhelmingly attractive, incorrigibly flirtatious." That sounded very like the Ambrose Philippa had met at Lockwood House. "I was smitten the moment I met him."

Philippa suffered a wave of jealousy. Miss Chandler had fallen for Ambrose, and they'd engaged in a torrid affair. But he'd painstakingly kept himself from Philippa. Suddenly her goal to make him fall in love with her seemed insurmountable.

Miss Chandler looked down. "So smitten that I wouldn't have noticed the tension between he and Nigel, except that Mrs. Oldham was quite vocal about it. Nigel returned from London intent on assuming a more managerial role at Beckwith. Ambrose didn't like that. He'd been raised to expect Beckwith and the title would be his. Nigel told me their father had made it clear the future of Beckwith depended upon Ambrose."

Philippa imagined a young man who'd felt entitled to a life that didn't really belong to him. A young man who'd been encouraged to succeed, driven to do so, but had then been told he was no longer necessary. "Ambrose felt betrayed."

"Yes, he felt as if his birthright was being stripped from him. At the same time, Nigel was bitter about Ambrose's strengths and the way everyone admired him. They'd been pitted— through no fault of their own—against each other."

"How awful for both of them. May I ask how Nigel died?"

Miss Chandler's eyes darkened, and her lips tightened. "He fell from Ambrose's horse."

Which was why Ambrose didn't ride. No wonder he'd seemed so unbearably apprehensive in the stables. It also explained his reaction to her touching the horse his brother had fallen from and probably his reaction earlier when she'd turned in the saddle. "Orpheus?"

Miss Chandler nodded.

That poor, magnificent animal. He clearly missed his master. And given Ambrose's horsemanship, he had to have missed riding all this time, yet he'd denied himself anyway. What else did he deny himself for the sake of guilt?

They walked a moment without speaking. Birds flew overhead, and the breeze stirred Philippa's hair. "The peninsula is so beautiful. Although you may have been stranded here, it can't have been a hardship." She looked at Miss Chandler with a half-smile.

Miss Chandler's lips curved up in response. "Not at all. It's home to me now. How long will you be staying?"

"Not long unfortunately, a week perhaps." Or less, if she was unable to make any progress with Ambrose. Right now, establishing a bond with him seemed as far-fetched as swimming the channel to France.

"Such a short time? If you leave, you can't come to my wedding."

Philippa wasn't sure attending Miss Chandler's wedding would be appropriate, but appreciated the sentiment. "I'm afraid I'm due at my Father's house. Depending on what happens with Ambrose, I'll be married in a month myself."

Miss Chandler's eyes widened. "You're betrothed to someone else?"

"Not formally, but my father has arranged a marriage. Since I've no other prospects, I must consider this option."

"You do have other prospects. You have Ambrose."

Philippa laughed, though she felt no mirth. Her situation seemed completely hopeless at the moment. "I 'have' nothing."

Miss Chandler stopped and turned toward Philippa. "That's not true. He proposed to you once. You're here—and he hasn't tossed you out. You're already far ahead of me."

Unfortunately, Philippa wasn't sure it was enough.

Chapter Nineteen

AMBROSE ran Demetrius across Beckwith until they were both exhausted. Ambrose's thighs protested, unaccustomed as they were to being in the saddle. But it felt good.

He hated that.

After Nigel's death, Ambrose had vowed never to ride again. Just as he'd vowed never to touch another woman after Lettice.

Depriving himself of his two favorite things had seemed a fitting punishment for his selfish behavior. And now, because the riding felt so damned good, he hated himself all over again. As if he'd ever stopped. How did one possibly manage all of that self-contempt?

By fighting whenever he was overwhelmed with pain. He needed a goddamned fight and not a practice session.

Or a really good fuck. Which was completely out of the question. He'd capitulated to riding, and he refused to do the same with sex. In spite of Philippa pushing him to the brink of his control.

A fight then. But not in Gerrans or Portscatho. He didn't want to venture into those towns. Not because he cared about his reception—people likely still despised him and he couldn't fault them for it. There were too many memories, too many shared experiences of a life he'd buried and which he preferred stayed that way.

And of course there was Lettice. If he could leave the Roseland Peninsula without seeing her, he'd count himself lucky.

Leave the Roseland Peninsula.

Though he'd ridden a few miles inland, the scent of the sea permeated the air. The sun was hot and bright. He removed his hat and let the heat seep into his scalp. He closed his eyes and listened to the birds, the distant bleat of Beckwith's sheep, the sound of his heart breaking anew. How he'd missed this place.

Five years was a long time to nurture regret. Had he really expected to spend the rest of his earthly existence over a tavern in London? Fighting and paying only cursory attention to his responsibilities?

He supposed not.

But neither had he given thought to what he might do with the years that stretched before him. Save his punishments and his avowal to never marry, he had no plans at all. No ambition. He was even content to let his second cousin inherit. Or so he'd schooled himself to feel.

His father had raised him to manage Beckwith and to establish himself as a leader within the Roseland Peninsula. Considering Ambrose hadn't been the heir, it had been a peculiar goal, though easily explained because no one had expected Nigel to live long enough to inherit. Including Ambrose.

Which didn't excuse what he'd done. Nigel had lived longer than anyone had predicted and might even still be here today if not for Ambrose's selfishness and entitlement.

The hell with it.

Ambrose turned around and started back, though at a slower pace than he'd come. Would he find Philippa where he'd left her? Had she returned to the stables or continued on her ride? He ought not to have left her like that, but one could expect little else from a selfish ass like himself.

What was he going to do with her? Try to ignore her the next week? Throw her out as he'd done with Lettice? No, she deserved better. Lettice had deserved better. At least he'd purchased her that cottage, not that it alleviated his conscience much.

When Ambrose finally arrived back at the stable yard, just before luncheon, Welch gave him a high-browed stare. He said nothing, but took Demetrius's reins, which was just as well because Ambrose had no desire to go into the stable and see Orpheus. Though he'd consented to ride today, he still wasn't sure if he'd do so again.

What bullshit. Now that he'd done it, he couldn't not ride again. It was as if he'd picked the wound open and couldn't staunch the flow of blood. Which meant he'd have to work twice as hard to keep himself from the other temptation—Philippa.

With that in mind, he decided to head directly to his bedchamber where he could banish her from his mind the only way he knew how, if only for a small while.

By the time he arrived upstairs, he was strung so tight he thought he might explode. But then he supposed that's exactly what he needed to do. Now, by his own hand. Anticipation coursed through him, brought his prick to attention.

He went to the windows on the other side of his bed and looked out over the ocean. So blue and pure. Full of possibility. Free of the past.

He stripped his coat and waistcoat from his heated body and cast them to the floor. The staccato of his breathing filled his ears as he unbuttoned his fall. He braced one hand on the casement and with the other pulled his cock from his drawers. Half-erect, he stroked his flesh until it hardened and heated beneath his fingers.

He inevitably thought of Philippa's dark sable hair and ale-colored eyes. Her pale, creamy flesh, the rise of her breasts and the pucker of her lush, pink nipples. Then he thought of her hand replacing his. He sucked in air as the blood flowed to his cock in earnest. He moved his hand faster, thinking of her lips stretching around him, taking him in her mouth, sucking him deep and hard.

He almost heard the soft rustle of her skirts, smelled the delicious scent of her lilac and honey perfume, felt the rush of her breath over him. Blood surged in his cock, urging him toward orgasm.

Cool fingers wrapped around his hand. His eyes flew open. She was *there*.

Philippa returned from her outing determined to make progress with Ambrose. After refreshing herself in her chamber before luncheon, she decided to exit through the sitting room that accessed both her and Ambrose's rooms.

The door to his room was not quite closed. She stepped closer. Was he there? She thought she'd heard someone, but it could've been any of the servants.

Or Ambrose.

Tentatively, she opened the door wider. Her breath caught. Silhouetted against the windows, his hand supporting his weight, he was…pleasuring himself.

Heat rushed over her, and her mouth went dry. She'd always found him attractive, enjoyed kissing him and touching him, but seeing this… She was overcome with the need to join him.

Slowly, anxiously, her breathing shallow, she crossed his room, her footfalls soundless against the dense carpet. His face was turned toward the windows. He gave no inclination he heard her approach.

His sharp, uneven breaths filled her senses. Her breasts grew heavy, and her legs quivered.

He still wore his breeches, but his penis was in his hand. Long and dark and hard, he stroked its length. His eyes were closed, the muscles of his extended arm bulged beneath the fine linen of his shirt.

She had to touch him. Now.

She slid her hand over his, stroking his shaft with him. He stopped. His eyes flew open. Glazed and unfocused, they turned uneasy upon seeing her.

"Why are you here?" His voice was low and broken, sounding as if it came from the back of his throat.

Philippa swallowed. She didn't think she could bear it if he turned her away. "I want to be."

"You shouldn't touch me," he rasped, though he didn't push her hand away.

There was no place for the word *shouldn't* in her mind just then. This moment was about need and satisfying herself—both of them—at last. "I have to."

"God, Philippa."

She dropped to her knees and moved her hand over his. He pivoted toward her. He put his hand on top of hers and showed her how to glide her fingers along his length.

His flesh was velvety soft, but it covered a rod of stone. She imagined what it would feel like slipping inside of her. She squeezed her thighs together and felt shockingly wet there.

He pressed her hand around him. "Harder."

She gripped him more securely, and slid her hand to the tip and back to the base again. A drop of moisture beaded at the end. She touched her thumb to it. Warm and a bit thick, she massaged it around the head.

"Faster," he urged.

She looked up at him. His gaze—glassy and hot—fixed on her. His features were taut. He appeared utterly enslaved.

Feminine power coursed through her. She squeezed him and pumped her hand along his shaft. Another bead of liquid rewarded her efforts. Emboldened by his stare, she leaned forward and touched her tongue to the tip. He tasted salty and masculine. Unbearably aroused, she licked at him and kissed the head.

He groaned then dropped to his knees.

She continued stroking him as he wrapped his arms around her. Then his mouth devoured hers, his tongue thrusting inside. He was hot and delicious and everything she never knew she wanted.

He gripped the back of her neck, holding her to his hungry kiss. He licked and sucked. She nearly died in ecstasy, amazed that a kiss could feel so good.

Vaguely, she still clasped his penis, but her movements had been arrested by all he was doing to her. She couldn't think, couldn't focus on anything but the sensations he gave her. Then he pulled back from their kiss and jerked at the front of her gown. With a few rough tugs, her bodice gaped and then his fingers were plucking the ties of her stays. Quickly, savagely, he laid her breasts bare. He looked his fill. Again, power surged through her.

With one hand, he rolled her nipple between his fingertips. She closed her eyes, glorying in his touch. Then he pinched her sensitive flesh and she lost herself completely, dissolving against him. She clutched at his shoulders, an anchor lest she drown.

He cupped both of her breasts. Firmly. Sensually. Yes, *yes*, this is what she wanted, what she needed.

His mouth came down on hers. Open, hot, greedy. She pulled at his neck and thrust her tongue against his.

He pushed her back until she was flat against the carpet. She opened her eyes as she stretched out beneath him. He threw his leg over her hips, straddling her on his knees. He bent over her and drove his tongue deeper into her mouth, filling her deliciously. She pressed up against him, seeking more of his kiss, more of his hand, more of everything.

His lips left hers and trailed down her neck. His hands continued their sweet torture. Her breasts ached, and she felt each stroke between her legs as a sharp, desperate need. She moaned shamelessly. "Please, Ambrose."

His mouth closed gently, reverently over her nipple, drawing on her heated flesh. She arched up to him and laced her fingers through his hair. *More. Don't ever leave me.*

His mouth clamped down and he suckled her. Heat rushed to her core, and she cried out. His fingers tightened around her other nipple, drawing on it. Sensation spiraled through her. She thrust her hips upward, seeking something to ease the ache between her thighs. An ache that intensified with each lick and caress.

"Please."

He bent low again and licked her other breast. She tugged on his hair, holding him close. His hand worked down her side and caressed her waist, then her hip. But there was still fabric between them. She wanted to feel him naked against her.

"Please," she said again, her voice small and breathless.

He pushed her skirt up. Baring her thighs. Again, he stared down at her as if he'd never seen such beauty.

Lightly, he stroked her inner thigh. She sighed softly, loving his touch. Then his fingers were there, against her core. So close… She opened her legs because it seemed necessary. He slid his finger inside of her, and she gasped at the sudden intrusion.

He froze, staring down at her. He withdrew his finger and sat back on his heels. His gaze locked on her again, but it wasn't the same. It was as if he didn't see her. He inched backward.

"Ambrose." She sat up and reached for him. "Don't stop."

His eyes were wide, frightened almost. What had happened? "What's wrong?" She wrapped her hand around his wrist.

He pulled away from her and scrambled to his feet, turning his back to her.

Cold air rushed over her exposed flesh. She pulled her bodice together and got to her feet.

"You should go." He sounded broken again.

No, she hadn't come all this way, hadn't finally breached the outer wall of his defenses to turn back now. "I'd rather finish what we started."

He kept his back to her. "I won't ruin you. Not that way."

She moved to stand behind him. "I'm already ruined, damn you. You might as well do me the courtesy of experiencing what that means!"

He spun around. His dark eyes were wild. He looked a bit mad. "I can't touch you. I won't. I won't *actually* ruin you."

Scrupulously, she stripped her clothes from her body and let them pool at her feet. She notched up her chin and held her breath at her daring. But she'd nothing to lose. Nothing she wasn't more than willing to give. "I'm asking you to, Ambrose."

His eyes glittered dangerously in the afternoon sunlight streaming from the windows behind her back. He swallowed then lifted his hand. He stroked his thumb down her throat. She arched her neck, casting her head back. She nearly moaned at the contact, but held her tongue, lest he retreat again.

His hand moved lower, sliding over her collarbone and stroking her breast. His touch was rough, and he tweaked her nipple. Her legs quivered, and she bit her lip.

He trailed his finger down the center of her belly, over her navel. He brushed horizontally over the top of the curls at the apex of her thighs. Slowly, agonizingly. His hand cupped her mound and pressed against her.

Unable to remain silent a second longer, she moaned and closed her eyes. His finger touched the top of her cleft. Exquisite sensation exploded. His finger didn't move, just stayed pressed against her.

She opened her eyes and saw that his eyes had slitted, and his mouth was drawn tight. He looked to be almost in agony. He'd been seemingly close to release when she'd first arrived. She reached for his penis and found it hot and hard.

He jumped back. "Go!"

She stared at him a moment, saw the fury in his gaze. With shaking hands, she plucked up her clothes and struggled into them. He had refastened his breeches and moved to stand at the fireplace with his back to her.

She'd pushed him too far. He wanted her, that was certain, but he was keeping himself from her and she was determined to learn why.

When she was decently clothed, she took a deep breath. *Patience and kindness, patience and kindness. Show him he can trust you.* "How was your ride this morning?"

He turned and glanced at her, glowering.

"I still haven't had a proper tour of Beckwith. Perhaps we could try again tomorrow."

He didn't look at her, but ran his hand through his hair until it boyishly poked this way and that. "I'll consider it." He turned and left.

She exhaled. *Patience and kindness.*

Ambrose's opponent's massive fist caught him in the chin. For the third time, Ambrose's skull jarred, and his teeth knocked together. He danced back, narrowly evading another strike.

A fight had seemed the perfect solution tonight for his frustrated mind and body, but for some reason he couldn't focus. He was slow, ineffective, distracted.

For some reason. he knew bloody well what reason: Philippa.

Though he'd avoided her the rest of the day, she'd been ever present in his mind. Even now when he was supposed to be chasing his agitation away.

He'd come so close to breaking his vow of celibacy. And so close to treating her as badly as he'd treated Lettice. Philippa deserved far more than a tumble or two with him.

His huge opponent—a brute called Weatherly—cornered him at the edge of the roped square and hit him in the ribs and the side. Ambrose moved left, sluggishly, and cursed his lethargy.

Vaguely he heard Oldham yelling at him to go down. He *should* put an end to this mockery of a fight, but goddamn it he hadn't gotten what he'd come for.

Snarling, he attacked the larger, wider Weatherly. He was bigger even than Hopkins. Ambrose would take him anyway. He drove several hits toward the man's face and head and chest, but despite his lumbering size, the bastard was fast. He connected with Ambrose's nose and that was it.

Blood gushed from Ambrose's nostrils, coating his lips, filling his mouth, dribbling over his chin. Christ, he hoped he hadn't broken his nose again. He went down on his knees, fury coursing through his defeated body.

Oldham, who'd been designated as his second, rushed into the square. "You all right?"

Ambrose touched his nose gingerly. Not broken, just bloodied. He nodded slightly, but tipped his head back in an effort to staunch the blood. "Towel."

Oldham rushed away and then returned. The count was up to twenty, Ambrose thought, but between the blood streaming down his face and the failure screaming in his head, he couldn't be certain.

A towel came down over his face as cheers arose. Weatherly must've been pronounced the winner. "Sorry," Oldham said. "Never been a second before."

"S'all right," Ambrose slurred. He spit out a mouthful of blood and dragged the towel over his lips. Then he bunched the fabric up and pressed it to his nose. "Up."

Oldham helped him stand and led him from the ring. Ackley and Oldham's son, Ned, awaited them outside the rope. Ambrose hadn't been overcome with such utter failure since the last time he'd lost a fight, at least four years ago.

"Hell of a show," Ackley said, his tone tinged with sarcasm.

Ambrose cast him a sidelong glance. "I was showing you what not to do."

"In that case, superior effort."

Ambrose considered punching Ackley. However, given his current inaccuracy, inefficacy, and overall inadequacy, he settled for glaring at his protégé. Not that Ackley was paying any attention. He was staring across the room at a stocky fellow with a wide brow and deep-set eyes. He returned Ackley's interest.

"That yer opponent next week?" Oldham asked.

Ambrose lowered his head enough to get a good look at their opposition. He was shorter, but wider than Ackley, with a decidedly mean countenance.

Ackley nodded. "It is."

The blood from Ambrose's nose had slowed to a trickle. He pulled the towel away. "Good, after seeing me tonight, perhaps he'll assume you're terrible."

Oldham snorted. "Is that why ye fought so bad?"

No. He'd fought so poorly because his every thought was consumed with Philippa. Her scent. The sparkle in her eyes. The silken feel of her hand wrapped around his prick. Christ, he was going half-erect for the thirtieth time that day.

As they made their way through the crowded room, located at the back of an inn in Truro, Ambrose overheard part of a conversation:

"Should've put me money on the giant."

"Eh, you always do bet on the weaklings."

From a woman, "He didn't appear weak. Shame his skill didn't back up his looks." The disappointment dripping from her tone was enough to thoroughly drench him in shame. Both because of his failure and because of his resulting anger. He ought to feel satisfied—hadn't he quit fighting to avoid people's admiration?—but no, he was furious. Irrationally livid.

The discontent curdling his veins all day boiled until every hurt he'd received in the fight blistered and burned. He stalked from the rear door of the inn into an alleyway that led around to the street. Ned brushed by him, going ahead to fetch the coach.

By the time they emerged on the street, Ambrose's nose had stopped bleeding.

Oldham eyed him. "Ye'll need cleaning up when we get back to Beckwith."

An almost fifteen-mile trip that would take them two hours or more in the dark. Ambrose was considering staying in town when a gentleman paused beside him.

"Ambrose?" The man swiftly removed his hat. "It's me, Thatcher."

Ambrose had recognized him immediately. They'd been friends at university.

"Blimey, it's been at least five years." Thatcher smiled broadly. "Grab an ale with me." And then, as if he'd just noticed Ambrose's face, his brow furrowed. "What happened to you?"

Yes, give me the ridicule I deserve. "I was in a fight."

Thatcher glanced around. "Where's the villain? I'll take care of him."

Ambrose blinked, unsure of what to make of that reaction. He wanted to take up for him?

"Nah," Oldham interjected. "His lordship fought at the inn."

"His lordship...right." Thatcher looked a bit sheepish. "I'd forgotten you're the viscount."

"Don't worry about it," Ambrose said. Their friendship had predated Nigel's death and thus Ambrose's inheritance. "Unfortunately we're returning to Beckwith, so perhaps another time."

Thatcher nodded, his gaze turning uncomfortable. "I hadn't even heard you were back. Yes, another time." He offered his hand. Ambrose took it and with the grasp came a flood of bittersweet memories. Before he'd ruined everything. He reflected on all the things he'd lost—friendship, respect, the joy of shared experiences—and tonight's defeat scorched him anew.

Thatcher passed on. Ambrose watched him walk away and wondered when it would ever be "another time."

Where was the goddamned coach?

Oldham stepped close to him, keeping his voice low so Ackley couldn't hear. "We could stay in town. Ye should get that ale with yer friend."

Thatcher wasn't his friend anymore. Hopkins and Saxton were the only people who could call themselves that, and after what had happened at Benfield Ambrose wasn't even sure about Saxton anymore. "That's not necessary."

"No, but it might be nice. I've noticed ye don't allow yerself much enjoyment. Ever since ye've been back, ye work, ye train with Ackley. Ye didn't even ride until today."

Ambrose scowled at him. "I don't need nice."

Oldham's dark brows drew together. "Ye keep talking about what ye need. What about what ye want? Ye used to be a fun-loving bloke. Before all that mess with yer brother, but don't you think it's time—"

"No, I don't think it's time, and you'd do best not to mention it to me again."

The coach rolled up then. Ned jumped down from the box and opened the door. Oldham took the rear-facing seat, while Ambrose and Ackley took the front-facing. Ned returned to the box beside the coachman, and the coach moved forward.

A half hour later, they were out of Truro making their way slowly in the dark. The moon was nearly full, which offered a bit of light in addition to their exterior lanterns. Ackley's soft snores filled the coach.

Ambrose couldn't relax enough to sleep. He couldn't relax enough to even find a comfortable position. He shifted in his seat, futilely trying to at least turn his mind off, if not find slumber.

"Do ye think yer brother would like the miserable bastard ye've become?" Oldham asked, his voice furious.

Oldham's words struck him like a flurry of blows. Ambrose welcomed his anger. "I'm certain he didn't like the selfish, arrogant prick I was and wouldn't give a damn what happened to me."

"I disagree. Yer brother loved ye."

The tension in Ambrose's body multiplied until his neck ached and his body thrummed with the need for release. "I told you not to talk about this."

"Someone's got to, otherwise ye'll have yer fight and go back to London." Oldham's tone had lost its edge, but he leaned forward intently. "Beckwith needs ye."

Nobody needed him. Or at least they shouldn't. "Beckwith has done fine in my absence."

"Aye, but it could be flourishing. The way ye teach and guide that boy, that's the way ye used to be. Ye could be that way again. Ye saw that bloke in Truro, he doesn't blame ye. What's past is past."

It couldn't be that simple. He didn't get to regain his life a mere five years after stealing Nigel's. Could his brother's memory be forgotten in so short a span? Ambrose wouldn't let it. "I blame me, and that's all that matters."

Oldham sat back with a wave of his hand. "Eh, I guess ye're still selfish. Go on then and wallow in yer self-pity. Ignore the people who need ye. If ye really wanted to honor yer brother's memory, ye'd stay and make things right again."

Fury and pain and shame exploded inside him. "I can't ever make things right!" Ambrose's chest heaved, his body shook. He grappled for air, for a shred of reason.

For a moment the only sounds in the coach were Ambrose's rapid breaths. Ackley had ceased snoring.

Ambrose felt a hand clap his knee. "Ye can make things better. Give these people—yer people—a chance."

Ambrose sat back against the squab, ice filling his veins. Was Oldham right? Was he being selfish by ignoring Beckwith? He'd thought to remove himself, that everyone preferred his absence. But what kind of man left his estate to the care of others and eschewed his responsibility for the sake of penance? A selfish coward.

The realization hit him harder than anything his opponent had delivered tonight. His shaking slowed, but he was still filled with dark apprehension. Not because of his anger or his unsatisfied need for self-punishment, but because he was afraid of finding satisfaction in life again, of forgetting nigel, of forgiving himself. What would happen to his soul then?

Chapter Twenty

PHILIPPA awoke the following morning with one goal in mind: find Ambrose and insist upon the tour he was "considering." She made her way to the breakfast room and stopped short at the threshold. Ambrose was eating at the table. He was never in the breakfast room.

He must not have heard her approach, for he didn't look up. Or perhaps he was purposefully ignoring her. Either way, she took advantage of the moment to simply watch him.

His dark hair was neatly combed, and from what she could see above the edge of the table, he was immaculately garbed with a white shirt and cravat, dark blue waistcoat, and a coat of nearly the same color. A shadow fell across his face, no, wait, that discoloration wasn't a shadow.

Philippa was beside him in a trice. "Were you in a fight last night?"

He looked up at her. His rich brown eyes raked her from head to waist until he seemed to remember himself and snapped his gaze to her face. "Yes."

His imperfect nose was bruised, along with his chin.

She wanted to touch him, to smooth away his pains, but had vowed to take things slow. "Does it hurt?"

He shrugged. "A bit."

"Was it a planned bout? I didn't realize you were still fighting. I thought you were training Ackley."

"I—" He hesitated. "I like to fight." His gaze was direct, unapologetic.

She'd seen him fight, had cared for him in the aftermath. "I can't imagine why."

He stood. A waft of sandalwood and sage tickled her senses. "That's not exactly a mark in my favor. Remember that when you're determining my worth. Have a good day." He inclined his head rather formally and departed.

She watched him go with a frown. She hadn't even had a chance to ask him about taking a tour today.

"Lady Philippa?"

Philippa turned at the sound of Mrs. Oldham's voice. "Good morning," she said with a cheeriness she didn't feel.

"Shall I bring your breakfast?"

"Yes, please." Though Ambrose's behavior was disappointing, she wasn't about to give up that easily. "Mrs. Oldham, where is his lordship going today?"

Mrs. Oldham's eyes lit, and her mouth curved up. Philippa had never seen the woman smile with regard to Ambrose. "He's going to visit with the tenants."

He was? From what Philippa had gleaned, he'd avoided his tenants at all costs. His ride yesterday had been his first foray onto the estate. What had changed to draw him out? Whatever the cause, Philippa recognized it as a good thing. Obviously Mrs. Oldham did too. She was beaming with satisfaction.

"You've been worried about him, haven't you?" Philippa asked.

The housekeeper nodded. "He's been gone a long time, and then to return for a fight and no other reason… That's not the Ambrose we remember."

It wasn't the Ambrose she thought she knew either. "Will you tell me about the Ambrose you remember?"

Mrs. Oldham's eyes took on a far-off cast. Then she smiled broadly. "He was so charming." Just as Lettice Chandler had said. "Always eager to help, a natural leader. The tenants admired and respected him. He'd organized many improvements and increased the sheep herd by more than half after he returned from university."

"He seems an excellent horseman."

"Oh, indeed. He's always been very athletic, so it's not

surprising he's such a successful pugilist." Her features darkened. "Though it's a sport I never would have thought he'd undertake."

"Why is that?"

"When Nigel—his brother—went to Oxford, he was routinely beaten by a group of boys. No one knew until Nigel came home at the end of his first year. Ambrose had vowed to thrash every one of them, though he was several years younger of course, but Nigel made him promise not to. Nigel didn't care for violence at all."

Philippa was confused. "Why would his brother's opinions affect him so much? Were they close?" Given what—granted, little—she knew, she'd assumed they weren't.

"Yes, quite. Until Ambrose came back from university. Their father had died, leaving Nigel as the viscount. Everyone assumed Ambrose would be the viscount one day. Nigel's health was so weak. He wasn't expected to survive to adulthood."

Miss Chandler had provided the same information, but it was satisfying to have corroboration. "Ambrose became bitter."

Mrs. Oldham nodded. "They argued often. Ambrose was thinking of leaving, but then Nigel went to London and things returned to the way they'd been before, with Ambrose in charge."

"Then Nigel returned with his fiancée, and things grew worse."

"Yes, Nigel tried to assert himself, which was absolutely his right. However, he didn't take his brother's role or his feelings into account. Though he wasn't the viscount, Ambrose *was* the master of Beckwith."

Philippa's heart ached for the brothers, both trying to carve their places and hurting each other in the process. "I believe I'll ride out today as well."

Mrs. Oldham nodded briskly. "I'll just fetch your breakfast." She turned to go, but then paused. She looked back over her shoulder. "You're a lovely young woman. I don't know what happened to bring you here, but I do hope his lordship will realize what's within his reach."

Philippa thought Mrs. Oldham meant her, but asked anyway,

just to be sure. "And what's that?"

"Love."

As Mrs. Oldham retreated to the kitchens, Philippa staggered to a chair. Yes, it was within his grasp, but would he take it? Philippa's life flashed before her—marrying Ambrose, loving him, but he didn't love her back.

Just like her mother had fruitlessly loved her father. And oh, how that hurt.

When Ambrose arrived at the stables, he jerked to a stop. Welch was leading Orpheus from his stall. The horse put his nose up and immediately began dancing toward him.

Welch gripped the lead tighter. "Sorry, my lord. Didn't know you were coming."

Ambrose swallowed, his throat suddenly tight. He stepped forward. "You're going to exercise him?"

Welch nodded. "Unless you'd like to do it?"

Orpheus whinnied and tried to move closer to Ambrose. Ambrose clenched his hands with resolve. Just as he couldn't continue to punish the tenants of Beckwith for his wrongs, he could no longer punish Orpheus. The fall that had killed Nigel hadn't been the animal's fault. It had been Ambrose's.

"I'll do it," Ambrose said.

The groom came forward and handed him the lead.

Orpheus nuzzled Ambrose's head. His throat closed tighter, but he managed to get out, "Fetch my saddle."

Welch's brow furrowed. "You'll ride?"

Was that a problem? "Someone's been riding him, yes?"

"I have, and so has Oldham, periodically."

"Yes, I'll ride."

Welch nodded and took himself off to the tack room.

Ambrose petted Orpheus's nose. He'd missed this animal. More notably, he'd missed this pull of emotion, this sense of fitting together. He'd had a taste of it with Philippa. He recalled that first night, holding her in the coach on the way to Herrick House, their series of disasters behind them. In that moment he'd belonged to her and she to him.

Orpheus whinnied louder and met Ambrose's palm with his questing nose. He allowed a small smile. "I've been an ass. None of this was your fault."

Orpheus nuzzled him and rested his nose against Ambrose's cheek. He closed his eyes a moment and patted Orpheus's dark head. He'd no idea how good forgiveness—albeit from a horse—could feel. He ought to try it with himself some day.

Welch returned. Carefully, as if he were completing an act of contrition, Ambrose saddled Orpheus. He spoke to him quietly, affectionately, slowly rebuilding their bond. When he was finished, Ambrose took him out into the yard. The morning was bright; pale clouds skimmed across the blue sky. The breeze was strong off the bay, carrying the salty tang of the sea. Ambrose was glad he'd left his hat behind this morning, preferring to feel the air through his hair.

He swung himself atop Orpheus, and they launched down the path as if they'd never been apart. He cut west across Beckwith's lands. His lands.

He took Orpheus to a canter, but only for a moment. Time and regret fell away, and they were moving at a full run.

The wind whipped over him and the fields blurred, his sheep white streaks as he and Orpehus flew by. Instead of going to see a tenant as he'd planned, he found himself at the ruins of the small cottage he and Lettice had used for their rendezvous. Though he'd ordered the building demolished, memories he'd kept long buried returned with blistering force.

Nigel throwing open the door. Lettice shrieking. Ambrose pulling on his breeches and following Nigel outside. Nigel shooting him in the shoulder and then riding off. Ambrose chasing him. The sickening crack of Nigel's head as it struck the rock.

Ambrose shook as he recalled the blood and his brother's unresponsiveness. Then the sheer horror of knowing Nigel would never wake up.

Hoof beats drew him to turn in his saddle. Philippa was bearing down on him.

He turned back, swearing. Every time he saw her, he was reminded of how he could barely control himself. How he'd ruined her and how he couldn't hope to fix the situation.

She rode up beside him and offered a brilliant smile that squeezed Ambrose's chest. "I was hoping to take that tour."

He walked Orpheus away from her. "I'm busy today."

She pressed her lips together. "Yes, I understood you were visiting tenants, but there aren't any around here, so forgive me if I argue you don't appear *busy*." Her brows drew together. "What happened to the Ambrose I met at Lockwood House? The one who leapt to my assistance, who kept me from harm and from scandal—at least for a while."

"That Ambrose is the same one who ultimately plunged you headfirst into ruin."

She inclined her head. "I like him just the same. As well as the one who somehow caused his brother's death."

Ambrose flinched. He turned Orpheus from her.

She followed him. "I see how tortured you are. I would help you. If you'd let me."

He pivoted to look at her. "I'm here for a prizefight, not to face the past." That had been his intent anyway, but he could not longer deny that he *had* to face it. That or leave his beloved home again.

"And I'm here to determine my future. Unless you'd rather I go before the ten days are up."

She sat very still, as if she were holding her breath. Allowing her to stay meant keeping his distance, physically. The one thing he couldn't go back on—at least not now—was his vow of celibacy. It was a five-year-old promise he'd managed to keep, and breaking it seemed somehow dishonorable. He feared doing so would make him feel less like the man he was trying to be.

"You can stay, but my sentiments haven't changed."

She nodded. "Would you at least let me try to help you? As your friend?"

As his friend. It was the most he could hope for. How he wished he'd met her at a different time, in a different life.

"How do you propose to do that?"

She shrugged, her frame seeming to relax. "Why don't we start with that tour?"

What harm could come from showing her around Beckwith?

He had calls to make anyway. "Let's go."

Three days later, Philippa accompanied Ambrose on a now-routine afternoon ride. In fact, the past few days had followed a welcome pattern. In the morning, Philippa walked to Gerrans and visited the market stalls. She chatted with the various merchants and met the town's residents who greeted her with kindness and warmth. They were delighted to meet a guest of Lord Sevrin's—nearly as delighted as they were to have him back on the peninsula.

After taking luncheon with Ambrose and Mr. Ackley, she and Ambrose rode around the estate, as they were doing now. They approached a cottage, and Ambrose motioned for them to dismount.

He helped Philippa from her horse. "I need to speak with Mr. Lerner. His shearing shed needs repair."

Philippa nodded. Each afternoon they listened to the tenants' concerns and complaints. Ambrose heard them all with interest and care, and often stayed to provide assistance. While he was busy, Philippa spoke to the tenants' wives who were universally complimentary of Ambrose's return and inquisitive about Philippa's presence. She merely smiled and said she was a guest from London.

Ambrose led her down the path to the cottage's door and knocked three times. Mrs. Lerner—presumably—answered.

She bobbed a simply curtsey. "Good afternoon, your lordship."

"Good afternoon, Mrs. Lerner. How are your boys?"

Philippa was amazed at how Ambrose recalled every tenant and every member of their family. She could see how he was truly master of Beckwith—or had been.

Mrs. Lerner regarded Ambrose skeptically. "Well, thank you. Mr. Lerner is out back."

Ambrose nodded once. "May I present my guest, Lady Philippa Latham? Will it be all right if she remains here while I speak with your husband?"

Mrs. Lerner eyed Philippa. "Certainly, my lord."

Ambrose leaned down to Philippa. "I won't be long." His breath caressed her ear, and she suppressed a delightful shiver.

After he left, Mrs. Lerner invited her inside and closed the door. "Would you care for tea?"

"Yes, thank you."

Mrs. Lerner retreated to a back room. Philippa moved further into the cottage, to a main living area furnished with a worn settee and three rather comfortable looking chairs. A few minutes later Mrs. Lerner returned with a small tray. She set it on a table and poured the tea. "Cream and sugar?"

"Yes, thank you." Philippa had been nervous during her first such encounter a couple of days ago, but everyone had been so welcoming, she now felt at ease.

Mrs. Lerner handed Philippa her cup then tended to her own. "It's good his lordship finally came home. Will you be staying here with him?" She glanced up at Philippa.

No one else had chanced such a forward question, but Philippa had been expecting it. And since thus far she had no cause to believe otherwise, she answered, "I'll be returning to London in a few days."

"Oh." Mrs. Lerner sounded a bit disappointed.

Philippa didn't know what to make of that and so she ignored the reaction. "Are the shed repairs extensive?"

"Not terribly, especially if Lord Sevrin helps. And I've no doubt he will."

Everyone commented on Ambrose's helpfulness. He tried so hard to paint himself as an unworthy blackguard, but such sentiments only supported Philippa's argument that he was a better man than he realized. "Lord Sevrin seems to do more than the usual landowner."

"He always did, even before he was the viscount. Especially before." Mrs. Lerner's face pinked.

Philippa sought to put her at ease. "It's all right. I'm aware of his lordship's past…problems."

Mrs. Lerner relaxed and sipped her tea. "We're all right pleased he seems to have overcome that awful tragedy. We need him here, though I imagine it's been difficult coming back."

Philippa wouldn't reveal how difficult. "I think so, but

everyone has been so kind and welcoming."

"We're a close community. What happened was awful, but his lordship's absence was far more troubling for us. I do hope he stays, as long as his duty allows."

Philippa hoped so, too. In fact, she'd mention it to him. After another quarter hour, she and Ambrose took their leave.

They returned to Beckwith where Ambrose helped her dismount. His touch was gentle, but brief. She could only wonder what he felt, but every time she was near him, she recalled that first afternoon here in his chamber or that day in the stables at Benfield or that episode in the closet at Lady Anstruther's ball and she became aroused. She wanted him, but as her days here were dwindling, she began to accept she'd never have him.

She was also loath to leave the Roseland Peninsula. "Beckwith is beautiful. I've enjoyed being here. Indeed, I'm not looking forward to leaving." In just four days. Her insides clenched, but she strove to focus on this moment instead of her murky future—though it was becoming less murky by the moment.

"I'm glad you like it."

They led their horses into the stable. Welch met them and took Matilda. Ambrose always cared for Orpheus now. Typically, Philippa would go to the house at this point and prepare for dinner. However, her conversation with Mrs. Lerner hovered in her mind.

She accompanied Ambrose to the tack area. "Mrs. Lerner says everyone is quite pleased to have you back. Indeed, they're hoping you stay. Will you? Once the prizefight is over?"

He removed Orpheus's bridle. "For a while. There are projects that require my attention."

"Such as helping Mr. Lerner repair his shearing shed?"

He nodded without pausing in his task. She ought to go, but she wanted him to know what Mrs. Lerner had said. Maybe it would help him. "She indicated you seemed to have overcome the tragedy that befell you and your brother."

Now he reacted. His brows dipped over his eyes, and his expression darkened. "I'm still here, the tragedy was all Nigel's."

A predictable response. She doubted he would ever relinquish any of that burden. "She told me what a good job you've done with Beckwith, how glad everyone is to have you back."

He unstrapped Orpheus's saddle, but said nothing.

Philippa waited another moment, but it became clear this was to be a one-sided conversation. "Ambrose, if you ever want to talk about—"

"I don't."

"It might help. You have all of this self-loathing, and really no one else blames—"

He looked at her sharply. "Have you been gathering information?"

Oh dear, she'd overstepped. "I've only listened to what people offered to tell me."

His eyes narrowed. "What people?"

Beneath the weight of his stare, she panicked. She'd no wish to get Mrs. Oldham in any trouble, nor did she particularly want to tell him she'd befriended his former lover. She could scarcely believe she'd done that herself. "No one in particular."

"Tell me who's been talking to you."

She brushed suddenly damp palms against her skirt. "Does it really matter when you won't talk to me? Everyone cares about you, Ambrose. They aren't telling tales behind your back, they're trying to explain a terrible situation. People have forgiven you, or don't you realize that?"

He glared at her. "You shouldn't be talking about it to anyone."

She refused to back down. Her time was running out. She had very few chances left to reach him. "You should be talking about it to me. I could help you find forgiveness. You and Nigel were in an awful situation, set up as you were to rival each other."

His lip curled. "Is that what you think? We weren't rivals." His eyes glittered dangerously. "I was his better. In every way. People shouldn't be wasting their forgiveness on me and neither should you."

His resolve to despise himself was beyond maddening!

"Don't tell me what I should or shouldn't do. You didn't mean for Nigel to die. Though I still don't know precisely what happened—"

"And don't ask me to tell you." He returned his attention to Orpheus. "Don't expect me for dinner."

She watched him another moment, but knew further conversation was pointless. She turned, her shoulders drooping. She was no closer to getting him to lower his guard than when she'd arrived. She'd been so sure the last few days had brought them closer, but he seemed as distant as ever.

It seemed he wouldn't ever forgive himself. Nor would he trust her with his pain. And she was damned sure he wasn't going to fall in love with her.

Later that night, Ambrose stepped out of his tepid bath. He was such a selfish ass. Philippa had been patient. She'd been kind. She'd been understanding. And he'd thrown her concern back in her face because he was too afraid to tell her what a beast he really was. If he talked to her about the past, if he revealed all that he'd done, she'd leave him. He didn't want her to leave him.

He owed her an apology.

He dried himself and donned a robe. Then he left his bedchamber and went into the sitting room. The door to Philippa's chamber was closed. He hesitated. He could apologize to her in the morning.

But his feet carried him to her door. He knocked softly.

"Enter," came her response.

His hand hovered above the latch. Then the door opened. She stood just over the threshold. In a silken wrapper over a night rail.

He swallowed in search of moisture for his suddenly parched mouth. "I, ah, I came to apologize." he croaked.

"Oh, thank you." She smiled softly. "Come in."

Yes, she was a siren because his mind screamed for him to run, but his feet stepped over the threshold, and he closed the door behind him.

She gave him a hooded, sultry look. "Actually, your arrival is rather fortuitous. I have a problem, and perhaps you can help."

He eyed her warily, every part of him—save one that was currently tenting his robe—screamed no. "Perhaps." That one part was apparently louder than the rest.

She retreated further into her chamber. A low fire burned in the grate, casting her in warmth and shadow.

She turned toward him. "Your face looks better. I heard you lost that fight."

Ambrose briefly considered sacking Oldham. Neither Ackley nor Ned possessed the nerve to share that information. "I did. Does that surprise you?"

"I'm certain it surprised you." How had she come to know him so well when he'd done everything to keep her at bay? She fidgeted with the tie of her wrap. "About my problem…"

He lingered near the door, afraid to move too close to her, as faintly clothed as they were and as furious as his cock was pulsing. "What do you need?" *And why couldn't you have asked a bloody servant?*

Her pink tongue darted over her lower lip. Ambrose sagged back against the door frame.

Delicately, she cleared her throat. "The other day in your room, you seemed close to…something. Goodness, this is embarrassing." She looked toward the fireplace, her cheeks flushing deep pink. "I've tried to do that for myself, but I can't seem to do it right." She managed to bring her gaze back to his. "Would you help me?"

Bloody hell. Was she asking him to help her pleasure herself? He could barely keep his hands from her now, but under the full weight of her feminine wiles he would very well be lost. He swallowed, with effort.

Her eyes glowed like amber in the firelight. "I know you'd prefer I leave you alone, but since we've done those other things, I was hoping you wouldn't mind telling me how to do it."

"Um, what have you tried?" His blood pounded in his temple, his ears, his cock.

"I touch myself." She placed a hand on her thigh where the edges of her dressing gown met. "And it feels…nice, but when you touch my breasts, when you…put your mouth on them, it feels different. Better." Her eyes were glassy, her breathing grew shorter. "Should I touch myself there?" She raised her hand to her breast, her fingers pressing against the top of her dressing gown and sliding between the fabric.

Her nipple hardened and his body came away from the doorframe like fire to oxygen. "Ah, you could. Maybe just cup the underside." She followed his direction. *What was he doing?* "And now touch the nipple." He gritted his teeth as her fingertips closed around the point.

She squeezed lightly and gasped. "It's so strange because I felt that down there. Between my thighs."

The same place he felt it, and he wasn't even touching her or himself. His prick threatened to burn through his robe.

"But when I touch myself there," her gaze flicked downward, "I can't seem to find the right place."

Oh, hell, he would surely regret this tomorrow, but she'd asked him for very little and offered so much. He couldn't say no.

"Lie on the bed."

She did as he commanded. She was the most provocative sight he'd ever beheld, cupping her breast while her dressing gown fell open to reveal a night rail that should've reached her knees, but was bunched up nearly to her sex.

He sat on the edge of the bed and untied the sash of her dressing gown. The contours of her body were quite deliciously visible beneath the gauze of her night rail. The firelight spread over her curves, highlighting the peaks and cloaking the valleys in mysterious, enticing shadow.

He took her free hand and guided it up under her night rail. The fabric rose, exposing her to his gaze. He looked up at her face. She watched him intently, her cheeks still flushed, but whether from embarrassment or desire, he couldn't know.

He guided her fingers to her clitoris and applied pressure. "Have you tried pressing here?"

She bucked up into his hand. A shudder wracked his body. "Yes, but it's not enough."

"Try this." He rotated their fingers over her flesh, manipulating her.

She ground up against him. "Oh, yes."

He took her hand from her breast and slid it beneath her night rail. "Squeeze your nipple again."

She pulled the flesh and cast her head back against the pillow. This was dangerously close to breaking his vow. He drew in a breath and tried to think of Nigel, of anything that would dampen his lust. But there was no room in his mind for anything or anyone but Philippa.

He continued stroking her, showing her a variation of movements and pressures. All the while, she surged against him, her hips seeking some sort of rhythm. He began to understand what she was missing. What *he* was missing.

"Have you moved lower?" He took her fingers and set them against her opening. Her flesh was alluringly damp. "Have you gone inside?"

She shook her head against the pillows.

Blood of Christ. His hand stilled. He shouldn't do this. *Why not?* He wasn't pleasuring himself, he was pleasuring her. Surely that wouldn't break his vow or his honor? A pathetic argument, but convincing nonetheless.

"Like this." Slowly, he pressed his middle finger into her flesh. She was tight and hot. Her hips fell back against the bed and her thighs closed around his hand. "Open, sweetheart." He coaxed her with his fingers, moving back up to her clitoris and stoking her desire—and his—anew.

She parted her thighs slightly, but he could feel her tension. She'd stopped caressing her breast. *No, don't stop.* Yes, he wanted to give this to her. So desperately.

He pushed her night rail up her abdomen, exposing the dip of her belly. He swallowed then moved the fabric higher. "Take it off," he rasped.

She opened her eyes and stared at him a moment before complying. Then the night rail went over her head and was thrust to the side.

God, she was exquisite. The firelight illuminated every graceful slope, every provocative hollow, the pale luster of her flesh, the rosy peaks of her breasts. He inhaled deeply, savoring not just her familiar honey lilac scent, but the new and delicious, musk of her desire.

Committed at least to helping her, he bent his head to her breast and blew across the tip. The nipple puckered and she sucked in air. He kissed her there, softly at first, then using his tongue to draw circles.

Her fingers tangled in his hair, and she pulled him against her. It was the end of his restraint.

He opened his mouth on her and drew her nipple against his tongue. He sucked and licked then cupped the soft flesh underneath. She tasted so good. Like sunshine on the brightest summer day. Like the sweet, salty breeze coming in from the ocean. Like home.

Gently, he began to move his fingers over her again, small circular motions meant to establish a rhythm she could latch onto. He applied a bit more pressure and widened his caress, going lower to stroke just the edges of her opening. His cock throbbed, but he wouldn't lose control. He would give her what she wanted.

Gradually, her hips fell open, exposing her to his fingers. Pressing his thumb against her clitoris, he slowly moved his middle finger along the length of her opening. She tightened up again and so he drew on her nipple. Moisture wetted his finger. "Yes, that's it," he murmured.

He slid his finger inside. Just a brief invasion. But she gasped and dug her fingers harder into his scalp.

She moaned. "More."

He climbed onto the bed and lay beside her. Inhaling deeply, he sought the strength to keep himself from covering her. After a moment, he allowed himself to stroke his finger into her again, more fully this time. He kept his thumb on her, moving over her, instilling that vital rhythm. Then he matched it with his finger, moving in and out of her with slow precision. Her hips rose to meet him again and again.

Vaguely, he recalled he was supposed to be tutoring her. "You see how the rhythm is important?"

Her hips rose faster as she began to demand more. He pumped his finger more purposefully, giving her what she wanted. He moved his mouth to her other breast, but kept his fingers on the first so he could pleasure them both. She gasped sharply and opened her legs wider, giving him greater access, urging him faster and deeper.

He worked his thumb harder as he thrust his finger in and out of her. Her breathing hitched and he could hear her coming release as much as he could feel it in the muscles clenching around his finger.

He squeezed one nipple and pinched it lightly as he suckled the other. Then he thrust his finger deep inside of her. She gripped his head and cried out. Her hips bucked up against him, losing their rhythm in favor of a shattering orgasm.

He continued to finger her, distantly aware that his own hips were grinding against the mattress beside her. He had to stop. But he couldn't, not until her spasms ceased.

At last she subsided.

And then, terribly, spectacularly, he came.

Chapter Twenty-one

AFTER several dark, blissful moments, during which she'd recaptured her breath, Philippa opened her eyes. Above her was the pale blue canopy of her bed. Beside her was the man who'd taken her to heaven after consigning her to so many days of hell.

She smiled and turned toward him, but when he abruptly stood, she feared nothing had changed between them. His dressing gown drooped, exposing the scar on his left shoulder. She knew without asking it had something to do with Nigel.

She shifted and her thigh met moisture on the coverlet. *His seed.* Pity they hadn't just done it together. Well, more together than *that.*

"I have to go." His voice, dark and hoarse, came over his shoulder, but he didn't turn to look at her.

Concerned and dismayed, she skirted the spot on the bed and went to stand behind him. "Ambrose, what is it? Didn't you…enjoy that?"

"Too much," he muttered so softly, she had to strain to hear. He turned to face her then, his eyes dark and a bit wild. "I have to go."

"I wouldn't mind if you stayed." *Or if you came back tomorrow night.* Becoming a wicked wanton didn't seem to bother her as it might have once. The girl her duplicitous parents had raised was well and truly gone, replaced by a woman with more desires than choices.

"I can't. And don't expect me for luncheon tomorrow. Or our ride."

"Oh." She couldn't keep the disappointment from her voice. "I was hoping to visit the beach tomorrow. I only have a couple of days left."

"You should do that. Good night." And then he was gone.

Though physically satisfied, Philippa awoke feeling emotionally cold. Every time she thought she'd made a bit of progress with Ambrose, he reminded her he was as shuttered as ever.

Ned Oldham entered the breakfast room as Philippa was leaving the table. "Lady Philippa, there's a letter for you." He handed her the missive.

Philippa's stomach dropped. *Exactly on schedule.*

She opened the parchment and read precisely what she'd expected:

Dear Philippa,

I am extremely disappointed in your decision to follow that blackguard to Cornwall. I have to assume that's why you've gone there. This changes nothing, except that I must disrupt my schedule to fetch you. I will arrive at Beckwith on the thirteenth. You will be ready to depart immediately. Sir Mortimer knows nothing of your impetuous flight to Cornwall and is most anxiously awaiting your arrival.

If you should sprout a conscience before the thirteenth, my itinerary is included so that you may meet me at any one of our scheduled stops. Such action on your part would greatly improve my disposition toward you.

Herrick

Cold, selfish, pompous—all qualities her father had always possessed, though Philippa had never realized their depth until he'd returned to London with *that woman*. Philippa gritted her teeth and crumpled the paper in her hand. Would her father perhaps understand she'd come here for love? Why not? He'd forsaken his family in the name of love for *that woman*.

He would've had to understand if she'd been successful in wooing Ambrose. But she hadn't been successful. He was no closer to loving her than she was to not loving him.

If only she could persuade him to see the man she did. A

man who clearly felt remorse for his actions, who had been forgiven by those around him, if not himself. A man who could love if he let himself.

She had just two more days in which to try.

She shoved the wrinkled parchment into her pocket. With brisk steps, she left the breakfast room and made her way from the house via the solar.

She tied the bonnet she'd brought to breakfast beneath her chin and exited the house. As she strode through the keep, Oldham greeted her near the stables.

He gave her a slight bow and tipped his cap. "Good morning, my lady. Where're ye off to this fine day?"

"Is his lordship about?"

"He's not, my lady."

She hadn't expected him to be, but was disappointed nonetheless. "Well, it's past time I visited the beach."

"I couldn't agree more. Mind ye don't turn yer back on the sea. She can be full of surprises." He winked at her.

"Thank you, I'll remember that." She smiled at him and continued on her way.

A quarter hour later she reached the path that descended down the cliff—not so much a cliff as a very steep hill. Slowly, she picked her way along the rocks and shrubbery. Tall grasses whispered in the breeze. The sun was warm, and she was glad she'd worn a light muslin frock. She stumbled, but caught herself by grasping the side of a large rock. *Lucky I wore sturdy walking boots, too.*

Another several minutes of painstaking navigation saw her finally at the base of the hill. The dirt had gradually given way to sand, and her boots sank into the soft ground.

The ocean was still dozens of feet away, but it rhythmically lapped at the shore. She stared, entranced, at the gentle waves rolling over each other and licking up the sand. The sea was more than just vast; it was powerful and beautiful and filled the air with sound and smell.

To the left were boats on the periphery of Portscatho. To the right were rocks with a bevy of seabirds flying overhead. In the distance was an endless stretch of blue, though she supposed

France was somewhere out there.

After several minutes, she tore her gaze from the sea and looked up the beach toward Portscatho. Maybe fifty yards distant was a cluster of flat rocks. A woman was kneeling near one of them. Curious, Philippa made her way in that direction. As she neared, she recognized Miss Chandler.

"Miss Chandler," she called, "good morning!"

Miss Chandler turned and shaded her eyes. Then she stood. "Good morning, Lady Philippa. What a pleasure to meet you here."

Philippa came to stand next to her and looked down at the pools of water surrounding the rocks. "What are you looking at?"

"Starfish, anemones, and such."

Indeed, the shallow pools contained black and iridescent shelled things, colorful anemones with delicate fringe waving in the water, huge-eyed fish with dark spots, brightly colored starfish.

Miss Chandler kneeled again and touched a starfish. "I never tire of finding such treasures." She looked up at Philippa. "Do you want to touch one?"

Why not? Lord only knew when she'd ever get another chance. She knelt beside Miss Chandler. "What does it feel like?"

"See for yourself."

Philippa touched the starfish and found it quite bumpy, but firm. Not at all slimy as she might've suspected. Miss Chandler touched an anemone and it swiftly closed up. Philippa jumped, but Miss Chandler laughed, pulling her fingers away.

"Did that hurt you?" Philippa asked, wiping her fingers on her skirt.

Miss Chandler laughed. "Not at all."

Philippa smiled. Her companion's delight was quite contagious. "Do you miss London?"

"Not in the slightest, which is why I never returned. That, and Father wouldn't have me in my ruined state. But even if he had, I wouldn't have left." She looked out at the horizon, her gaze wistful, her lips curved up in satisfaction. "I love the sea."

"Why?"

"It makes me feel insignificant." At Philippa's frown, she continued. "In the best way. It reminds me my problems are small and relatively meaningless. It helped me recover from Nigel's death and my part in it."

Philippa nodded slowly, appreciating the sentiment, but she was still so curious about what had really happened with Nigel and how Ambrose had sustained that scar. "What do you mean by your 'part'? And how did Ambrose get that scar on his shoulder?"

Miss Chandler's gaze sharpened. "You don't think I caused it?"

Goodness, Philippa had made it sound that way, and that hadn't been her intent. Philippa rushed to reassure her. "No. I was just thinking about it and thought I'd ask you. Ambrose is frustratingly close-mouthed. I've tried to show him he can trust me, but he's buried under a mountain of self-recrimination."

"Can you blame him?"

No, she couldn't.

Miss Chandler shaded her eyes from the sun and looked beyond Philippa. "Here he comes now." She dropped her hand and focused on Philippa. "I should go before he gets here."

Miss Chandler was several yards away before Ambrose arrived. He stared after her departing figure. "Who was that?"

Philippa tensed, wondering what his reaction would be. "Miss Chandler."

His eyes shuttered. "Did you just meet?" He continued to stare after her.

"We met in town last week. The day after I arrived."

He turned his gaze to hers. He looked surprised. "You didn't mention it."

She arched a brow at him. "I thought you preferred to avoid discussion of the past."

He nodded once. "I'm... How did you find her?"

"Did you know she's to be married in a few weeks?"

His brows shot up, and he looked down the beach once more. "I did not."

Philippa waited patiently, though she wondered what he was thinking. Was he sorry he hadn't gotten a chance to greet her?

Was he glad she was getting married? "You haven't seen her?"

He turned his head to gaze out at the sea. "No. I didn't want to." He moved his attention to Philippa and she shivered at the intensity in his eyes. "You understand what happened with her? There are no good memories. Knowing she lives here is one of the reasons I never came back."

Philippa wanted to soothe him, touch him, tell him she understood, but she did nothing. This was more than he'd ever given her. More than she'd dared hope for. She wound her fingers together in a tight grip. "She was showing me the tidal pools."

He looked down at the water amongst the rocks. "And what do you think of them?"

"They're unlike anything I've ever seen. The Roseland Peninsula is astonishing."

He nodded. "Do you want to put your feet in the ocean?"

She glanced at the waves hitting the shore. "I don't know. Do I?"

"You really should, since you're here." His gaze turned mock-stern. "However, I must warn you, it's quite cold."

She laughed softly. "Then why do it?"

He arched a brow at her, and giddy sensations raced up and down her body. This was her Ambrose. "Because you've never put your feet in the ocean." He took her hand and guided her to a rock. "Sit."

She perched on the edge of the rock. He kneeled before her, and her heart beat faster. His hands came under the hem of her gown and unlaced her boot. It was a fairly innocuous manner of touching someone, but she felt every brush of his fingers, every whisper of his movements as a seductive caress.

He moved to the second boot and, once removed, deposited both beside the rock. Then he reached up to her knee where her stockings were tied, and Philippa nearly melted into her own tidal pool.

This touch was far more intimate. Still utilitarian, but it bore the promise of so much more. He pulled the cotton down her calf. The fabric slid along her skin. Sparks of anticipation shot up her leg. Heat bloomed between her thighs.

When his fingers found the ties of her second stocking, he looked up. Their gazes connected and locked. She saw heat and need, an exact mirror of what she felt. How easy it would be to launch herself into his arms, but she kept herself rigid. She was deathly afraid of frightening him away, of ruining this moment.

The tapes came free, tickling the back of her knee. His fingers trailed along her flesh, slowly dragging the stocking down. He wasn't removing her stockings, he was driving her mad with desire. Did he have any idea?

He took both stockings and set them atop her boots. Then he stood, breaking the trance.

She refused to feel disappointed. This was progress. He wasn't shutting her out, and he wasn't leaving. In fact, he was removing his own boots and stockings.

A moment later, he was barefooted. He wiggled his feet in the sand and smiled. A genuine smile of joy that nearly drew a sob from Philippa's throat. Swallowing, she forced herself to remain serene.

He took her hand. "Come."

She stood. "Oh!" The sand was warm and soft against her feet. Tiny granules found their way between her toes, creating friction as she wiggled them as he had. She looked up at him and giggled.

"Feels strange?" he asked.

"A bit."

"Wait until we reach the wet sand." He tightened his grip on her fingers and led her toward the waves.

This was about as close to perfect as she'd ever experienced. Walking hand in hand with Ambrose on a nearly deserted beach where they could be exactly who they were. No one to fear, no one to judge, no one to keep them apart.

Her feet felt light and wondrous upon the sand, as if she were gliding beside Ambrose. Then they reached the damp, compacted sand where the waves had swept during high tide. It was much cooler and didn't come up between her toes. The further they walked, the wetter the sand became. The waves were breaking just ahead, maybe twenty or so feet in front of them.

She slowed her pace. "How does this work? Do we stand here and wait for the waves to come?"

He was a few steps in front of her, still holding her hand. He turned his head to look at her over his shoulder. "We can, or we can walk up to them."

"Is it safe?" She suffered a moment of trepidation recalling what Oldham had said about the sea being full of surprises. "Oldham cautioned me not to turn my back."

"Excellent advice. It's perfectly safe where we are and where we'll be. The water will not come above your calves."

She turned her head and looked up at him. "What about my dress?"

"You'll have to hold it up. Or let it get wet. Your choice."

She batted her eyelashes at him. "Lord Sevrin, are you trying to entice me to dampen my skirts?"

He laughed, and she grinned at the sound. Her chest expanded and suddenly the day seemed brighter, warmer, more vivid in every way.

"You're a terrible flirt, Lady Philippa." With his free hand he pointed out at the water. "The waves crash out there, falling over each other. See the white?"

Philippa nodded, transfixed by the ebb and flow. It really was quite beautiful. She moved to stand beside him, her feet sinking into the squishy sand.

He leaned his head down next to hers and spoke against her ear. "Then they roll in, some very gently so that they barely lap at the shore and others—oh, here comes one—with more purpose."

Philippa tried to back away, but Ambrose held her fast. "I've got you."

She turned her head. His cheek was so close. She could kiss him if she dared—

She gasped as frigid water rushed over her feet, wetting the hem of her gown.

"You forgot your dress," he said, turning to look at her. Then he swept her up so quickly, she automatically threw her arms around his neck for safety. This wave—so quick on the heels of the last—came higher, to his upper calf. She'd be drenched if he hadn't picked her up.

They stared into each other's eyes as the water receded. Slowly, he set her back on her feet. She cursed her failure to prolong the embrace.

"Now," he said, "Are you ready to jump the next one?"

Jump? "Whatever do you mean?"

He took her hand again and led her forward. "Mind your dress this time."

Philippa grasped her skirt and lifted the hem.

"When the next wave comes, jump over the edge."

The water came up again, softer than the one that had gotten them wet.

"Now!" Ambrose tightened his grip on her hand and jumped as the edge of the wave came at them. Philippa jumped with him, and they came down into the shallow water. Cold droplets splashed their ankles and calves. Philippa laughed. Ambrose joined her, his dark eyes sparkling with delight.

No, there was no more perfect moment than this.

They spent the next quarter hour jumping the waves and running from the ones that were particularly robust. Philippa considered tripping so that he might sweep her up again, but didn't want to tempt her advantage. This had been far more wonderful than she'd ever imagined. She could almost convince herself that marriage with him was possible.

That hope and her dwindling timeframe drove her—perhaps foolishly—to say, "It's almost time for me to make a decision. About our future."

He cast her a sidelong glance. "Your feet must be freezing." He led her up the beach, but didn't take her hand this time.

She'd overstepped. Again. "Did you hear what I said?"

He stopped. They'd just reached the dry sand, and Philippa was aware of all of the tiny grains sticking to her wet feet.

He turned. The mischievous spark had disappeared from his eyes. "I don't deserve a wife."

"Not even me?" She actually bit her tongue trying to reel those words back into her mouth.

He pivoted and took a step up the beach. "Not even you."

Again, she didn't think before blurting, "Would you consider taking a mistress?"

His gaze snapped to hers. "God, no. Why would you even ask?"

Because I'd like the position. If only for a couple of days. "Miss Chandler was your mistress. Why not take another?"

"She wasn't my *mistress*." He ran his hand through his hair. "Christ, Philippa, you know how that turned out."

She stopped and dug her heels into the sand. "I do. But I'm not her. And Nigel's not here."

He stared at her, stupefied. The muscles in his jaw worked. He opened his mouth then closed it again. "I can't do that with you."

"Why not? What makes me inferior to Miss Chandler?" It was a risky question, comparing herself to the other woman he'd ruined, but she was desperate. She'd thrown all of her cards onto the table and put all of her money into the pot.

He sucked in a breath then let it out slowly. He raked her with a thorough and heated gaze. "Absolutely nothing. Trust me when I say it's a concerted and exhausting effort to keep my hands off you. It has been since the night we met."

She squeezed her eyes shut for a brief moment as his words settled over her. Hope bloomed in her chest and she stepped toward him. "Why do you, then? I'm here. Willing. Eager. I want you, Ambrose."

His face paled, and the heat growing between them dissipated. Philippa wanted to reach out and grab him, seize the moment that was rapidly fading, but he stalked toward their boots and stockings.

Defeated, she turned and followed him.

He sat on the edge of the rock and pulled his stockings on with quick jerks. Then he shoved his feet into his boots. He stood and stared down at her, his eyes as inscrutable as the sea.

"I swore a vow of celibacy after what I did to my brother. I took his future wife as my lover and drove him to his death. There is no coming back from that, Philippa. I'm broken and you've no cause to try to fix me."

"Don't tell me what I shouldn't do. I lo—"

"No!" He took a step back from her, his face paling. "Don't

ever say that to me. I can't do this anymore. You have to leave me alone." He turned and stalked away.

The sand felt as if it were cemented to Philippa's feet. She was affixed to the beach, as incapable of following him as he was of staying with her.

That was it then. She'd put everything out, left her very heart within his grasp. And he'd chosen his guilt instead.

She bent down and plucked up her stockings then dropped her rump onto the rock. She squeezed her eyes shut against the tears that threatened.

She had only herself to blame. She'd taken a risk and it had failed miserably. Better to know now than after they'd married. She could easily have found herself in her mother's position—unhappily married to a man who only made her miserable.

After Philippa had donned her stockings and boots, she pulled her father's letter from her pocket. He'd be here in three days. If she left tomorrow, and because she knew his travel plans, she could meet him along the way.

She stood and started back toward the hillside path.

Chapter Twenty-two

LATER that afternoon Ambrose stood outside Lettice Chandler's door, his hand poised above the wood. He'd left Philippa intent on visiting with one of his tenants, but he'd ridden around aimlessly instead. Until he'd ended up here.

If Philippa could talk to Lettice, why couldn't he? Why *shouldn't* he? He wasn't precisely sure what had driven him here, but it somehow felt necessary. Apparently the time had come to settle accounts.

He knocked.

He dropped his hand and stood rigid. His stomach twisted with nausea and his skin turned cold and clammy. The door opened.

She looked older, of course, but not just in years. Experience and emotion—perhaps sadness or regret—had carved tiny lines around her eyes and mouth. She was still beautiful, but not in the carefree, vibrant way she'd been five years ago. Her eyes did not sparkle, and her mouth was not half-curved in a saucy smile. He'd never considered she might have been suffering. He'd never considered her at all.

"Ambrose. Come in." She opened the door wider and invited him inside.

He peered into the interior, but his feet suddenly felt like lead. "I don't know why I'm here."

"It doesn't matter. I'm glad you came. Would you like tea?"

"No." *Go inside. Apologize. Make this right.* He stepped over the threshold, and his muscles loosened.

She moved inside, and he shut the door. His anxiety ramped up again. They were alone. As they'd been so many times. But he didn't want to touch her. The thought of touching her was awful, repellent.

"I'm sorry." The words sounded small and insignificant to his ears, but they were all he had.

Her eyes drooped with sadness. "I know. I'm sorry, too. If I could take it all back, I would."

He nodded because further speech had become quite blocked by the apple-sized ball in his throat.

"It's good you've come back." She led him into a small sitting room. It was cozy, feminine, and with its modicum of furniture, quite solitary. He'd consigned her to a life of loneliness. But no...

"You're to be married?"

She sat in the single chair, an outmoded affair with a patched arm. "Yes. To Mr. Daniel Sedley. Do you remember him?"

"He owns several fishing boats in Portscatho."

She smoothed her skirt, a serviceable muslin of lesser quality than she'd worn five years ago. "That's right."

He nodded, glad for her but unable to say so. It seemed wrong they were having this discussion, that she was planning a future when Nigel lay in the churchyard just up the High Street.

"What about you?" she asked. "Are you going to marry Lady Philippa?"

Ambrose stared at her. "Why would you think that?"

She shrugged. "You couldn't do better. And she's in love with you."

He wanted to argue, not because he didn't believe her, but because he didn't want it to be true. Yet he'd heard Philippa on the beach, had stopped her from saying it. "She told you that?"

"It's obvious."

Ambrose hadn't intended to stay, but his legs gave out just as his emotions threatened to flow free. He sank onto her narrow settee. "I don't deserve her." God, it felt good to finally let something out.

She smiled, but there was regret in her eyes. Eyes that had once been full of flirtatious vitality, but now looked weary. "I understand. It took Daniel years to convince me I deserved him. I give him a lot of credit for persistence."

Philippa was trying, in her own way, to do the same. She'd come here to see if they'd suit. She'd asked him again today about marriage, coming just shy of proposing to him herself. And he'd repaid her efforts by repeatedly shutting her out. "I haven't been fair to her. It's just that… I'm not sure I'm ready. I haven't—" He glanced at her briefly. "I haven't been with another woman since…"

Lettice sucked in her breath. "Oh, Ambrose."

He felt the anguish in her tone all the way to his bones. Unable to tolerate her empathy, he looked away. "It's the only way I could manage. The only way I could allow myself to live after what I'd done. I don't know if I can change that for Philippa. Maybe in time."

"You don't have much of that."

"I know. She's leaving after the prizefight. But perhaps I can persuade her to stay."

Lettice shook her head. "I don't think so. She's to be married."

He snapped his gaze to hers. "She told you that?"

"Her father arranged something. I think she came here hoping to avoid it."

He'd done nothing but shove her away.

He stood. "I have to go."

"Good. Perhaps you can both attend my wedding."

He arched a brow at her, surprised to feel a bit like his old self—a remarkable accomplishment given his present company. "I'm not sure that's advisable. You might've forgiven me, but I'm sure Sedley would skewer me on sight."

She shook her head. "No, Ambrose. Everyone's forgiven you. It's only you who needs to forgive yourself."

He nodded, suspecting she was right, but still unsure of how to do it. He left her cottage a few minutes later. He'd been intent on returning to Beckwith, but to do what? Ask Philippa to marry him? He wasn't ready for love—she deserved nothing less—and might never be. But the thought of her marrying someone else made him weak to his soul. Or what shred was left of it.

He pulled himself astride Orpheus and rode down to Portscatho and then back along the beach toward Beckwith. He still couldn't ride through Gerrans, not past the churchyard where Nigel was buried.

By the time he rode into the stable yard, he was desperate with longing. His brain screamed for him to stop and think, but the protestations grew weaker and weaker. Welch met him, and Ambrose tossed the reins in his direction. Wordlessly, Ambrose turned and strode to the house, his gait eating up the path.

He had to see Philippa, needed to hold her before she left him forever. He moved into the drawing room and took the stairs two at a time. Onward to the door to her chamber, where, with a shaking hand, he rapped three times.

The door opened to reveal her maid who bobbed a curtsey. "Your lordship."

Philippa emerged from the doorway to her dressing chamber garbed in nothing but a chemise. Her hair was loose, gently waving about her shoulders and grazing the tops of her breasts. He'd never seen her with all of her hair down.

He couldn't take his hungry gaze from her but spoke at the maid, "Leave us."

Philippa nodded at the girl, who skirted Ambrose and left the bedchamber.

Ambrose went to stand before Philippa. His ragged breathing filled his ears; his furious heartbeat clogged his throat. She looked up at him, her eyes wide, luminous, trusting.

Salvation was right here. He had only to touch her. To accept what she offered—trust, solace, love. The argument in his head died away, leaving him open and vulnerable.

He shoved his hands into her hair and cupped her head. She was soft and warm and smelled like just-bloomed lilac drenched in honey, as if she'd bathed that afternoon.

He dragged his thumb along her cheek and settled it against her lower lip. Her tongue darted out and licked the pad and he was lost. He held her head captive while he slanted his mouth across hers. She was ready. Hot, wet, eager. Her arms snaked around his back and held him close.

The knowledge that he was about to break his long-held vow

made him quake, both with fear and with wanting her so badly. How would he even perform? It had been so long.

No, he didn't want to think right now. Only to feel. To luxuriate in this woman who'd given herself so completely to him. This woman he was completely unworthy of, but whom he so desperately wanted to deserve.

She licked at his mouth, inviting him to devour her. Her fingers dug into his back, a reflection of his own need. He picked her up as effortlessly as he'd done at the beach and took her to the bed.

He tempered his lust, setting her gently onto the coverlet. Waning sunlight streamed through the windows, setting her skin afire with gold. "You're exquisite," he breathed, unable to find the volume to speak aloud amidst his overwhelming humility.

She reached up for him, and he was impatient to be next to her. He quickly removed his coat, waistcoat, boots, and stockings. She sat up and pulled at the ends of his cravat. The silk whispered against his neck as she tugged it free and cast it aside. He swept his shirt over his head in one fluid movement.

When his gaze found hers once more, he stilled. Her eyes were wide, focused on his bare chest. No, on his shoulder. His scar. Would she ask him about it again? He didn't want to spoil this, was afraid of the intrusion of anything but what they could give each other right here, right now.

She kneeled before him on the edge of the bed. With halting fingers, she touched the five-year-old blemish. Gently, she traced the circle where Nigel's bullet had pierced him.

Ambrose reveled in her nurturing silence. He'd never imagined he could one day associate that wound with anything good. But her touch and her care were absolution for his sins. Succor, joy, contentment seemed not only possible, but within his grasp.

Because of her.

That she said nothing about the scar, asked nothing when he owed her so much, humbled him even more. He pressed his lips to her forehead. Her breath sighed against his collarbone, warm and soft. Comforting.

She drew her chemise up over her head. With her arms

raised, her breasts rose high, tempting him with their tight pink buds. Without pretense, he drew a nipple into his mouth. She gasped and lowered her arms to his shoulders, her chemise rippling against his back as it fell from her grasp.

He cupped her breasts, holding her to his mouth. Her hands clasped his head as he suckled her. She was a feast, and he was starving. He licked at her and grazed his teeth along her nipple, then moved to the other, repeating his erotic ministrations.

Her hands were suddenly at the waistband of his breeches. Already wildly aroused, his cock strained against his drawers. She fumbled with the buttons and he impatiently took over, making quick work of shedding both his breeches and his undergarments.

He guided her back against the mattress, or did she pull him? It seemed a mutual action, taking each other where they needed to be.

He lay against her side and drew his finger along her lips, across her jawline, down her neck. He traced the elegant slope of her collarbone and pressed a kiss to the hollow of her throat where her heart beat strong and fast.

He dragged his fingers down to her breasts, not touching the sensitive peaks, but sweeping around the curves and valleys. Slowly, intently, he circled one breast, teasing her flesh. She arched up, begging him wordlessly to give her more. He closed his fingers over the nipple and lightly tugged. She gasped and her hips came off the bed, signaling how deep her arousal had reached.

Reluctantly but purposefully he left her breast and trailed his fingers down her belly to the indentation of her navel. She sucked in her breath. He recalled the night they'd met when she'd said she was ticklish. Most definitely.

He slid lower, skipping the bounty between her thighs—for now. He glided his palm over her hip. She was supple and smooth and powerful, the muscles of her legs defined and athletic.

Her body told him so many things. How she lived, what she wanted, how he could pleasure her. And that was paramount to him. Not his own satisfaction—which after denying himself so long would be easy enough—but hers. She was a gift he would not take lightly.

He explored the arc of her thigh, the pocket behind her knee, where he knew she was also ticklish, the sleek curve of her calf. Intermittently she made soft, whispery noises when he grazed a sensitive spot.

Time to map that most intimate part of her, the part he longed to touch and taste. He brought his hand up between her thighs. Her initial reaction was to clamp them shut, but she quickly relaxed her muscles and even widened her legs. So responsive.

Dark curls cloaked her sex. With a light touch, he delved through them and found the pink folds, damp and warm with her arousal. "Beautiful," he breathed.

He stroked along her cleft, gathering moisture. Her thighs widened further, inviting him, enchanting him. God, she was so wet already. He needn't do what he was about to, but he couldn't help himself. Her sweet musk and soft flesh were more than he could stand.

He leaned down and kissed the skin above her curls. She inhaled sharply, and her buttocks came off the bed. The movement drew his fingertip inside eliciting a soft moan from her lips. He slid further in, and she thrust her hips.

Quickly, he resettled himself between her legs and pressed his mouth to her clitoris. "*Ambrose.* What on earth are you doing?"

Of course she would ask him.

He smiled against her flesh. "Pleasuring you."

"Oh."

He licked her as he worked his finger inside and pumped once. Twice. "Is this all right?"

She threaded her fingers in his hair. "God, yes."

"Good."

He showed no mercy then. He pushed her thighs open further, exposing her innermost flesh to his greedy gaze. Pink and wet. Delicious. He kissed her fully, his tongue delving deep into her passage.

She bucked up, crying out as he made love to her with his mouth. Her muscles contracted around him, her thighs tensed as her hips thrust. She'd paid attention when he'd instructed her about rhythm, but her movements were jerky, uncontrolled. He returned his finger to her channel and gave her the rhythm, evening out her thrusts and driving her steadily toward the pinnacle she sought.

He put his thumb on her clitoris and splayed his hand over the top of her sex. He pressed against her as he feasted. Her fingers gripped the back of his head. Her muscles clenched and she shuddered. Once. Twice. A third time. He thrust his tongue into her and devoured her, his own cock in danger of spilling its seed.

A small but insistent voice said, *you can stop now.*

No, he couldn't.

Yes, you can. You haven't yet broken your vow.

He sat back as her orgasm faded. Her eyes were closed, her lips parted to allow ragged breaths to escape.

Leave now and you'll have nothing to regret.

Her eyes flew open. The wonder in her gaze instantly turned to apprehension. She sat up and clutched his hand. "Don't you dare leave me."

Chapter Twenty-three

SHE'D seen that look before. That fear and revulsion—not for her, but for himself. She wouldn't let it take him, not this time. She tugged his hand, trying to pull him down onto the bed with her.

His face shuttered, his eyes dulled, he resisted her touch. "I ought to go."

"No, you ought not. It would be highly ungentlemanly to leave a lady in this situation."

His gaze regained focus and settled on her. "My vow is important."

She scrambled up onto her knees and took his other hand, holding him tight in her grasp. "I can see that, and I don't mean to dishonor it. But tell me, why is it important?"

His eyes narrowed, and his voice was dangerously soft. "You know what happened. I seduced my brother's fiancée."

"And that was horrible, but it's also in the past."

Roughly, he pulled his hands from hers. "He died, Philippa! He found me with her, shot me in the shoulder, which is less than I deserved, and then rode off on Orpheus. Which he would've survived if I hadn't chased him down and caused him to fall." The anguish lined in his face, the ragged desperation punctuating each word twisted her heart.

She found his hands again and stroked her thumbs over their backs, willing peace, understanding, forgiveness into his tortured soul. "It was an accident. A terrible, tragic accident. If you were meant to die too, you would have."

His eyes widened, giving him the appearance of a boy facing his fear. "But look what I did to you. No good can come from me."

She laughed softly, for his logic was quite flawed. She cupped his jaw line. "Plenty of good comes from you. You saved me, Ambrose—not from a ruined reputation and not from danger. You saved me from the cold life my parents orchestrated." After tonight she could never marry Sir Mortimer. She'd choose an isolated cottage filled with the ghostly memories of her love for Ambrose before she'd wed another man. Which seemed likely because though he might give her his body, he'd never promised his heart or his soul. She wanted, no, she *needed* both.

Cautiously, she lay back, offering her body, her comfort, her love. "Show me what else is good."

He visibly swallowed, his gaze moving over her like a gentle caress. She waited, breathless, for his decision.

He leaned down and kissed her mouth. A painstaking brush of his lips over hers. Delicate, sweet. She relaxed and brought her hands up to his shoulders, thrilled by his courage.

His mouth opened over hers. He slid his tongue into her as he settled his body over hers. She kissed him back, slanting her mouth, meeting him, wanting him.

The connection of his bare chest against her breasts made her gasp into their kiss. To have him against her—skin to skin—was everything she'd craved. Nothing between them save heat and desire. He pressed his hips down, grinding his hard length deliciously against her.

She opened her thighs, ready to finally make him hers. His sex nestled hers, and though she'd just found her orgasm moments ago, she was more than ready again. Achingly so.

His fingers found her most sensitive spot and worked the flesh a moment. She clutched at his waist, trying to pull him harder against her. His fingers delved lower, and he positioned his shaft at her opening.

"Sweetheart, I do believe this is going to hurt a bit."

He pushed inside, opening her farther than she'd ever stretched. He slid in slowly, his thumb massaging her clitoris. She rotated her hips needfully and clasped his hips, seeking that all-important rhythm that would lead them to ecstasy.

He was going too slow. This didn't hurt in the slightest. She tightened her grip on his hips and pulled him down as she pushed up. "Oh!" Pain burned as her muscles stretched in a way they'd never done before, and she dug her fingers into his buttocks.

"Shhh," he murmured, taking his hand from between them and smoothing her hair back from her face. He looked into her eyes as he rotated his hips the barest amount. He didn't move, just kept himself still, filling her, allowing her to accommodate him. He was so beautiful to her, his eyes dark and seductive in the sunset, his skin glistening with damp.

The burning faded, and pleasure reclaimed her. He kissed her lightly and began to move. A slow withdrawal followed by an equally slow penetration.

He kissed a path to her ear and whispered, "Open your thighs wider, that's right, open to me, love."

His words only increased her desire, her need. She'd wanted this moment so badly. He plunged deeper on the next thrust—still gentle, but with a bit more force. She gasped and clutched at his back.

"Now wrap your legs around me."

She looked up at him, not sure what he meant.

He reached down and lifted her left leg then guided it around his hips, opening her even more to him. He pressed forward and, dear Lord, but the sensation was intense. He was so deep, the precision of his entry and withdrawal so perfect. She wrapped her other leg around his hips, and he began to move faster. He tilted his hips forward, grinding against the top of her sex, abrading her most sensitive flesh. She moved with him, urging him to go faster, drive harder.

"More," she demanded in husky tones.

He quickened the pace, driving in and out of her with ruthless grace. There was no pain, only a building bliss similar to before, but completely different. He filled her and yet she didn't feel full enough. Tiny whimpers escaped her throat as she sought to find that thread of pleasure that would carry her to the other side.

He thrust harder and then claimed her mouth, conquering her with his tongue as he plundered her with his sex. He moved faster, rising above her, breaking their kiss. He lifted his hand and grabbed the top of the headboard.

"Come with me now, Philippa. Come with me."

His hips stroked a desperate pace. She began to break away. Sparks danced behind her eyelids and she realized her eyes were shut tight. She wanted to see him.

She opened her eyes and watched the tension in his face. He ground low against her and hovered the barest moment. Then he pulled away from her and rolled to his side. He cried out, a deep, guttural sound.

His abrupt departure reminded her she'd been in the middle of her own release. Her muscles spasmed, and she missed the pressure of him against her and inside of her. She put her fingers against herself and massaged until the shocks subsided.

When her breathing slowed a bit, she turned to her side. He lay on his back with his hand thrown over his eyes.

She watched him a moment then looked down at his shaft. His flesh glistened with moisture.

He'd stopped himself from leaving his seed inside of her. She supposed that was fair, given they'd made no plans for the future, no promises. Still, emptiness invaded her soul and reminded her that though he'd given her his body, she'd received nothing else.

A knock on the door startled them both. He sat up, his eyes flicking to the door and then to her.

"Probably Feeney come to see if she can help me finish getting ready for dinner."

Ambrose arched a brow. "She'd be that obtuse?"

Philippa's lips curved up. "No. Who could it be then?"

The knock came again followed by, "Yer lordship? Ye've a visitor downstairs," Oldham called through the door.

Philippa stood on legs made wobbly by blissful satisfaction. "I'll go into the dressing chamber."

Ambrose nodded as he climbed off the bed.

She left the door opened a sliver. She wanted to hear whatever Oldham said.

She found a towel in a stack of linens and cleaned herself. The scent of him clung to her body and she smiled at the hint of ownership she felt. He might not be hers forever, but he'd been hers tonight.

After tidying herself, she went back to the door and listened.

"Tell Jagger I'll be down shortly. And he's not invited for dinner."

She frowned. Jagger?

Once she heard the door latching shut, she stepped back into her bedchamber. "Jagger's here?"

Ambrose had donned his breeches and shirt. He was now plucking up his other clothing. "For the fight."

"You invited him to stay here?" No, that didn't make sense. Ambrose had just said Jagger couldn't stay for dinner.

"No. There's some sort of problem. I need to get downstairs and see what it is. Take your time."

The hell she would. She wanted to know what was going on. "Please send Feeney up?"

He nodded, his clothing draped over his forearm.

She padded over to him, marveling at how comfortable she felt exposing herself to him. She stood on her toes and pressed a kiss to his cheek. "Thank you." She spoke softly against his ear. "I know that wasn't easy, but you've given me a great gift. I'll cherish it—and you—always."

His free hand came swiftly up her neck and cupped the back of her head. He kissed her fiercely, deeply. But it was over much too quickly. Too bad they couldn't spend the entire evening in bed. There was always after dinner…

He turned and left, and she hurried back into her dressing chamber, anxious to see what Jagger wanted. Her joy ebbed as she realized it probably wasn't good.

Ambrose didn't have time to reflect upon the loss of his celibacy. He cleaned up and dressed quickly, and a scant quarter hour later he descended the stairs. He only hoped Philippa took a lengthy toilet. He didn't want her around Jagger or his unscrupulous employees, two of whom were seated on his mother's favorite settee. Seeing them there—two criminals staining his mother's memory—negated the bliss he'd so recently enjoyed.

Jagger stood near the fireplace, a glass of whisky dangling from his fingertips.

Ambrose took the last few steps loudly so that all three of his guests turned to look at him. "What the hell are you doing in my house drinking my whisky? I don't recall inviting you."

Jagger laughed and then held up his glass in mock toast. "Such charming hospitality." He took a drink and pressed his lips together. "Fine stuff, Sevrin. I hate to bother you, but we've a problem with tomorrow's bout. Ackley's opponent tripped down a flight of stairs yesterday and broke his arm."

Bloody hell. Ambrose frowned, unaccountably disappointed. "They canceled the fight?"

"No, they found a replacement for him. Giant bloke called Weatherly."

Christ. The mammoth Ambrose had fought in Truro. "He's a bit advanced for Ackley. He needs a few fights before he can face someone like Weatherly."

Jagger sipped his whisky. "Good thing he won't be fighting Ackley then."

A cold sliver of apprehension shot down Ambrose's neck. "What do you mean?"

"His one condition for fighting tomorrow is that you're his opponent."

Because the bastard was certain he could beat Ambrose.

The two men on the settee moved their heads back and forth, watching the conversation like a tennis match. Perversely, Ambrose wanted to knock their skulls together. Their presence in his drawing room only served to remind him how far he still was from becoming a worthy master of Beckwith. He was a fighter. And now a degenerate debaucher of virgins. He grasped the newel post at the base of the stairs until his knuckles whitened.

Jagger took two steps forward. "Did you hear me?"

Ambrose moved away from the stairs and toward the sideboard, to the whisky. "I did."

"And?"

Ambrose took his time pouring a glass of his father's decades-old whisky. He swirled the amber liquid before taking a leisurely sip. His initial response was yes. Though he'd sworn off prizefighting, a rematch with the man who'd beaten him was rather enticing.

Finally, he turned toward Jagger. After all the bastard had done, Ambrose wanted to torture him, just a bit. "You've nothing to force me."

Jagger's brows met as they dipped low over his stern gaze. "I didn't realize I needed to." He stepped toward Ambrose and spoke in a placating, almost deferential tone. "Consider it a training exercise for Ackley. He can watch you and learn. It would be most beneficial."

Ambrose bit back a laugh since they'd already done exactly that. His pulse accelerated as he continued to contemplate the rematch. A rematch in which Ambrose was focused, with his eye on winning instead of losing himself. He wasn't sure he'd ever fought a bout that way.

Though, he despised the notion of helping Jagger in any way. It was one thing to shepherd Ackley—which also benefited Jagger of course—and quite another to satisfy the man who'd threatened Philippa on multiple occasions.

Jagger swaggered around the settee where his lackeys reclined. Thank God they weren't also sampling Ambrose's whisky. "I gather you don't want to resume your fighting permanently, and I swear I'll never ask you again." He shrugged and smiled a thief's smile. The kind that was meant to disarm while he stole your valuables from under your nose. "You have a reputation to regain. I imagine the local townsfolk would cheer for their champion."

Ambrose's neck prickled. Jagger was frightfully well-informed regarding Ambrose's current position.

Jagger moved around the settee and stalked toward Ambrose, stopping just shy of him. He regarded Ambrose with a challenging stare. "Come on. Fight. *Win*. You know you want to."

So damn much. Ambrose curled his free hand into a tight fist.

"I'll do it."

"No!" Philippa's feet tapped down the stairs with a staccato rhythm. "You're not fighting."

All heads in the drawing room swung to watch her descend.

Damn. She'd repaired herself—to astonishing effect—in record time. Her cheeks were still rosy, but he didn't know if it was from her earlier pleasure or her current pique. Whatever the cause, she stirred his blood as if he hadn't made love to her less than an hour before.

She paused at the bottom of the stairs and took in the occupants of the room. Her face paled as her gaze fell on the men seated on the settee. These men had attacked and abducted her in the past.

Ambrose moved quickly to her side. He put his arm around her and faced his visitors. "Out. You've overstayed."

"I've gotten what I've come for." Jagger set his glass on the sideboard. He gave a gallant bow to Philippa. "Delightful to see you, my lady. May I say how lovely you look?"

"You may not," Ambrose growled. "You may not speak to her at all, in fact."

Jagger turned and gestured for his men to follow. "Come along, you dolts."

They stood and followed their employer from the drawing room. One of them, however, cast a lingering glance at Philippa. Ambrose fought the urge to trail him outside and beat him into Beckwith's drive.

Philippa shivered. He turned toward her, cupping her face.

Her gaze was frantic, pleading. "Please don't do this, Ambrose."

"I want to fight. I need to."

She gripped his upper arms. "Why? Forget Jagger. He has nothing to hold over us."

How could he make her understand? "After Nigel died, fighting was all I had. It was the only thing that kept me human. It kept me alive. I can't subsist without it."

Her fingers dug into his arms. "You can. You have me."

Did he have her? Aside from the physical sense? She'd made her inclination for marriage clear. He had only to propose and he *could* have her. In all sense of the word. Forever. A chill rattled his bones as he realized there was such a thing. For so long, he'd only thought about getting through the day. "It's not the same, Philippa. Fighting is intrinsic to who I am."

She pressed her lips together. "You'd choose violence above me."

He wished she hadn't put it like that. There was no comparing the two. "There's no choice. I can't *not* fight."

Darkness crept into her eyes. She nodded once, but Ambrose didn't think she truly comprehended. How could she? Fighting had literally saved his life.

She let him go, dropping her arms between them. She nudged her cheek away from him so that he was no longer touching her face. "So, you'll fight a man who beat you a matter of days ago for a man who twice abducted me."

He inwardly cringed. However, it was precisely because Weatherly had beaten him that Ambrose was so committed to fighting him again. Jagger's involvement was an unfortunate coincidence he wouldn't allow to trouble him. Besides, he posed no danger to Philippa anymore.

Further debate was pointless. Instead, he asked, "How did you know I fought him before?"

"Ackley mentioned him by name. How predictable of you to deflect the conversation away from yourself. From your feelings." She stepped backward, well outside of his reach. "Please tell Mrs. Oldham I prefer to eat in my room this evening."

His body thrummed with pent-up energy. It was as if the bone-melting bliss he'd experienced such a short time ago had never been. "Will you still come to the fight tomorrow?"

"No, I've had quite enough of watching you hurt yourself. I'll be preparing to leave." She set her hand on the staircase railing. The veins in her wrist were taut as she gripped the wood.

He was afraid to ask it aloud, but had to know for sure. "You're going to your father's? To marry?"

Her eyes flickered with surprise. "How did you know?"

It was true. "Lettice told me." More surprise. "I saw her this afternoon," he added.

"Good, maybe now you can start to heal." She paused, but looked as if she might say something more. Then she pressed her lips together. Finally, she turned from him, murmuring, "Good night, Ambrose" as she ascended the stairs.

He nearly went after her. In his mind, he was already following her to her chamber, begging her to take him into her bed one more time. But what was the point of that when it would only be one more time? What he really ought to do was beg her not to marry whomever her father had chosen. If she could just wait a little longer, perhaps he could be the man she deserved.

No, it was good she was leaving. If she stayed with him, his selfishness and his passion would surely destroy her just as it had done Nigel.

He would focus on the fight, on winning. Then he'd come back to Beckwith and fulfill his duty. Alone.

Chapter Twenty-four

LATE the next afternoon Philippa and her maid packed the last of her belongings. Ambrose, Ackley, and Oldham had left for Truro a few hours ago and would be staying overnight at an inn. Philippa planned to leave early in the morning to meet her father. He'd be furious when she told him she wouldn't marry Sir Mortimer, but he'd just have to learn to live with disappointment.

As would she.

Her heart ached every time she thought about not seeing Ambrose again. Didn't he realize he didn't need to fight anymore? She understood he'd needed it at a desperate time in his life, but he'd finally begun to recover from Nigel's death—she was sure of it. He'd faced Lettice. He'd ridden Orpheus. He'd opened himself to her.

But he couldn't move on until he decided it was time. And she wouldn't watch him continue to punish himself. Not when he saw violence as more essential than love.

One of the two footmen she'd brought from Herrick House came to retrieve her last piece of luggage. She nodded at him and then left her bedchamber.

Mrs. Oldham was waiting for her in the drawing room. Her face was pale and drawn. She clutched her hands together. "You're really leaving then?"

"I have to. My father is expecting me. Indeed, he's due here tomorrow, but I'm going to meet him on the road. I just can't stay here another moment." It was too painful.

Mrs. Oldham nodded. Then she dropped her hands with a huff. "I wish I could kick that boy square in his posterior!"

Philippa startled at the housekeeper's vehemence. "I beg your pardon?"

"His lordship. He ought to be marrying you."

"You mustn't be angry with him." Philippa wasn't. Only disappointed. "He didn't invite me here, and I came with no illusions. Things have turned out as they were meant to."

Mrs. Oldham frowned. "I'd rather hoped you would be staying. Will you be stopping in Truro for the fight? I admit I almost wish I'd gone with Mr. Oldham."

She had? "Why?"

"I can't imagine his lordship fighting like that. I suppose I wanted to see it. Half of Gerrans and Portscatho are there."

"They are?"

The housekeeper nodded. "They want to cheer him on."

Philippa thought about watching him in Dirty Lane. Instantly, as if she were watching him now, her breath grew short and her heart hammered. She curled her fingers into her palms. "I've seen him fight. It's brutal." And yet, she hadn't been able to look away.

She suddenly regretted not going. If half of the peninsula was there, she wanted to be too—she cared about him at least as much as they did. *More.* She loved him. She had to see for herself that he would be safe. What difference would it make if she departed from Beckwith or Truro to meet her father? "Mrs. Oldham, how would you like to accompany me to Truro?"

The housekeeper's eyes lit. "Give me ten minutes to change."

The journey to Truro seemed to take forever instead of an hour and a half. They arrived in the Middle Row—Truro's main thoroughfare—just as the fight was due to start. Philippa could only pray it didn't begin on time.

The Middle Row was a noisy, smelly place, and the journey along the street took them an additional ten minutes. When they reached the Red Lion Inn, which was hosting the fight in its stable yard, Philippa fairly jumped from the coach.

They had to pay their admission and pass through an archway to get to the yard. A stage had been built in the center, and a

multitude of lanterns illuminated the space. Ambrose and
Weatherly circled each other. Philippa stopped and stared.

Mrs. Oldham took her by the hand and pulled her through
the teeming crowd. Shouts and jeers jostled her senses as much
as the ever-moving cluster of people. Above the din, she heard
the distinct sound of flesh hitting flesh. She stood on her toes
and just made out Weatherly stumbling backward. Her heart
surged.

She and Mrs. Oldham continued on until they reached her
husband standing on the stairs leading up to the stage. There was
a small platform at the top, just large enough for Ackley, who
was acting as Ambrose's second.

"Mrs. Oldham!" her husband called as he pulled her up the
stairs to stand beside him. He grinned. "I'm so glad ye came!"

Mrs. Oldham turned and gestured toward Philippa. Her
speech was lost in the noise, as Philippa turned to watch the
fight. Standing on the second stair, she now had a clear view of
the fight in the wide space between the slats of the railing that
surrounded the stage.

Ambrose was focused on his opponent. His eyes were sharp,
his fists positioned in front of his chest. He didn't seem to have
sustained any injuries. Yet. She went to wrap her gloved hands
around the stair rail, but realized there wasn't one. She scooted
forward and clasped the bottom rung of the stage rail.

A bell sounded. "Can't touch the railing!" came a loud voice.

Philippa jerked back. All eyes—including Ambrose's—turned
to her. His fists fell a bit, but then the fight had been halted
because of her error. His gaze connected with hers, and she felt
the hungry fire in their depths all the way to her soul. He looked
alive in a way she'd never seen him. Perhaps he *did* need this.
And did that leave any room for her?

The bell rang again, and Ambrose's attention snapped away
from her. He moved forward, lightning fast, and struck
Weatherly in the chin and again in the eye. The massive man—
and he was *huge*—retaliated with a jab toward Ambrose's middle.

Ambrose danced to the left. She noticed his feet were bare as
they'd been at the end of the fight in Dirty Lane. He moved
faster, easier than his opponent. Philippa let out a gust of air as

her anxiety began to fade.

Too soon.

Weatherly was also fast. He followed Ambrose to the left and delivered a series of blows meant to overwhelm. Finally the fourth or fifth caught Ambrose's ear. But Ambrose was undaunted. He drove forward, his mouth compressed, his eyes narrowed. A fake punch to Weatherly's side followed by one to his cheek that connected. Another fake to his chin followed by a hit to his ribs.

Philippa leaned forward and just caught herself from touching the railing again. She gaped at Ambrose's speed and agility. He'd been astonishing in Dirty Lane, coming back from near defeat, but this was something else. He was on fire, possessed. And it was shockingly thrilling.

Ambrose continued his assault. Unable to mount an offense, Weatherly was only blocking punches and even that defense was faltering. Blood trickled from the side of his mouth. Ambrose hit him in the cheek. Weatherly's head jerked with the blow. Saliva and blood streamed from his lips. His arms flailed briefly and then he fell. Hard. Right in front of Philippa.

She stared at his face pressed against the wood. His eyes were closed, one of them already blackening.

The count started. Ambrose stood in the opposite corner, but he wasn't looking at Weatherly. He stared at Philippa, giving her the intensity he'd directed at his opponent. She shivered.

The count continued, and Philippa's pulse increased apace. Her breathing drowned out the sound of the crowd so that it seemed only she and Ambrose were present.

The count reached twenty-five. Ambrose walked to the center of the stage, his gaze never leaving hers.

She spared a glance for Weatherly. Still unconscious, his second on the floor beside him, trying to rouse him.

Thirty.

The umpire met Ambrose at the center of the stage and raised his arm. "Lord Sevrin!"

The resulting cacophony was unlike anything Philippa had ever heard. People pushed at the stage; now the fight was over they were free to touch the railing. Two large men, however, positioned themselves at the base of her staircase and prevented anyone from coming up.

Then Oldham grabbed her wrist and pulled her up the stairs. She joined Ackley on the platform. Ambrose was at the edge of the stage, his stare still intense. Still focused on her.

With a cry, she threw herself against him.

Ambrose hugged her close, heedless of the sweat coating his body. Her arms were clasped tight about his neck, and for a moment he forgot about the cheering crowd, their very public and visible position. He kissed her soundly on the mouth, taking her giddy laughter into himself like a tonic for his healing soul.

"Come with me," he whispered against her ear.

Firmly, he clasped her hand and led her down the stairs. Ackley squeezed aside. Oldham met Ambrose's gaze and nodded. He took Mrs. Oldham by the hand, and they led Ambrose and Philippa through the screaming crowd.

Ambrose recognized faces from Gerrans and Portscatho. Tenants from Beckwith. Thatcher from his last visit to Truro. All grinned widely and shouted their congratulations. For him. Winning had never felt this good, this satisfying.

Their progress took several minutes, but finally they entered the back door of the Red Lion into a small corridor. Ambrose had let a room upstairs.

Oldham closed the door behind them then clasped Ambrose's arm. "I'll procure a room for Lady Philippa." His brow quirked up. "Or at least for her maid." He and Mrs. Oldham continued along the corridor.

Ambrose turned and led Philippa through a low-mantled doorway that led to the servants' staircase. As soon as they were in the small space at the base of the stairs, he shut the door. He recalled their encounter in the closet at wherever that ball had been. Keeping himself from her then—no, *every* time he was near her—had nearly killed him. And now, now there was no need to stop himself. Couldn't if he tried. He pushed her back against the wood and seared her mouth with his.

She met his kiss, tongue for tongue, lips and teeth mashing

together in a mad, lustful frenzy. Her hands splayed against his bare chest, kneading and stroking his muscles. Her nails dug into his shoulders, pulling him savagely against her.

His cock raged and he positioned himself squarely between her legs. But those damned skirts... He pulled them up and clasped her thigh. She spread her legs for him, and his fingers delved into her curls, finding her heat...

She wrested her lips from his. "Upstairs."

"What's wrong with here?" He slipped his finger into her tight sheath and her eyes fluttered close.

She cast her head back against the wood. "Nothing," she gasped out. The muscles of her sex clenched around him, and moisture flooded her channel.

Here was fine, but upstairs would be better. He swept her into his arms and took the stairs two at a time. No easy feat given the narrow space and low ceiling.

At the top of the stairs was another door, which he shoved open with his shoulder. He turned left down the corridor until he reached the end where his chamber was located.

He had to set her down to open the door. She pressed against his back as he fumbled with the latch. Her hands came around and stroked his rigid cock through his breeches. He turned and ruthlessly took her mouth. She pushed into him and he stumbled backward into his room, falling onto his back.

She landed on top of him, her eyes wide. "Are you all right?"

He grinned. "Never better." He stretched out his foot and managed to kick the door closed.

She straddled him, pulling her skirts up so that her bare flesh rode against his prick. He grabbed her waist and ground her down as he thrust up. She braced her palm over his chest and dug her fingertips into his skin.

Impatient and desperate, he shoved his hands beneath her skirts and unfastened his breeches. Her hand joined his, closing around his flesh. His head fell back against the floor and he closed his eyes in ecstasy. She stroked him once, twice. God, that was impossibly good.

And then she was gone.

He opened his eyes to find her bent over his waist, her gaze focused on his erection. One hand was wrapped around his prick and the other was exploring his testicles. Light, curious touches. He wanted to tell her to stop, that he may not be able to control himself, but words simply wouldn't come.

He dropped his head back and lost himself in her touch. She stroked and massaged him, her fingers working around his tip and then descending to the base with delightful precision.

His eyes flew open again when he felt something wet against the head of his cock. He looked down and the sight he beheld— Philippa's mouth poised around him—nearly made him come. He wound his fingers in her hair, pulling the pins free, desperate for the satiny curtain of sable to cloak his thighs.

Her mouth bobbed down then up, her tongue laving his flesh. How did she know how to do this? His balls clenched. He wouldn't last long.

She sucked him deep into her mouth and when she came up again, he grabbed her shoulders and sat up with her. Then he picked her up again and tossed her atop the bed.

He stripped his breeches and drawers from his heated body. "You. Are wearing far too many clothes."

"You'll have to undo my dress." Her voice was deep, seductive. She turned and held up her disheveled hair to give him access.

He jerked the—thankfully few—laces free and put his mouth on the back of her neck. He opened her dress, trailing his lips along her flesh, kissing and biting each place he exposed.

She shrugged the dress down to her waist and he pulled it off entirely. Kneeling, she started on the laces of her stays. He would've taken over, but he didn't think he'd work as efficiently as her. And he wanted her naked. Now. Instead, he stayed behind her and worshipped her back with his lips and tongue. When the stays were loose, she tugged the garment free and tossed it aside. He dragged her chemise over her head, leaving her nude save her stockings. She'd lost her slippers somewhere along the way and he worked quickly to divest her of her last garments, finally exposing her to his starving gaze.

She made to turn, but he gripped her shoulders and held her still. He trailed his mouth down her spine, licking a path to the delicious contour at the base. She shivered as he drew his finger over the round curve of her buttocks. He pressed her face down onto the bed and lay beside her. He slid his finger down, down until he met her damp sex. He thrust inside of her and she opened her thighs, giving him greater access. Welcoming his touch.

Her hands came up and clutched the coverlet on either side of her head. He stroked in and out, giving her what she craved. What he craved. Her hips came back off the bed, meeting his thrusts. He considered taking her this way, but he wanted to see her face when she came.

He flipped her over. She instantly pulled on his shoulders and arched up to kiss him, her mouth hot and open, her tongue demanding entry.

She parted her thighs and he buried himself between them. There was no need to position himself, no need to guide his way in. Her hands moved down his sides and clasped his buttocks, pulling him into her. But he needed no direction. He speared himself inside of her with one long, bold stroke.

She fell back on the bed and brought her legs up until her heels dug into the backs of his thighs. God, she was so tight, so hot, so unbearably divine.

She met his thrusts with eager jerks. Her hands and feet dug against him, urging him deeper and faster.

Her breaths grew short, frenzied. Soft moans and gasps escaped her mouth. Her eyes were closed, her lips parted in ecstasy. "Yes," she cried. "Yes, Ambrose."

And then her muscles squeezed viciously around him as her orgasm swept her away. Her cries grew frantic, incoherent. He squeezed his eyes shut at his impending release. His balls drew up and his cock surged. He meant to withdraw, but her heels were still pressed tight against his thighs and her hands dug into his buttocks. He couldn't move except to drive deeper and spill himself inside of her.

With a loud cry, he pitched forward, catching his weight before he settled against her, their hearts beating against one another.

Chapter Twenty-five

PHILIPPA rose as dawn broke through the narrow gap between the window curtains. Ambrose slept behind her, his arm thrown over her hip. She closed her eyes for one more minute of comfort in his embrace.

Lying with him again changed nothing. He hadn't promised her anything, nor had she asked. He wasn't ready to move forward—with her—and she had to. Alone.

If he had a change of heart he could always come after her. But she doubted he would.

She scooted away from him and left the bed. Chilled without his body to warm her, she quietly found her clothing and dressed, save the laces at the back of her gown. She plucked up her slippers and cast one final look at Ambrose. Love welled in her heart and threatened to spill from her eyes, but she turned and left. She would not be ruled by regret. She'd seen firsthand how remorse had ruined him, and she refused to let it ruin her.

In the corridor, she paused, unsure where to go. She'd left her footmen and Feeney with her coach when she and Mrs. Oldham had gone to the fight. Ambrose had asked the Oldhams to procure another room, and presumably that was where she'd find Feeney. She made her way down the main staircase into the inn's common room. A footman greeted her at the bottom.

She tried to ignore her embarrassment given her not-quite-dressed-state, not to mention the condition of her hair, but her face grew hot anyway. "Excuse me," she said then had to clear her sleep-jagged throat. "Could you please direct me to my chamber? I'm Lady Philippa."

"Of course." He led her back up the stairs and then in the opposite direction from Ambrose's room. He paused and inclined his head toward the third door.

"Thank you," Philippa said. "Do you know where my footmen are staying? I should like to have my coach ready as soon as possible."

"I'll see to it, my lady." He bowed and departed.

Philippa knocked softly on the door and was quickly answered by Feeney who looked more than a bit relieved to see her mistress.

Less than a half hour later, Philippa and Feeney stepped outside the front of the inn. Philippa was still occupied with tying her bonnet as she made her way to the Herrick coach.

She put her foot on the first step and sniffed. What was that smell? Above the general scent of waste associated with a town the size of Truro was the unmistakable stench of unwashed male. She turned her head toward the footman holding the door and froze as cold fear drenched her body.

Swan, his familiar rotted-tooth grin splitting his round face, winked at her. As before, he was garbed in stolen livery, except this time it was Herrick's. "'Morning, my lady. Seems we're to have our tête-à-tête after all."

Feeney opened her mouth, but her scream never came. The other "footman", who was really Jagger's second employee, had come down from the box and had slapped his filthy hand over the lower half of Feeney's face.

Feeney dropped to the ground in a dead faint.

Philippa lurched toward her, but Swan grabbed her elbow in a vice-like grip. He gestured at Feeney's crumpled form. "Tie 'er up and stow her with the other blokes."

Philippa's footmen?

The other criminal picked Feeney up, tossed her over his shoulder, and swaggered away with her down the street.

Hope for not only her safety, but for that of her retainers, surged inside of Philippa as the Red Lion footman came from the inn and stopped short. "Is everything all right, my lady?"

"No." Philippa elbowed her would-be captor in the stomach.

He grunted but retaliated by backhanding her. She took the blow across her face and fell against the side of the coach.

The Red Lion footman rushed forward and the unmistakable steel of a blade in Swan's hand glittered in the morning sun. Swan lunged toward the footman's stomach. The footman gasped and pitched forward.

Philippa shrieked. Swan was upon her in a trice, his hand grinding against her mouth. "None of that now!" He pulled a dirty length of cloth from his pocket and tied it around her face, gagging her. Then he spun her about and pulled her arms behind her back and tied them tightly together with a length of rope he'd grabbed from the floor of the coach. "Time for a ride." Swan hefted her up the steps and tossed her inside the vehicle. The door slammed shut, shrouding her in darkness since the curtains on the windows were drawn.

A few moments later the coach moved forward, leaving the Red Lion—and her hope—behind.

Ambrose awoke to early morning light filtering into his room. Smiling languidly, he reached for Philippa, but his hand met an empty bed. He sat up and rubbed the sleep from his eyes. He scanned the floor where her clothes had been and found that, too, empty. She must've gone to her own room.

He dragged himself from the bed and stretched, relishing the warm satisfaction thrumming through his body. He'd won the fight, and Philippa's presence had made the victory that much sweeter. Suddenly, he was desperate to see her. He hated waking up without her at his side and resolved he'd never do it again. He dressed quickly and headed downstairs in search of someone who might tell him where she was.

He was in luck for the Oldhams were seated in the common room downstairs. Mrs. Oldham was sipping a cup of tea while Mr. Oldham was talking with the inn's proprietor.

Ambrose made his way to the table, but by the time he'd arrived, the innkeeper had moved on. Mrs. Oldham acknowledged Ambrose's presence with a scowl.

Ambrose sat. "Why are you looking at me like that? What

have I done now?"

"She's gone."

Ambrose didn't require clarification as to who "she" was. "Gone?"

Mrs. Oldham nodded. "Her coach, her servants. Just as she'd planned, I suppose. I thought... That is, I'd hoped after last night she'd be staying." She glared at Ambrose, her scowl turning to thorough disdain.

He too had hoped Philippa would've stayed, but perhaps she preferred marriage to the other man. And who could fault her? He'd given her nothing. "She's to be married." God, saying those words turned him inside out.

Oldham slapped his palm on the table. "To someone else? She should be marrying you."

"I'm sure this other man is preferable." Ambrose's spine threatened to curl in on itself.

Mrs. Oldham set her cup in her saucer and delivered Ambrose a frosty glare Saxton would've been proud of. "I doubt that. She loves you."

He knew it was true. Why then had she left? Because he'd been a selfish ass. Again.

As if Mrs. Oldham could hear his thoughts, she leaned over the table, her eyes searching his face. "When are you going to stop this nonsense and let the past go? Nigel would never want this for you."

Pain streaked through him, but—shockingly—not as keen as before. "Nigel's not here to say."

Oldham grunted. "And more's the pity, but it was still likely he wouldn't have been here in any case. The lad was on borrowed time."

How he hated to hear that argument. As if Nigel were to blame for living beyond everyone's expectations. "So everyone always said, yet there he was."

"Only because he was driven to succeed," Mrs. Oldham said. "Just like you."

Ambrose stared at her.

"You think he wasn't? He was always jealous of you. How couldn't he be? And when he inherited, he finally had the chance to show everyone what he could do, but you were already so firmly entrenched in Beckwith's operations, it was impossible for him to find a footing." She laid her hand over the top of Ambrose's. "And that's not your fault. If you must blame someone, blame your father. He planted a rivalry that was bound to hurt someone."

"I did more than 'hurt' Nigel." He swallowed and finally gave voice to the fear that haunted him. "What if I wanted Nigel to die? So that I could inherit?"

Mrs. Oldham's eyes clouded. She squeezed his hand tightly. "Oh, you dear boy. I would never believe that of you, and you mustn't either. You made mistakes, but so did he. And so did that woman he brought home. It was a terrible mess, and the result was tragic." She dashed her free hand over her eyes. "You can turn your back on all of us, on Nigel's legacy—because whatever happened, you inherited from *him*—but do *not* turn your back on Lady Philippa. She loves you, and I daresay you'll never find that again."

Self-recrimination and doubt were so rooted in his soul, he couldn't see past them. He felt small and sad, completely lost. "What if I hurt her? I don't know if I'm capable of loving her in the way she deserves." Mrs. Oldham had no idea what Philippa had endured watching her parents' farce of a marriage.

Mrs. Oldham cocked her head to the side. "Do you love her?"

Was love that feeling of supreme satisfaction when he'd awakened this morning? That sorrow when he'd found her gone? The searing pain that sliced through him as he thought of her marrying someone else? "Yes." It came out as a near-whisper. "Yes," he said louder as certainty inflated his chest.

But what did that mean? Could he simply forget the things he'd done and move forward? He closed his eyes and pictured his brother's face, which had become more difficult to summon in the years since his death. Instead, he recalled Nigel's laugh, the way his brow furrowed as he worked on the estate ledgers and the haunting notes he'd created from his violin.

Ambrose smiled. For the first time, he thought of his brother and smiled. Nigel would've liked Philippa. He would've appreciated her humor and intelligence, her independence. Things Ambrose loved about her.

The idea of going back to the way things were before—living at the Black Horse in London, wandering at the edge of acceptability, belonging nowhere and to no one—filled him with a suffocating despair. God help him, he wanted so badly to deserve even a small part of her.

Was there a chance for him? Philippa had maintained for so long that he was a good person. Could there be a morsel of truth to that? Could he find whatever remained of his decency?

"What are ye going to do?" Oldham asked.

"The only thing I can." He brought Mrs. Oldham's hand to his lips and pressed a kiss on her knuckles. "Thank you."

Tears glistened in her eyes. "Go and find her."

Unfortunately that directive proved far easier to utter than carry out. No one knew at what time she'd left or in which direction she'd departed. Ambrose supposed she'd gone east since her father's house was in Somerset, but preferred to speak with the footman who'd been on duty to glean more information. Unfortunately that footman had strangely disappeared.

The innkeeper was furious, but the footman had been relatively new and, apparently, sometimes the new ones snuck away from their posts for a drink or two, or ten. The innkeeper sent men out in search of the lad, both at his home and at the local pubs.

Ambrose preferred action to inaction. Fortunately, he'd ridden Orpheus to Truro yesterday in advance of the coach in which Oldham and Ackley had traveled. He saddled his horse in the Red Lion's stables and rode out into the Middle Row as a coach pulled to a stop in front of the Red Lion.

Ambrose didn't move. He'd recognize the Herrick crest anywhere. It was the exact coach Philippa had been waiting in that night on the Haymarket.

A liveried footman opened the door and Philippa's father stepped down. Ambrose frowned and he dismounted. He handed Orpheus's reins to a footman belonging to the Red Lion.

"Herrick," he called.

Philippa's father turned, and his ridiculously bushy eyebrows gathered low over his eyes. He strode toward Ambrose, his fists clenched at his sides. "You. Where the bloody hell is my daughter?"

"She's on her way to you. You didn't meet her on the road?" Fear curdled Ambrose's stomach. Where the devil had she gone?

"No." Herrick began to look alarmed. "You've lost my daughter?"

Never mind Herrick had somehow allowed his daughter to travel to Cornwall unchaperoned. Ambrose, was, as always, the villain. Except that he wasn't in this case, and he was growing more certain that someone was. His mind raced and settled on Jagger. Where was that filthy bastard? He had a room at an inn down the street. Ambrose turned, intent on finding the criminal.

Just then a Red Lion-garbed footman ran toward him. "My lord, my lord! We found her ladyship's maid and retainers. They'd been bound and stuck in a tack room at the mews." The mews where the Red Lion's customers stored their vehicles. Ambrose vaulted onto Orpheus's back and tore off down the street.

A few minutes later, he jumped down and stalked into the mews. A footman wearing the Red Lion's livery was laid out on a pile of straw while Philippa's maid—sobbing—held a piece of fabric against his side.

"Who's that?" Ambrose asked.

Philippa's footmen, wearing only their undergarments, stood nearby massaging their wrists. "He's from the Red Lion. Tried to stop them from taking her ladyship and was stabbed for his troubles."

"They've sent for a physician," the other footman put in.

Ambrose pinned them both with a furious stare. "Who took her?"

The first one answered. "There were two of them, my lord. A stocky fellow and a taller bloke. They took our livery and the coach."

Dark, uncontrollable rage simmered in Ambrose's heart. "Where did they take her?"

"Not sure, my lord. Their plan didn't seem very well thought

out. They argued a bit. The stockier one—Swan was his name—
he only wanted to be alone with her ladyship to—" The footman
swallowed, and he glanced at the crying maid. "You know."

Ambrose did know. And he'd kill the son-of-a-bitch as soon
as he found him. First, however, he had to find him, and Swan's
advantage was at least a few hours. Where could he have gone
that wasn't in the direction Philippa's father had come? The
other roads out of Truro led west and northeast. The northeast
was less traveled and the population along it was fewer than to
the west. If Ambrose were trying to abduct someone and get
away with it, he'd go northeast. But was Swan that smart?

"Where's the master of the mews?" Ambrose asked.

A man with graying hair and sharp, bright eyes ambled
toward him. "Aye, my lord?"

"The liveried men who took out Lady Philippa Latham's
coach this morning, did they ask anything?"

"Aye, my lord. Wanted to know what lay west and
northeast."

"You told him?" At the man's nod, Ambrose continued,
"And did he tell you which way he went?"

"Nay, my lord. But if I had to guess, I'd say northeast. He
looked over at his cohort when I told him there'd be less that
way."

Ambrose was already halfway back to Orpheus when he
called, "Thank you," over his shoulder.

Ten minutes later he was racing away from Truro via the
northeast road.

Chapter Twenty-six

PHILIPPA had hoisted herself onto the seat shortly after the coach had left the Red Lion, but that had been hours ago. Midmorning had passed before they finally stopped. The door opened, and bright light spilled into the interior, momentarily blinding her.

Swan stuck his head inside. "Come on then." He reached in and grabbed her upper arm then pulled her viciously from the coach.

She tripped down the stairs, but he caught her before she fell to the dirty track. She looked around, blinking. "Where are we?"

"Far away."

There were no buildings in sight. No people. No animals. Not even the distant bleat of a sheep. What had happened to the other criminal? "Are we alone?"

Swan jerked his head toward a hedgerow. "Brewer's gone to take a piss. I imagine ye'll need to relieve yerself. Best take care of that before we get to our business." He leered at her, his gaze fixating on her breasts. He brought his hand up and squeezed her flesh through her gown.

Her stomach heaved. Rescue seemed hopeless. She'd have to find a way to run or overpower her captors. Hysterical laughter bubbled in her throat, and she swallowed sharply then coughed.

"Brewer!" Swan yelled. "What's keeping ye?"

Silence answered him. Swan frowned. "Idiot."

He took the length of rope that dangled from her hands and looped it securely around the wheel of the coach. "Don't go spooking the horses, else ye'll get dragged." He cackled then smacked his lips against hers before going to the hedgerow.

Philippa spat into the dirt several times. She frantically tried to get her hands free, but her wrists were already raw and bleeding from her efforts in the coach. Tears squeezed from the corners of her eyes. To end up here, like this, after last night. Why had she left Ambrose? She loved him, and surely he felt something for her. She should have demanded he marry her. Marriage to him and whatever that brought was preferable to a life without him.

The hedgerows rustled, and Swan came running from them at full speed. Ambrose followed on his heels. Philippa surged forward. The horses stepped nervously, and Philippa steadied herself.

Swan grabbed one of the horse's bridles. "Come any closer, and I'll have them drag 'er," he warned.

Ambrose's gaze swung to Philippa and her position tied to the wheel. Fury and anguish lined his face. "Let her go, and I'll let you live."

"How about ye leave now, and I'll take the lady and go?"

Ambrose bared his teeth menacingly. "When I can no longer draw breath. And maybe not even then."

A shadow of fear passed over Swan's features. He tugged the bridle, and the horses stepped again.

Ambrose reached out, but didn't move. He glanced at her, and she saw stark fear in his eyes.

She stared at him intently. "Ambrose. The horses are from Holborn." Hopefully he would know what that meant. That as coaching horses bred by England's finest stable they wouldn't run. They might dance a bit, but they wouldn't run unless truly in danger. She would've just blurted it out but determined any advantage she could give him would be welcome.

Realization lit Ambrose's eyes. He pressed his lips together and then he moved. As quick as during last night's fight. Faster even. His fist drove straight into Swan's throat. The villain's head snapped back, and he fell to the ground. As expected, the horses moved. Swan had landed beneath one of them, and his arms flailed as his mouth furiously opened and closed in search of air.

One of the horses stepped on his thigh and reared up in response. The coach rolled forward and Philippa's shoulder and arm dragged along the dirt track. "Ambrose!"

Ambrose grabbed the bridle and stilled the animal. Thank God for his knowledge of horses. He leapt to her side. "Are you all right? He hit you." His hand stroked the angry weal on her face where Swan had struck her earlier.

She nodded, her eyes swimming with tears. "But nothing else. Oh, Ambrose." She buried her face in his neck, relief coursing through her veins so that she sagged against him.

He fumbled with the rope on her wrists and after a moment frowned. "This is impossible to untie."

"He had a knife earlier."

Ambrose stood. "He dropped it when I came after him." He ran to the hedgerow and found the blade then quickly returned to saw her free from the rope. His fingers gently stroked her wrists. "Philippa." He sounded broken, lost.

She brought her hands up to his face and smiled through her tears. "I'm fine." She glanced toward the hedgerow. "What about the other one?"

"Unconscious on the other side of the hedgerow."

She shivered, dropping her hands. "Is Swan dead?"

Ambrose turned his head toward Swan who was no longer moving. "I didn't think. I reacted. He took you from me and meant to rape you."

His eyes were wild. She felt secure and safe again, but he hadn't yet found the ground beneath his feet.

"Ambrose, are you all right?"

"I didn't mean to kill him. I—" He wiped his hand over his mouth and looked away from her.

She thought maybe she understood. The fear in his eyes, the dread quivering through his frame. She put her hands at the base of his throat and directed him to look at her. "It's not like Nigel. It's not the same at all."

"But *I'm* the same. It was me. I killed him."

"You didn't kill Nigel. It was an accident. You have to stop blaming yourself. Please." She leaned her head against his chest.

"Just breathe with me, Ambrose. Let go of this. Let go of Nigel."

They stood like that for several minutes. His hands loosely wrapped around her back, her arms twined about his neck. She listened to his heart beat against her cheek. It gradually slowed, and she thanked heaven for that.

Finally, his lips brushed her forehead like that long-ago night when he'd taken her home. The night she'd begun to fall in love with him.

Suddenly she couldn't live another moment without telling him. "I know you don't want to hear this, but I love you." She pulled back to look up at him. There were no guarantees, but he was worth waiting for. Worth *fighting* for. "And I know you don't want to marry me, but I won't have anyone else. I want you, and you're just going to have to—"

His lips found hers and he kissed her softly, gently. "Shhh," he breathed against her mouth. "Even before I knew that bastard had taken you, I'd decided to come for you. I can't bear the thought of living without you. My life has been such a misery. I'd forgotten how to live, how to love. If I ever really knew how." He looked into her eyes. "You are my life, my love, my reason for breathing. Philippa, if you don't marry me, I'll simply spend the rest of your life destroying your reputation until you do."

She kissed him, laughing against his mouth. "I will."

He slanted his mouth over hers and slipped his tongue past her lips. She kissed him back, squeezing him tightly.

He pulled back after a moment and rested his forehead against hers. "How can you be so certain about me? What if I hurt you?"

That he was finally opening his soul to her filled her heart with joy. "You won't. You'll learn to trust yourself as much as I do."

He shook his head. "How did you ever find a reason to trust me? Even last night when you begged me not to fight, I did it anyway."

"That wasn't very fair of me. I didn't understand. Fighting seemed a way for you to punish yourself, to banish the pain in your heart with physical pain."

"You understood perfectly."

"Why you *started*." She'd thought an awful lot about this during her nightmare carriage ride. Of all the things she would say to him if she ever had the chance. "But after watching you last night, I saw that fighting helped you heal. It was something for you to hold on to. Something that didn't judge, something that wouldn't hurt you beyond the physical."

He held her tight. "You're an amazing woman."

She snuggled against his chest. "Just someone who loves you." She leaned up and kissed his cheek. "What are you going to do about the man behind the hedgerow?"

"I'll tie him up. Then we'll take Orpheus back to town and send someone to clean up." He flicked a glance at Swan and froze.

Philippa turned. Swan's leg twitched. Ambrose rushed to the downed man and knelt beside him. Philippa followed.

Ambrose touched Swan's neck for a moment then looked up at her. "He's alive."

Philippa felt a surge of relief. Not because Swan hadn't died, but because now Ambrose didn't have to live with knowing he'd killed him. A man could only bear so much.

Ambrose fetched the rope and dragged Swan to a tree at the side of the road. Then he went and hefted Brewer to the same tree. When he had them both in sitting positions, he tied them to the trunk. While he worked, Philippa led the horses and coach a short distance to a shaded spot on the opposite side of the road.

Ambrose came to stand beside her. "Now, we can go."

She took his hand and they walked toward Orpheus. "Thank you for saving me," she said. "Again."

He smiled down at her with love shining in his gaze. "It was you who saved me."

Epilogue

ONE month later, Ambrose rode into Gerrans, his wife at his side. They dismounted in the churchyard and left their mounts to graze. In one hand, she clutched a bouquet of roses from Beckwith's gardens. With the other, she twined her fingers through Ambrose's.

He smiled down at her, still marveling almost constantly at how she'd changed his life. How she'd changed him.

They'd visited Nigel's grave a few times. She always brought him flowers and always spoke to him as if they'd been acquainted. She settled the roses next to his headstone. "Good afternoon, Nigel. 'Tis a beautiful day. We finished the new gate yesterday. Now Beckwith has a fine entrance to the keep and stables."

Ambrose imagined his brother admiring the work, even though he couldn't have helped build it. Strangely, he was able to see Nigel's face more clearly now, but maybe that was because Philippa had insisted upon hanging the portrait of them as children in Ambrose's study.

With her at his side, forgiveness for his sins was coming, at last. He still had dark moments, but she guided him through them with love and care. He'd never deserve her, but he'd spend his life trying.

Just as he'd pledged to shepherd Beckwith to its fullest

potential. For Nigel.

She turned to him. "Ready?"

He nodded, and they turned from the grave and walked back to their horses.

She curled her hand around his forearm. "I meant to ask you about Hopkins's letter last night, but you quite distracted me." She narrowed her gaze seductively, clearly recalling their post-dinner activities in the solar when he'd made love to her on the settee facing the gardens at sunset.

And now he was the one distracted. "Pardon?"

"The letter you received yesterday from Hopkins?"

He dragged his thoughts from disrobing her. Such inappropriate meditations in a churchyard. "Ah, yes. All is well at the Black Horse." Hopkins had taken over the club and Ackley's training.

They reached their horses and walked them out to the High Street.

"Do you miss it?" she asked.

Shockingly, he didn't. "No." After rescuing her from Swan, Ambrose hadn't once had the urge to fight. He leaned over to her and brushed his lips against hers. "All of my physical urges are currently being met, and I don't anticipate that changing any time soon."

She arched a brow. "'Any time soon?'"

"Ever," he clarified. He'd never get enough of her. With that in mind, he said, "There's a little cove not too far past Portscatho. We could go down and watch the sea. Among other things." He trailed his lips along her jaw.

"You want to do that on the beach? With all that sand?" She wrinkled her perfect nose. "That sounds frightfully uncomfortable."

He snagged her earlobe between his teeth. "Actually, there's a rock. I thought I might sit you on the edge—"

"You're not trying to seduce me in public again, are you?"

He raised his head. "Sweetheart, that's what scoundrels *do*. But make no mistake—you seduce me with every look, every touch, every breath. And I humbly beg you to never stop."

She sighed in mock exasperation. "All right, if I must." She traced her finger along his crooked nose. Her eyes shone with adoration. "I love you so, Ambrose."

"I love you."

She grasped his lapels. "Don't ever stop."

Just before his lips met hers, he whispered, "Never."

The end

Thank you so much for reading *To Seduce a Scoundrel!* I hope you enjoyed it! Read on for an excerpt from the next book (a novella) in the Secrets and Scandals Series:

To Love a Thief

To set things right, she has to be very wrong...

Former constable Daniel Carlyle hasn't the foggiest notion how to be a viscount. No one is more shocked than he when his father's second cousin *and* his son die on the same day. When a prominent earl offers to guide Daniel through Society and the House of Lords, he's grateful to have a champion. Things seem to be falling into place when he meets a lovely young woman he intends to make his viscountess. Until he catches her stealing from his mentor.

The moment Jocelyn Renwick glimpses her family's stolen heirlooms in the possession of a wealthy earl, she demands their return. He dismissively insists they've been in his family for generations, and she privately vows to get them back at any cost. But the law-abiding Lord Carlyle foils her plans, and she reluctantly partners with him to solve the theft of her property. When they discover the earl is up to his ears in criminal acts, he threatens to link Daniel to his gang of thieves. Jocelyn must decide if justice for her family is worth risking a chance at love.

Chapter One

May, 1818, London

JOCELYN RENWICK had loved a good ball—the dancing, the decorations, the costumes, the breathless excitement as guests arrived—during her very brief Season two years before. She'd been full of wonder and anticipation for a future that had seemed rife with possibility. Now, as a paid companion, she adorned the wall, and the balls she'd once enjoyed had become sadly lackluster.

It wasn't that the balls themselves had suddenly turned dull. It was her situation. With no close relatives to turn to after her father's death, she'd become the ward of a family friend, who'd inherited Papa's property and meager estate. While her guardian had taken care of her, he hadn't offered to finance another Season, and her trust wasn't sufficient to cover the expense. And since there was no one marriageable—at least in her opinion—in her small village in Kent, Jocelyn's options were limited.

She'd jumped at the chance to serve as paid companion to her guardian's great-aunt, Gertrude Harwood. She was a charming, elderly widow, and Jocelyn was delighted to accompany her for what she said might be her final Season.

Unfortunately, Jocelyn's Season so far hadn't included meeting any eligible bachelors or any dancing. The only people she mingled with were Gertrude's friends, who were even now clustered about.

The edge of Mrs. Montgrove's monstrous fan—it was the size of a dinner plate with ostrich feathers jutting at all angles—caught the side of Jocelyn's head, dislodging a lock of hair.

"Oh!" Mrs. Montgrove turned to Jocelyn with eyes widened in horror. "I'm so clumsy. Look what I've done to your coiffure. Here, let me fix it." She tried to smooth the hair back up toward the rest of the curls styled atop Jocelyn's head. However, judging from the tickle against her ear, the wisp wouldn't stay put.

Mrs. Montgrove's brow furrowed.

"Just tuck it behind her ear," Gertrude said with a wave of her fan, which was decorated with small diamond-shaped mirrors.

"Let me." Mrs. Dutton removed her glove and then licked her finger. When her digit moved toward the wayward lock, Jocelyn had to fight to keep from ducking.

Instead, she held up her hand. "I think I'll just repair to the retiring room for a spell before the rest of my hair falls apart."

They all stared at her, and Mrs. Montgrove looked stricken.

Jocelyn rushed to add, "It's not your fault. My hair has a mind of its own." She gave all of them her sunniest smile before turning on her heel and picking her way through the ballroom. She hadn't meant to imply that Mrs. Montgrove had caused a hair disaster. Someday she would perhaps learn to think before she spoke; however, the task seemed especially difficult when neither Mama nor Papa were around to offer loving reprovals.

Oh, how she missed her parents. Tears blurred her eyes as she meandered through the crowd. Mama had been gone a very long time, but Papa's death just two years ago was still fresh enough to elicit a sharp twinge of melancholy, if only for a moment.

She shook the emotion off. Her eyes refocused, and she attempted small smiles as she passed people she'd met two years before. Some made eye contact, while others simply looked away or stared right through her. There was nothing like an aborted Season followed by two years of mourning and adjusting to a life without family to make one feel insignificant.

Oh, Papa. Jocelyn made it out of the ballroom before her throat dried up and constricted. Perhaps she'd returned to London too soon. Perhaps she shouldn't have come back at all.

By the time she reached the retiring room she'd mostly recovered her equilibrium, locking her grief in the recesses of her mind. Pasting a pleasant expression on her face, she opened the door and immediately stepped to the side as a woman departed. She skirted by Jocelyn without making eye contact.

Invisible. No one saw her and they never would, for she hovered at the fringe of polite Society as a paid companion. Still, it was better than nothing, and without the funds to finance a second Season, the best she could hope for. She was young, and perhaps she'd yet marry.

Straightening her spine and again banishing her maudlin thoughts, Jocelyn closed the door and moved into the retiring room. An attractive brunette was patting her hair before a mirror. She turned upon hearing Jocelyn's approach and offered a friendly smile. "Good evening."

Jocelyn was momentarily surprised. Her lips curved up in response and then froze as her gaze settled on the necklace around the woman's neck. Three strands of pearls were held together by an oval, ivory pendant, which bore a hand-painted scene of two lovers in a boat beneath a sweeping willow tree. Her *mother's* necklace—it had to be—the one Papa had commissioned as an engagement gift. Jocelyn squinted, looking for the scratch in the glass over the ivory—damage caused by her tiny fingers when, as a toddler, she'd knocked it off Mama's dressing table.

Seeing the small defect, Jocelyn was instantly transported back two years to the night she and Papa had returned home after a musicale to find their house ransacked, their retainers bound together in the scullery, and all of their most prized possessions gone. The panic and fear came back to her in a wave, as did the shock of her father's heart attack that had occurred as a result.

But that was then. Now she was safe and whole, even if Papa wasn't.

Somehow, Jocelyn found the ability to speak calmly though

her heart was racing. "What a lovely necklace. Wherever did you find such a treasure?"

The woman's fingers came up to touch the pendant, and Jocelyn had to suppress the urge to snatch the piece from her neck. "My dear husband gave it to me. It's quite special, isn't it?"

Before Jocelyn could make further inquiries, the woman swept past her and exited the retiring room. Jocelyn whipped around and made for the door. It opened inward, causing Jocelyn to jump back to avoid being caught by the edge of the wood.

Two women, deep in tittering conversation, bustled in, forcing Jocelyn to step to the side before she was trampled. Invisible again.

As soon as the way was clear, she rushed into the corridor, but didn't see the woman wearing her mother's stolen necklace. She hurried back to the ballroom, desperate to find her. Once inside, she stopped short. Blast! There were so many people. And too many blue gowns. Jocelyn's quarry wore a cerulean gown with ivory flounces at the hem.

Keeping her gaze moving over the crowd, Jocelyn made her way in the direction of Gertrude and her friends. With her attention so focused on her hunt, she failed to notice the foot she trod upon until it was too late to avoid.

"Pardon," said a deep, male voice.

Jocelyn nearly stumbled, but a strong hand clasped her elbow and kept her from sprawling face-first in the middle of the ballroom. She regained her balance and turned toward the man she'd offended.

An exceptionally white cravat met her gaze. She looked up and up—he was quite a bit taller than she, an easy feat given her diminutive stature—and stopped when she met his dark blue-gray eyes. She'd expected to see annoyance and was surprised, for the second time that evening, when they crinkled in amusement.

"You look as if you're on a mission. May I be of service?" He offered his arm.

Jocelyn stared at his sleeve as she tried to pull her thoughts from finding the woman in her mother's pendant and refocus them on the first gentleman she'd met in two years.

He leaned down slightly and whispered, "Please take it lest someone think I'm waiting for a bird to land."

Unused to a gentleman's attention, let alone one with a sense of humor, she arched a brow at him. Then she quickly wrapped her hand along his forearm. "We wouldn't want that," she murmured.

"Now, where may I escort you?" In addition to being tall, he was quite handsome, with broad cheekbones and a wide chin with a small cleft in the center. "Or, shall I be lucky enough to secure a dance?"

A dance? The first dance she'd been offered in two years and she said, "No, thank you, I need to find someone." The flicker of disappointment in his gaze made her rush to add, "I should be delighted to dance with you after I find…" Her brain stalled a moment as she tried to think of something to say other than "the woman who stole my mother's necklace." "My friend, Mrs. Harwood. I am just returned from the retiring room and want to ensure she doesn't worry after my absence."

He inclined his head, which was covered in thick dark hair cut a trifle shorter than was fashionable. It suited him. "Just tell me where to go so we may reassure your Mrs. Harwood, and then we'll have our dance."

Drat. Or maybe not. She could use the opportunity of their dance to locate the woman in the blue gown without wandering the room alone. And, oh, to dance again! "Just over there, near the corner," she said.

He guided her through the throng. "I realize we haven't been properly introduced, but I'll accept your assault on my toes as an adequate reason to dodge propriety, if you don't object?"

The whole was said with such wit that she smiled in spite of her anxiety over seeing her mother's pendant. "I can't possibly object to that. Thank you for your generous consideration, sir."

"Lord Carlyle at your service," he intoned deeply with a nod of his head that was surely meant to take the place of a bow, which he couldn't possibly execute during their cross-ballroom circuit.

Lord Carlyle … Jocelyn searched her memory for the name

from her Season. She hadn't heard of him at all, which wasn't surprising. She'd attended only a half-dozen social events before her world had turned upside down.

"I'm Miss Renwick," she said, dipping her knees as they walked, in a sort of awkward, mobile curtsey. Perhaps she should have just inclined her head, too.

"A pleasure to make your acquaintance." His voice was deep and a bit raw. That is, his tone was not the same as other gentlemen she'd met in Society. She couldn't quite put her finger on it, but Lord Carlyle was somehow different. He even looked different. Oh, his cravat was perfectly tied, but there were no jewels sparkling from the folds, no ring adorning either hand, and no watch fob to spark conversation. An image of the fob Mama had given Papa as a wedding gift flashed in her mind. It, too, had been stolen.

Remembering her mission, as Lord Carlyle had called it, she glanced about for the woman in the blue dress. Where had she gone?

They broke free of the crowd as they came to the less-populated corner of the cavernous ballroom. A handful of potted trees were clustered like a makeshift forest, in which Gertrude and her friends were gathered.

Gertrude's head bobbed up and down. Her body sometimes succumbed to fits of shakiness due to her age. "Ah, there you are, dear. And you've brought a friend." She cast an approving glance and then offered her hand to Lord Carlyle.

Jocelyn released Carlyle's arm. "Lord Carlyle, this is Mrs. Harwood."

He executed an immaculate but somewhat stiff bow, one that looked as if he'd practiced it to perfection. There was definitely something different about Lord Carlyle. "Good evening, Mrs. Harwood."

Gertrude tittered. "Good evening, my lord. So charming! You *must* dance with Jocelyn!"

He cast a smile in Jocelyn's direction. "I plan to, ma'am."

Gertrude, and indeed all of her friends, sent congratulatory looks at Jocelyn. Just then, Jocelyn caught the sweep of a vivid blue skirt to her left. She turned her head and saw the woman wearing her mother's necklace approaching the terrace.

She pivoted toward Carlyle and smiled up at him. "I believe I'd like a bit of air first. My lord, would you mind taking me for a turn on the terrace?"

"Not at all." He looked to Gertrude and when she nodded her approval, he offered his arm again.

Jocelyn strolled with him to the terrace, her feet moving perhaps a bit too quickly in her haste.

"In a hurry?" he asked.

"Sorry, I'm so short, I'm used to walking rapidly to keep up." It was the truth, but also provided a convenient excuse.

They stepped out onto the terrace. A few couples were enjoying the warm May air, including the woman in blue. Her companion turned at that moment, and his gaze fell on Carlyle. "Carlyle!" he called jovially. "I've been looking for you."

Jocelyn slid a glance at her escort. He knew those people?

Carlyle led her to the couple and performed another exemplary bow. "Lady Aldridge, you look lovely this evening."

She smiled at him and lifted a coy shoulder, which sent her dark ringlets swinging against her neck. "Carlyle, you are too kind. But then that's one of the reasons Aldridge and I adore you so."

Lady Aldridge squeezed the man's arm as she said the name, which meant he must be her husband. But he was at least two decades older than Lady Aldridge, who couldn't be more than a few years Jocelyn's senior. Indeed, at first glance, the man appeared to be Lady Aldridge's father.

"Lord and Lady Aldridge, allow me to present Miss Renwick. Miss Renwick, this is Lord and Lady Aldridge."

He *did* know them. Her estimation of Lord Carlyle dipped. Although she didn't know the circumstances behind Lady Aldridge's possession of her mother's necklace, Jocelyn couldn't help the outrage that washed over her every time she looked at the ivory pendant. She forced herself to relax and be rational. It wasn't Lord Carlyle's fault he was acquainted with people who were inexplicably in possession of stolen goods.

Lady Aldridge smiled, revealing even, white teeth and a dimple in her right cheek. She was very lovely. "Miss Renwick, how nice to make your acquaintance. Carlyle, I do believe you promised me a dance tonight, and I hear a new set starting."

Carlyle flicked a glance at Jocelyn, clearly looking for a way to claim their dance instead, but Jocelyn wanted the opportunity to question Lord Aldridge about her necklace.

She gave him a reassuring nod. "Go ahead. We'll dance the next."

Lady Aldridge's brow puckered as she turned her gaze to Jocelyn. "Truly, you don't mind? I haven't danced at all this evening. Aldridge's knees are paining him, you see."

Jocelyn hadn't danced in two years, but she bit back an unladylike retort and nodded her approval instead. "It's quite all right." She removed her hand from Lord Carlyle, who gave her another splendid bow and then led Lady Aldridge into the ballroom.

Armed with the wrath of the righteous, Jocelyn turned to face Lord Aldridge. Possessed of a light complexion and thinning gray hair, he was broad-shouldered and tall. But then everyone was tall to her.

She wasted no time launching her interrogation. "I encountered Lady Aldridge a few minutes ago and complimented her necklace. It's so unique. She said it was a gift from you. Do you mind telling me how you obtained it?"

He glanced to his left, toward the ballroom, before piercing her with an arrogant stare. "It's been in my family for generations."

Of all the pompous liars! Her heart thumped an erratic rhythm. "Indeed? It's exactly like a necklace that was stolen from my family two years ago. *Exactly*. Right down to the scratch in the glass. Are you quite certain of its origin?"

Aldridge glanced back toward the ballroom and then over his shoulder, as if ensuring no one could hear them. Then he stepped closer and spoke softly, but his eyes glinted dangerously. "You're mistaken, my dear. It's a family heirloom. I'm sorry for your loss, and I'm sure your necklace is somehow similar. Lady Aldridge's pendant, however, is not the same one." His tone was so patronizing, so *superior*, Jocelyn could only stare at him.

He started to move past her, but she did the unthinkable

and grabbed his elbow. He turned a surprised glare on her. "I beg your pardon, Miss Renwick."

She let go of his sleeve, a bit shocked by her own cheek, but she was desperate. It simply wasn't possible the pendant had been in *his* family, not when she'd worn it at her very first ball! "My apologies. However, you must understand how important this is to me. Is there any chance you purchased the necklace? Perhaps you've confused it with another piece?"

Aldridge's face reddened, and his forehead took on a sheen of perspiration. "I said you were mistaken, young lady. Do cease your impertinent questions."

His reaction told her far more than his words. He didn't like her inquiry at all and was discomfitted by it. Why? "My lord, I don't believe my questions are impertinent. Several valuable pieces of heirloom jewelry were stolen from my family two years ago. I merely wondered if you had perhaps purchased stolen property—unknowingly of course." She added the last when the flesh around his mouth paled.

"I assure you, Miss Renwick, I haven't purchased any stolen property—unknowingly or otherwise. Do you have any idea who I am?" He moved closer to her, which only served to make him tower over her like an ancient oak.

She squeezed her hands into tiny fists. He clearly believed her vulnerable to intimidation given her stature, but it was precisely because of her smallness that she refused to be bullied. "I'm afraid I've only just met you, my lord, so you must forgive my ignorance. I believed you to be the gentleman in possession of my late mother's necklace."

That did it. His nostrils flared and his lip curled. Fury rolled off him in waves. "I am not to be trifled with, gel. I do not take your insinuations kindly and advise you to desist any further pursuit of this topic."

And then he marched into the ballroom without a backward glance, mopping his forehead with a handkerchief from his pocket as he went.

Well, that had gone rather poorly. Jocelyn frowned after his retreating figure. She was as certain Lady Aldridge was wearing her mother's pendant as Lord Aldridge was that Jocelyn was mistaken. Was it possible he'd purchased a stolen item and was now too embarrassed to admit it? Perhaps, but he hadn't seemed embarrassed. He'd seemed furious and guilty, as if she'd caught him red-handed.

Jocelyn allowed the cool night breeze to soothe her temper. At length, she returned to the corner of the ballroom Gertrude and her friends still inhabited.

"There you are," Gertrude said, her gaze searching the space around Jocelyn. "But where's Lord Carlyle?"

Jocelyn inclined her head toward the dance floor. "Dancing."

Gertrude's mouth dipped in disappointment. "I thought he was going to dance with you." Her gaze traveled past Jocelyn's shoulder, and her lips curved up. "The set is just ending. He's coming this way! Stand up straight, dear. Smile!" Gertrude assembled her expression into something a bit more sedate, but her eyes sparkled with excitement.

Jocelyn faced the dance floor, and indeed, Lord Carlyle was walking toward them. While she'd dearly love a dance, she wasn't sure she wanted to partner with someone who was on such friendly terms with the perfidious Lord Aldridge.

Carlyle arrived and gave a bow to Gertrude and her friends, who were lingering in the background. Then he directed the full intensity of his eyes upon her. And yes, intensity was the right word, for Lord Carlyle could probably look a hole clean through a person. Indeed, perhaps he could see through Aldridge's lies. "Are you still amenable for our dance?" he asked.

Her stomach gave a little flutter as she contemplated what else Carlyle might be able to see. "Yes." The acceptance slid from her lips before her brain had made up its mind. As they walked toward the dance floor, the strains of a waltz began, and Jocelyn was glad she'd agreed.

He took her waist and clasped her hand as he swept her into the music. His touch was light and gentle. Comforting.

Comforting?

She was not about to think of this gentleman as anything other than a potential adversary. Not given his acquaintances. Best to get to the bottom of that, then. "Lord Carlyle, how do you know Lord and Lady Aldridge?"

He turned his powerful gaze upon her again. Goodness, but she could stare at his eyes for an unseemly amount of time. She refocused on his shoulder.

"Perhaps you know I'm relatively new to Society?" he asked. "I only inherited the viscountcy within the past few years. Before that I was, ah, not raised as a viscount's son. Lord Aldridge has been kind enough to help me adjust to my new role. Indeed, I don't know where I'd be today without his assistance and generosity."

Oh, dear. That was quite a bit more than acquaintances. "He's a close friend, then?"

"More like a relative, actually. I had a loving father, God rest his soul, but I suppose Lord Aldridge has behaved in that capacity for some time. Yes, I daresay he's been rather parental in his care and solicitation."

And with that, her *potential* adversary became her Adversary. How unfortunate, because she really could have lost herself in his eyes.

Other Intrepid Reads Authors

Books by Emma Locke

The Naughty Girls Series
The Courtesans
The Trouble with Being Wicked
The Problem with Seduction (Winter 2013)
The Art of Ruining a Rake (Winter 2013)

The Hoydens
The Danger in Daring a Lady (Fall 2013)
The Importance of Being a Scoundrel (2014)
The Hazards of Loving a Rogue (2014)

To receive updates on future book releases, sign up for Emma's
mailing list at http://www.emmalocke.com.

Books by Erica Ridley

Historical Romance
Too Wicked To Kiss
Too Sinful To Deny
Born To Bite

Contemporary Romantic Comedy
Love, Lust & Pixie Dust
Wands, Wishes & Genie Kisses (Spring 2013)
Fate, Fire & Demon Desire (Fall 2013)

To learn more about Erica, her books, or to sign up for her
mailing list for contests, freebies, and new releases, visit
http://www.ericaridley.com.

About the Author

Darcy Burke wrote her first book at age 11, a happily ever after about a swan addicted to magic and the female swan who loved him, with exceedingly poor illustrations. An RWA Golden Heart® Finalist, Darcy loves all things British (except tomatoes for breakfast, or any other time of day, actually) and happy ever afters.

A native Oregonian, Darcy lives on the edge of wine country with her devoted husband, their two great kids, and three cats. In her "spare" time Darcy is a serial volunteer enrolled in a 12-step program where one learns to say "no," but she keeps having to start over. She's also a fair-weather runner, and her happy places are Disneyland and Labor Day weekend at the Gorge. Visit Darcy online at http://www.darcyburke.com where you can sign up to receive her newsletter, follow her on Twitter at http://twitter.com/darcyburke, or like her Facebook page, http://www.facebook.com/darcyburkefans.